THE LAST GOODNIGHT

THE LAST GOODNIGHT

KAT MARTIN

KENSINGTON
PUBLISHING CORP.

www.kensingtonbooks.com

KENSINGTON BOOKS are published by

Kensington Publishing Corp.
119 West 40th Street
New York, NY 10018

All Kensington titles, imprints, and distributed lines are available at special quantity discounts for bulk purchases for sales promotion, premiums, fund-raising, educational, or institutional use. Special book excerpts or customized printings can also be created to fit specific needs. For details, write or phone the office of the Kensington Special Sales Manager: Attn. Special Sales Department. Kensington Publishing Corp, 119 West 40th Street, New York, NY 10018. Phone: 1-800-221-2647.

Library of Congress Card Catalogue Number: 2021939154

ISBN-13: 978-1-4967-3679-6
ISBN-10: 1-4967-3679-6
First Kensington Hardcover Edition: November 2021

ISBN-13: 978-1-4967-3796-0
ISBN-10: 1-4967-3796-2
First Kensington Trade Paperback Edition: November 2021

ISBN-13: 978-1-4967-3682-6 (ebook)
ISBN-10: 1-4967-3682-6 (ebook)

10 9 8 7 6 5 4 3 2 1

Printed in the United States of America

THE LAST
GOODNIGHT

CHAPTER ONE

*K*ADE LOGAN STOOD ON THE BANK, WATCHING THE SHERIFF AND his deputies haul the mud-covered vehicle out of the lake. The crane groaned as the auto tilted upward, the rear end lifting into the air, the front wheels dragging across the spongy earth. Brackish lake water poured out through the open windows, along with weeds and silt. Even a few silver fish had made the car their home.

For eight long years, Kade had been haunted by the mystery of what had happened to the dark green Subaru Forester that had belonged to his dead wife.

Oh, he knew where Heather was. In a grave in the old hillside cemetery in Coffee Springs, the small town closest to the ranch. Her body had been found in a shallow depression up in the hills at the base of the mountains outside Denver.

Heather had been beaten and strangled. Any signs of rape had faded as her body decayed, but as beautiful as she was, Kade was sure sex had been involved.

Her killer had never been caught.

"You okay?" Sam Bridger, Kade's best friend, stood beside him, a tall blond man Kade had known for years. Kade had been too lost in thought to hear him approach.

"She's been dead eight years, Sam. So yeah, I'm okay." But the rage he felt had never lessened. It should have. At the time of her death, their marriage was already on the rocks. The second time Kade had caught Heather cheating, he had filed for divorce.

"Maybe they'll find something in the car that'll give them a reason to reopen the case," Sam said.

"Maybe." Kade hoped so. He wanted Heather's killer to be found and punished. No matter how things had turned out between them, he owed her that much.

His gaze went back to the car being lifted onto the flatbed of a diesel truck with an Eagle County Sheriff's emblem on the side. The truck pulled away from the edge of the lake, tires churning through mud made worse by last night's rain. The motor groaned as the vehicle slogged along the little-used, rutted lane to the asphalt road leading toward Eagle, the county seat.

The last time Kade had seen the dark green SUV was the night Heather had left him. That night, she had packed her things, taken the car, and driven away without a backward glance. Kade had never seen her again.

At the time, like half the residents of Coffee Springs, he'd believed Heather had run off with one of the men she'd met in the town's only saloon, or maybe a guy in Vail, the ski area frequented by the rich and famous only an hour's drive away, where Heather sometimes went to ski with her girlfriends.

Kade had believed it too. For a while. Then, two years later, a couple of hikers had found a body in a shallow grave, the dirt washed away by a recent storm. The victim, a female, turned out to be Heather Logan, a shock that had sent Kade into a tailspin.

By then, he'd accepted the likelihood that Heather had been a victim of foul play. She hadn't left with some big spender from Vail and simply started a new life, as she had threatened to do. She had been murdered.

Since then, Kade had been tormented by guilt. He lived each day with a terrible sense of failure that he had let Heather down. At the very least, he should have found the man responsible for her death.

And made the bastard pay.

"I've seen enough," Kade said. "I'm heading back to the ranch."

"That's it?" Sam asked, a blond eyebrow edging up. Sam and Kade had gone to school together, worked side by side during the summers when they were kids. Sam knew Kade well enough to know it was far from over.

Kade thought of Heather and felt the old rage burn through him. "Over? Not by a long shot." He started striding away, the bottom of his brown, oiled-canvas duster kicking up behind the heels of his muddy cowboy boots.

"What are you going to do?" Sam asked, falling in beside him, matching him stride for stride.

"First, I want to see what the forensic experts find in the car. Then I'm heading into Denver." A friend in the city owned a company called Nighthawk Security. Kade's father had known Marcus Delaney. The current owner, a war hero, was his son. Kade trusted Conner Delaney to recommend a competent investigator.

Though Kade had tried that before.

A month after Heather had disappeared, when she hadn't made contact with any of her friends, he'd begun to worry that she hadn't just run off with a man, as everyone believed. He'd filed a missing-persons report with the police, but they'd never found any trace of her.

After her body was discovered and her disappearance became a homicide investigation, Kade had hired a retired police detective, but the case was cold by then. He began to accept that if the cops and his private investigator couldn't find the man who had murdered her, maybe it was time to let go.

Still, the rage inside him remained. A cold fury that wouldn't leave him till the day he found the man responsible for his wife's death.

And dispensed the justice the killer deserved.

CHAPTER TWO

ELEANOR BOWMAN SAT AT AN OAK DESK NEAR THE FRONT DOOR OF the office. The building that housed Nighthawk Security, a two-story brick structure on Acoma Street, had recently been remodeled. The interior was done in pleasant tones, with comfortable brown-leather sofas in the waiting area, a conference room, and an employee lounge in the back.

Photos of local wildlife hung on the walls—elk, deer, a big black bear—along with autographed photos of celebrities the company had done business with at one time or another. The faces of Tom Selleck, Clint Eastwood, Denzel Washington, and Kevin Costner looked down from sturdy oak frames.

Aside from providing private investigation services, Nighthawk offered a top-rate security team that specialized in personal and business protection. Conner Delaney, the man who owned the company, was former military, tall, dark-haired, and just flat hot.

Though most of the guys on the security team also held PI licenses, Ellie was one of only four private investigators and, along with Conn's sister, Skye, the only other woman who actually worked out of the office. They were all independent contractors, and though there was room for additional personnel, Conner was very selective. Only the best got a job at Nighthawk.

Ellie was fully licensed, owned a Glock 19 semiauto and a .38 Smith and Wesson revolver. But she wasn't a former police detective like Skye or an army ranger like Trace Elliott, Conn's right-hand man. Her specialty was undercover work, and she was good at it. Embezzlement, larceny, fraud—Ellie went in covertly and ferreted out the guilty parties, information that went to the person who had hired her, who decided what course of action to take.

She rarely came into the office. Anonymity was an important part of her work. But Conn believed she'd be the right person for the job he had in mind.

Since she'd just finished a case, she was looking for something to do. She hoped for something interesting, but work was work. She didn't want her savings account to dwindle.

She looked up at a noise at the front of the office. The glass door swung open, and a tall, broad-shouldered man wearing a dark brown Stetson walked in. People thought of Denver as a western town, but it had been years since Ellie had seen a guy in a cowboy hat who looked like it belonged on him.

Dressed in crisp, dark blue jeans that fit snuggly over a pair of narrow hips, brown lizard-skin boots, and a white shirt with pearl snaps on the front, the man removed his Stetson, revealing neatly trimmed, golden-brown hair, and strode toward the desk closest to the door, which happened to be hers.

"My name's Kade Logan." He had a lean, muscular build and the long, powerful legs of a bulldogger. His deep, masculine voice fit him as perfectly as his hat, and his hard, handsome face could rival any of the celebrities hanging on the office walls. "I have an appointment with Conner Delaney."

"Yes, Conn mentioned he was expecting someone. I'll let him know you're here." The office was small enough that they didn't need a receptionist. Ellie rose from behind her desk, wondering if Kade Logan could possibly be the client Conn had in mind for her.

In a cinnamon pencil skirt and matching jacket, a pale yellow silk blouse, and a pair of four-inch, dark brown heels, fall colors for the season, she started for Conn's office, leaving her jacket draped over the back of her chair. Kade Logan's eyes, the same golden-brown as his hair, followed her across the room.

Ellie knocked and opened the door. "Mr. Logan's here to see you."

Conn rose behind his desk. He was as tall as Logan and, like most of the guys in the office, really built. He was also engaged to be married, though Ellie had her doubts.

"I need to speak to him first," Conn said. "Then I'll introduce you."

"So he's the client you were telling me about?"

"That's right. Kade's father and mine were friends. He owns a ranch called the Diamond Bar."

"I'll send him in." Turning, she headed back to where Logan stood waiting, long legs braced slightly apart, turning his hat in his big, calloused hands. No question this guy was for real. She wondered what kind of help he needed.

She smiled up at him. A little under five-foot-four, she was at least ten inches shorter than Kade. "Go on in. Conn's waiting."

He gave her a cursory nod, then disappeared inside the office. She looked down at her skirt and blouse, the business attire she had chosen to meet a new client, and wondered if she should have worn a pair of jeans.

Ten minutes later, she found out.

"Kade, meet Eleanor Bowman."

His eyes narrowed, forming tiny sun lines at the corners. "You're Eleanor Bowman?"

"I'm Ellie." She smiled and stuck out a hand. "Pleasure meeting you."

His jaw tightened for an instant before he reached out and accepted her handshake.

He turned back to Conn. "Eleanor. With a name like that, I thought she'd be an older woman, someone with more experience. Either way, this is a bad idea."

"What idea is that?" Ellie asked.

"Eight years ago, Kade's wife was murdered," Conn answered for him. "Her body was discovered in the mountains outside Denver, but the killer was never found. Two weeks ago, the car Heather was driving when she disappeared was discovered in a lake near Coffee Springs. That's the town closest to the ranch. The police now believe she could have been picked up by someone who knew the area, someone who lived there or had ties to the community. It's possible the killer abducted her, dumped the car in the lake, then drove her somewhere and murdered her. Afterward, he disposed of her body, then returned to Coffee Springs."

"Maybe the killer wasn't a local," Ellie said. "Just someone passing through, someone who lived in Denver or a nearby town."

Logan glanced off toward the window. "We were in the middle of a divorce when she was killed. I knew she was seeing someone, but I didn't know who. He could have been local or someone from out of town. Either way, the sheriff was never able to figure out who it was."

"And that's the reason you want to hire me? To find out who murdered your wife?"

His gaze swung to hers. "First off, I don't want to hire you. Conn thought it would be a good idea. He said your specialty is working undercover, but the last thing I need on my ranch is a woman snooping around. You'll stick out like a sore thumb."

Irritation bubbled up, and her spine went straighter. "Did Conn tell you I was born in Wyoming? I was raised on the Grass Valley Ranch near Jackson Hole. Did he tell you I can ride just about anything you have in your remuda, or that I moved steers up into the mountains and back down into the valley every year. And the weather doesn't bother me. I know ranching, Mr. Logan. I can fit seamlessly into your operation. I can do whatever job it takes to make people accept me and gather the information you need."

Silence fell.

Conn Delaney's lips twitched in amusement. "I think you can see why I thought Ellie was the right person for the job. I think you should hire her, Kade."

A muscle worked in Logan's square jaw. He raked a hand through his hair, mussed a little from the hat.

"I need some time to think about it."

"Are you sure?" Ellie asked. "Because if you want to find your wife's killer, you've already had eight years to think about it."

Kade's golden eyes narrowed, seemed to burn into her green ones. "I need to know who my wife was seeing at the time she was murdered. I'm happy to pay whatever that information costs. You really think you can do it?"

"If you want me to succeed, I'll need straight answers to any questions I ask. If you're willing to do that and if the information is out there, I'll find out who it was."

He frowned. Clearly, he didn't like the idea of her asking him questions about his personal life. On the other hand, he wanted answers.

Kade nodded. "All right, we'll do it your way."

Going in undercover was a good idea, and apparently Logan was smart enough to know it.

"It's a hundred fifty miles from Denver to the Diamond Bar Ranch," he said. "If you go out I-70, with traffic, it's about a three-hour drive from here to Coffee Springs. I'll text you the directions from there out to the ranch."

"All right."

"What kind of car are you driving?"

"Whatever kind I need. I have a friend in the used car business. We have an arrangement. He rents me whatever I think is best for the case I'm working. For this, definitely something with four-wheel drive."

For the first time, she caught a glimmer of respect in Logan's eyes. "When can you start?"

"I can be there tomorrow, but we need to figure out the best place for me to fit in. That way, I'll know what I need to bring."

His hard mouth edged up. "You mean besides your pistol?"

"You better make that plural." She flashed him a phony smile. "Remember, Mr. Logan, I'm from Wyoming."

Logan seemed to find that amusing, and some of the tension went out of those wide shoulders. "You'll need to call me Kade. Same as everyone else."

"Kade then." She didn't smile. She wasn't thrilled to be working for a guy who didn't want to hire her because she was a woman.

"You can use the conference room," Conn said, rising.

Ellie walked ahead of Kade out of Conn's office, and she led him into the glass-enclosed room next door. She wondered what sort of cover job he planned to dredge up for her and reminded herself she didn't have to take the case.

As she studied Logan's solid jaw, the gleam in his world-weary eyes, and his hard, sexy mouth, it occurred to her she would be making a far safer decision if she turned him down.

Kade stretched his long legs out beneath an oak conference table surrounded by ten brown-leather captain's chairs and studied Ellie Bowman. When he'd called Conn Delaney and asked about hiring a detective, it never occurred to him Conn would suggest a woman.

And a damn pretty woman at that. A little shorter than average, she had a small waist, slender hips, and shapely legs. Dark copper hair, clipped neatly at the nape of her neck, curled softly down her back, gleaming in the sunlight streaming in through the window.

He'd felt a jolt the moment he had walked into the office and seen her sitting at her desk. He was a man of strong sexual appetites, and he'd been single for the past eight years. He noticed women, and Ellie Bowman definitely was one.

"I can bunk in with the hands," she said. "This time of year, you're probably still looking for strays and moving them down to the lower pastures."

Kade inwardly groaned. *The bunkhouse?* Not likely. A good-looking woman would be nothing but a distraction to the hands.

"I don't suppose you can cook," he said. "Mrs. Stenson is leaving for a month-long visit with her son and his family in Phoenix. Be a place you could easily fit in."

One of those smooth reddish eyebrows slid up. "Why am I not surprised the only job you think I can handle is in the kitchen?"

Irritation trickled through him. He wasn't being disrespectful.

His mother had taught him better than that. With an opening in the kitchen, hiring her would be believable. Simple as that.

"Cooking won't be a problem," she answered before he had time to respond. "My mother cooked for our ranch hands. I pitched in whenever she needed me."

He managed to nod. "Mabel has a helper, so you won't be left to do all the work yourself. In fact, Maria usually does most of the heavy lifting now that Mabel is in her seventies."

"If that's what you think works best, that's what I'll do. It's your money. I'm sure you'd like to get the best results for the dollars you spend."

"True enough." She was pragmatic. Heather had been exactly the opposite, spending ridiculous sums of money on herself. "Taking over the kitchen will give you an excuse to be in town. You'll be feeding a six-man crew plus my foreman and me, a few part-time hands, a stable boy, and anyone else who happens to be around. Mabel went in for supplies a couple of times a week. That should give you a chance to get to know some of the locals."

Ellie's full lips curved in the first real smile he had seen. He wondered what she'd taste like. *Damn.*

"Actually, standing in for your cook is a good idea," Ellie said, surprising him with the admission. Kade reassessed some of the assumptions he'd made.

"I haven't cooked for a while," she said. "But it's kind of like riding a horse. Once you're back in the saddle, you remember how to do it."

He clamped down on the heat those words generated and the stirring in his loins beneath the table. He'd like to give Ms. Ellie Bowman a ride—the kind neither of them would soon forget.

Kade scrubbed a hand over his face. This was a bad idea on every level. Except that if the lady was as good as Conn said, it might actually work.

Kade straightened in his chair. "Anything else you need to know?"

"Where will I be staying?"

"Mabel moved into a cabin behind the ranch house a couple

years back. Her old room is down the hall from the kitchen, off the mudroom."

"That'll do."

He nodded and rose from his seat. "If you think of anything else, you can call me on my cell phone."

"All right." Ellie put his number in her contacts, and he put hers in his. There was something intimate about it Kade didn't like.

"I'll see you tomorrow."

"I'll be there no later than three."

He frowned. "We get up early on the ranch. Cook's the first one up."

She smiled, and he caught a glint of humor in her eyes. "Maybe I should charge you a little extra for ruining my beauty sleep."

Kade actually laughed. Looked like Ms. Bowman had a sense of humor. Good thing to have on a ranch. "You find my wife's killer, and I'll give you a ten percent bonus. That pay for your beauty sleep?"

Ellie stuck out a hand. "You're on."

Kade accepted the handshake, his big palm wrapping around her smaller one. Surprised at the strength he felt there, he settled his hat on his head and tugged the brim down low. "I'll see you tomorrow, Ms. Bowman."

"Ellie," she said in a voice that made him think of clean sheets and his big, four-poster bed.

That was the moment Kade knew he was in trouble.

CHAPTER THREE

*E*LLIE DROVE THROUGH THE BIG TIMBER GATE THAT MARKED THE entrance to Kade Logan's property. The sign at the top, between two racks of sun-bleached elk antlers, read DIAMOND BAR RANCH.

After she'd met Logan yesterday, Ellie had done some research. The man owned over 19,000 deeded acres plus 18,000 grazing acres near the tiny town of Coffee Springs. The ranch house and pastures sat in a valley surrounded by forested mountains that rose up from the valley floor.

As she drove the last few miles down a well-maintained gravel road, Ellie looked up at the swath of pine trees stretching all the way up to snow-capped peaks. The grass in the valley had turned golden brown, and the leaves on the aspen trees shimmered in red and orange on the sides of the hills.

Fenced pastures ran along both sides of the road, and as she neared the house, she saw wooden corrals, a few log cabins, and several barns clustered around a newer structure fashioned of stone and chinked square timbers under a dark brown metal roof.

The ranch was beautiful, like something out of the old West. Except for the house, which, with its huge, plate-glass windows, tall stone chimneys, and inviting covered porches, appeared to be no more than twenty years old.

Ellie pulled her rented white Jeep Cherokee around to the back of the house, figuring the temporary cook she was pretending to be wouldn't likely arrive at the front door. She made her way up onto the back porch and knocked, stepping back when a slender young woman with glossy hair in a loose black braid opened the door.

"You must be Ms. Bowman," the young woman said.

"I'm Ellie Bowman, the new cook." She smiled. "At least until Mabel gets back. You must be Maria."

"*Sí*, I'm Maria." She pulled the door open wider. "Please come in. It's good to meet you."

"Good to meet you, as well, and please just call me Ellie." As she stepped into the steamy interior, delicious aromas drifted toward her. "Something sure smells good."

"That's the meat and onions I fried for the casserole. It's all finished, in the pan and ready to go into the oven. The men will be in before dark for supper."

"What can I do to help?"

"I think Señor Kade expected you to come in through the front," Maria said. She was in her early twenties, a Latina or perhaps part Native American. "He wanted to see you in his study before you settled in, but something came up, and he was called away. He said to tell you he'd be back soon."

"Is that what I should call him? Señor Kade?"

Maria smiled. She was a beautiful girl. "No, no. That's just what I call him. My mother worked for him. I've known him since I was a girl. Señor Kade is still how I think of him."

Ellie smiled, liking the young woman already. "I can bring my stuff in later. Tell me what you need me to do."

Maria flicked a glance toward the seating area off to one side. There was a long rectangular wooden table with benches on both sides, room enough to seat ten or twelve people, plus a chair at each end.

"Mabel left last night," Maria said. "I'm not used to cooking by myself. You could help by setting the table. Then I won't have to do it later. Just the basics, silverware, paper napkins, water glasses, and coffee mugs. The men serve up their own meals."

"All right. I can do that. It'll give me a chance to figure out where everything is." Ellie set to work opening cabinets and drawers, mentally cataloging supplies and cookware, memorizing where things were located. In minutes, she had the table set using vinyl, red-checked placemats and red paper napkins to give it a cheerful look. Maria seemed pleased.

They worked together to cut up tomatoes, onions, and cucumbers for a big crisp green salad to go with the casserole.

"The men won't be in for a while," Maria said. "I'll help you bring in your things."

"Great. Thanks."

But Kade Logan appeared first. Shoving through the back door and stepping into the warm kitchen, he shed his tan Carhartt jacket and hung it on a peg beside the door. The hat he was wearing was the same brown felt as before, but this one was crimped and stained, a working cowboy's hat.

Her gaze traveled over him, and her stomach contracted. She had forgotten the impact the man had had on her the first time she'd seen him. The broad shoulders and long legs, the square jaw and hard mouth, the slightly mussed golden-brown hair. The feeling was even stronger today.

Kade Logan was a man's man, and her hormones seemed to know it.

The notion grew when he turned and saw her. She could have sworn his nostrils flared. Ellie forced herself not to turn and run back out the door.

It was ridiculous. Kade Logan was only a man. In her line of work, she dealt with men every day.

"I see you made it." The deep male voice sent a tingle of awareness up her spine. "We had a little trouble or I would have been here to greet you."

"What kind of trouble?" She was a private investigator. Curiosity came with the job.

"Why don't we get our business finished? Then you can get settled in. My study is down the hall."

She followed his long strides out of the kitchen, traveling over polished wood-plank floors, past a dining room lit by an antler chandelier and furnished with a copper-topped table surrounded by eight high-backed leather chairs. A wine cellar with a glass door was tucked into one wall, something she wouldn't have expected.

His study reflected the same combination of mountain and western décor, with beautiful oil paintings, dark wood furniture, and colorful Indian throw rugs on the floor.

Kade didn't sit down, just closed the heavy door.

"What's going on?" Ellie asked.

"You'll hear about it anyway. Not many secrets on a ranch. Someone shot a steer up in the north pasture. Probably just some hunter who couldn't tell the difference between a cow and a deer, but the men have all been told to stay alert."

"Did you call the sheriff?"

He nodded. "Sheriff Glen Carver. He's working on it, but the ranch covers a lot of acres, and it's been raining, which destroys any footprints or tire tracks. With luck, the guy is long gone and won't be bothering us again."

"I'll keep my eyes and ears open just in case." She smiled up at him. "No extra charge."

Amusement touched his lips, and Ellie felt it in the pit of her stomach.

"I assume Maria showed you your room."

"She was busy working on supper. I'll bring my stuff in later and ask her to show me."

"I'll help you bring it in. I saw where you parked. Let's go."

They walked back into the hall but turned the opposite direction, went through a mudroom, and out a door leading onto the wooden deck that wrapped around this side of the house. As they headed for the Jeep, a black-and-white border collie raced up to Kade and gave a single bark.

"That's Smoke. Short for Smokin' Joe because he can run like the wind. He's friendly. You don't have to worry."

She knelt and stuck out a hand so Smoke could sniff her fingers. Ellie ran her palm over his glossy coat. "He's your dog?"

"He's the ranch dog. He kind of belongs to everyone, but I watch out for him."

She loved dogs. If she lived there, she'd have at least two or three.

Kade grabbed both her bags out of the rear of the Jeep and started back toward the house while Ellie slung her laptop case over her shoulder, grabbed her big leather purse, and fell in beside him.

Kade went back inside through the mudroom and opened a door off the hall. There was a nice big bedroom with a small sitting area off to one side and a private bath. An old-fashioned quilted spread covered a queen-size bed with an ornate wrought-iron headboard.

"I'll leave you to it," Kade said. "I think I'll head back to the kitchen and find something to eat. Maria always keeps something around for strays." The door closed, shutting out Logan's tall frame. It felt as if the air had gone out of the room.

Ellie sank down on the bed. Kade Logan had an amazing presence. He had money and power and a sexual aura that was hard to resist.

Ellie wondered why his wife had left him.

Supper was over. It was dark out, the moon covered by a thick layer of clouds. Sitting behind the desk in his study, Kade looked up at a light knock on the door. "Come in."

Ellie Bowman walked into the study, closing the door behind her. "I need to talk to you."

"I figured that when I heard the knock."

"Now that I'm settling in, I have questions. Until I have answers, I can't do my job."

He capped the pen he was holding as he went over the monthly bills. His CPA took care of the day-to-day money side of ranch business, but he still liked to keep an eye on things like income and expenses, watch for ways to make improvements.

"Have a seat."

She sat down in one of the wing-backed, brown-leather chairs across from him. She'd shown up today dressed for ranch living, in a pair of jeans and a yellow-plaid western shirt that stretched over a pair of breasts that threatened to pop the snaps. The humidity in the kitchen left wispy strands of fine, dark auburn hair curling around her face. Kade felt the same pull of attraction he'd experienced the first time he'd seen her and cursed the arousal tightening his jeans.

He leaned toward her across his big oak desk. "So what would you like to ask?"

"I think we can agree the fewer people who know why I'm here the better. After you left, I asked Conner to make a few phone calls. He spoke to Sheriff Carver, got some basic information on the case, and emailed it to me. Once I knew your wife's body was found in Boulder County, I was able to go online and get a copy of the autopsy. Since I'm sure you know the details and hearing them again must be painful, I won't enumerate them here."

"She's been gone eight years. I can handle whatever you have to say." Not exactly the truth. He could handle the details. He knew them by heart. But every time something new came up, the rage resurfaced, the way it had the day they'd found her car.

"Her body wasn't discovered for two years after she died," Ellie continued. "Which destroyed all but the most basic evidence."

Kade said nothing.

"Bones broken in her skull indicated she'd been beaten. The hyoid bone in her neck was broken, which says she was strangled to death."

"Yes."

"There was nothing in the car," she said. "The police believe she took her bags and her purse with her. They weren't with her when they found her body, so the killer must have disposed of them elsewhere."

"Good a guess as any." His jaw felt tight. "They don't know if she was raped. Once I know who the guy is, I'll find out." *Before I kill him.* Kade wondered if Ellie recognized the hard look in his eyes.

"I can get the facts of the case," she said. "I'll read everything I can find about your wife and the murder. What I need to know are the things I can't find in a report."

Wariness trickled through him. "For instance?"

Ellie looked him straight in the face. "Why did your wife leave you?"

Silence fell. Irritation had him sitting up straighter in his chair. "You think Heather was the one who wanted the divorce?"

"You said she'd started seeing someone. Sometimes when a man sleeps around, the woman wants payback."

His jaw tightened even more. "Tit for tat. Is that it?"

"Was it?"

He leaned back in his chair, rocking a little on the springs. "Since you've already formed an opinion, why bother asking me?"

Faint color rose in Ellie's cheeks. She took a deep breath. "You're right. I'm being unfair. It isn't like me. Let's start over. Tell me why the two of you were divorcing."

Kade clamped down on his emotions. He hated this. Hated talking about the past. "You really need to get into my personal life? Can't you just be satisfied knowing the marriage failed?"

"I have to know as much as I can about your wife in order to find out what happened to her. You promised to give me the information I need." She cocked one of her reddish eyebrows. "Or do you want to end this right here?"

Kade's hand tightened around the leather armrest of his chair. He didn't want to talk about his marriage. It had been painful eight years ago when he'd first filed the divorce papers. It was nearly as painful now.

He didn't want to talk about it—but he wanted to catch a killer.

"You want to know what happened, but it's not an easy question to answer. Heather and I were high school sweethearts. She was a cheerleader. I played varsity football. We were prom king and queen, that kind of thing. Heather was beautiful. When we met, I was a senior, and she was a sophomore. The first time I saw her, I fell a little in love."

"You were the star quarterback, right? Most popular guy in school? Or am I jumping to conclusions again?"

He'd been an all-star quarterback, so he didn't correct her.

"I wanted her to marry me as soon as she graduated."

"And Heather wanted that, too?"

"Heather wanted to go to college first. I didn't want to wait. In the end, we compromised. We got married, and she went to the community college in Vail instead of going away to a four-year school."

Ellie studied him. "I think I see where you're going with this."

"Do you?" He leaned toward her. "Heather cheated because I boxed her in. It was my fault. I pressed her to marry me. Her parents pressed her. I was heir apparent to the Diamond Bar Ranch. My family had money, social position. Heather craved freedom. I should have seen it, but I was too busy making plans for the future. Too busy working to build the ranch I'd someday own."

"And after you were married?"

He scrubbed a hand over his face, weary of the conversation. He hadn't talked about Heather and his failed marriage since the day she'd walked out. Hell, he'd never really talked about it.

"My father died a year after we married, and I took over running the ranch. I'd been working on the Diamond Bar since I was a kid. It was all I ever really cared about. I worked long hours, didn't spend the time I should have with Heather. After a few years, she got restless and started cheating. The first time I found out, I pretended not to know. The second time I caught her, I filed for divorce."

He sighed. "Maybe if I'd tried to work things out, she'd still be alive."

"Or maybe not. You had certain expectations when you married her. I imagine she knew what those were."

"She knew I wasn't the kind of man who would tolerate a woman who cheated, if that's what you mean."

"Would you have let her go if she'd been the one to ask for a divorce?"

He'd thought about it after Heather had left. "I'd loved her since high school. I would have let her go if it would have made her happy."

Ellie's big green eyes remained on his face. "Then your failed marriage wasn't entirely your fault. Heather knew the rules. She decided not to play by them."

He just stared. No one had ever said anything like that to him before. He had blamed himself, and no one had ever disagreed. Not Heather's family. Not his mom, who had died a few years after his dad. Not his brothers, who mostly stayed out of his life. Not even Sam. Kade looked at Ellie, and something loosened in his chest.

He rose behind his desk. "If we're done here, I've got a ranch to run."

Ellie stood up across from him. "Thank you for being so honest."

"I assume our conversation won't leave this room."

"You don't have to worry about that, Kade. Not about this or anything else you say to me."

He just nodded.

"You may not realize it, but you've given me a mental picture of your wife. I'll talk to other people, add to the image. It'll help me sort out the kind of man I might be looking for."

"Like I said, Heather was beautiful. Guys pretty much fell at her feet."

"I'm not looking for men who would have wanted Heather. I'm looking for men Heather would have wanted." Turning, she walked out of the room and silently closed the door.

Kade sat back down in his chair. His pulse was hammering. His chest felt tight. He had a strong suspicion he had underestimated Eleanor Bowman.

CHAPTER FOUR

*E*LLIE ENTERED THE KITCHEN BEFORE DAWN THE NEXT MORNING thinking of Kade and their conversation in his study. She had jumped to conclusions when it was her job to remain objective. She'd figured a handsome man like Kade who exuded authority, charisma, and virility wouldn't be satisfied with just one woman.

Halfway through the interview, she'd realized her judgment was colored by her past. She was divorced from a man who had been deceptive and unfaithful. Mark Jeffreys was a handsome attorney, educated at Harvard and incredibly charming. She'd been in love with Mark, too blind to see him for the man he really was.

When she'd walked into their apartment and found him in bed with the wife of one of his clients, she was forced to face the truth she had suspected since a few months after their wedding. Mark was far from the perfect husband she had believed him to be.

And it was past time to file for divorce.

Being single again turned out to be a blessing. Ellie built a new life for herself and reclaimed her independence. She would never give up that independence again.

She thought once more of Kade. She didn't want to like Kade Logan. If she did, the attraction she felt for him would make her job even more difficult.

Last night, she'd had a dozen more questions she'd wanted to ask, but she could see his patience was thinning. She needed his cooperation to find the man she was hunting. She'd have to take it slow.

Ellie grabbed a dark green apron with a Diamond Bar brand printed in white on the front and tied it around her waist. Outside the kitchen windows, a gray dawn was beginning to lighten the sky. Maria arrived while Ellie was turning on the big Viking eight-burner stove.

"I'm glad you're here," Ellie said. "I wasn't sure if you lived on the ranch or in town."

"I live with my grandmother in a cabin a few miles down the road. My mother passed, and my grandmother was lonely."

Ellie smiled. "It's nice that she has you for company."

Maria seemed pleased.

Ellie reached into a cupboard and took out a big frying pan. "We'd better get started. It's only my second day, and I'm still trying to figure things out."

But she had already taken a couple of cartons of eggs and a mound of bacon out of the big Sub-Zero refrigerator. The kitchen was huge and modern, all stainless steel with long stainless counters, glossy white cabinets, and commercial-grade appliances.

This was a working ranch miles from the nearest café. Every day, there was a hungry crew to feed.

Maria started frying bacon while Ellie scrambled the eggs, the two of them sliding into an easy routine. Ellie hadn't cooked for a crowd in years, but as she'd figured, it all came back without much effort.

"I heard some gossip in town," she said as she stirred the eggs, brown shells with bright yellow yolks from ranch chickens. Kade had actually been the source of some of the information, but she needed to keep him out of it. "I guess Kade's late wife's missing car was recently discovered. I heard she was murdered."

Maria nodded. "*Sí*, she was killed years ago, but the sheriff only just found her car. Señor Kade was very upset."

"They say the husband is always the first person the police suspect. I'm surprised they never considered Kade could have done it."

"Oh, for a while, they thought he did. After his wife's body was found, the police were here almost every day. But there was no proof Señor Kade was involved." She looked up at Ellie with big dark eyes. "If they'd seen the way he grieved, they would have known he was innocent."

But Ellie had seen the guilt he still carried. Was it possible after he'd caught Heather cheating, he'd been angry enough to kill her?

It was unlikely the man who had killed her would hire a detective to find out the truth, and from what Kade had said, since his wife had gone missing, she was the second investigator he had employed.

"So you've worked for Kade for quite some time?" Ellie asked, watching the eggs thickening in the skillet.

Maria nodded. "I've known him since before I started high school. My mother worked for him. I helped her after school and on weekends. After my mother was killed in a car accident, I moved in with my grandmother. Señor Kade hired Mabel, but he let me keep my job here on the ranch. He's been very good to my family and me."

Ellie filed the information away.

"Did you know his wife?" One thing about two women working together, talking was a natural way to pass the time.

"*Sí.*"

"What was she like?"

Maria flipped the bacon sizzling in the pan. "It's not good to speak badly of the dead, but I did not like her."

"Why not?"

"Ms. Heather always wanted attention. She flirted with the men and liked to make trouble. Señor Kade's a good man. He deserved someone better."

"I see." Breakfast preparations continued with only a few minor catastrophes, which Ellie figured would smooth out as she got used to the job. Maria told her they made sack lunches for the men's midday meal, since they were often too far away to come all the way back to the house. The Diamond Bar was a far bigger spread than the small ranch she had been raised on.

She glanced at the clock on the wall. At five a.m., the men started filtering in from the bunkhouse, removing their hats and coats one by one, hanging them on the coatrack next to the door. Last night at supper, Kade had introduced her to all of them.

"Mornin', ma'am." Roy Cobb was tall and beanpole thin, with a cowlick in the middle of his forehead. Ellie had a very good memory and a knack for recalling faces.

"Good morning, Roy."

"Ms. Bowman," another man said. Seth Ackerman, early forties, curly brown hair and crooked bottom teeth.

"Seth."

Each man greeted her. Slate Crawford, not bad-looking, with linebacker shoulders as wide as Kade's but more thickly muscled, and short brown hair neatly trimmed. He had all the markings of a lady's man, and she couldn't help wondering if he had been one of Heather's lovers. Then she remembered Kade's hard jaw and the dark look in his eyes when he had talked about this wife.

Probably not.

Turtle Farley was short and stout, round-faced and always grinning.

Alejandro Ramirez followed him in, tall, well-built, jet-black hair and eyes, just enough of a Spanish accent to sound sexy. He was incredibly good-looking. Maria blushed every time Alejandro glanced her way, though he didn't seem to notice.

Riley Parker was engaged to be married to a girl who lived down the road. He had a mop of blond hair he constantly shoved back from his forehead.

Last man in, Kade's foreman, Wyatt Knowles, was older, maybe sixty, with silver hair and a handlebar mustache that curved around his mouth and turned up at the ends. He was quiet-spoken and always watchful, which likely made him good at his job.

The men were sitting at the table, wolfing down their meals, when Kade walked into the kitchen. The room momentarily went silent, his larger-than-life persona briefly capturing everyone's attention. Then they returned to shoveling food into their mouths.

Kade walked toward her, his jaw solid, his hat pulled low. Ellie felt a hitch in her breath that she determinedly ignored. Kade surveyed the kitchen, saw most of the mess had already been cleaned up, then glanced over at his men.

"Doesn't look like they've got any complaints about the food."

Ellie shrugged. "It's breakfast. Bacon and eggs aren't much of a challenge."

"Not if you know how to cook them without setting the kitchen on fire."

She smiled.

"I'm glad you're settling in." Kade's eyes caught hers in silent communication. "I'm heading into town a little later. Why don't you make a list of the supplies you need and you can ride in with me? Save you having to drive in yourself."

She'd been planning to make the trip into Coffee Springs no later than tomorrow. "That would be great." She could dig around, begin asking the raft of questions that crowded her mind. Unfortunately, for every one that got answered, another question came up.

Still, it was a start, and she appreciated Kade making it easy for her.

He served himself a plate of breakfast, took off his hat and sat down with the men, ate, then disappeared down the hall. Ellie and Maria doled out sack lunches and sent the men on their way. They had just finished the final cleanup when Kade returned.

"You ready to go?"

"I'm ready." Ellie flicked him a glance as she grabbed her purse and puffy down jacket. She felt a little zing as he walked up behind her, and both of them headed out the door.

Kade started around to help Ellie into his big, metallic brown, diesel Ford dually pickup, pausing for a moment to give Smoke a quick rub. When he looked up, she was stepping on the running board, hoisting herself into the passenger seat without any help.

Kade rounded the truck and slid in behind the steering wheel, both of them buckled up, and he started the engine. It was ten miles into Coffee Springs, but once they reached the main road, it was paved the rest of the way, so it wasn't a bad drive, and he never grew tired of the beautiful scenery, the open pastures, forested hillsides, and snow-topped mountain peaks.

"So what do you think of the place?" he asked.

Ellie pulled her gaze away from the same landscape he was admiring. "Your ranch is beautiful, Kade. You've really taken care of it."

"My dad left the place in my hands. I couldn't let him down."

"So you were an only child?"

"I've got two brothers, Gage and Edge, but they've never been interested in ranching. They wanted to see the world, make their own way. Gage is, well, I guess you'd call him an adventurer. Travels all over the world looking for one thing or another. Edge is in the military, deployed God-only-knows where. What about you? Any siblings?"

"Nope, only child. My dad died when I was in college. My mom died a few years after I graduated. I still miss her."

He nodded as if he understood. "Why'd you go into law enforcement?"

"Actually, I'm mostly into the investigating part of the business. I go in and figure things out, give the information to my client, and let them take it from there. Sometimes they go to the police; sometimes they handle it a different way."

He wondered what she'd do if she knew he planned to administer his own deadly justice to the man who'd killed Heather. "Seems like an interesting job. How'd you get started?"

"It was kind of an accident. I took a drama class in high school and found out I was good at playing different roles. But I had no desire to actually become an actor. A few years back, I got sucked into helping a friend who had a problem with one of his employees. I played the part of a new hire, managed to find out who was embezzling company money, and realized I had a particularly useful skill set." She looked at him and smiled. "Now here I am."

He started to ask something more when his cell phone started ringing. The service out there was spotty at best, but it was better than nothing.

"Logan."

"Kade, we got another dead steer. Same as before, bullet in the head. I figured you'd want to take a look."

He muttered a curse. "On my way." Tossing his cell up on the dash, he slowed and began to make a U-turn. "Change of plans. That was my foreman. Looks like you're going to have to make that drive into town tomorrow."

"What's going on?"

"Another dead steer. That makes two. Not much chance it's a hunter now, but I need to take a look. It's closer if I just drive straight from here. You all right with that?"

"Absolutely. I'm an investigator. Maybe I'll see something you miss."

It was possible, he supposed. He drove back the way they'd come but turned the pickup onto a rutted dirt road a half mile back.

He'd expected Ellie to badger him with questions. Instead, she rode silently beside him. In the easy quiet that settled between them, some of his tension eased.

Wishing it hadn't rained last night, Kade drove along the fence line until he spotted a couple of bay horses and a big Appaloosa tied to a post and three of his men grouped together in the pasture. He pulled the truck to a stop. He and Ellie got out and walked toward the men.

Kade crouched next to the steer to get a closer look. A single bullet had penetrated the animal's skull. He turned the steer's head, saw that the bullet had gone all the way through from the side. Not much chance of finding it.

"Nice clean shot," Slate said. "Guy was no amateur."

"My guess, steer's been here a couple of days." Wyatt smoothed his silver mustache as he stared down at the carcass. "Probably killed the same day as the first one."

Kade studied the dead Hereford. With their curly red coats and snowy white faces, he had always thought they were beautiful animals. "He shot one, moved, then killed another one."

"He might have figured the gunshot would alert someone,"

Ellie said. "It's pretty far away from anything, but maybe he was being cautious."

Kade cast her a glance. "Sounds about right. The question is why?"

"We took a look around," Turtle said. "Didn't see any more dead animals in the area."

"What about signs of the shooter?" Ellie asked.

"If he left any trace, the rain washed it away," Wyatt said. "If I was going to pick a place to take the shot, I'd be up on that knoll over there." Wyatt pointed. Ellie nodded in agreement and started walking in that direction.

Kade turned back to his men. "I'll take it from here. Ride on up toward Blowout Canyon. Seth spotted a bunch of strays up there before he rode in last night."

"You got it, boss." The men headed for their horses, swung up in their saddles, and nudged the animals off through the grass at an easy lope.

Kade took a last look at the steer, then strode off to catch up with Ellie. She had slender hips, but the kind of round, sexy behind that drew a man's attention. He cursed the heat that slid into his groin as he followed her trail and walked up beside her.

"I don't like losing stock to predators, especially not the two-legged kind."

Ellie flashed him a sympathetic glance and kept walking, head down as she searched the ground on the way to the knoll and began to circle around it. Kade carefully approached the ground at the top. No brass casings. No footprints. Or if there had been any, they'd been washed out by the rain.

Ellie broadened her circle, glancing from the knoll to the road, picking the shortest route between the two. She turned and started walking, and just as she reached the fence, she paused.

"What is it?" Kade asked, catching up with her again.

"Looks like a piece of red flannel." She plucked it off the single strand of barbed wire that ran along the top of the fence. "He must have caught it as he was arriving or leaving."

"Could belong to anyone."

Ellie studied the direct line between the knoll and the road. "It could be, but I'm betting it doesn't."

Kade took the small red square out of her palm. His fingers clenched around it. "I'm going to find him. And when I do, he's going to wish he had never trespassed on my land."

CHAPTER FIVE

With their trip to town canceled, Ellie returned to the kitchen while Kade phoned Eagle County Sheriff Glen Carver. He showed up an hour later, a broad-shouldered man in his late-thirties with thinning brown hair cut short. Ellie wandered out as Kade talked to him about the shooting. Carver asked all the right questions, said he'd take a ride out to look at the second steer, but there was something in his eyes when he looked at Kade that made her wonder about him.

She went back inside and worked with Maria to put supper on the table, a meal of ham and lima beans with cornbread and honey butter, apple cobbler for dessert.

When supper was over, Ellie went to her room to check her email. Her laptop sat on the pretty Victorian writing desk in the sitting area. She sat down in the small, ornately carved chair in front of the screen and pulled up her mail. Conn had sent her a copy of the police report, which dated to the time Heather's body had been found, but there wasn't much in it.

At the time, Sheriff Carver had interviewed some of the locals, but by then the case was cold. Two years earlier, everyone, including Kade, had assumed Heather had taken off for parts unknown and simply disappeared.

Needing a little fresh air, Ellie wandered outside, crossing the yard toward the barn, a big two-story, metal-roofed, wooden structure painted brown. Darkness had settled in. In the quiet, she could hear the soft sound of branches rustling in the breeze and horses moving around in the pasture.

Smoke trotted up beside her, and she scratched behind his ears as she walked through the open sliding double doors. The familiar smell of hay and horses greeted her, along with the shuffle of hooves in one of the stalls.

A dainty little bay mare nickered and stuck her head over the top of her enclosure. Ellie rubbed the velvety nose and straightened the horse's topknot. "Aren't you a pretty girl?" The mare nickered softly.

"Her name's Buttercup." Kade's deep voice came out of the shadows. "The vet gave her a tetanus shot for a cut on her hock, but she's almost healed. She'll be fine in a couple of days. Maybe you'd like to ride her sometime."

She couldn't see his eyes beneath the brim of his hat, but she would have recognized that iron-hard jaw anywhere. A tingle of awareness slipped through her. She told herself to go back to the house, but her legs refused to move.

"I haven't ridden since I left Wyoming," she said, working to keep her voice even. "I used to love it. I had my own horse. His name was Rusty. The bank claimed him as part of the assets when they foreclosed on our ranch."

Kade moved out of the shadows. The snaps on his denim shirt glinted in the moonlight coming in through the open barn windows. "That had to be tough. I know how I'd feel if I lost the Diamond Bar."

"In a way, it killed my dad. I mean, he just got so depressed. Then he got sick and died."

She didn't tell him that she and her mother were left with nothing. That she had worked two jobs to help her mom pay the rent on the small apartment they'd been forced to move into. Or that after her mom finally got a decent job, Ellie had worked to put herself through college.

She didn't say that the hardships they had faced were the reason her independence was so important. She had only given it up one time, when she had married Mark, and that had been a disaster. She wouldn't let it happen again.

"I came to tell you I'd drive you into Coffee Springs tomorrow," Kade said. "I can drop you off in town before I head into Eagle to see the sheriff. Hopefully this time nothing will happen to postpone the trip."

"I'm looking forward to talking to some of the locals."

"Remember to keep an eye open for a guy wearing a torn red flannel shirt."

She glanced up at him. "You don't really think . . . ?"

Amusement lifted a corner of that hard sexy mouth. Her insides curled as a thread of heat slipped through her.

Lust, she thought. It's just a normal response. What woman wouldn't lust after a handsome, ruggedly virile male like Kade Logan. "I'll be sure to keep watch," she replied with a smile.

She turned away and started back toward the barn door, and Kade fell in beside her, slowing a little to match his long strides to her shorter ones.

They crossed the yard, but he stopped her at the base of the steps leading up to the porch on this side of the house.

"I appreciate your insight on the shooting. You've got a good eye for analyzing a situation."

"Thanks. It's a learned but very useful skill." She opened the door and stepped into the hall that led to the mudroom on the other side of the kitchen. She could hear the sound of Kade's heavy boots behind her. Ignoring the uptick of her heartbeat, she turned into her room and firmly closed the door.

Ellie leaned back against it. Her pulse was throbbing, and heat tugged low in her belly. She hadn't dated in months, hadn't had a relationship serious enough to include sex in years. She would have to be careful. She couldn't afford to indulge her off-the-charts attraction to Kade.

Ellie sighed. The last thing she needed was a controlling man like Kade Logan, a man used to running his domain with an iron hand. She needed to do her job and get back to Denver.

Before she made another mistake.

* * *

As he strode down the hall to his study, Kade's mind went back to the moments he had spent with Ellie in the barn. Watching her with the mare, her gentle touch and the softness in her voice, he'd wanted to pull her into his arms and kiss her until her legs went weak.

It wasn't like him. He didn't mix business with pleasure. But as he'd followed her out of the barn, his gaze slid down to her hips, and his palms itched to cup that round behind. He was still hard beneath the fly of his jeans.

He sighed. He wasn't exactly sure how he felt about Eleanor Bowman. He sure as hell knew he'd like to take her to bed.

He walked down the hall into his study and closed the door. It was past time he made a trip to Vail. He usually stayed at the Four Seasons when he needed to get away, needed a place to escape the burdens of running a ranch the size of the Diamond Bar. Or when he needed a woman.

The resort wasn't cheap, but he didn't indulge himself often, and he could afford it. Kade had never brought a woman to the ranch. The ladies he had sex with weren't the kind you brought home.

Grace Towers was the exception. She was classy and smart, a woman he had met in the bar at the resort. Grace was thirty-four, wealthy, a pretty blond divorcée who lived in Denver but also owned a condo in Vail. He'd been up front with Grace from the start. He'd already had one disastrous marriage. He wasn't interested in anything serious.

For almost a year, Grace was okay with that. They'd seen each other whenever their plans coincided, enjoyed a non-exclusive, no-strings relationship. Then she'd wanted more.

Three months ago, he had ended the affair. Since then, he'd slept with a couple of other women, ladies out for a good time in one of the trendy bars in Vail, women who thought it would be cool to sleep with a real Colorado cowboy. He was pretty sure he hadn't disappointed them.

Taking a seat in the leather chair behind his desk, Kade scrubbed a hand over his face, feeling the roughness along his jaw. One-night stands really weren't his style. And the truth, whether he liked it or not, was that Ellie Bowman was the woman he wanted, the first woman he'd been attracted to on more than a physical level in years. Didn't mean he was ready for anything of a serious nature.

Kade leaned back in his chair. From the vibes she was throwing, he didn't think Ellie was any more interested in a serious relationship than he was. Which might just work in his favor. If she felt half the attraction for him that he felt for her, maybe they could enjoy each other for as long as she was there, keep things simple, then go their separate ways with no hard feelings.

He had plenty of time to wait, plenty of problems to keep him occupied while he let things play out. Maybe Ellie Bowman would be worth it.

CHAPTER SIX

WITH BREAKFAST OVER THE FOLLOWING MORNING, ELLIE WATCHED the last of the hands walk out the door, striding off toward their horses or one of the four-wheel ATVs. For a while, Smoke ran along beside them. Then the dog turned and trotted back to the barn to join his friend Billy.

Ellie had met the stable boy, Billy Harris, last night. He was fifteen years old, with light brown hair and blue eyes. The boy worked after school, on weekends, during school breaks and summers, mucking out stalls and doing general cleanup around the property.

According to Kade, his home life sucked, so he spent as much time at the ranch as possible, even stayed in the bunkhouse if the weather was too bad for him to ride his dirt bike back home or one of the hands couldn't drop him off.

As Ellie watched Billy and Smoke through the window, memories arose of her years in Wyoming. In a lot of ways, ranching had changed since she was a girl. In other ways, the business was as rough and tumble, as grueling and demanding as ever.

Droughts, blizzards, cattle theft, disease, falling beef prices. Kade Logan faced those problems every day. She couldn't help admiring him for the success he had made of the Diamond Bar.

He walked into the kitchen just as she and Maria finished cleaning up, and an unwanted flutter rose in the pit of her stomach. *Not good.*

"You ready to make that trip into town?"

More than ready, she thought. The sooner the mystery of Heather's murder was solved, the sooner she could go back to Denver, get away from the temptation Kade Logan posed.

"I'll just grab my stuff."

Thirty minutes later, Kade pulled his dual-wheeled Ford into the parking lot in front of Rocky Mountain Supply, a big metal structure with a row of gas pumps out front. The only other businesses in town were the Coffee Springs Café, the Elkhorn Bar and Grill, Murray's Grocery, the Coffee Springs Bed and Breakfast, and Fred's Gun Shop and Dentistry.

A post office the size of a bedroom sat at the end of two-block-long Main Street, next to an old white, wood-frame house.

"I'll be back in time to buy your lunch at the café," Kade said as Ellie climbed down from the passenger seat.

"Okay, I'll see you there."

Kade touched the brim of the dark brown Stetson he wore for dress and drove off toward Eagle, thirty miles away. He wanted to talk to Sheriff Carver, he'd said. Ellie figured the trip there and back, plus time to take care of his business, gave her a couple of hours to order supplies and wander the tiny town to see if she could come up with any useful information.

Groceries were her first priority. She walked into Murray's Grocery, which reminded her of the store in the small town of Grassy Meadows near their ranch in Wyoming, narrow and old-fashioned, the shelves crowded, but neat and very clean. She headed toward the man behind the front counter, who looked up as she approached. She noticed he had beautiful blue eyes and a handsome face.

"May I help you?" he asked.

"I'm Ellie Bowman. I'm new to the area. I just started working at the Diamond Bar Ranch."

He smiled. "Welcome to Coffee Springs, Ms. Bowman. I'm Jonas Murray. I own the store."

"Nice to meet you, Jonas. I'm taking over the kitchen while the regular cook's on vacation. I came in to pick up supplies."

"Pleasure to meet you." His gaze went to her ringless left hand, then back to her face. He was in his forties, about six feet tall, a snug-fitting navy blue Henley hinting at an athletic body. "Coffee Springs is always happy to have new people. Where are you from, Miss Bowman?"

"It's just Ellie, and I'm from Denver." She glanced around the store. "Kade said the Diamond Bar had an account here. He said just to put whatever I needed on the bill."

"No problem. Did you bring a list?"

"Sure did." She dug the list out of the leather purse slung over her shoulder and handed it across the counter.

"All right, I'll have my son, Sean, put the order together for you. He's on his way in right now."

"I've got some other shopping to do, so there's no real hurry."

He looked down at the list, sizing up the number of items. It was amazing how much a ranch crew could eat. "An hour should be plenty of time."

"Thanks." She shifted the purse up on her shoulder, which pulled her jacket open, and Jonas's gaze went to her breasts. Interest crept into those blue eyes. Apparently he liked what he saw.

His attention returned to her face, and his smile returned. "You're new in town. What do you think so far?"

Ellie shifted, letting the jacket fall open a little wider. In her line of work, a woman's femininity was a valuable tool, something she had learned long ago. In Jonas's case, apparently it was working.

"It's beautiful here," she said. "Unfortunately, I'll only be at the ranch a few weeks, till Kade's regular cook gets back from vacation."

"Mabel mentioned she'd be gone for a while."

"She's visiting family in Phoenix."

Jonas's gaze drifted down then back up. "So . . . you and Kade are . . . friends?"

She shrugged. "Not really. We met in Vail a few years back. He said if I ever needed work to come see him." Let him speculate, wonder if she had slept with Kade, if she might be easy prey, see where the idea led.

"Mabel came to town a couple of times a week," he said. "She never missed. Maybe next time you come in, I could buy your lunch." His smile widened. "We'll be working together. Give us a chance to get to know each other."

Falling into the part she'd decided to play, Ellie returned the smile and made it softly inviting. "I'd like that . . . Jonas."

His blue eyes gleamed. "Then it's a date." He glanced toward the back of the store. "I think I heard my son walk in. I'll give him your list."

"I'll be back later to pick everything up. Great to meet you, Jonas."

His mouth practically watered. "You too, Ellie." Jonas strutted off toward the back of the store, and Ellie walked out the front door, onto the wooden porch. There weren't many men in Coffee Springs, even fewer who would attract a woman as beautiful as Heather Logan.

But Jonas Murray was a handsome man and clearly a player. He'd wasted no time in pursuing Ellie. Jonas had just found a place at the top of her suspect list.

From the market, she walked into the big metal building next door, Rocky Mountain Supply, which seemed even larger inside. The front section of the store was a minimart, with rows of candy bars and snacks, magazines and paperback books, a coffee bar and a beverage counter.

The rest of the space was a general store, with all sorts of farm equipment, saddles and horse gear, racks of clothing, including heavy Carhartt work clothes and western wear. There was a section of camping equipment and RV supplies.

She could see a sign that read FEED AND GRAIN above a door at the back. Rocky Mountain Supply was the only game in town, the only store for miles around that catered to ranchers, outfitters, tourists, and sportsmen.

A steady number of customers moved around inside.

"May I help you?" A stout, gray-haired older woman had noticed her wandering about.

"Yes, thank you. I'm new to the area. I just started working in the kitchen at the Diamond Bar Ranch."

"I heard Mabel took off to visit her son and his family down in Phoenix." The woman smiled. "I'm Frances Tilman. Everybody calls me Fran. Welcome to Coffee Springs."

"I'm Ellie Bowman. It's nice to meet you, Fran. I'm happy to be working at the ranch. It's a beautiful place, and the people there all seem really friendly."

"Oh, they are. I've known most of them since they were kids. Seth Ackerman is engaged to my niece."

Ellie smiled. "That's the nice thing about small towns. Everybody gets to know everybody."

"True, and it's one of the things that make Coffee Springs such a great place to live."

"Sure seems like it."

"So you aren't married?"

"No. Though it would be nice to have a family someday." *If she could ever find a man she could trust, one who wouldn't try to control her.*

They chatted amiably for a while, talked about the weather, about the scenery. Fran showed her around the store, and Ellie selected a few items just to keep her talking: a pink paisley western shirt, a quilted down vest, and a pair of Montana Silversmith earrings.

"I just met Jonas Murray," she said to test the waters.

Fran's silver eyebrows pulled together. "I'm not surprised."

"What do you mean?"

"You're new in town. Not many gals around as pretty as you. Men like Jonas . . . sometimes they try to take advantage."

"Really? Is he married?"

"Was till his wife left him some years back. I suspect Jenny caught him with his pecker somewhere it shouldn't be."

Ellie laughed. She wondered how long ago that was and if the woman he was having the affair with could have been Heather Logan. She'd take a look at county divorce records, figure out the timing.

"Jonas was very nice, and I'm not married either. He asked me to lunch. That ought to be safe enough, don't you think?"

Fran shrugged her plump shoulders. "You're both adults, both single. I don't suppose there's anything wrong with it. Just remember what I said."

Ellie nodded. "Oh, I will."

Fran seemed satisfied her advice had been taken. She was clearly the town gossip, or maybe it was just that there were so few people who lived in the area that gossiping was a sort of recreation.

"You know there is one thing that bothers me about living out at the ranch," Ellie said as they headed for the checkout register.

"What's that?"

"I heard Kade Logan's wife was murdered and they recently found her car. It kind of makes me nervous, you know? I mean, they've never found the woman's killer. He could be right there on the ranch."

"Well, you don't have to worry about Kade. That man worshipped his wife." Fran sighed. "She was the most beautiful creature you ever did see. Tall and blond, like an angel. They were high school sweethearts, you know."

"I heard that. Maybe now that they've found her car, they can find the guy who killed her."

Fran leaned toward her. "Just between you and me, that woman was lucky someone didn't kill her sooner. Why, she was always flirting with some fella. Didn't matter if he was married or not. Liked to make men jealous. Kade just seemed to close his eyes. He didn't want to lose her, I guess."

"You think she and Jonas were . . . ?"

"No idea. If they were, I never heard."

They reached the register, and Fran went behind the counter to ring up Ellie's order. She paid for her purchases and left the store. As she walked down the street, she smiled. For her first few days on the case, she had gleaned a surprising amount of information.

She wondered what Kade would say about her upcoming lunch date with Jonas Murray.

CHAPTER SEVEN

KADE SAT BEHIND THE WHEEL, WITH ELLIE IN THE PASSENGER SEAT as he pulled the pickup around to the back of Murray's Grocery. Jonas's son, Sean, was waiting, and the two of them loaded the food and supplies into the bed of the truck.

"Thanks, Sean," Kade said when they were finished. He liked the lanky teenager, who was a hard worker and always friendly.

Kade returned to his seat and cranked the engine, firing the truck up again. "Hungry?" he asked Ellie.

"Starved."

He drove the truck out from behind the grocery store into the street. "So how'd it go? Learn anything useful?"

"Maybe. People were easy to talk to. I remember that's the way it was when I was growing up in Wyoming. Frances Tilman over at Rocky Mountain Supply could be a well of information."

"You got that right. Woman's got her nose stuck in everybody else's business."

"She talked about you and your wife, among other things."

Irritation trickled through him. He didn't like the idea of people talking about him behind his back. "What did she say?"

Ellie slanted him a look. "If I tell you this stuff, I want your word you won't mention where you heard it, and you won't confront the people who told me. Once I break their trust, I'll never get it back."

He frowned. "I don't gossip, never have. Whatever you say goes no further."

"Fran said Heather liked to make men jealous. She said you pretty much ignored it because you didn't want to lose her."

A muscle jerked in his cheek. "She was my wife. I took a vow. I planned to keep it."

"But there is only so much a person should have to take. I know because I divorced my husband for cheating. And I don't regret it one little bit."

He turned his head to study her from beneath the brim of his hat. Why a man would want to cheat on a woman who looked like Ellie he couldn't imagine.

He slowed the truck and pulled into the parking lot of the Coffee Springs Café. "Maybe if Heather hadn't been murdered, I wouldn't regret it, either. Unfortunately, I'll never know."

Ellie's eyes, green as spring hay, shot to his. Today she'd pulled her glorious auburn hair into a pony tail that swung appealingly back and forth across her back. He tried not to imagine what those shiny curls would look like spread over his pillow.

They climbed out of the truck and went into the café, which had old-fashioned molded-tin ceilings and branding irons on the walls. Kade waited till Ellie slid into one of the red-vinyl booths, sat down across from her, and picked up a menu, though he knew it by heart.

"So what else did you learn?" He perused the menu, trying to appear casual. He didn't really like hearing what people said about him. It was none of their business how he ran his life, but he needed answers, and it looked like Ellie might actually have a chance of getting them.

"Well, I met Jonas Murray when I was getting groceries. When I asked Frances about him, she said he was a real hound dog. That's the reason his wife divorced him."

"I could have told you that."

"Jonas asked me out. He said Mabel came in at least a couple of times a week. I've got a lunch date with him the next time I come in for groceries."

The news hit him like a punch in the solar plexus. Jealousy was an emotion he'd learned to control when he was with Heather.

He'd thought he'd buried it completely with his late wife. "What the hell?"

"Take it easy. There's a chance he had an affair with Heather. If he did, that puts him on our suspect list."

Kade leaned back against the seat. He tolerated Jonas Murray, but he didn't really like the man. Jonas was a good-looking, athletic guy women were drawn to. Kade didn't like the idea of Jonas with Ellie.

Kade closed the menu. When the waitress walked up, Ellie ordered a salad, and Kade ordered a burger. Both of them ordered coffee. Wendy, the daughter of the café owners, Sally and Chill Cummings, filled their cups with the steaming brew. A few minutes later, she returned with their orders, set them down with a thud on the table.

She smiled. "Nice to see you, Kade. It's been a while."

"Wendy, this is my new cook, Ellie Bowman. She's taking Mabel's place till she gets back from Phoenix."

Wendy darted a quick glance across the table. "Good to meet you, Ellie."

"You too, Wendy."

Her attention returned to Kade, and her smile broadened. "Anything you need, just let me know."

"I will. Thanks."

Wendy sashayed away, hips swinging. She had a great figure, and she knew it.

"That woman has the hots for you," Ellie said.

Kade nearly lost the mouthful of coffee he had just taken.

"She's Chill Cummings's daughter. She's only twenty-two."

"So? You're what, fifteen or sixteen years older? Thirty-seven or eight?"

"Thirty-seven. The way I feel lately, I'm surprised you didn't think I was a lot older than that."

Ellie laughed. It was a soft rumbling, sexy sound that sent his blood heading south.

"So . . . you prefer more mature women?"

Was she flirting? He could only hope. He wasn't interested in twenty-two-year-old Wendy Cummings, but he was sure as hell interested in Eleanor Bowman.

"A lady about your age would do just fine."

Faint color rose in her cheeks. She took a drink of coffee. So did Kade.

He set the china cup down on the table. "If you want to meet some locals, there's a country western band plays at the Elkhorn on Friday nights. Just a couple of musicians who drive up from Eagle, but they're really not too bad. I'll take you if you want to go."

She eyed him across the table, clearly reluctant. "That's a good idea, but it might be better if I went by myself."

Kade picked up a french fry and dabbed it in the ketchup he'd squeezed onto his plate. "Women around here don't go to bars alone. That might be old-fashioned, but that's the way it is."

Ellie's forkful of salad paused halfway to her lips. "You're right. I don't know what I was thinking."

Kade knew exactly what she was thinking. That she didn't want to go out with him. It didn't take much for a man to recognize that look in a woman's eyes. He stopped eating as a thought suddenly occurred. "You don't think I killed Heather, do you?"

Her gaze met his and didn't move away. "From what I'm hearing around town, you definitely had motive. But I doubt you'd be dumb enough to hire two different detectives to find Heather's killer if you were the guy who did it."

He relaxed back in the booth, more relieved that he should have been. He thought of the way she had looked at him in the barn last night. He wasn't an expert on women, but he was pretty sure the attraction was mutual.

"All right," he said. "Then we'll go to the Elkhorn on Friday night, and I'll introduce you around."

Ellie just nodded, obviously not excited at the prospect. If she really wasn't interested, he'd find out Friday night.

She went back to work on her salad. "What did Sheriff Carver have to say?"

"I asked him if there were any other reports of cattle being killed in the area, but so far, there haven't been any."

"So maybe the shooting was personal."

That's what Kade had been thinking, though he hadn't come right out and said it, didn't really want to believe it. "You could be right. I was hoping it was just some bastard who got a kick out of shooting a moving target, but it could be he's zeroed in on the Diamond Bar."

"Or you, specifically. You're a powerful man in the area. You must have enemies. You need to make a list, Kade."

He nodded. "You're right. I wish you weren't."

"Maybe whoever you pissed off will consider two dead steers enough of a payback."

"I sure as hell hope so."

They finished the meal, and he followed her out to his truck. They were just driving out of town when his cell phone rang. The call came out through speakers on the dashboard.

"Kade, this is Will Turley. We've got a problem out at the mine."

"Since when do you call me about a mining issue?"

"Since someone blew up one of the shafts and damn near killed one of my men. You're the leaseholder, so I figured you'd want to know."

Kade's hand tightened around the steering wheel. "You're right. I'm on my way." He turned to Ellie. "Phone Maria and tell her to go ahead and start making supper. You're going to be late getting back."

Ellie pulled out her cell and made the call, then settled back in the seat. "I didn't realize you owned a mine. I guess I should have done a little more research."

"The mining operation is owned by Red Hawk Mining, which is part of Mountain Ore, a big international conglomerate. They lease the mine, but the claim sits on the original Diamond Bar homestead, 619 acres south of Copper Mountain down in Summit County. Dad moved the ranch headquarters when he bought the acreage up near Coffee Springs."

"How far away is it?"

"From here, about an hour and half." Kade rubbed a hand over his jaw. "Two dead steers and now this. There's always problems to deal with on the ranch, but this feels different. I don't like it."

"You're thinking there's a chance killing the steers wasn't enough payback after all."

That was exactly what he was thinking. Ellie seemed to have a knack for reading his thoughts. His glance strayed to the tempting swell of her breasts beneath her pale blue turtleneck sweater. He hoped to hell she couldn't tell what he was thinking right now.

He fixed his gaze firmly back on the road. "You're a detective. You made some solid observations at the scene of the shooting. Maybe you'll pick up on something at the mine the rest of us miss."

"I'm on your payroll. Up to you to decide where I can be the most useful."

His mind slid immediately into the gutter. Kade clamped down on his lustful thoughts. He had more important matters to deal with than the throbbing in his groin.

Kade stepped on the gas.

CHAPTER EIGHT

*E*LLIE SETTLED BACK FOR THE DRIVE FROM COFFEE SPRINGS TO THE Red Hawk Mine. The case she'd undertaken had turned out to be far more complicated than she'd expected. And far more intriguing.

She was too much of a professional not to wonder if the dead steers and the explosion at the mine were connected. She'd know more once they got there and she took a look around. In the meantime, she planned to sit back and enjoy the ride.

Kade drove Highway 131 from Coffee Springs to I-70, took the interstate east through Vail, past Copper Mountain, then turned south on 91. A sign read LEADVILLE and GRANITE. Their route had started in high mountain country, dropped down to a drier, more arid landscape, then started climbing again, winding through soaring mountains, clear, glassy lakes, and deep green, forest-lined canyons.

It was in those canyons that silver, copper, and lead were discovered in the 1870s and '80s, producing huge amounts of ore, creating the great Colorado silver boom. Some of the mines were still producing today.

Which was about all Ellie remembered from her history classes.

The pickup pulled onto a single-lane asphalt road that ran parallel to a rushing stream and climbed slowly higher. At one point, it forked, and she could see a timber gate just like the one leading into the Diamond Bar, with a pair of elk antlers on each end of the sign. Instead, the pickup took the left-hand fork in the road.

"The old ranch is that way." Kade pointed toward the gate. "The original cabin is still there, built by my great-grandfather, along with a couple of outbuildings and the original barn."

"Do you still use the cabin?"

"I usually stick close to home in case I'm needed, but whenever I get the chance, I come up here and stay a few days, do some hunting and fishing. Sometimes getting back to basics feels really good."

"So you keep the buildings maintained."

He nodded. "Seems like I owe that much to my family, the men and women who came before me. It took a lot of hard work to build the homestead into the ranch it is today. Besides, it's good to have a place to get away once in a while."

"You ever bring anyone up here with you?" she asked, though she didn't think the cabin sounded like Heather's kind of place.

He sliced her a look from beneath the brim of his hat. "You mean like a woman? No. Heather would have hated it, and there hasn't been anyone else I wanted to spend that much time with."

She didn't say more as the pickup began to climb a steep gravel road that wound through a narrow canyon. Kade pulled up in an open area in front of a group of wood and metal buildings and braked to a stop. Off to one side, Ellie could see the mine entrance, a dark hole in the steep side of the mountain.

"It's a small operation," Kade said. "The claim started producing in the 1890s. It closed after World War Two for about thirty years. When prices went up, Mountain Ore Mining bought the Red Hawk, renewed the lease, and started production again."

He cracked open the pickup door and stepped out of the truck. Ellie got out and walked around to his side of the vehicle.

"I assume this is a silver mine," she said as they crossed the open area toward a wooden building with a sign that read OFFICE above the door.

"Mainly silver, lead, and zinc. Also some sphalerite, galena, and pyrite, a little gold."

"Gold?"

"Not enough to be profitable. It's the other stuff that makes the money."

She glanced around the operation, watched a group of miners at work. A skip loader rolled one way and then another, picking up rocks and carrying them from place to place. One of the workers, a tall, lanky man with curly red hair, broke away from the others and strode toward them.

"Kade, thanks for coming." He stuck out a hand Kade shook.

"You wouldn't have called if you hadn't thought it was important."

"The mine is on your land. That gives you a certain liability. This wasn't an accident. I figured you'd want to know."

Kade turned. "Will Turley, this is Ellie Bowman. Will's the supervisor here. Ellie works for me at the ranch. She was with me in town. Faster to come straight here."

Turley tipped his head in her direction. "Nice to meet you, Ms. Bowman."

"Ellie," she corrected.

Turley smiled. "Ellie."

"Where'd this happen?" Kade asked.

"Follow me." Turley started striding away, and Kade followed, while Ellie hurried to keep up with the two tall men.

Turley led them toward the hole in the mountain and disappeared inside. Kade followed, but Ellie hung back. Her heart was pounding, her palms sweating. Her breath hitched in and out a little too fast.

She was hoping it wouldn't happen, but she'd had a fear of tight places since she was a kid. Since the dirt-and-log fort she'd built and played in with her dog, Tuff, had caved in on her. She'd been buried up to her neck for hours when the rain had started, turning the dirt to mud. She'd been sure she was going to die that day.

Kade paused and looked back. "You coming?"

She moistened her lips and nodded. She could do this. The accident had happened a long time ago. She just needed to take a few deep breaths. She followed Kade and Will Turley into the mine, which felt cool and damp, the air heavy with the scent of moist earth.

Kade fell back to walk beside her. "You okay?"

"I'm not crazy about places like this, but I'll be all right."

"You can wait in the truck if you want."

"I'm fine." He kept an eye on her as they headed deeper into the main shaft. She could see quite a way down the tunnel, which was lit by a string of overhead lights. A compressor pumped air along a tube that ran deep into the mountain.

When Turley halted, Ellie forced herself not to turn around and run back outside.

"There." Turley pointed toward a dark hole off to one side. "That's a tunnel we just started digging off the main shaft. The explosion turned it into a pile of rubble. A small crew was preparing to go in. Dick Murphy had just started to check the air when the explosion went off. We drove him to the hospital. He was hurt real bad."

"Sorry to hear that."

"Did any of the miners see anyone unusual in the area?" Ellie asked.

"They were all busy working. It was early, so I figure whoever did it was up here last night."

Kade walked over to examine the pile of rocks that had collapsed into the tunnel but hadn't completely sealed it off. Turley climbed to the top of the rocks and ducked through the low opening that led to the other side.

Ellie thought of the dark hole Turley had gone into, and her chest clamped down. Kade handed her his Stetson.

"Why don't you go back and take a look around outside? I'll be out in a minute."

Ellie didn't argue. She was doing her best not to hyperventilate. "Okay," she said a little breathlessly.

Still, she waited until Kade had climbed the rubble pile and disappeared inside to join Turley. Just watching him sent her anxiety up another notch.

Fortunately, her school nurse had known a lot about anxiety. After the accident, Mrs. Scarsdale taught her some tricks to help her control the panic attacks.

Ellie took a deep breath and slowly released it as she headed back toward the light at the mouth of the tunnel, grateful to feel the sun on her face as she walked outside. She took a couple more calming breaths, then started toward the pickup.

She glanced down at Kade's hat, which still held a trace of his body heat, the brim marked with the faint imprint of his callused fingers. There was something about the hat, something intimate and strangely sensual that made her stomach contract with an odd sort of longing.

Ellie hurried to the truck, set the hat on the seat, then turned and started toward the group of miners who were busy doing their jobs, whatever they might be. She approached an older, silver-haired man standing off by himself with a can of Pepsi in his big, gnarled hand.

"So I guess there was an accident here this morning," she said. "What happened?"

His gaze flicked toward the tunnel. "Not sure yet. There was some kind of explosion. Things like that can happen in a mine, but there was no gas buildup, nothin' like that, and none of us was using any explosives."

"How's the man who was injured?"

"Dick Murphy. He might lose his leg. We're all hoping he'll be okay."

"I hope so, too."

The man looked away and took a long swallow of soda. Being a miner was a dangerous job. The explosion must have brought that truth home to the men.

Kade walked out of the tunnel, and Ellie headed over to meet him.

"Summit County sheriff will be out to take an incident report," he said, his expression grim. "But it won't happen till later today. Meantime, I need to get back to the ranch." He didn't say more till they were inside the truck, just picked up his hat, settled it on his head, and started the engine.

Kade flicked Ellie a sideways glance. "What happened to you in there?" He drove away from the mine and started back down the narrow road toward the valley below.

"I'm kind of claustrophobic. It started after an accident I had as a kid." She went on to explain about the log fort collapsing, being half-buried and terrified. "It was dark by the time my dad finally found me. I was only ten. I thought I was going to die."

"You should have said something."

She shrugged. "I'm over it mostly. I mean, elevators don't bother me, stuff like that. The mine . . . that was different."

He grunted. "It's not my favorite place, either."

"The guy I was talking to said the man who was injured might lose his leg. Did you figure out what happened?"

Anger glittered in those golden-brown eyes. "Looks like it was an IED. Murphy kicked a rock and set it off. If he'd stepped on it directly, he'd probably be dead."

Her stomach squeezed. "IED? Are you sure?"

"Turley's a marine. Served in Afghanistan. He hasn't put the information out to his men or anyone else, but he's sure."

"Maybe it was a disgruntled employee," she said. "Someone he fired."

His gaze slanted to hers. "Someone who wanted payback?"

The knot in her stomach tightened. "Maybe."

"The mine sits on Diamond Bar property. I'm not a big believer in coincidence."

Ellie glanced back toward the mine. "Neither am I."

Two days later, Kade drove Ellie in for supplies and her lunch date. It burned him to think of her with Jonas Murray. Murray was the biggest womanizer in Coffee Springs. Once Heather was gone, Kade had managed to block the notion the guy could have been sleeping with his wife. He figured Heather would have had better taste. Now Ellie had forced him to face that very real possibility.

As he drove down the road, Kade thought of their earlier conversation. Ellie had wanted to drive herself into town, but Kade had told her he had a Cattlemen's Association meeting in Eagle, which fortunately was true.

"I'll be done about the time you're finished," he'd said. "Save us taking two vehicles." It was an excuse, and the look in Ellie's green eyes said she knew it.

"You told me yourself the guy is at the top of your murder suspect list," he added. "I don't like the idea of you being alone with him."

"I won't be alone, and even if I am, I've got a gun in my purse, so you don't have to worry."

It made him feel better, but not much.

"I'll see you back here in an hour and a half," he said. "You've got my number. Text me if you need more time."

"All right."

He wanted to lean over and kiss her, leave her with the imprint of his mouth over hers as she talked to Murray. Fortunately, he came to his senses.

Kade looked in the mirror as he drove away, saw Ellie disappear into the grocery store, and cursed.

CHAPTER NINE

*E*LLIE GAVE JONAS HER LIST OF SUPPLIES, WHICH HE HANDED TO HIS teenage son, then they walked over to the Coffee Springs Café.

Dressed in jeans, a dress shirt, and a navy wool jacket, Jonas looked good, his perfectly styled brown hair barely moving in the wind blowing down off the mountains.

Wendy Cummings took their orders. The pretty blonde was friendlier this time, probably because Ellie wasn't with Kade. She and Jonas talked about the weather, always a safe place to start, progressed into a little local gossip, and then Jonas mentioned he had heard someone had shot two of Kade's steers.

"Word travels fast," Ellie said, forking up a bite of chicken Caesar salad.

"Probably just some rowdy kids wanting to shoot at something besides a paper target."

"You think so? I was thinking more along the lines of a disgruntled employee taking it out on Kade."

Jonas shrugged. "Could be, I suppose. Kade always brings in a bunch of part-time hands to work the fall roundup. Maybe one of them got pissed about something."

"That certainly sounds possible." If Kade would make a list of the men he'd hired, they could discuss it, find out if he'd had problems with any of the men.

Jonas finished the first half of his corned beef sandwich. "You're out at the ranch. Heard anything new on Heather's murder? I imagine Kade's pushing hard now that they found Heather's car."

It was the perfect opening to discuss the subject.

Ellie gave him a conspiratorial smile. "Kade doesn't talk about it, but everyone else does. I heard her stuff wasn't in the car when they pulled it out of the lake."

"Which means she must have gone with the killer willingly."

"That's what I was thinking." Ellie leaned toward him. "It's kind of exciting, don't you think? Being involved in a murder investigation? Did the cops ever talk to you about her?"

He nodded, picked up the second half of his sandwich. "After they found her body, one of the Eagle County deputies came into the store and asked me some questions. Nobody's come around since they found the car."

"I saw her picture. She was really beautiful."

Jonas looked wistful. "Yeah, she was."

"I hear she got around. Liked to flirt and make guys jealous. Did you ever . . . you know, sleep with her?"

Color crept into Jonas's face. "No, of course not."

"I guess I shouldn't have asked. Kade might go after you if he ever found out. You could end up getting hurt."

Jonas's chin jutted out at belligerent angle. "I'm not afraid of Kade Logan."

Ellie grinned. "So you did sleep with her."

The corner of Jonas's mouth kicked up. "I didn't say that, did I?" But he had the smug look of a man who was proud of the conquest he had made.

Ellie took another bite of salad. "Was Heather the reason you and your wife divorced?" She'd gone online and looked at county records, seen a copy of Jonas's divorce papers. Jennifer Murray had filed the petition eight years ago, around the time Heather had disappeared.

Jonas shook his head. "Not really. We'd been having trouble for a while."

They finished their meals, and Wendy refilled their coffee

cups. Jonas took a sip of coffee. "We've talked about me too long. What about you? You're not married, right? Beautiful woman like you? Why not?"

Ellie shrugged. "I like being single. I like having my independence, being able to do whatever I please." Though she was playing a role, it was true. She liked her life for the most part. Still, there were times she wished she had someone who cared about her the way Kade had cared about Heather.

Jonas reached over and took hold of her hand where it rested on the table. "Maybe sometime you'd like to come over for supper. Surely you get a day off once in a while. I make a mean pot of spaghetti." He smiled. "Add a nice bottle of chianti, who knows what might happen."

"Ellie doesn't have time to date," Kade said darkly from beside her, the conversation around them having muffled his approach. Ellie's head came up, and she jerked her hand out of Jonas's grip.

"She's only going to be here a couple of weeks, and I need her on the ranch," Kade said.

She pasted on a smile and slid out of the booth, trying to hide her annoyance. "I guess it's time to go. Thanks for lunch, Jonas."

Jonas cast Kade a disapproving glance, then smiled at Ellie. "I'll see you in the store on your next trip to town."

Ellie just nodded. "Thanks again." She started walking toward the door, felt Kade's big hand at her waist, and ignored the warmth spreading through her.

She climbed into the truck and slammed the door, silently fuming as Kade slid into the driver's seat. She pinned him with a glare.

"Why on earth did you do that? Jonas was just beginning to trust me enough to talk."

Kade's golden eyes zeroed in on her. "What about you, Ellie? You beginning to trust him, too?"

Her eyes widened. "Are you kidding? I'm not interested in Jonas Murray. I'm trying to find out if he killed your wife!"

A flush rose in Kade's lean cheeks. "You think he did it?"

Ellie blew out a frustrated breath. "My instincts say no. He's a chaser, not a killer. But I need to do a little more checking before I can be sure."

Kade leaned back in his seat. "Look, I'm sorry. I don't know what the hell happened. I saw you through the window, and I thought about the way he treats women, the way he talks about them behind their backs. I don't like the bastard and never have."

She didn't tell Kade that Jonas had very likely slept with his wife. She didn't want to be responsible for the grocery store owner winding up in the hospital.

"You going to his house for supper?" Kade asked.

"No. I would have politely declined. But thank you for saving me the trouble."

He flicked her a glance that held a trace of amusement. "My pleasure," he said.

Kade sat hunched over his desk that night, staring at the screen on his laptop. Ellie wanted the name of the men who had worked part-time during the roundup, or anyone he might have pissed off enough to kill two of his steers.

He had just finished perusing the list one more time when a light knock sounded at the door. He already recognized the knock as belonging to Ellie, and anticipation he didn't want to feel poured through him.

"Come on in." He felt a little kick as he watched her cross the room and sit down in the leather chair across from him.

"Did you make the list?"

He studied the screen on his laptop. "I pulled up the names of the part-time guys on the payroll at the time of the roundup. I know most of them. They've worked for me before. They're good men. I can't remember having a beef with any of them. Or any-one else."

"Are you sure? Maybe it was something that seemed unimpor-tant to you but was a big deal to one of them."

He looked down at the computer screen but nothing stood out. He shook his head. "I don't see anything that rings a bell."

"How about someone who didn't make it to the end of the pay period? Someone who might have been paid before the roundup was over and left?"

He thought about it, and a memory surfaced. "Frank Keller. Older guy, always bitching about something. We were short a few men. Seth found him in town and brought him out to the ranch. I remember he only worked a week or so before he got into an argument with Alejandro. Used a racial slur, said he wouldn't take orders from someone like him."

"So you fired him?"

"Wyatt sent him packing, but Keller confronted me before he took off. Said he deserved extra pay for changing his plans and driving all the way out here. I told him to forget it. He was a troublemaker. He'd get paid what he'd earned but not a dime more. I told him the only thing he deserved was a punch in the mouth and I'd be happy to give him one."

Ellie laughed. "Not a good idea to go around assaulting people, Kade. Someone might press charges, and you could end up in jail."

He didn't bother to reply. He hadn't hit the guy, so it was no big deal.

"You wouldn't happen to know if Frank Keller was ever in the military?" Ellie asked.

"No idea."

"I'll find out. Anyone else you can think of besides Keller who might hate your guts?"

Kade grinned. "No."

Ellie laughed. She rose from her chair. "It's getting late. I've got to be up early, and as you once pointed out, I don't want to miss my beauty sleep."

He remembered, and desire slipped through him. He knew exactly how to give the lady a very good night's sleep. "I'll see you at breakfast."

He watched her cross the room to the door and tried not to notice the way her jeans cupped that round behind. His groin tightened. Damn, he needed a woman.

Unfortunately, he had reached the point where only one woman would do. He wanted to pursue the attraction, but with the two of them working together, it wasn't a good idea. Ellie walked out of the study. The door closed quietly behind her, and Kade softly cursed.

CHAPTER TEN

*T*HE WEATHER CHANGED, GREW OMINOUS. THICK BLACK CLOUDS rolled in over the valley. Lightning erupted, and heavy sheets of rain poured down, turning the pastures to mud. Then the winds swept in, gusts up to sixty miles an hour, heralding an early winter storm of epic proportions that no one had expected.

Kade had been up twenty-four straight hours, most of them in the saddle. He and the men were moving stock from one pasture to another in search of safe havens from the battering wind and rain. When Wyatt, Alejandro, and Roy Cobb showed up to take their shift, Kade, Seth, and Turtle headed back to the ranch.

The men rode into the barn to take care of their horses. Kade swung down from the saddle, rain dripping from the brim of his hat onto his yellow rubber slicker, and Billy ran up to take the reins of Kade's big buckskin, Hannibal.

"Rub him down real good, Billy, and make sure he gets an extra scoop of grain."

"Yes, sir."

As the men headed for the bunkhouse to change out of their wet, muddy clothes, Billy led the tired animal away, and Kade headed for the kitchen. Wearily climbing the steps, he removed his wet hat and slapped it against his thigh.

He was wearing his fringed leather chaps against the cold and the yellow rain slicker that helped keep him dry. Stepping into the kitchen, he hung his hat on the rack, along with his slicker and the Carhartt jacket underneath.

"Kade! You're back." *Ellie.* "Come in and get warm. We've been worried about you." The concern in her voice warmed him more than the temperature in the kitchen.

"*Sí,* you should've come in sooner," Maria chided, and if he hadn't been so tired, he might have smiled. "I'll get you a cup of coffee," she said.

"We made a big pot of beef noodle soup and a stack of roast beef sandwiches," Ellie said. "We figured when the hands rode in, we'd have something warm for them to eat."

"That's good," Kade said. "Beats the hell out of a sack lunch. Thanks." He sat down tiredly at the table, and Ellie brought him a bowl of hot soup and a sandwich piled high with beef and cheese on whole wheat bread.

"How's it going out there?" she asked.

"Riley's horse took a fall, broke Riley's leg. We splinted the leg, and Slate took him in. They're on the way to the clinic in Eagle."

"Oh, dear. I hope he's going to be okay."

"The break looks pretty clean. With any luck, he'll be fine."

Ellie frowned. "With Riley gone, that puts you one man short. Two until Slate gets back."

He just nodded. Losing Riley was going to make a tough situation a whole lot tougher. He dipped into his soup, which, at the moment, tasted better than filet mignon. A couple more mouthfuls and he glanced up to see Ellie standing next to him.

"Maria can handle the cooking. Until the storm passes, we won't be doing anything fancy. I can take Riley's place."

For a second, he thought his hearing was faulty. "You got any idea what it's like out there?"

Ellie's gaze went to the steamy glass panes battered by slashes of rain. "I've got a pretty good idea just looking out the window."

"Yeah, well, it's worse than it looks. It's nice of you to offer, but—"

She gently squeezed his shoulder. "I'm from Wyoming, Kade. I've worked in conditions like these. You need a hand. I can do the job."

He didn't want her to do it. He already had a man down, and he didn't want Ellie getting hurt. He started to shake his head.

"Let me help you, Kade," she said softly.

He scrubbed a hand over his face, felt the roughness along his jaw. "I need a couple of hours' sleep. Seth and Turtle came in with me. They need to eat and get a little rest before we go back out. If you're still willing, I'll have Billy saddle you a horse."

"I'll get my things together. I can do this, Kade. If I wasn't sure, I wouldn't have offered."

Already regretting his decision, he finished his meal and headed upstairs to bed. Two hours later, his alarm went off. Ignoring the wet, muddy clothes he had discarded in a pile on the bathroom floor, he put on his long underwear, jeans and boots, and a heavy flannel shirt, snapped his chaps up the sides, and went back down to the kitchen.

Seth and Turtle were already there. Kade paused long enough to down a mug of hot coffee and grab a couple of fresh-baked chocolate chip cookies. He set the empty mug on the kitchen counter as Ellie arrived in jeans, a turtleneck sweater, and a pair of scuffed brown cowboy boots. He could tell by the fuller shape of her body that she was wearing long underwear, which told him he had spent way too much time checking out her sexy curves. At the moment, he was just glad she was dressed warmly.

"Looks like you're all ready to go," he said.

"I was raised on a ranch. I came prepared."

Turtle cast a sideways look at Ellie. "Boss, you sure about this?"

"Kade might not be sure, but I am," Ellie said. "I'm ready any time you are."

Kade strode to the door, grabbed his hat and tugged the brim down low. Ellie grabbed a heavy down jacket off the back of a chair and slipped it on.

"You got a hat?" he asked.

She picked up a battered felt cowboy hat off the table next to the coat and settled it on her head as if she had done it a thousand times.

Kade looked at the woman in front of him, and heat rushed straight to his groin. *Jesus.* The shot of lust was totally unexpected, completely out of place, and definitely unwanted.

"Rain gear?" he asked.

"Seth found me a slicker that'll work."

"All right, let's go." The men walked outside into the pouring rain. Kade stopped Ellie as she started past him. "Stay close. Where I go, you go. Okay?"

She just nodded and headed out the door. Kade followed, the rain slamming into him as he walked next to her toward the barn. Billy had saddled four fresh horses. The kid stood just inside the barn holding the reins, Smoke close beside him. He'd be staying in the bunkhouse till the storm quieted enough for him to go home.

Kade strode toward his second mount, a big bay gelding named Kojak. Billy had saddled a spotted mare named Painted Lady for Ellie—a good choice, Kade figured. The mare was strong, dependable, and easy to manage.

Ellie made a cursory examination of the equipment, checked the bridle, the front and back cinches, and the length of the stirrups Billy had shortened to fit her. Kade blinked when she ignored the stirrups, grabbed the horn and vaulted into the saddle, then looked over at him and grinned.

Kade laughed. He was freezing his ass off, his eyes gritty from lack of sleep. The rumble of mirth coming from his chest completely surprised him. And he appreciated it more than she could know. He touched the brim of his hat in salute, gigged the bay, and they rode out of the barn into the rain.

Kade wasn't laughing an hour later when the wind picked up and the rain turned to sleet, then snow, blowing sideways in a full-on Colorado Rocky Mountain blizzard.

Ellie had forgotten how cold a snowstorm like this could be. Now her fingers and toes were numb, her cheeks chafed and burning. Her hat was gone, replaced by a wool cap pulled low over her ears. She drew up the handkerchief that had slipped down around her neck and nudged the paint horse forward.

She knew Kade was somewhere close by, but she couldn't see him though the blinding white. She nearly missed the calf that had slid into a depression filled with mud and was almost completely hidden by the falling snow.

Ellie climbed down from the mare, grabbed the coil of rope off the horn, and slogged her way through the tall drifts to the downed animal. She slipped a noose around the calf's neck, remounted, and dallied the rope around the horn.

Tugging lightly on the reins, she urged the mare backward, her gaze on the calf. "Come on, sweetheart, get on your feet." The rope went taut, and the calf slid a little out of the icy mud, but the animal was half-frozen and barely able to move.

She started to dismount when a second loop dropped over the calf's head; then the rope went taut as Kade's bay horse moved backward. Working together, they pulled the calf out of the slushy mud. The calf bellowed and struggled to its feet. Kade removed the ropes, and the little guy trotted off toward its mother, who stood a few feet away.

"Let's move them back with the others," Kade said. "We'll push them all up into the draw out of the wind."

Ellie nodded, and they drove cow and calf back to the herd in the north pasture, then pushed the animals up into the canyon, where the wind wasn't so deadly. Ellie sighed in relief as Kade rode up beside her.

"Let's head in. You've done more than your share, and the snow's letting up. Most of the cows have been moved someplace they can weather the storm. That's all we can do for now."

Ellie just nodded, too weary to speak. It was dark as she rode next to Kade across the pasture back toward the barn. The rest of the hands were also heading home, nothing more than fuzzy dark spots in the distance.

As they reached the fence line nearest the house, Ellie spotted a small, dark shape lying on its side, almost completely covered by snow. She touched Kade's shoulder, pointed to the fallen calf, rode over, and swung down beside it.

Dread rose as she recognized the black-and-white pattern of Smoke's heavy coat, his face barely visible beneath a layer of snow. Her eyes burned as she crouched and ran a hand over the dog's cold, still body. She looked up to see Kade standing beside her, long legs splayed, rain slicker blowing in the wind, his jaw as hard as granite.

"It's Smoke," Ellie said. "He's dead." Her throat felt raw and so tight she could barely force out the words.

Kade crouched beside her, leaned over, and brushed the snow off the dog's familiar face. Ellie started to help so Kade could take Smoke home when a faint whimper escaped.

"He's alive!" Ellie shouted into the wind.

Kade scooped the animal into his powerful arms, lifted Smoke against his chest, and started striding toward his horse. "It's okay, boy. I've got you now. We're going to get you home, and you're going to be okay."

Kade stepped into the stirrup, swung a leg over the horse's rump, and settled in the saddle, holding the dog against his chest.

"Go ahead," Ellie said. "I'll be right behind you."

Kade whirled the big bay and thundered away as Ellie swung up on Painted Lady and hurried to catch up with him. He paused to look over his shoulder, making sure she was all right. Then the big horse leaped forward as Kade raced for the house.

Billy was waiting. It was Friday night. The boy had spent the night instead of going home. His mother worked at a bar in Eagle and didn't pay much attention to where he was or when he got back. Kade looked out for Billy and kept him safe.

"Is that . . . is that Smoke?" the boy asked. "What . . . what happened? How bad is he hurt? Is he . . . is Smoke gonna be okay?" Billy loved Smoke even more than Kade did. Ellie's heart went out to him.

"We're going to do our best, son." Kade dismounted and strode toward the house, the dog secure in his arms. By the time Ellie had helped Billy take care of the horses, Kade had a blanket draped over the kitchen table. Smoke lay silently on top while Kade examined him.

"Can you tell what's wrong?" Ellie asked as she walked up to him.

His jaw firmed. "I can tell, all right. Smoke's been shot. Got to be the same bastard who killed my steers."

"God, Kade. How bad is it?"

"The bullet entered just in front of his right front leg and kept going. It tore the muscles and tendons, but it didn't break any bones. He's hypothermic, and he's lost a lot of blood."

"Can we get the vet out here?" Ellie asked.

"In this weather? Not a chance. I'll clean the wound and stitch him up while we try to get him warm. Best we can do." His eyes found hers, and she could read the anger he was fighting to hold inside. "I could use your help."

"Of course. I'll put some water on and find some towels, get things ready for you. Just let me know what you need."

Kade nodded. He'd been raised on the ranch. Ranchers handled all kinds of animal emergencies. Ellie wasn't surprised that Kade planned to tend to Smoke's injury, which included sewing him up.

Maria appeared in the doorway, her arms full of towels, what looked like an old sheet, another blanket, and a heating pad. She set them on the end of the breakfast table.

"Thanks, Maria," Kade said.

Billy shoved open the kitchen door, letting in a blast of icy air. "I brought the vet kit. Can you fix him?"

"Thanks. I'm going to need that. We're going to do everything we can to take care of him." Kade looked down at the dog, whose chest barely rose and fell. "He's still alive, still responding." He started cleaning the wound, cutting away the fur and swabbing the area around the bullet hole with alcohol. "Keep him covered except where I'm working."

Ellie and Billy held Smoke steady while Kade gave him a shot of lidocaine to numb the area around the wound, and also a shot of penicillin.

"Once I get him stitched up, we've got to get his body warmed up to room temperature." But at the moment, the cold was working in their favor, keeping the dog sedate while Kade worked over him.

While Kade finished cleaning the wound, Ellie threaded a needle. Kade wasn't the only one who'd been raised on a ranch.

She handed him the needle, and he began pulling it through the dog's flesh, sewing the entry wound good and tight, then the exit wound. When he finished, Ellie moved the heating pad up to cover a little more of Smoke's body, then covered him with a blanket.

"Best we can do for now," Kade said. "Once we get him warm, we can move him to his bed in my study."

Maria turned and started for the door. "I'll go in and get it ready for him, make sure it's clean and warm."

Kade just nodded.

Ellie watched the careful way his hand gently smoothed over Smoke's body. The shooter had chosen a precious target tonight, one dangerously close to the ranch house. How far was the man willing to go? Who would be his next victim?

Kade took a last long look at the dog who meant so much to him and everyone on the ranch. At the hard glint in his whiskey-brown eyes, Ellie knew exactly what he was thinking.

She felt no pity for the man who had become Kade's enemy.

CHAPTER ELEVEN

*T*HE STORM RAGED FOR ANOTHER TWO DAYS, BUT THE WINDS HAD died down, and the temperature had risen enough that the cattle were no longer in danger of freezing. Aside from a few stray head that the hands rounded up and drove back to herds in various pastures, the danger had mostly passed. Keeping track of four thousand cows wasn't an easy job, but the men were used to it, Kade included.

And every day Smoke continued to improve. He was still sleeping in his dog bed in the study, but he was alert and eating. Kade figured that by tomorrow the dog would be up and moving around. With Billy hovering over him, Smoke couldn't be in better hands.

Riley Parker was back at work. He couldn't ride a horse, but he was in good spirits and eager to help. He could drive an ATV. Wyatt had come up with a dozen jobs he could handle.

Hungry and tired at the end of the day, Kade joined the men in the kitchen. Ellie was back working with Maria. Tonight they served a hearty meal of roast beef, mashed potatoes, and gravy, with berry cobbler for dessert. After the long hours the crew had been working, the food tasted especially good.

The men were just about finished, relaxed and joking, when Kade pushed back from the table. He still had work to do in his study, and he wanted to check on Smoke. He flicked a glance at Ellie and felt a familiar stirring.

He'd wanted Ellie Bowman since the day he'd walked into her office in Denver. That want had only grown stronger during the time she had been working on the ranch. With a frustrated sigh, he went into his study to check on Smoke. The dog was peacefully sleeping. Kade ran a hand gently over Smoke's thick coat, then sat down behind his desk and got to work.

A few minutes later, a familiar knock had him lifting his head. *Ellie.* His pulse kicked up. "Door's open. Come on in."

She walked in and closed the door, her gaze going to Smoke. "How's he doing?"

"He's sleeping. Looks like he's going to be okay."

"That's great, Kade." She was wearing a soft yellow sweater that clung to her full breasts and sent arousal burning through him.

"I just got a call from Conner," she said. "Conn tracked down Frank Keller's military records."

Kade rose from his chair. "Tell me."

"Keller was army E.O.D, Kade. Explosive Ordinance Disposal."

Kade thought of the bomb in the mine that had wound up costing a man his leg. He thought of Smoke and how close the animal had come to dying. "That rotten sonofabitch. The explosion in the tunnel, the shootings . . . has to be him."

"Keller was dishonorably discharged four years ago for failing a drug test. According to Conn, because of the danger involved in handling a bomb, EOD is especially concerned with that."

"Drugs. Not smart in his line of work."

"That's for sure. Last known address was an apartment in Denver. Moved out the end of summer."

"Before he came here."

"No record of where he is now."

Kade grunted. "Somewhere close enough to kill two steers, blow up a mine shaft, and shoot my dog. I'll call Carver and let him know." He'd phoned the sheriff the morning after they'd found Smoke, but with the severity of the storm, Carver was up to his ass in alligators. Kade understood that. Now he had the name of a likely suspect. With any luck, Carver would find and arrest him.

"I'm heading into town in the morning," Ellie said. "I know you have plenty of work to do here."

He couldn't argue. "That's an understatement. I haven't really had a chance to thank you for what you did out there." He rounded the desk and walked toward her. He closed his hand into a fist to keep from reaching out to touch her.

Ellie looked up at him. "I'm glad I could help."

"I promised to take you dancing at the Elkhorn," he reminded her.

Ellie smiled. "The storm had other ideas."

He wanted to say more, tell her how impressed he had been with the way she'd handled herself, how grateful he was for what she had done. He looked into her pretty face, but instead of speaking, his hands encircled her waist, and he pulled her against him. In less than a heartbeat, his prized control faded, and his mouth came down over hers.

Ellie stiffened for an instant, then her lips softened under his. Her palms slid over his chest, and she kissed him back, opening to invite him in. She tasted sweet as honey and a little bit naughty, and the desire he'd been fighting broke free.

Kade deepened the kiss, turned it wet and hot and erotic. Cupping her round behind, he lifted her into the vee at the front of his jeans and let her feel his arousal. Ellie moaned, and her nipples budded. He was hard and throbbing as he slid his hands beneath her sweater and unhooked her bra, then filled his palms with her soft, full breasts.

He wanted to put his mouth there, feel her smooth skin against his tongue. He wanted to strip her naked, drag her down on the rug, and bury himself inside her.

"I want you so damn much." He kissed her again, a deep, taking kiss that Ellie returned full measure. Lust pumped like a drug through his veins, and his groin tightened. Ellie's fingers dug into the muscles across his shoulders, and a soft moan slipped from her throat. Her body melted into his, fitting him even more perfectly than he had imagined. Then she broke away.

"Kade . . . I-I . . . can't. We can't do this." She was breathing hard, and so was he.

"Why the hell not? You don't want me? Because I think you

do." He pulled her back into his arms and kissed her again. Ellie softened and kissed him back, then turned away.

"Please don't, Kade."

Reluctantly, Kade let her go. "You don't have to worry. I'm not the kind of man who takes what a woman isn't willing to give."

Ellie sighed. "I know that. It's just . . . you're a hard man to resist, Kade, and even if you were interested in a relationship, which I doubt, I'm not the docile, meek sort of woman you need. I value my independence too much."

Amusement trickled through him, easing some of his frustration. "You think that's what I need? A meek, docile woman I can boss around?"

"Well, you can't deny you're used to giving orders."

"True enough. But one of the things I like about you, Eleanor Bowman, is your strength. Unlike most of the women I know, you're not the least bit intimidated by me."

"Well, no, but—"

He bent and kissed her softly one last time. "Think about it, Ellie. Maybe you being you and me being me might work out just fine." He ran a finger down her cheek, turned and walked over to the door. Kade pulled it open. "I'll see you at breakfast."

Ellie moistened her lips, which were plump and pink from his kisses. His erection throbbed as she walked past him out of the study.

A tired sigh escaped. Even if Ellie were interested in a no-strings sexual relationship, Kade couldn't afford the time. There was too much going on. Too much at stake. The storm damage was costly and needed to be repaired. And there was still a shooter out there. Until Frank Keller was arrested, people could get hurt.

Add to that, he had hired Ellie for a reason, and it wasn't to warm his bed. Heather's killer was out there somewhere, and Eleanor Bowman was his best chance of finding him.

Still, he'd dream about her tonight. And wish things could be different.

* * *

While Kade worked with his men to repair the storm damage and move the cattle back into more open pastures, Ellie drove toward town on the pretext of buying supplies. She hadn't seen Jonas since they'd had lunch, but she had done more digging into his past.

Turned out Jonas had an alibi for the night Heather Logan disappeared. According to Fran Tilman, he'd gone off for a few days with the girl he'd been seeing, a college student name Cissy Winters. The affair had been going on for several months before Jenny Murray found out. According to Fran, it was the final straw in the destruction of his marriage.

The sheriff might have known, but it wasn't in the police report. Either way, unless something new turned up, Jonas was off her list.

From the start, she had been looking into the ranch hands, the men closest to Kade, men who also had access to his wife. So far, she'd found nothing suspicious. The Diamond Bar hands all appeared to be trustworthy, hard-working men. As she came to know them, she could better judge whether one of them would have gone behind Kade's back with Heather. At this point, Ellie didn't think so.

She turned the rented Jeep Cherokee onto the paved road and continued toward Coffee Springs, though she didn't plan to stop in town. Kade had said Heather's two best friends were women who'd gone to college with her. They were married now, but still living near Vail. Both of them had agreed to talk to her.

Ellie was glad for the chance to escape the ranch. She'd been attracted to Kade Logan since the moment she'd first seen him, an attraction that had grown stronger every day. She admired the way he ran the ranch and the way he handled his men.

He was also tall, solidly muscled, and the most ruggedly handsome, sexiest man she had ever met. Her stomach contracted just thinking about the kiss they had shared in his study last night. She wouldn't easily forget the feel of his mouth moving hotly over hers, his lips so much softer than they appeared. When his big hands cupped her breasts, every bone and muscle in her body had turned as soft as melted wax.

She wanted more of him, wanted him to kiss her again, touch her all over, wanted to touch him. She wanted Kade to make love to her.

But what would happen if he did? Kade wasn't looking for a relationship. On the other hand, neither was she. And as he had said, with both of them being such strong, self-reliant people, maybe it could work. At least for the time she would be staying at the ranch.

Setting out beneath a bright morning sun and the crystal shimmer of snow along the edges of the road, Ellie drove the Jeep to the turnoff near Coffee Springs and headed southeast on Highway 131 into the Vail valley. Her first appointment was with Gretchen Kneedler, blond and pretty from her Facebook photos, though it looked as though Gretchen had put on a few pounds since her college days.

After a pleasantly warm welcome, they sat drinking coffee at the kitchen table.

"So what was she like?" Ellie asked.

"Heather was the most popular girl in school," Gretchen said. "Every man on campus wanted her. Women wanted to be with her because she was such a guy magnet. She could have just about any man she wanted, but during those early years, she always felt she belonged to Kade."

Ellie took a sip of coffee, which Gretchen had brewed from bold, freshly ground beans. "From what I understand, she cheated on him more than once."

Gretchen wrapped her fingers around her coffee mug as if she needed the warmth. Her friend was dead. And talking about murder was always chilling.

"Heather needed constant attention," Gretchen said. "Kade was busy working the ranch. She really didn't start cheating until after they'd been married a while. To tell you the truth, it wasn't entirely her fault."

Exactly what Kade had said.

"Do you have any idea who she might have been seeing when she disappeared?"

"The last time we talked, she told me she had met someone, but she didn't say who it was. I know she met him while she was here on a ski trip. She and Anna Marshall and I skied together a few times every winter. That winter I was making plans to get married. I was so busy planning the wedding, we drifted apart for a while. She didn't tell me the guy's name, but she might have told Anna. You think that's who killed her?"

"That's what I'm trying to find out." Ellie finished the last of her coffee and rose from the table. "Thanks, Gretchen. I really appreciate your help."

The women walked together to the door. "Nobody deserves to die the way she did," Gretchen said. "I hope you find the rat bastard who killed her."

"Me too."

From Gretchen's, Ellie drove to an address near Avon and turned onto a winding road that led to a gray, wood-frame house trimmed in dark green. A petite woman, at least part Asian, opened the front door.

"You must be Ellie Bowman." Anna Marshall smiled. "It's nice to meet you." She stepped back to invite Ellie into her neat, modestly decorated two-story home.

"Why don't we sit in the living room?" Anna suggested. "There's a nice view and still enough snow that it's very pretty outside."

"That sounds great."

Anna had glossy black hair cut in a bob that framed her face, very smooth skin, and dark eyes. "Would you care for something to drink?" she asked.

"I had coffee at Gretchen's, so I'm fine."

They sat down on a gray tweed sofa and chatted for a while. Anna had two children, both at school and not due home for a while.

"So let's talk about Heather," Ellie said after Anna had begun to relax. "She was one of your best friends, right?"

"That's right. Heather and Gretchen and I met the first week of college. Something just clicked between the three of us, and we stayed friends over the years." Anna reminisced about their days as students, then the early years of their lives after graduation.

With a little gentle prodding, she confirmed what Gretchen had said, that Heather had slept with a number of different men. Yet the picture the two women painted of the lonely woman Heather had been gave Ellie a different perspective.

"She and Kade were completely ill-suited," Anna said. "Heather was beautiful, but she was very insecure and very needy. Kade needed someone he could depend on."

"Apparently, she met someone new around the time she disappeared. Did Heather ever mention him?"

"We talked about guys whenever we got together. We'd been best friends since college. Some things don't change."

"So you knew she was seeing someone."

"I knew she'd been seeing the same guy for a while, but I'm pretty sure their affair had ended. I know she'd recently met someone while she was skiing with us in Vail. I don't know if they ever hooked up."

Same thing Gretchen had said. "Did she mention his name?"

"No. I just remember her talking about him one day after we'd been on the slopes. I know she was excited about seeing him again, though."

"What about the other guy, the one she'd been involved with before?"

Anna looked down at the hands resting in her lap. "It was a long time ago. I don't want to get him in trouble."

"You wouldn't have agreed to see me if you didn't want to find Heather's killer. I give you my word I won't tell anyone unless I find out he had something to do with her death."

"You can't tell Kade," Anna said, looking up at her.

"I won't tell Kade unless I have no other choice. I promise."

"She had an affair with Glen Carver."

The sheriff? Ellie's pulse took a leap.

"Glen wasn't sheriff eight years ago, just an Eagle County

deputy. I don't know how serious it was between them, or exactly when it ended, but I know Heather was involved with him for at least a couple of months."

Ellie had sensed something off about Carver. Now she knew what it was.

"You think it was her idea to end it, or his?"

"It was always Heather's idea. She was married to Kade. I don't think she ever planned to leave him."

"She must have been surprised when he filed for divorce."

"Part of her was devastated. In her own way she loved him. Another part seemed wildly relieved."

"Maybe she felt a sense of freedom she'd never had before."

Anna nodded. "Yes, I think that was it."

They talked a while longer, then Ellie rose, and Anna walked her to the door. "Thank you for your honesty," Ellie said.

"About Glen Carver . . . Glen's a nice guy. What I told you could damage his career."

"Unless he's somehow connected to the murder—"

"He's a sheriff. He wouldn't kill anyone."

Ellie just nodded. "I'm sure you're right." But passion made people do crazy things. Sheriff Glen Carver had just become her number one suspect.

Unfortunately, there was no way she could discuss it with Kade.

CHAPTER TWELVE

THE WEATHER IMPROVED, RETURNING TO THE BRISK, CLEAR DAYS OF fall. Kade strode toward the barn, his mind on the work that needed to be done. Earlier that morning, he had phoned Glen Carver and told him about Frank Keller. Said he believed that Keller, a disgruntled former employee, was the man responsible for the shootings on the ranch.

Kade told Carver that Keller could also be responsible for an explosion at the Red Hawk Mine, which operated on Diamond Bar land.

"You think your dead cattle, your dog, and the incident at the mine are connected?" Carver asked.

"Yeah, that's what I think."

"The mine's in Summit County. I'll call Gil Worthington, the county sheriff. Bring him up to speed on Keller and see what information he might be able to share on the mine explosion."

"Thanks."

"I'll get back to you," Carver had said.

Kade was replaying the conversation in his head when he looked across the yard to see Wyatt bent over the saddle, riding his horse like hellfire across the pasture toward the house. Kade's senses went on alert, and he rushed to intercept him.

"What is it? What's happened?"

Wyatt reined his horse to a sliding halt. "The bastard shot Alejandro. We were working in the east pasture. They're bringing him here in the back of Slate's pickup."

Kade clenched his hand into a fist, the leather glove biting into his palm. "You call for a chopper?" There was a clinic in Eagle, but anyone with a serious injury was airlifted to the hospital in Vail.

Wyatt nodded. "They're on the way. The pasture is close to the house, so they're coming directly here. I tried your cell, but the call dropped and I couldn't get through."

Fury warred with fear for Alejandro, a man Kade liked and respected. "How bad is it?"

"He was back-shot. Entered through his shoulder and came out through his chest, but we were there when it happened, and we got the bleeding stopped right away."

"What about the shooter?" Kade asked.

"Turtle and Roy went after him. Last call I got, they hadn't found him."

Kade clamped down on the rage burning through him. He wanted Keller, but taking care of his men came first. Kade made another call to the sheriff, told him Alejandro Ramirez, one of his ranch hands, had been shot and that he was being airlifted to the hospital in Vail.

"I'll need to talk to Ramirez," Carver said. "I'll check in with the hospital, speak to him as him as soon as he's stable."

"You need to find this guy, Sheriff. Before he kills someone."

"I'll find him. As soon as I have the information I need, I'll put out a statewide BOLO."

"I'll let you know if I find out anything else," Kade said.

"This is police business, Kade. You need to stay out of it."

Fat chance of that. "I have to get going. Keep me posted, Glen." Kade hung up the phone.

Now that he'd notified law enforcement, he needed to be sure his men were protected, which meant he needed to set up security patrols. Then he was going after Frank Keller. He could track a man as easily as he could a cougar or a bear. He'd find Keller and deal with him—one way or another.

The thought had barely formed when he spotted Slate's white Ford F-250 barreling toward them down the dirt road, flinging muddy slush where the snow had melted. It was October, not yet winter. With any luck, the snow would be gone and not return until next month.

Kade strode over as the pickup braked to a stop. Shoulder to shoulder, Slate and Kade walked to the back of the truck. A bedroll had been spread open, and Alejandro lay on top, his eyes closed, his swarthy face washed out to the color of glass. Riley rode next to him, the cast on his leg sticking out in front of him.

Kade reached down and took hold of Alejandro's limp, dark hand. "Chopper's on the way. You hang in there, you hear? You're gonna be okay."

Alejandro's black eyes cracked open. "Did they catch the *chingadero* who shot me?"

"If they don't, I will."

Alejandro managed a nod, and his eyes slid closed. A *whop whop whop* signaled the arrival of the life-flight helicopter. It also told the household staff that something was going on. Maria rushed out of the kitchen, wiping her hands on her apron as she raced toward him.

"What's happened?" The pickup tailgate was down, and she could see Riley sitting in the back.

"It's Alejandro. He's been shot."

Maria made a high-pitched sound in her throat, turned, and ran toward the truck. Kade knew the girl had feelings for the handsome Latino. There was no way to mistake the blush in her cheeks whenever he was near. Alejandro hadn't seemed to notice. Which Kade figured was better all around.

Maria climbed into the truck bed, picked up Alejandro's hand, and pressed it against her cheek. "You'll be all right, Alejandro. Señor Kade will make sure, and I will pray to the Blessed Virgin. You'll see."

Alejandro's eyes opened, and a faint smile touched his lips. "So pretty . . . and so . . . sweet . . ." His features went slack as he drifted into unconsciousness.

A sound of pain slipped from Maria's throat, and Kade sighed. Alejandro was a ladies' man. Half the women in the county had warmed his bed, and the other half wanted to. Until today, Alejandro had been careful to keep his distance from Maria, a young woman he liked and respected. Who knew what would happen now that the girl had openly revealed her affections?

Kade thought of Ellie and the hot kiss in his study. Whatever happened, he was in no position to throw stones.

Maria held onto Alejandro's hand as the chopper set down in the widest part of the yard, the doors slid open, and a pair of EMTs jumped out carrying a stretcher. Kade watched the men at work, grateful they had arrived so quickly.

He turned at the sound of a car engine pulling up the drive. The motor went off, and Ellie got out of her rented Jeep Cherokee and hurried toward him.

"What's going on?" she asked.

"Alejandro's been shot."

"Oh my God, is he going to be all right?"

"We'll find out once we get to the hospital. Get Maria, and let's go."

Ellie's gaze went to the black-haired woman standing in the yard, tears streaming down her face. Ellie walked over and wrapped an arm around her shoulders. "Come on. Kade's driving us to the hospital."

"I'm going with you?" Maria looked at her with big, wet, hopeful eyes. "What . . . what about supper?"

"The guys can make do for one night," Kade said as he joined them. "In the meantime, I need to set up security patrols around the ranch. You think Delaney can handle that?"

"Nighthawk has a team that specializes in protection of just about any kind. They're the best or Conn wouldn't be using them. I'll call him, tell him what's going on and what you need."

Kade nodded. "Wait here, and I'll get my truck."

* * *

The Vail Hospital was a well-staffed medical facility in the Vail valley, a four-story brick and stucco building on West Meadow Drive. Ellie waited while Kade talked to the receptionist, telling her they were there for Alejandro Ramirez. The woman behind the counter sent them up to the surgical floor, where a nurse guided them down the hall to a room in which several other worried families waited impatiently for news of their loved ones.

Seated on a pale blue vinyl sofa, Maria clung to Ellie's hand, barely holding it together.

"Alejandro . . . he's such a good man."

"He's going to be all right," Ellie said. "You just need to keep telling yourself that."

"I'm praying for him. I pray you're right and he'll be okay."

But the hours slipped past, and the only news of Alejandro's condition came from a nurse who told them he was still in surgery.

Finally, a weary-looking doctor in wrinkled green scrubs walked through the door, and Kade, Ellie, and Maria all rose to meet him.

"I'm Doctor Sawyer," he said. Average height, thick gray hair, deep lines around tired eyes. "You're Alejandro Ramirez's family?"

"As much family as he has around here," Kade said.

The doctor nodded. "He's out of surgery, recovering in the ICU. The bullet that entered his body took out a portion of his lung."

Maria stifled a sob, and Ellie squeezed her hand.

"The fast action of the men who were with him prevented him from losing too much blood. We repaired the torn tendons and muscles, but the lung was the most serious injury."

"He going to be all right?" Kade asked.

"In time, he should be fine. But he's going to need some care while he recovers. A quiet place with someone who can change his dressings and see to his needs till he gets back on his feet would be best."

"He can stay in the main house," Kade said. "I'll have a nurse brought in."

"I'll take care of him," Maria said firmly. "I can do my work and still have time to look after him."

Kade frowned. Ellie figured he was worried about Alejandro taking advantage of Maria's tender feelings, but considering the polite way the ranch hand had always treated the girl, Ellie didn't think he would.

"Fine," Kade said. "Maria, are you sure this is what you want?"

"Sí, Señor Kade. I promise he will get the best of care."

"Oh, I'm sure he will," Kade said with enough sarcasm to send warm color into Maria's cheeks. "You can stay in one of the guest cabins. The one with two bedrooms," he added pointedly.

Maria glanced away. "Thank you."

"Mr. Ramirez won't be awake for at least a few more hours," the doctor said. "I suggest you all go home and come back in the morning."

Maria's chin firmed. "I'd like to stay here tonight. I don't want Alejandro to wake up alone." She looked at Ellie. "But I don't want to leave you with too much work."

Ellie smiled. "Supper's handled. It's just breakfast. I'll be fine."

"I'll have one of the men come into town in the morning to get you," Kade said. "He can drive you back to the ranch to get your car, and you can return to the hospital anytime you want."

Maria looked relieved. "Thank you. Thank you both so much."

"You just watch over Alejandro," Kade said. "The rest will take care of itself."

They left Maria and headed back to the ranch, both of them quiet along the way. From the set of his jaw, Ellie knew Kade was thinking about Frank Keller.

"It'll be dark by the time we get home," Kade said. "In the morning, I'll ride out to the pasture where the men were working, have Wyatt show me exactly where Alejandro was shot. With any luck, I can figure out where the bastard was hiding and be able to track him from there."

"I'll ride with you," Ellie said. "We can go over the crime scene together. Two of us tracking Keller puts the odds in our favor. And if you run into trouble, you'll have backup."

"I can take one of the men."

"You're down two men already. I'm a detective. I have my own weapon, and I'm a damned good shot. Let me do my job."

Kade looked as if he wanted to argue. In the end, he gave her a single stiff nod. Tomorrow they were going hunting.

CHAPTER THIRTEEN

AT BREAKFAST THAT MORNING, KADE SPOKE TO THE MEN ABOUT Frank Keller. They remembered him from the short time he had worked the roundup. Kade told them he believed Keller was behind the shootings and an explosion that had happened up at the Red Hawk Mine. He told them the sheriff would be out sometime today to ask questions and take a look at the crime scene.

He asked Wyatt to handle the sheriff, then told the men he was going after Keller himself. With the ranch so shorthanded, he was taking Ellie as backup. She had proved herself during the storm, he explained, had shown herself to be as capable as any of the hands, and she had volunteered for the job.

Roy Cobb grumbled a little. Wyatt cast Kade a long, searching glance, but in the end, the men accepted his judgment. Kade had thought about telling them the truth, that Ellie was a private investigator from Denver he had hired to look into his wife's murder. These were men he trusted. Men he had known and worked with for years.

But Heather had been killed eight years ago. Roy and Seth had both come aboard after her death, but the other guys were all working on the ranch at the time. Was it possible one of them had murdered her? He didn't believe it, but until the killer was found, there was no way to know for sure.

Add to that, he didn't want Ellie's true purpose leaking to anyone in town. It wouldn't be fair, not when she was doing her best to track down the killer.

"What's the situation with Delaney and the security we need?" Kade asked Ellie as she finished cleaning up the breakfast dishes, with Turtle Farley pitching in to help. Kade had a hunch Turtle was infatuated with the pretty redhead. Fortunately, he was smart enough to know his interest wasn't returned.

"Conn's sending a team out today. They'll need someone to show them around and find a place they can stay."

"They can use the other guesthouse. I'll talk to Slate, have him show the men around." Kade left with the hands, talked to Wyatt about the day's assignments, and returned to the ranch house.

"You ready to head out?" he asked Ellie.

"I just need to grab my gear, some food, and my weapon. I'll be right back."

Kade watched her walk away, her ponytail moving with the same tantalizing rhythm as her hips. Which returned his thoughts to the hot kiss in his study. Jesus, he couldn't remember wanting a woman the way he did this one. Not even Heather. But he had been younger then, without much experience with women. In the years since his wife's death, his sexual needs had changed. He was a man now, not the boy he had been back then.

A man who needed a woman, and the woman he wanted was Eleanor Bowman.

A weak sun lit the horizon by the time they all set out, Kade on Hannibal, his big buckskin, Ellie riding Painted Lady. She and the brown-and-white mare had already bonded. Ellie trusted the horse, and the horse trusted her. They made a good team, both of them spirited and unique.

The hands split up a half mile down the dirt road and headed off to tend herds grazing in different pastures. Wyatt led the way to the place the men had been working when Alejandro was shot, a grassy meadow surrounded by hills that rose to mountain peaks.

Kade didn't like it. The pasture was way too close to the house.

"First the steers, then the mine, Smoke, and now one of the men. He's getting bolder."

Ellie nodded. "He escalating—or he's trying to draw you out. Which is exactly what's happening right now."

A muscle tightened in Kade's cheek. "Well, if that's his plan, he's in for a big surprise when I find the sonofabitch."

"You need to be careful, Kade. There's every chance he's lying in wait somewhere to take you out."

Kade studied Ellie from beneath the brim of his hat. She was right. She was smart and good at her job. He was paying her top dollar for her skills. Still, he hated the idea of putting her in danger.

Wyatt rode to a spot in the meadow and dismounted. "We were working right here." He collected his horse's reins. "Clearing a downed tree at the edge of the pasture."

Kade dismounted. He noticed a set of tire tracks where Slate's pickup had driven across the wet field to pick up the injured man. The meadow was muddy, and there were still patches of snow on the ground.

"This is where Alejandro went down, right?" Ellie led the paint horse close to the spot and looked up at Wyatt.

"That's right." Wyatt smoothed his handlebar mustache as Ellie crouched to examine a dark patch of blood on the ground and the area around it.

She rose and studied the landscape. "Which way was he facing when the bullet struck?"

"We were talking. I was here, so he was looking north. Bullet had to have come from the south."

Ellie nodded, as if that was what she'd been thinking, and tugged on Lady's reins, leading the mare toward a cluster of trees on a far-distant ridge.

"You think he's that good a shot?" Kade asked as he and Hannibal walked beside her. Wyatt and his horse followed.

Ellie paused and looked around, her gaze moving along the southern perimeter. "Where would you have been if you wanted to hit your target and get away clean?"

Kade studied the ridge, turned to see if he could find a better position. "You're right. The ridge was his best option." He turned to Wyatt. "You've got things to do. I'll call you, let you know if we find what we're looking for."

Wyatt nodded, but both of them knew cell service was sketchy out there. Wyatt swung up on his horse and reined the animal toward the road, riding off to catch up with the hands.

Kade and Ellie continued toward the ridge, both of them keeping an eye on the line of sight between where Alejandro had been shot and where the bullet must have been fired.

Keeping watch in case the guy was still up there somewhere.

Once they reached the trees, they tied the horses to a branch and spread out to study the ground, looking for any sign the shooter might have left. Twenty minutes later, Kade stared down at a set of muddy boot prints that led to an impression on the ground behind a granite boulder.

"Over here!" he shouted.

Ellie looked up from her search and hurried toward him. "What is it?"

"Boot prints leading up to that rock. Looks like he knelt right here." He pointed to the depression in the dirt. "Used the boulder to steady his rifle and also hide his position."

Ellie studied the scene. "No rain last night to wash away his tracks." She looked up. "Or maybe he wants you to find him."

Kade's jaw hardened. "Then let's give him what he wants."

They followed the boot prints south, the tracks ending where hoofprints began. The shooter had been on horseback, a relatively silent way to travel and easier for him to disappear in rough country.

Leading Hannibal, Kade followed the shooter's tracks higher up into the hills. At one point, the hoofprints disappeared into a rocky outcropping of granite, forcing him to pause. He and Ellie spread out, searching the ground, hoping to pick up the trail on the far side of the boulders.

Kade spotted hoofprints in a patch of mud, returned and signaled for Ellie to follow, and quietly led the way over the rocks and down the other side, where he'd picked up Keller's trail.

They mounted and followed the prints, winding up on a game trail Keller had used to climb higher up the mountain. Kade swung down from the buckskin and crouched on the ground to make a closer examination.

"Looks like he came through here last night. The mud has dried a little. He's still heading south. He keeps going, he'll hit Copper Spur Road. If he's got a truck and trailer parked somewhere nearby, he could load his horse and just disappear."

They rode for two more hours, taking a short break to water the animals and eat the sandwiches Ellie had packed, then continuing south, exactly the way Kade figured.

At one point, the shooter had ridden into a stream to hide his tracks. Kade dismounted and walked the bank, first heading north to be sure the guy hadn't backtracked. Seeing no sign of him, he led Hannibal south along the bank and finally found the place where the shooter had ridden out of the water.

Kade mounted and waited for Ellie to catch up with him. They had stopped talking a while back, just to be safe, and were using hand signals to communicate. There was a chance the guy had set up camp somewhere in the area. Or was lying in wait along the trail.

They finally reached Copper Spur Road, just a narrow lane, most of the pavement washed out over the years and never replaced. Ellie pointed to a wide spot that served as a turnout. Tire tracks marked the place where a vehicle had been parked, and the trail of hoofprints ended there.

Kade cursed. "He's gone. We've lost him."

"At least now we know he's pulling a horse trailer. We need to tell the sheriff."

Kade nodded, pulled out his phone, and looked down at the screen. "No service."

"We'll call as soon as we get in range."

That's when the first shot rang out.

CHAPTER FOURTEEN

*E*LLIE'S HEART JERKED. SHE AND KADE QUICKLY LED THEIR HORSES down a slope off the road into a copse of trees dense enough to provide some measure of cover. Two more shots rang out, then two more.

"Stay here. I'll take a look." Kade handed her Hannibal's reins. Ellie wasn't used to staying behind, but two moving targets were easier to hit than one, and Kade was already on his way. She watched him weaving between the rocks, staying low as he made his way toward the ridge where the shots had come from. She caught occasional glimpses of his brown canvas duster and the crown of his hat before he disappeared.

Ellie chafed to go with him. Time ticked past, and her worry increased. Tying the horses to a tree branch, she prepared to follow Kade and make sure he was all right. Just then he reappeared.

"Couple of kids target practicing."

Ellie breathed a sigh of relief.

Kade glanced back at the muddy road. "He's got wheels now. No way we can track him very far." He untied Hannibal's reins, raised them over the horse's thick neck, and swung up into the saddle. "We've got a long ride back. Might as well head on home."

Ellie swung up onto Painted Lady. She was tired and a little stiff, but after the hours she had spent in the saddle during the storm, her muscle memory had returned. She hadn't ridden much the last few years, but she'd practically been raised on the back of a horse.

They set out at an easy canter, the return trip not nearly as difficult as the one out. Kade knew the area, so they were able to travel the fastest, easiest route. Still, it was a long day on horseback and dark by the time they got home. Ellie was bone-tired, and she could tell Kade was angry and disappointed.

As it was a school night, Billy had already gone home, so they unsaddled and put away their own mounts. Wyatt came out of the bunkhouse to talk to them, and Kade filled him in on the day's progress—or lack thereof.

"The security team arrived," Wyatt said.

"That's good news."

"Six guys, including Delaney, all former military or police. Slate spent part of the day with them, getting them acquainted with the layout of the ranch. They seem extremely efficient, happy to live on MREs, but I figured we'd be able to come up with at least one meal for them a day. They'll be working in shifts, so we won't know exactly when they'll be coming in." He looked over at Ellie.

"I'll keep something in the kitchen for whenever they show up. It won't be a problem."

"Looks like Delaney gives the orders. He said not to expect to see them around. Staying out of sight is part of their job. That's how they work."

"Sounds like they know what they're doing," Kade said. "Which is a helluva relief. I don't want anyone else getting shot."

Wyatt turned to Ellie. "Turtle made dinner tonight. Said he cooked on a ranch as a kid." Wyatt smiled. "It wasn't half bad. Not as good as your cooking, ma'am, but not half bad."

Ellie returned the smile. "I'm grateful for the help." While the men finished talking, Ellie went on up to the house. Turtle had left food on the stove, the last of a pot of stew, but Ellie was too tired to eat.

Something was bothering her about all of this. Shooting a couple of steers? Maybe a guy who got fired would be angry enough to go that far. Shooting Kade's dog was definitely personal. But setting off a bomb in a mine? Shooting one of the ranch hands?

Why would a guy go that far? If the shooter was Keller, it had to be more than just getting back at Kade for firing him.

The question stayed with her as she showered and got ready for bed. She needed to talk to Kade, see if there was something else he could tell her, maybe something he had forgotten.

She brushed out her hair, pulled on a soft fleece robe, and headed barefoot down the hall to his study. There was no light beneath the door. He had probably gone up to bed.

She thought of the day they had spent, the ease with which they had worked together. She thought of the way her gaze kept drifting over him, the wide shoulders and long legs, the way he sat his horse, as if he and the buckskin were one inseparable being.

She thought of the competent way his big hands held the reins, imagined how they would feel skimming over her body. In scuffed boots, a long canvas slicker, and a battered cowboy hat, he looked as if he'd walked off the set of a western movie. The chaps he occasionally wore outlined the masculine bulge at the front of his jeans and made her feel hot all over.

Several times during the day, she had noticed him watching her the way she'd been watching him. She hadn't missed the heat in those golden-brown eyes.

Ellie shook off the notion. She couldn't risk getting involved with Kade. She didn't trust men in general, especially not one who undoubtedly had left a string of broken hearts in his wake.

She looked down at her fleecy robe. She wasn't dressed for seduction. She just needed to talk to the man.

Renewing her resolve, Ellie climbed the stairs and knocked on Kade's bedroom door. When he abruptly pulled it open, she stumbled forward into his arms.

"Ellie." Barefoot and shirtless, he wore only a pair of faded jeans so soft they clung to the muscles in his long legs and hugged his narrow hips. His chest was all lean muscle, his biceps thick and solid. A working man's body, darkened to teak by the sun. Ellie's mouth went dry.

Kade's gaze slid over the fluffy robe that covered her from neck to toe, modest by any standard, and the dark copper curls that hung down her back. The gold in his eyes glittered with heat. Kade pulled her into the room and closed the door.

"Ellie . . ." he repeated as a hard arm wrapped around her waist and he dragged her against him. Kade slid his fingers into her hair to anchor her in place, and his mouth crushed down over hers.

Heat enveloped her, like warm honey sliding through her veins. Ellie moaned. The kiss went on and on, coaxing at first, then deeper, more demanding, wild and reckless and completely irresistible. Her arms went around his neck. Kade parted her robe and filled his hands with her breasts.

"Jesus, I want you." He toyed with her nipples, turning them pebble-hard, then lowered his mouth to suckle one aching tip while his hand kneaded and caressed the fullness.

"Kade . . ."

"I need you, Ellie. Don't say no."

She couldn't have said no if a gun had been pointed at her head, not with her mouth so dry and her body so hot and wet. *No* was the last word on her mind. She could think of several dirty words she wanted to say, blushed just thinking about them.

"Yes . . ." she said. "Yes, Kade," and arched her back to give him better access.

Kade groaned. He returned to her breasts, suckled and tasted until she was begging for more. "I need you too," she whispered. "Please, Kade."

He left her a moment, then returned with a handful of condoms he tossed on the nightstand and started kissing her again. "I've been hard for you half the damn day." He slid the robe off her shoulders, let it pool at her feet. She was naked underneath. Maybe she'd dressed for seduction after all.

Kade kept kissing her, plundering her mouth as he plundered her body. A hand slid down to the curve of her waist, moved lower to cup her bottom and pull her into the vee at the front of his jeans, letting her feel his erection. He was thick and hard, straining against his zipper.

Ellie whimpered as he stroked her, kissed her again, and just kept kissing her. She was wet and ready when he lifted her, wrapped her legs around his waist, and unzipped the fly of his jeans.

"I can think of a dozen ways I want to have you, starting right now."

She made a sound in her throat as he filled her, slowly, then more deeply. Backing her up against the wall, he drove into her, out and then in, easy at first, then faster, deeper, harder. Ellie made a sound low in her throat and just hung on, her heart pounding, her breath coming in short, sharp pants. Her insides lifted on a swelling tide of need, and her belly tightened as she exploded into climax.

Kade didn't stop, just kept pounding into her, coaxing her toward the peak again, riding her hard, demanding she respond.

Heat burned through her, hot waves that sucked her under and wouldn't let go. Pleasure deep and erotic had her sobbing his name. She came hard, and Kade came with her, their mating as violent as the storm they'd endured, Kade taking her mouth again in a final kiss that went on until the tide of passion finally abated.

Ellie slumped against him, her arms still around his neck, her fingers entwined in his thick brown hair. She lifted her head off his shoulder as Kade carried her across the room and settled her in the middle of his big four-poster bed. He left to deal with the condom, returned, and began to strip off his jeans. As he climbed into bed beside her, she saw that he was still hard.

"I didn't come here for this," she said, looking up at him.

"I figured. Doesn't matter now, does it?"

She whimpered as he lowered his head and kissed her, started kissing his way down the side of her neck.

"I-I'm on the pill," she said, "but—"

"You don't have to worry." He pointed toward the string of foil wrappers he had brought from the bathroom. "We've got plenty for tonight." He kissed the side of her neck. "I promise I'll make it good for both of us."

Dear God, she had no doubt of that.

As Kade settled his big, hard body between her thighs, she thought he would take her more gently this time, make love to

her with slow, tender care. Instead, he touched her as if he owned
her, kissed her as if she belonged to him. He made love to her as
if she had no choice but to give him what he wanted.

It shocked her to realize it was exactly what she wanted too.

They slept for a while, spoon-fashion, his broad, powerful chest
against her back. She wasn't sure how much time had passed
when she felt his hand stroking over her hip, arousing her. Soft
and easy turned to wild and frenzied, and finally to completion.

She'd had sex before, but not like this. Not this wild, reckless
passion that demanded everything she had to give and more.
Like a dangerous drug in her system she hadn't known she craved
until now.

But as he worked his magic to give her the kind of pleasure
she'd never known, she sensed the dark fire inside him that she
had recognized from the start.

She wondered if that fire would incinerate them both.

Kade felt the mattress dip as Ellie slipped out of bed. She
grabbed her robe off the floor and dragged it on, then moved
quietly to the door and disappeared into the hall.

Kade let her go. He'd had her three times last night and again
before dawn. Beneath her reserve, he'd discovered a wildly passionate woman whose needs matched his own. Just thinking
about the things he had done to her, the things he still wanted to
do, had him hard beneath the sheets.

He hadn't gotten nearly enough of Ellie Bowman, wasn't sure
he would anytime soon. But as much as he wanted her, a voice inside warned him to be wary.

Kade didn't trust women, hadn't since Heather had played
him for the perfect fool. For years, he'd been the laughingstock
of Coffee Springs, so busy building the ranch into a bigger, more
powerful empire, he'd blindly ignored the signs of her betrayal.
They'd been together since high school. No way would she cheat
on him. Or so he had thought.

But the web of lies and deceit could only go on so long. He'd
ignored the truth the first time, convinced himself it would never

happen again. The second time, he'd confronted her, and Heather had admitted her betrayal. The men she'd been with thought she was beautiful, she'd said. They wanted her in a way Kade never had.

Kade had filed for divorce the next day. No amount of tears or begging could convince him to forgive her. Kade had watched her drive off that night filled with an anger that still hadn't left him.

But he'd never thought it would be the last time he'd see her. Never expected that she would be brutally murdered and the sonofabitch who killed her would never be brought to justice.

One thing Kade knew. He would never be free of the guilt that rode him like a ravenous beast until Heather's killer was dead.

Alone in the room, he glanced at the clock on the nightstand and rolled out of bed. Catching the scent of sex in the sheets, his morning hard-on returned. He still wanted Ellie—maybe more than he had before.

And he needed her. He'd hired her to help him find Heather's killer. That hadn't changed.

His mind remained on Ellie as he strode naked into the bathroom, turned on the shower, and stepped beneath the warm, soothing spray. Ellie was pretty as a picture, not as glamourous as Heather, but in some ways even more attractive. She had an openness Heather had never had, and she seemed to really care about people. She was intelligent and good at her job.

And with her plump, milk-white breasts and that round feminine behind, she was sexy as hell.

But Ellie was still a woman. Kade had vowed long ago that no female would ever dupe him again. It was a vow he intended to keep.

CHAPTER FIFTEEN

ELLIE SERVED BREAKFAST TO THE HANDS; THEN SHE AND TURTLE cleaned up the kitchen. Kade didn't appear. Maria had called to say Alejandro was being released today. She was waiting for the paperwork to be completed, then driving him back to the ranch. Ellie couldn't help wondering what Alejandro thought of Maria's newly revealed affections.

For both their sakes, Ellie hoped it would work out.

With the kitchen spotless, Turtle closed a kitchen drawer, hung up his apron, and headed for the back door. "You have a good day now, ma'am."

"It's just Ellie, Turtle."

He grabbed his hat off the rack and crammed it onto his round, balding head. "Yes, Ms. Ellie."

Ellie laughed as he walked out to join Wyatt and the rest of the men. She tried not to think of Kade and what had happened between them last night, but it was impossible. The sex had been hot and raw and unbelievably satisfying. But there was an underlying darkness in Kade, a simmering anger that never completely left him, not even when he was making love.

She wasn't sure who the anger was aimed at, but she had a feeling it was mostly himself. He blamed himself for his late wife's death, or at least for not bringing her murderer to justice. Maybe, working together, they could find the man who had killed her.

Kade still hadn't come down to eat. Ellie was sure he'd been awake when she'd left, but he hadn't said a word. He was avoiding her, ignoring what had happened between them. Clearly he wasn't interested in a "morning after" conversation. Or maybe one night of uninhibited passion was enough for him.

A flicker of something that felt like regret slid though her. Kade wasn't interested in more than a physical relationship. He'd been honest about that from the start. Ellie was no longer sure what she wanted from Kade. For the moment, she told herself, sex was enough.

She sighed as she wiped her hands on a dish towel, took off her Diamond Bar apron and hung it on a hook near the stove. Whatever Kade was thinking, they still needed to talk about Frank Keller, try to figure out if there could be another motive for the attacks. They needed to be certain Keller was the man responsible, because so far they had no proof.

And there was the not-so-small matter of solving Heather's murder—the job Kade had originally hired her to do.

She glanced up at a noise in the hall, saw him walk into the kitchen, and felt a sweep of sexual desire it was ridiculous to feel after last night.

Kade's eyes locked with hers and seemed to glitter with heat. "Good morning," he said, his voice a little rough. "I see you got the men fed and watered."

Her lips twitched. "They aren't livestock, Kade, but yes, the guys left for work a while ago."

"I want you to know, Ellie, I appreciate the job you've done here. Nothing more important to the ranch hands after a hard day's work than a hearty, good-tasting meal. When I suggested you work as cook, I figured Maria would do the actual labor and you'd just sort of pitch in as cover for the job you're really here to do. Instead, you took over at a time we really needed you, and I'm more grateful than I can say."

She was touched by his words, certainly hadn't expected them. "Thank you."

His eyes found hers across the distance between them. "So . . . about last night—"

Ellie's raised a hand, cutting off whatever he'd planned to say, hoping he wouldn't notice the color rising in her cheeks. Talking about the intimacies they'd shared wasn't easy for her, either.

"You don't have to say anything, Kade. We enjoyed ourselves. That's all that matters."

One of his dark eyebrows went up. "That's it, then? One night was enough for you?"

Heat tugged low in her belly as she remembered the things they had done. "Was it enough for you?"

He walked up behind her, slid his arms around her waist, and eased her back against him. She gasped at the feel of his heavy erection against the curve of her behind.

"Hell, no, it wasn't enough." He pressed his mouth against the nape of her neck. "I want you. That hasn't changed." His voice thickened, grew husky. "If I had my way, darlin', I'd bend you over the kitchen table and have you right here."

Shock widened her eyes, and a little sound came from her throat. When she turned to look up at him, he briefly kissed her lips.

"Don't worry, it's not going to happen. We can't let this thing between us interfere with our work. I have a ranch to run. You're here to find my dead wife's killer. I think you understand that— probably better than I do."

She released a breath of relief. She wasn't sure if it was because he understood the situation—or because he still wanted her.

"I understand completely. Which reminds me of the reason I came to see you last night."

His mouth edged up at one corner. "You mean before things got a lot more interesting?"

She ignored a rush of warmth. "I came to talk to you about Frank Keller."

His eyes sparkled with what could only be male arrogance. "I guess we got sidetracked."

Ellie clamped down on the memory of Kade's hard body pressing her down on the mattress. "I guess we did."

"Before we get started, I need a cup of coffee." He eyed the round metal baking pan covered with foil sitting on top of the stove. "If those are biscuits, I could sure use a couple."

"I can cook you something."

"Biscuits and coffee will do."

Ellie poured some of the dark brew into a mug, which Kade carried over to the table. Ellie took him some biscuits, butter, and raspberry jam, carried her own cup over, and sat down across from him, wondering if she'd ever be able to look at the kitchen table without remembering what Kade had said.

"You wanted to talk about Frank Keller." He took a drink from his mug.

"That's right. All the way back to the ranch yesterday, I kept thinking about him. I don't have any trouble believing a guy you fired would be angry enough to kill a couple of your steers. Shooting your dog was definitely personal, something an angry man might do. But setting off a bomb in a mine? Shooting one of the ranch hands? It had to be something more than just payback because he was mad at you."

Kade sipped his coffee. "I've thought about it, that's for sure." He set the mug down on the table. "Wyatt said Keller refused to take orders from Alejandro because he was Latino. That could definitely have made him a target."

"True. Attempted murder seems a little over the top, but I guess it's possible. Still, it was the mine explosion that convinced us Keller's the man we're after."

"The guy is an explosives expert. Army EOD. There can't be many of those around."

"I think we should talk to Will Turley up at the mine. See if he's ever heard of Frank Keller. Maybe there's a connection we don't know about. If not, maybe he can give us the name of someone else."

"Good idea. I could phone him, but I'd rather talk to him in person. Seems like you usually get a better take on things face-to-face."

"I agree. Sometimes something useful comes up that wouldn't have if you were on the phone."

Kade nodded. "Speaking of which, I got a call from Delaney. He wanted to check in, let me know he and his men are settled in and on the job."

"I'm glad they're here."

"So am I." He glanced around the kitchen. "You're finished here. Let's take a drive up to the mine. I'll call Turley, make sure he's there." Amusement crinkled the sun lines at the corners of his eyes. "In the meantime, I promise to keep my hands off you—at least until we get back home."

The pickup dipped and swayed as it lurched along the steep gravel road winding up the side of the canyon to the mine. The crew was busily working when Kade pulled into the open area surrounded by wood and metal buildings and turned off the engine. Men shuffled in and out of the dark hole in the side of the mountain that was the entrance to the mine.

As he and Ellie climbed out of the pickup, Will Turley walked toward them, curly red hair gleaming in the sun. Ellie's hair was a darker shade of red, her curls loose and silky. Kade flicked her a glance, wishing he could free those luscious strands from her ponytail and slide his fingers through them.

"Always good to see you, Kade," Will said. He turned, looking surprised to see him with Ellie again today. Kade never mixed business with pleasure. He told himself this time he had no choice.

Will smiled at Ellie. "Kade didn't say he'd be bringing you along, but it's nice to see you again." The knowing gleam in his eyes said he could guess what they'd been doing in the bedroom last night. Kade's hand unconsciously fisted.

Ellie smiled at Will. "I had an errand to run in Vail, so I came along." Her motive for the trip was none of Turley's business.

Turley's attention returned to Kade. "So what can I do for you?"

"How's the investigation going? Any idea who blew up the tunnel?"

"Not that I've heard," Will said. "But the investigation is ongoing. I don't think the sheriff would tell me if he had a lead."

Kade nodded. "Ever hear of a guy named Frank Keller?"

Will's answer was drowned by a skip loader backing up, setting off a loud beeping. Men scrambled to get out of the way.

"Why don't we go inside where we can talk?" Will suggested.

They followed him into the office, and Turley closed the door. Kade's jaw tightened at the way the man's eyes lingered on Ellie's breasts as she took off her puffy jacket.

Jealousy was an emotion Kade had learned to ignore when he had been married to Heather. Somehow it felt different with Ellie. Maybe because she wasn't flirting with the other man to purposely spark his temper.

His gaze went to Turley. Ellie was a beautiful woman. Turley was just a man. Kade's temper eased.

He sat down next to Ellie in folding chairs in front of Turley's metal desk. The office was cluttered by metal shelves against the walls filled with an assortment of ore samples, heavy chunks of rock containing silver, lead, zinc, and any of a half dozen different substances, all covered with a fine layer of dust.

Turley sat down across from them behind his desk. "You asked me about Frank Keller."

"That's right," Kade said. "You recognize the name?"

Will nodded. "Keller worked here for a while. He was our blast technician when we started the new tunnel. It was a while ago, though. At least six months."

"Did you give the sheriff his name after the explosion?"

"It never occurred to me Frank would be involved. Like I said, he's been gone for at least six months, and he never gave us any trouble. We parted amiably, and that was the last I saw of him."

"Why'd he quit?"

"We got to a point we didn't need him, and he'd only been hired for a specific project. He completed the work, we paid him, and he left."

"Did he say where he was going?" Ellie asked. "Or leave a forwarding address?"

"He said something about a job in one of the mines in southern Colorado. Didn't say which one. That's all I know."

Kade rose from his chair. "Thanks for the help, Will. If you think of anything else, I'd appreciate a call."

He didn't mention the dead steers or what had happened to Alejandro. Those were ranch problems, and so far he had no proof Keller was involved. If Keller hadn't blown up the mine, maybe the events weren't connected.

They left the mine supervisor's office and climbed into the truck. Ellie's seat belt clicked into place as Kade slid behind the wheel and fired the engine.

"Maybe Keller isn't our guy," Ellie said.

"Maybe not. We need to know more about him. He only worked the roundup a week or so before he was fired. Around the middle of September, I think."

"If he was working in a different mine somewhere before that, why would he come back to Coffee Springs?"

"Good question. Maybe he was raised around here. He knew how to ride, how to handle himself out there or Wyatt wouldn't have put him to work."

"I'll get on it as soon as we get back," Ellie said. "I know someone who might be able to help."

CHAPTER SIXTEEN

*E*LLIE HAD A SECRET WEAPON WHEN IT CAME TO INFORMATION. Zoey Rosen was a friend from college, her roommate in the dorm their first year at the University of Colorado. They'd shared an apartment in the years that followed and become even better friends.

The good news was Zoe was an internet whiz. She'd majored in computer science in school and now worked as a systems security engineer. Zoe knew her way around the digital world. She'd been fascinated by computers, gaming, and the internet since she was a kid so she could find just about anything. Legally or otherwise.

Ellie didn't want to take advantage of their friendship, but Zoe loved a challenge, and she was always glad to help. In this case, there was a man out there who could be setting off explosives and shooting people, possibly a man named Frank Keller. Though the sheriff had put a statewide BOLO out on Keller as a person of interest, so far he hadn't been found.

And she planned to ask Zoe about the sheriff himself. Carver had been secretly dating Heather Logan. If she had ended things, maybe the sheriff hadn't taken the news so well. Maybe they had fought about it and he had killed her. It was worth checking out.

Ellie watched the passing scenery as Kade drove his big Ford truck from the mine back toward home. The mid-October weather was chilly, but the sun was shining as he turned onto the road just south of Coffee Springs out to the ranch. Twenty minutes later, the big timber gate welcomed them. On the slope of the hill, the tall stone chimneys, plate-glass windows, and covered porches of the ranch house loomed ahead.

Kade pulled in behind the house and turned off the engine. Ellie climbed out as he rounded the front of the vehicle and walked toward her, all long legs, snug jeans, and cowboy boots, his hat pulled low on his forehead.

Kade stopped in front of her, and her gaze slid over him. Kade didn't miss much, and unfortunately, he knew exactly what she was thinking.

He propped his hands on his hips, his silver belt buckle gleaming. "I hope you like what you see, darlin'."

Color washed into her cheeks, and she glanced away. "Sorry, my . . . umm . . . mind was wandering."

Kade's eyes slid over her breasts, making them peak inside her sweater. "Mine too," he said gruffly.

Embarrassed, she glanced away, spotted the black-and-white border collie rising from the blanket he had been lying on in the sun. "Looks like Smoke is doing a little better."

Kade's attention swung to the dog limping toward them, his head cocked as he looked adoringly up at Kade.

"Easy, boy." Kade stroked his thick black-and-white fur and gently rubbed behind his ears. "You can stay out a little longer, but as soon as the afternoon starts getting colder, you gotta come inside."

Ellie smiled. "You think he knows what you're saying?" She reached down and ran a hand over Smoke's furry head.

"Probably. He's pretty damned smart."

As Kade continued to pet the dog, Billy walked up. "I been taking real good care of him, sir. You don't have to worry."

"I know that, son. I never worry about Smoke when he's with you."

Billy gazed down at the injured dog he clearly loved, and his features hardened. "I wish I'd been there when Smoke got shot. I would have gone after that guy myself."

"He's a dangerous man, Billy. Better to let the cops deal with it."

"You and Ms. Ellie went after him."

"We did. Unfortunately, we didn't find him."

Billy looked hard at Kade. "You won't give up, will you?"

Ellie knew the boy had a bad case of hero worship, which, on occasion, she fought not to feel herself.

A muscle ticked in Kade's jaw. "Not a chance."

Apparently satisfied with Kade's answer, Billy and Smoke wandered away, the dog hobbling along beside his friend.

"That's Maria's car," Kade said, spotting the older-model Honda compact SUV in front of one of the log cabins. There were three on the property. One belonged to Mabel. The other two were used for guests.

Kade started walking, with Ellie beside him. He stepped up on the porch beneath the overhanging roof and knocked.

Maria opened the door. "Señor Kade. Ellie. Please come in. Alejandro's sleeping. If you want, I can wake him."

Kade took off his Stetson and held it in his hand. "I hate to do that, but I need to talk to him. How's he doing?"

Maria smiled wistfully. "Alejandro's a very good patient. He's been no trouble at all."

Ellie bit back a smile. She figured the man could behave like the devil himself and Maria would still think he was wonderful.

"What about you?" Kade asked. "You doing okay?"

"Sí, I am fine. They were very nice at the hospital. They put a cot in Alejandro's room so I'd have a place to sleep."

Kade's eyebrows pulled together. He was worried about Maria's infatuation with a man who, according to rumor, collected women like exotic butterflies. So far, Kade hadn't interfered.

At a noise from inside the bedroom, Maria glanced toward the door. "Alejandro must be awake. I'll tell him you're here." Smoothing a strand of glossy black hair back into her single long braid, Maria disappeared into the bedroom.

She returned a few minutes later. "Alejandro would like to see you, Señor Kade."

Kade nodded. Hat in hand, he walked into the room, and Ellie followed. She hadn't been hired to investigate the shooting, but she was involved in it now. She wanted answers as much as Kade did.

The room was sunny and cheerful, with a dark green quilt on the big, king-size log bed and framed petit-point pictures on the yellow pine walls. Alejandro rested comfortably, a pillow behind his back propping him up a little. His face looked pale, his black hair was mussed, and a scruff of dark beard lined his jaw. It only made him more handsome.

The sheet was pulled up to his waist, and a bandage was wrapped around his chest and shoulder, the white making his olive skin look even darker.

"I didn't figure they'd let you out for at least another few days," Kade said.

"I hate hospitals," Alejandro grumbled as if that explained everything. "Maria told them she'd look after me at the ranch, so they let me go."

"How are you feeling?"

"Like a cattle truck ran over me."

Kade moved closer to the bed. "You ready to talk about what happened?"

Alejandro sighed. "There isn't much to say. I was working with the men on that downed tree in the east pasture. I heard a gunshot and felt a punch in my back that slammed through my chest like a cannon ball. I went down hard. I don't remember much after that. I saw Wyatt running toward me, then Slate was there. I remember Wyatt tearing open my shirt. Then I must have passed out. That's all I remember."

"Doc said the boys did a good job patching you up. Stopped the bleeding and got you back to the house. Ellie and I went after the shooter, but we couldn't find him."

"I wish I could tell you more."

"Don't worry about it. We'll find him. In the meantime, you just get well."

"Is there anything special you want?" Ellie asked. "Maybe some cookies or something?"

"No, Ms. Ellie." All the guys called her that now. She thought it was kind of cute. "I don't need anything. By the time I think of something, Maria already has it for me." His black eyes wandered toward the door, where the girl stood watching, anxious for her patient's welfare. A look passed between them, and Maria's cheeks went pink.

Maria was as beautiful as Alejandro was handsome. The attraction between them shouldn't have been a surprise.

"Alejandro needs to rest," Ellie said, picking up the vibes. "We should go."

Maria looked at Ellie. "I'll get Alejandro settled, then be over to help with supper."

"The important thing is for your patient to get well," Ellie said. "You don't need to worry. Turtle's been helping me in the kitchen. Between the two of us, we've got it under control."

Kade looked at Alejandro. "Let me know if you think of anything else. In the meantime, just rest and take it easy."

Turning, he started for the door, waited for Ellie, and followed her out, then fell in beside her as they walked back to the house and went in through the kitchen. Ellie forced herself not to glance at the oak table as they walked past.

"I've got some work to do on my computer before I start supper," she said. "I'll see you later."

Kade's golden-brown eyes sparked with heat. "I'm looking forward it."

Ellie's stomach curled.

A problem came up that afternoon. Roy rode in to say something seemed to be wrong with the waterhole up near Bear Tooth Ridge. With all the trouble they'd been having, Kade was afraid the water might have been poisoned. Grabbing a sample kit, he and Wyatt set out on ATVs to take a look. Slate joined them on his own ATV, pulling a small trailer with enough makeshift fencing to keep the cattle away from the drinking hole.

Unfortunately, by the time they got there, two of the cows were down, bawling in pain, alive, but clearly sick.

"Sonofabitch," Kade said.

"We need to get that water sample, see what's going on," Wyatt said as they turned off their four-wheelers' engines.

Kade pulled a pair of glass vials out of the kit he'd brought and knelt at the edge of the drinking hole. The surface was smooth and flat. The water was clear and looked clean, but there was no way to tell without testing it in a lab.

Kade filled the vials and put them back in the kit. "We need to get these two cows back to the barn so the vet can have a look at them." *If they stay alive that long,* he thought, and silently cursed.

"I'll go back and get a truck and trailer," Slate said, "bring it around through the gate at the far end of the pasture."

"Sounds good." But it would take a while. In the meantime, there wasn't much they could do for the animals without knowing what was wrong with them. They needed to keep the other cows away from the water until they found out what was going on.

While Slate headed back to the ranch, Kade and Wyatt unloaded the fencing and went to work erecting a barrier around the waterhole.

Wyatt smoothed his handlebar mustache and glanced over at Kade. "You think the guy who shot the steers poisoned the water?"

"Could be," Kade said. "Other ways it could have happened too." Using a post hole digger, he dug a hole, set one of the fence posts, shoveled the dirt back in, and tamped it down. "Won't know for sure till we get the lab report." Had Frank Keller poisoned the cows? Or was the man smart enough to be long gone from the area?

The test results would take a few days. In the meantime, even with the security patrol he'd hired, the hands needed to stay alert. Nineteen thousand acres was a big chunk of land. Fortunately, the cattle had been brought down to the lower pastures for the winter, which meant the patrol was less spread out.

Slate returned with the pickup and trailer. They loaded the sick cows, and Slate drove them back to the ranch. Kade and Wyatt finished building the fence, then drove the remaining cattle north toward another waterhole they hoped would be safe. They didn't find any sick cows in the area, and the second waterhole was more remote, which made it somewhat safer.

By the time they were finished and on their way home, it was pitch-dark. There was no moon and only a few stars overhead.

Kade's stomach growled. Supper was long over, but with any luck they'd find something left for them in the kitchen. He thought of Ellie and what he'd had in mind for her tonight. He was hungry, but not just for food. Unfortunately, it was after midnight when he and Wyatt walked tiredly into the ranch house kitchen.

Ellie was nowhere in sight, but a platter of roast chicken and potatoes waited for them in the oven. There was a salad in the fridge and hot rolls in the warming drawer. Kade smiled. A detective who could cook and run a kitchen. Best luck he'd had in some time.

Thinking of why Ellie had come to the Diamond Bar had his smile slipping away. She was there to find a killer. She'd been sidetracked into helping him track down Frank Keller, but there was nothing more either of them could do right now.

In the meantime, tomorrow was Friday. He had promised to take Ellie to the Elkhorn Bar and Grill. She had come to Coffee Springs in search of a murderer. She wanted to meet some of the locals, eliminate them as suspects, if nothing else. He could help with that.

And when he brought her home after the dance, they could continue where they had left off. He'd have Ellie back in his bed, and until this was over, he planned to convince her to stay there.

It was a thought that would get him through a long, worrisome night.

CHAPTER SEVENTEEN

ELLIE WAS GRATEFUL TO HAVE MARIA HELPING AGAIN IN THE KITchen. The hands ate breakfast and set off for work, while Kade went over the books in his study. When Maria left to take a plate of ham and eggs to Alejandro, Kade returned.

"We've got security covered and the hands on the lookout for Keller, but unless someone spots him or the sheriff comes up with something, there's nothing more we can do right now."

Ellie looked up at him. "I'm waiting for a call from a friend. She's a whiz at digging up information. I'm hoping she can come up with something useful. But you're right. Unless something turns up, we've got nothing."

"There's one thing we can do."

"What's that?"

"I promised to take you to the Elkhorn, introduce you around. You came here to do a job. Maybe that will help you do it."

Ellie started nodding. Kade was right. She needed to get back to the murder case she was there to solve. "All right. That sounds good."

Ellie's eyes widened when Kade framed her face between his hands, leaned down, and captured her lips in a very thorough kiss. "I'll see you at supper."

Her heart was racing. The man could just look at her and make her want him. She watched him stride across the kitchen, long legs encased in his worn, rough-out chaps. They outlined the heavy bulge beneath the fly of his jeans, and Ellie bit back a moan.

Kade grabbed his work jacket off the coatrack, plucked his battered cowboy hat off a peg, settled it on his head, and tugged it low. With a last hot glance, he turned and walked out of the kitchen.

Ellie took a deep breath. She was in way over her head with Kade Logan. Kade wasn't interested in more than a physical relationship. Which should be exactly what she wanted.

She didn't trust men, not after her lying, cheating ex-husband. She'd had the same bad luck with every serious relationship since college. She'd met David Richmond her third year. He was the love of her life—or at least so she'd thought. David had professed eternal devotion and hinted at marriage. All the while, he was screwing one of the grad students.

Two years later, the promising relationship she'd had with a young doctor turned sour when she found him cheating with one of his patients. It seemed the word *gullible* was stamped on her forehead.

The woman Ellie was now refused to let herself be fooled again. Added to that was the not so small matter of her independence. She would surely lose it with a man like Kade. Better to keep her distance from him, enjoy that hard male body and all that masculine virility, and say goodbye when the time came.

The sound of her cell phone returned her thoughts to the moment. She had called Zoey Rosen last night, but her friend hadn't picked up. Unlike Ellie, Zoe never let a man make a fool of her. She took what he offered and felt no remorse when she ended things. Zoe dumped her lovers without a second thought.

Ellie grabbed the phone off the kitchen counter and checked the caller ID. "Hey, Zoe, thanks for calling me back."

"I'm glad you phoned. It seems like it's been forever. What's going on?"

"Actually, I'm on a job." Phone against her ear, Ellie left the kitchen and headed for her bedroom, where she wouldn't be overheard if Maria came back to the house. "I'm working undercover on a ranch, trying to find the guy who murdered the owner's wife eight years ago."

"Wow, that sounds like an interesting case."

"You could . . . umm . . . say that."

"Okay . . . what's that I'm hearing in your voice? What's going on? Aside from work, I mean?"

There was no way to avoid the truth with Zoe. They'd been roommates for years, best friends for what seemed like forever.

Ellie sighed. "I'm sleeping with the owner. It's highly unprofessional, I know, but somehow it just happened."

"What's his name?"

She hated to answer. Zoe would be on the internet the minute they hung up. "Kade Logan. He owns the Diamond Bar Ranch near Coffee Springs."

Zoe was already typing away on her keyboard. "Oh, my God. Seriously? If he looks half as good as his picture, you'd be crazy *not* to sleep with him."

Ellie thought of Kade's hungry kiss that morning, and her stomach contracted. "It's just physical. Neither of us is interested in a relationship."

"Be careful, girl. You can tell yourself you aren't interested in anything but sex, but part of you has been searching for the right man since you broke up with David."

"Yes, and look where that got me. I married Mark, and he turned out to be a total snake. I'm not falling for Kade. With any luck, I'll find the person who killed his wife and be on my way back to Denver."

"After some great, very hot sex, I hope."

"Exactly. What about you?"

"I'm dating a guy named Chad Wilson. We met at a gaming convention. He's really great. Especially in bed."

Zoe was petite, with short blond hair, a generous mouth, and an upturned nose that made her look like a pixie. Her nickname in college was Tinkerbelle.

"So this guy, Chad," Ellie said. "Sounds like you really like him."

"I do."

"Then maybe you should give him a chance. He might turn out to be Mr. Right this time."

"Yeah, maybe." But Zoe didn't sound convinced. She was even less trusting than Ellie. "So how can I help with your investigation?"

"Actually, there are two things going on at the ranch." She explained about the shootings and the mine explosion. "I need you to look at a guy named Frank Keller. We think he's behind the trouble Kade's been having." She gave Zoe everything she had on Keller, including the fact he was army EOD.

"What else?" Zoe asked.

"I was hired to solve Heather Logan's murder. She disappeared eight years ago." She gave Zoe the details, which included the discovery of Heather's body two years after her disappearance, then the police recently finding the woman's missing car.

"I need you to look at the Eagle County sheriff, Glen Carver. He was having an affair with Kade's wife a few months before she died, might even have been seeing her when it happened."

"So Heather was cheating."

"That's right. And Carver wasn't the only one. Apparently, she was involved with half the guys in Coffee Springs and maybe some in Vail."

"And Kade didn't know?"

"Not at first. He didn't want to believe it, I guess. Once he was sure, he filed for divorce. The night she packed up and moved out of the house was the night she disappeared and possibly the night she was murdered."

Silence fell. "No wonder Kade's gun shy."

"Including you and me, that makes three of us."

Zoe laughed. "Okay, I'll get on it. Things are kind of busy at work right now, so it might take a while, but I'll make it a top priority."

"Thanks, Zoe, you're the best."

Zoe hung up the phone.

Kade returned to the ranch in time for supper. He'd found Conner Delaney, who now sported a dark shadow of beard along his jaw, and they'd talked about the security detail.

"I've got men patrolling the area twenty-four seven," Conn said. "They'll be watching for any sign of this guy—on foot, in a vehicle, or on horseback. I've shown my men a photo of Keller, so they know who they're looking for. He shows up, we'll be ready."

Delaney was a professional, and it showed. The hands had all worked with Keller and would recognize him; they'd be watching for him too. "You see anything suspicious, I need to know."

"Will do," Conn said. The men who worked with him all wore camo, which was no big deal out here. Half the guys in Coffee Springs hunted in the fall, along with the passel of hunters who came up from Denver each year.

Delaney took off on an ATV, and Kade went in to join the men for supper, along with a couple of the security guys who had just come in off patrol. Ellie and Maria set out the food, a macaroni-and-cheese casserole made with baked ham. The guys served themselves and sat down at the table.

Kade fidgeted, anxious for the meal to be over so he and Ellie could be on their way to town.

"I'm going upstairs to change," he said as soon as the men had walked out the door. "We'll leave for the Elkhorn around seven, if that works for you."

"Okay, I'll be ready."

He let his gaze wander over her, didn't hide what he was thinking. He wanted this woman. And tonight he planned to have her.

"I'll . . . umm . . . see you at seven," Ellie said with a hitch in her voice that told him she'd received his message loud and clear.

Arousal heated Kade's blood. If he had his way, he'd cancel their plans for the evening and haul her directly upstairs.

It wasn't going to happen. He wanted Heather's killer even more than he wanted hot, erotic sex with Ellie Bowman.

But not by much.

The Elkhorn was just getting wound up when they arrived. It was a country bar at the end of Main Street, a log building with pine ceilings, walls, and tables. Even the top of the long bar was made from a slab of ponderosa pine, varnished to a glossy sheen.

Kade escorted Ellie to one of the wooden bar stools, and she climbed up on the brown-leather seat. She'd hung her coat on the rack beside the door, and he had hung his sheepskin jacket beside it. Underneath, she wore a short denim skirt with her boots, showing off her pretty legs, and a white sweater cut low enough to reveal the soft mounds of her breasts and the deep cleavage in between.

Looking at her made his mouth water.

A buxom blonde sauntered toward them behind the bar. Maisie Gaines was a few years older than Kade, a good-looking woman he had known for years. He'd slept with her a few times the year after Heather had left, but the sparks just weren't there. They decided they made better friends than lovers, and Kade considered Maisie as good a friend as he had in Coffee Springs.

"Well, look who the cat dragged in," Maisie drawled in a voice that sounded like the smoker she had been when she was a kid. Her eyes slid over him in a more than friendly manner, but it was a game she played with all the men who came into the bar.

"Maisie, this is Ellie Bowman. She's running our kitchen while Mabel is visiting family in Arizona. Ellie, this is Maisie Gaines. She owns the place."

Maisie turned her shrewd gaze on Ellie. "Pleasure to meet you, Ellie."

"You too, Maisie." Ellie's big green eyes were equally assessing. Kade had a hunch she was just as shrewd as Maisie. How a woman knew which particular lady a man had taken to bed he would never know, but clearly these two were reading each other perfectly.

"What are you drinking, darlin'?" Kade asked, hoping to move the situation in a different direction.

"Jack and Coke," Ellie said.

Kade almost smiled. He'd bet it wasn't her usual alcoholic beverage. But when in Rome . . .

"Make that two," he said.

Maisie mixed the drinks and set them on the counter. "Enjoy." She winked at Kade and sauntered off to help a cowboy at the other end of the bar.

"Old friend?" Ellie asked dryly.

"Exactly that and nothing more, as least not for a long time. Just so you know."

Ellie relaxed a little. "Not my business."

"At the moment, it is."

Her eyes met his. He didn't hide the desire he felt for her. He wasn't interested in another woman. Not Maisie or anyone else.

Kade glanced around the room, which was more than half full. Cowboys in jeans, western shirts, hats, and boots; women in tight jeans and sexy tops. Turquoise jewelry glittered here and there around the room.

More people drifted in. Dark came early, and this was ranch country. The band started playing at eight o'clock on the nose—a guitar, fiddle, and drum. They started with an Alabama fiddle tune to warm up the crowd. The next song was a Texas two-step, George Strait's "Does Fort Worth Ever Cross Your Mind?"

"Let's dance," Kade said as couples poured onto the dance floor. Any excuse to hold her.

"One dance," Ellie said. "Then I need to get to work."

"Fine." Hauling her off the bar stool, he swept her onto the dance floor to join the other couples circling to the music. Ellie had no trouble following his lead, and in seconds, they were dancing together as if they'd done it a hundred times. She felt good in his arms, fit just right.

He thought how well they would fit together once he had her in his bed, and the blood began to pound in his veins. Arousal slid through him, and he started getting hard. Kade silently cursed. They had a long evening ahead, and he needed to focus on the reason they were there.

The song came to an end. Kade glanced toward a table in the corner. "I see some friends sitting in the back. I'd like you to meet them."

"All right."

He led her over to where Sam Bridger sat with the petite blonde he had been dating. Kade hadn't talked to him since the day the sheriff had pulled Heather's car out of the lake.

"Kade," Sam said, rising. "Good to see you."

"You too." They shook hands. "Sam, this is Ellie Bowman." He debated telling Sam the truth about who she was, then decided against it since his friend wasn't alone. "Ellie's filling in for Mabel while she's down in Arizona." Kade turned. "Ellie, this is my good friend, Sam Bridger. He owns the Bridger Ranch down the road from the Diamond Bar."

"Nice to meet you, Ellie," Sam said.

"And I'm Libby," the woman said with a smile.

"Nice to meet you both." The couples talked briefly, and then she and Kade started back to their seats.

"They both seem nice," Ellie said.

"I've only met Libby a couple of times. Sam just met her this summer. She had some trouble when she first got here, but it all worked out." Kade glanced back at the two blond heads bent close together. "Looks like he's got it bad."

Ellie laughed. "How long have you and Sam been friends?"

Kade didn't miss the speculation in her eyes. "You aren't thinking Sam was one of Heather's conquests?"

Ellie looked back at the tall, good-looking blond rancher dressed in jeans and boots, like most of the guys in the bar. "You don't think so?"

"Sam and I have been friends since we were boys. He saved my life once, pulled me out of a swimming hole after I took a shallow dive and hit my head. Sam never approved of Heather. I think he knew what she was doing. The reason he never said anything is because he's my best friend."

Ellie made no reply. Kade figured she would be on the computer first thing in the morning, looking up information on Sam Bridger. But Sam was the one man in Coffee Springs Kade didn't have to worry about.

"Who's the other bartender?" Ellie asked as they crossed the room back to their seats.

Kade glanced over. On dance night, it took two people to handle the drink orders. "Name's Rance Sullivan." A guy Kade didn't much like.

Sullivan was a handsome bastard, with too-long black hair and an olive complexion. He was always spouting off about being part Native American, but it was just a line he fed to the ladies. Kade had wondered for years if Heather had been one of Rance's women. If she had, part of him didn't want to know.

"How long has he been working here?" Ellie asked.

"His family's from Eagle. Claims he's part Arapahoe, but I doubt it. He's worked here off and on for years."

"Since before Heather's disappearance?"

His jaw tightened. "Yeah."

As Ellie settled herself on the stool in front of her drink, she flashed Kade a look of warning. *Remember, I'm here to work*, that look said.

He almost smiled. She was right, so he nodded, though she hadn't said a word. "I see a couple of guys I know. I'm going over to say hello."

"Take your time," Ellie said pointedly. She turned around and casually took a sip of her drink.

As Kade started toward the local veterinarian and his wife, he watched Sullivan easing his way down the bar in Ellie's direction, a predatory gleam in his black eyes.

Kade's hand unconsciously fisted. Looked like Sullivan had set his sights on Ellie tonight.

Kade's temper inched higher. The notion of Sullivan with Ellie stirred a hot, dark feeling inside him. He didn't understand it. He had never been a jealous man. Or at least he had learned to control it. Until now.

Kade forced himself to keep walking.

CHAPTER EIGHTEEN

*E*LLIE TURNED A WARM SMILE ON THE BARTENDER. SHE'D BEEN
watching him since they'd walked in. Rance Sullivan was tall,
dark, and handsome. He had the kind of persona that promised a
ride on the wild side, a broad-shouldered, well-muscled body, and
a masculine gleam in his eyes that said he'd be good in bed.

He paused in front her, mopped the bar with a white terry-
cloth towel. "I haven't seen you before. You must be new in town."

She smiled. "Ellie Bowman." She held out a hand, and Rance
shook it, held it a little too long. "I just started working out at the
Diamond Bar Ranch."

"Nice to meet you, Ellie. I'm—"

"You're Rance Sullivan. I know who you are. A friend of mine
mentioned you. But it was a long time ago."

"A friend, huh? What was his name?"

She glanced surreptitiously over her shoulder as if she wanted
to be sure Kade couldn't hear. He was talking to a couple of cowboys at the back of the room. "Her name was Heather Logan. She
was married to Kade at the time. We met in Vail."

Sullivan's black eyes followed her gaze to the back of the room,
checking to see where Kade had gone. "Heather mentioned me?"

"That's right. I guess you guys were . . . umm . . . seeing each
other for a while."

His gaze sharpened. "That what she said?"

Ellie shrugged. "We got to be pretty good friends, always skied together when she came to Vail." She smiled. "Heather had a real thing for you. Said you were tall, dark, handsome as sin, and wicked as the devil in bed. She told me you were the best she'd ever had."

Sullivan's shoulders subtly straightened. "I'm surprised she told you."

"Like I said, it was a long time ago."

His white teeth flashed. "Truth is, we did have a few good times."

Ellie felt the rush of satisfaction that came with uncovering information. She took a sip of her drink. "When I started working at the ranch, I wondered if you'd still be here." She smiled. "And what do you know, here you are."

Ellie didn't miss the wolfish gleam in his eyes that shifted from friendly to hungry. "Heather and I . . . it was wild and hot, but it didn't last long. With Heather it never did."

"So she dumped you?"

Anger glinted for an instant. "I wouldn't call it that, more a mutual parting of the ways." The smile he summoned looked forced. "But you aren't Heather, are you? You're a beautiful woman, and if you're in the market for a good time, I'm happy to oblige." He tipped his head toward the man at the back of the room. "Unless you're more interested in your employer."

"Kade just gave me a ride into town since I'm new to Coffee Springs."

The hungry gleam was back. "I promise you, sweetheart, I can give you a far better ride than Kade Logan."

Ellie smiled at him from beneath her lashes. "I'll give it some thought." She watched Rance swagger off to wait on a customer at the other end of the bar, amazed at how easily people gave up information. Then again, time changed everything. After eight years, Sullivan wasn't worried about being linked to a murder investigation. He just wanted to get laid.

Which Kade seemed to realize as he strode up to the bar, his square jaw in a rigid line.

"I thought you wanted to visit with your friends," Ellie reminded him.

"I talked to them. They're fine." He took her arm and urged her down from the bar stool. The band was playing Willie Nelson.

"I want to talk to Maisie," she said.

"Later. There's something I want to show you." His eyes were dark and hard as he led her down a hall at the back of the bar.

"Where are we going?"

Kade opened the door to a storeroom, dragged her inside, closed the door, and turned the lock. Ellie gasped as he pulled her into his arms and his mouth crushed down over hers. Firm soft lips mixed with iron-hard determination, and heat engulfed her. Dampness slid into her core. She found herself gripping the front of Kade's western shirt, kissing him back with the same hungry need she sensed in him.

His hands moved down to her breasts, cupping them over her sweater, then sliding underneath, reaching around to pop the hooks on her bra, filling his palms with the fullness. He abraded her nipples, turning them diamond hard, and she moaned.

Kade's hat fell off as he deepened the kiss, turning it hotter and even more demanding. She felt dizzy and out of control. She was in a storeroom in the back of a bar. Through the fog of lust, it occurred to her that Kade's former lover was the owner and that he had probably done the same thing in here with her.

Ellie broke away, her breath coming in quick sharp pants. "Did you bring her here? Did you have sex with Maisie in this storeroom?"

"Hell no. The few times I had sex with Maisie was in her house, not the bar. I never wanted Maisie the way I want you." Then he fisted a hand in her hair to hold her in place and kissed her deeply again, ravishing her mouth as his other hand slid over her body.

Ellie's legs went weak. She clung to Kade's broad shoulders and kissed him back. The next thing she knew, he was shoving aside a stack of bar towels piled on a counter, wrapping his hands around her waist, hoisting her up, and setting her firmly on top. Her skirt rode up as he moved between her legs and started kissing her again.

Kade tugged her sweater off over her head and tossed it away, followed it with her bra, and captured a breast in his mouth. Moaning, she slid her fingers into his hair and arched her back to give him better access.

Restless hunger poured through her. "I need you, Kade," she whispered as she clung to him, her body aching and on fire.

"Just hold on, darlin'."

Hearing the buzz of his zipper, Ellie gripped the front of his white western shirt and jerked it open, popping the row of pearl snaps on the front. Her hands slid over his powerful chest, savoring its strength and breadth. Wanting to taste all that warm male skin, she pressed her mouth over his heart.

Kade hissed in a breath. Lifting her chin, her lowered his mouth to hers and kissed her, then positioned himself between her legs, tore off her red thong panties, and stroked her until she was sobbing his name. Kade slid inside her, his hard length filling her completely, promising the same pleasure he had given her before.

Kade paused, a shudder rippling through him as he fought for control. "Damn, I want you. Watching you smile at Sullivan, I wanted to rip his head off and shove it down his throat." Kade drove into her, hard enough to lift her a little off the counter. "He doesn't touch you. Nobody touches you but me." Kade kissed her.

She should have been angry, should have been worried at the wildly possessive note in his voice, maybe even frightened. Instead, she raised her hips to take more of him, urging him to move deeper, faster, harder, wildly exhilarated that in some way he claimed her.

Kade took her and took her, the sound of their lovemaking hidden beneath the music pounding through the walls of the storeroom. Ellie came with a rush so sweet and hot that tears filled her eyes.

She cried out as a second climax struck. Seconds later, Kade's jaw clenched and his whole body tightened as he followed her to release.

For long seconds, neither of them moved. Kade just held her, his forehead tipped against hers. He cupped her face and kissed her one last time.

"Are you all right?"

She didn't know what to say. She wasn't all right. She felt as if she had fallen under some dark, powerful spell Kade Logan had cast over her. She had never felt this kind of wild, erotic hunger. She wasn't sure if she could handle it, or if she should just run away.

"I-I'm okay."

He took care of the condom she had barely noticed he'd put on, then turned back to her. There was something in his eyes, something dark and turbulent.

"I don't know what happened. One minute I was watching you talk to Sullivan. I knew what he was saying. I knew exactly what he wanted from you, and the next thing I knew I was dragging you in here." He sighed and ran his fingers through his hair. "I feel like I should apologize, but I don't regret what happened, so it wouldn't really be sincere."

Ellie might have smiled, but there was nothing funny about what had happened. It had shown her just how deeply she was entangled with Kade. Still, she didn't regret it either. "It's all right. I could have stopped you. I never doubted that."

He grabbed his hat off the floor and tugged it on, bent his head, and pressed a last brief kiss on her lips. "No matter how much I want you, I'd never hurt you, darlin'."

Ellie studied his handsome face. The turbulence remained, but it was softened by some other emotion she couldn't read. "I think it's time we went home."

Kade lifted her down from the counter and set her on her feet. They both rearranged their clothes, and Kade straightened her skirt. He didn't say more, but the heat in his eyes had barely dimmed. She was pretty sure he planned to take up where they'd left off when they got back to the ranch.

Ellie told herself she should back away before it was too late. But as he urged her out of the storeroom, she was pretty sure that wasn't going to happen.

Kade followed Ellie across the dance floor toward the front door. "What about Maisie?" he asked. "I thought you wanted to talk to her."

Ellie glanced over at the blond woman behind the bar. "Probably not the best time," she said dryly.

Kade followed her gaze to Maisie, who watched them with a smug smile on her face. Ellie's dark copper curls were mussed, her white sweater smudged with dirt, and her denim skirt wrinkled. She looked as if she had just rolled out of some cowboy's bed. Which basically she had.

Kade felt the heat creeping into the back of his neck. "You're probably right." They grabbed their coats off the rack by the door, put them on, and stepped out into the cold evening air.

Kade walked Ellie around to the passenger side of the pickup and helped her climb in, then headed for the driver's side. As he started the engine, he tried to remember a time in his younger, wilder days when he'd dragged a woman into a back room somewhere and had steamy, uninhibited sex with her.

Definitely never happened.

It bothered him that Ellie could make him lose his highly valued control. Hell, he'd barely noticed the men Heather flirted with. Kade asked himself why that was. What was the difference between the two women?

The only answer that came to mind was that after the first few years, he and Heather had pretty much just cohabitated. After dating through high school, marriage was the next logical step. And this was Coffee Springs. Kade needed a wife. Heather was beautiful, and there weren't a lot of women to choose from.

Ellie was different. She was her own woman. Independent,

smart, hardworking, and sexy as hell. Kade had to admit he was fiercely attracted to her, more than any woman he could recall. Hell, more than any other woman he'd ever known.

He was in deep trouble with Ellie Bowman, and unsure how to proceed. The feeling was new to him. He warned himself to tread carefully, but as he cast her a sideways glance and felt his body coming to life again, he wasn't quite sure how to make that happen.

CHAPTER NINETEEN

*E*LLIE SPENT MOST OF THE NIGHT IN KADE'S BED. AS THE CLOCKED ticked toward four a.m. and Kade lay beside her fast asleep, she was surprised at how reluctant she was to leave.

You can't afford to get any more involved, a little voice warned. *It's too big a risk.*

Easing back the covers, she dressed and quietly left the bedroom, went downstairs, showered, and went to work. As she set out the basics for breakfast, she thought again of the night she had spent with Kade, and another thought surfaced. Kade had told her he'd never been jealous of Heather. But he'd been beyond jealous of Ellie last night.

He doesn't touch you. No one touches you but me.

No man had ever made those kinds of demands on her. Not her ex-husband, not a boyfriend or anyone else. Not that it was a problem since she didn't sleep with other men when she was involved with someone—no matter how brief a time the relationship lasted.

Still, it made her wonder. Was there a chance Kade had murdered Heather in a fit of temper? Infidelity was certainly a trigger for Kade.

As breakfast ended and she and Maria cleaned up, Ellie tried to imagine a version of Kade who would kill his wife, but the entire concept of Kade using violence against a woman just didn't fit.

She thought of the people in his life—Wyatt, Alejandro and

the ranch hands, Maria, young Billy. If anything, Kade was overly protective of the people he cared for.

True, the man was wildly demanding in bed, but he had never threatened her physically, and she had never been afraid of him. In truth, when they'd been having passionate sex in the storeroom, she had encouraged him—a thought that sent hot color into her cheeks.

Still, she would find a way to take a look at Heather's medical records, see if there was any evidence of abuse, and also ask Zoe to take a look at Rance Sullivan, see if anything suspicious popped up.

Ellie wiped her hands on a dish towel and glanced over at Maria. "Looks like we're done here," she said. "You should take breakfast to Alejandro. How's he doing, by the way?"

Maria gave her the dreamy smile she had been wearing since she'd been staying in the cabin with the handsome Latino.

"He's getting better every day."

"That's good to hear. So . . . what about the two of you? Do you think you'll get together after he's well?"

Maria's soft smile faded. "He thinks he's too old for me."

"How old is he?"

"Thirty-one." Two years older than Ellie. "I told him ten years is nothing. But he thinks I should go out and see the world, enjoy life before I think about settling down."

"Maybe he's right," Ellie said.

Big brown eyes locked on her face. "My world is here in Coffee Springs. My grandmother is here. My family is close by. I don't care about seeing the world. There's no other place I'd rather be."

There wasn't much Ellie could say to that. Heather was the kind of woman who had craved freedom. Maria was a homebody who just wanted a man who loved her and a family of her own.

"Give him some time. If he cares for you, maybe he'll figure it out."

Maria's eyes welled. "I thought I could make him fall in love with me. It's not Alejandro's fault." A drop of wetness rolled down her cheek as Maria turned away, grabbed the foil-wrapped platter of food she had prepared, and hurried out the door.

Ellie sighed. Secretly she had always dreamed of a love story with a happy ending. Now that she was older, she'd be happy just to see one of her friends find that kind of love.

She thought of Kade and his moodiness that morning, the few words he had said to her before he'd left the house. He seemed to have the same doubts about their relationship she had. *Gun shy*, Zoe had said.

The happy ending wasn't going to happen. Not for her and probably not anyone else.

With a breath of resignation, she forced her thoughts back to the murder case she was supposed to be working, crossed the kitchen, then went down the hall to her bedroom. Her laptop perched on the little Victorian writing desk in the sitting area. Ellie sat down and went to work.

Starting with Rance Sullivan, she dug around on Google and checked half a dozen places where his name might pop up. He had no criminal record that she could find. On his Facebook page, she learned that Sullivan was a member of the Elk Foundation, an organization that supported wildlife habitat and hunting. Also the NRA, so he undoubtedly owned a gun, but so did half the men in Coffee Springs, and Heather had been strangled, not shot. He definitely had a lot of women friends.

Zoe would be able to go deeper, but Ellie didn't see any red flags where Sullivan was concerned. At eleven o'clock that morning, she heard a car pulling up behind the house. Since most visitors came to the front door, she went to the window to see who it was.

A silver Mercedes convertible gleamed in the sunlight, steam rising from the engine in the cold. A stylishly dressed woman in designer jeans and a cashmere sweater got out. Early thirties, sleek, shoulder-length blond hair turned under, no tell-tale dark roots, a face bordering on beautiful, eyebrows perfectly plucked, lips full and painted a sexy red.

Ellie's insides knotted. She headed for the kitchen, opened the door, and stepped out onto the porch. "May I help you?"

"I'm Grace Towers. I'm a friend of Kade's." Her gaze ran over Ellie in her worn jeans, scuffed boots, and red-plaid flannel shirt. "You must be the cook."

That and a whole lot more. "I'm Ellie Bowman. Is Kade expecting you?"

"I thought I'd surprise him. Would you mind telling him I'm here?"

"I'm afraid he's out with his men. He usually comes in around noon to work in his study for a while, but not always. If he's in cell range, I might be able to reach him on his phone."

Grace flashed a perfect white smile. "That would be lovely. Thank you, Ellie."

"No problem."

Pulling her phone out of her pocket, Ellie punched in Kade's contact number. He picked up on the second ring.

"Ellie. What's the problem?"

With all the trouble that had been happening, and since she rarely called, he had to figure it was urgent.

"Everything's all right. I just wanted to let you know you have a visitor."

"Who is it?"

"Your friend Grace Towers. She drove out to surprise you. *Surprise.*"

"Very funny. Tell her I'm fifteen minutes out."

"Will do, boss." Ellie hung up the phone.

Kade gritted his teeth. *Women.* He shoved the phone into his back pocket. The last thing he needed was more woman trouble. But after the ass he had made of himself in the Elkhorn last night, he had no right to fault Ellie.

He waved at Wyatt. "I'm heading in. Keep your eyes open." The shooter could still be out there, which all of them knew.

"Will do," Wyatt called back, his mouth a worried line beneath his silver mustache.

Kade climbed onto the ATV he had ridden to the north pasture and started back to the house. He didn't see any of the security men on patrol, but he was sure they were there. These guys really knew what they were doing. He felt safer knowing they were watching his back as he drove the four-wheeler down the muddy, half-frozen lane back to the ranch house.

Where Grace was waiting, he reminded himself, and silently cursed. Ellie had met one of his former lovers last night. She was perceptive enough to know Grace was another.

Kade remembered meeting the wealthy, thirty-four-year-old divorcee at the Four Season's bar in Vail, a lady on the lookout for company. He'd gone home with her that night, and they had enjoyed each other. Kade had told her he wasn't interested in anything permanent, and Grace had adamantly informed him that she wasn't either.

They'd dated off and on for almost a year, whenever Grace was in Vail and lonely for male companionship. When she'd started pressing him for more than just no-strings sex, Kade had ended the affair. Now she was here.

He rode the four-wheeler up to where Grace stood next to Ellie and turned off the engine. He couldn't help comparing the two women. One tall, sleek, and sophisticated. The other smaller, with a full-busted, sexy figure, and gorgeous dark copper hair. One so perfect she seemed synthetic. The other a real woman in every way.

He clamped down on a memory of hot sex in the Elkhorn storeroom last night. Now was definitely not the time.

He strode forward. "Grace. It's good to see you." He didn't lean down and kiss her cheek as he might have done before. "How long's it been? At least three or four months." He flicked a glance at Ellie to be sure she got the message.

"Three and a half months, darling. Way longer that it should be. That's why I'm here." She linked her arm through his. "Why don't we go inside so we can talk somewhere private?"

Ellie gave him a phony smile. "That sounds like a good idea." She walked over and opened the door, stood waiting as the two of them approached. The door slammed solidly behind him, and Kade winced as he led Grace into the house.

As soon as the study door was closed, Grace slid her arms around his neck and tried to kiss him, but Kade turned his face away. He caught her hands and eased them from around his neck as he stepped out of her embrace.

"I thought we'd both decided to move on, Grace."

"You decided, Kade. I thought it was just a misunderstanding. I thought once we were together again, you'd realize your mistake."

"It wasn't a mistake, Grace. I've moved on, and so should you."

One of her blond eyebrows went up. "By moved on, you mean you're sleeping with your cook?" She scoffed. "I thought you had higher ambitions."

"I don't have any ambitions when it comes to women. I sleep with whoever I want, as long as that's what the lady wants too."

"You could do far better. Surely you can see that." She reached out and pressed her hand against the fly of his jeans. "We were good together, Kade. Admit it."

He caught her wrist and moved her hand away. "We had some fun. Now it's over. I'll walk you out to your car."

Her lips thinned. "Fine. If you're determined to behave like a fool with a woman so clearly beneath you, there's nothing more to say." Turning, she huffed across the study, pulled open the door, and marched out into the hall.

She didn't wait for Kade, who followed her out, just headed back to the kitchen. When she reached the door, she paused to look at Ellie.

"Enjoy him while you can. He's a great fuck, but he doesn't really give a damn." Grace slammed out the door.

Kade's gaze locked with Ellie's. "I ended it three months ago. It was never serious."

"It's none of my business." Words she had said last night.

But there was a note of regret in her voice he had never heard before. Kade looked at her, and something tightened in his chest. He strode toward her, pulled her into his arms. When she tried to turn away, he caught her chin, forcing her to look at him.

"Grace was just another woman. She never meant anything to me. Whatever happens between us, you're special, Ellie. I've never met anyone like you." Bending his head, he kissed her, didn't stop until her ripe lips softened under his and she was clinging to his shoulders.

He didn't know what was going on between them, but whatever it was, that was the moment Kade decided it was worth finding out.

CHAPTER TWENTY

*E*LLIE TOLD HERSELF TO PACK UP AND LEAVE. THERE WAS ALWAYS another job. Quitting would be the smart thing to do. She didn't trust herself where Kade Logan was concerned, and she didn't want to risk getting hurt again.

But Ellie had never been a quitter. She would stick it out until the job was done. And something had happened today, something she hadn't expected. Was it possible Kade had feelings for her, something deeper than the lust they both shared?

Because Ellie was beginning to realize how deep her feelings ran for Kade. Watching him with Grace Towers had made her physically ill.

But Kade had said he wasn't interested in Grace. He'd said Ellie was special. Did he mean it? Or was it just a typical male line?

The ringing of her cell ended her thoughts. She pulled the phone out of her pocket. *Zoey.*

"Hey, Zoe."

"I've got news, Ellie. Actually, I've got a couple of things to report."

"Starting with . . . ?"

"You already know Frank Keller worked for Red Hawk Mining."

"That's right. I know the mine's owned by Mountain Ore Mining Consolidated, but I haven't had time to check them out."

"Mountain Ore is a huge corporation, family-owned, with mines in other parts of Colorado, but also South America and

Africa. After Keller got out of the army four years ago, he worked for Mountain Ore in several different locations. His first job was in Brazil, but he ended up back in the States, working in southern Colorado."

"When did he quit?"

"Not sure he ever actually did. From his employment records, it looks like he worked whenever the company needed him. He was contract labor. Sometimes he went months between jobs."

"You said Mountain Ore is family-owned."

"Mose Egan is head of the clan. He's CEO. Other family members have jobs there, all VPs of something or other, his daughter, Jane, and her husband, Phillip Smithson, and Mose's son, Richard. International headquarters are in Denver."

"Anything pop up that explains why Keller was looking for work in Coffee Springs?"

"Frank was born in Denver, but he's got a second cousin in Phippsburg, so he's familiar with the area. His cousin's name is Earl Dunstan. No address, just a post office box."

"Maybe Phippsburg's where Frank's hiding out. That's great work, Zoe. I'll make sure the sheriff knows."

"And speaking of Sheriff Carver . . ."

"Yes . . . ?"

"The guy has a solid reputation, but I found old photos of him and Heather posted on one of his friend's Facebook pages. At the time the pictures were taken, the two of them looked very hot and heavy. The date was a month before she disappeared."

"So Carver's still a suspect."

"Looks that way," Zoe said.

"Send me the photos."

"Soon as I get off the phone. Oh, there is one more thing." An excited note rose in Zoe's voice. "I quit my job."

"Wow, really? I know you said it was just a way to earn a living until something more interesting came along, but—"

"Something more interesting came along. Conner Delaney offered me a job doing digital forensics for Nighthawk Security."

Silence fell. "Are you sure you want to do that? My boss can be, well, he isn't exactly a rule follower."

Zoe laughed. "And you think I am?"

Ellie smiled. "Point taken, and when you put it that way, I think you'll really enjoy the challenge."

"The good news is, from now on you don't have to feel guilty when you ask me for help. I'll be getting paid for it."

Ellie chuckled. "I remember introducing the two of you, but I didn't realize Conn knew how talented you were."

"Apparently all the bragging you did about me worked. Plus, he gave me a couple of test problems, and I solved them."

"No surprise there. Will you be working in the office?"

"Conn's setting up a space for me, but I'll also be working at home. No set hours. I'm really excited about it."

"So am I."

"Listen, I gotta run. Now that I've got a new job—"

"Now that you're on the payroll, there's something else I need."

Zoe laughed. "What is it?"

"Any chance you can get into Heather Logan's medical records, see if there's any sign of abuse?"

"Wait a minute. You're thinking your guy, Kade, was a wife beater? I don't like the sound of that."

"I can't imagine Kade ever hurting a woman, but it's my job to be sure."

"I'll check it out."

"Also, there's a bartender named Rance Sullivan. Works at the Elkhorn Bar and Grill in Coffee Springs. He's one of Heather's conquests. I didn't see anything suspicious, but you might."

"I'll take a look."

"Thanks, Zoe. Can't wait for a girlfriend lunch."

"Me either. Talk soon." Zoe hung up the phone.

Working at the computer on his big, dark oak desk, Kade looked up as Ellie walked through the open study door.

He rose from his chair and walked toward her. "I'm sorry about this morning . . . about Grace, I mean. Like I said, I haven't seen her in months."

A burnished eyebrow went up. "Any other female surprises in store for me?"

The back of Kade's neck went warm. "No." Not unless one of the females he had slept with in Vail a few months back showed up. The sex had been hot, the release satisfying, but he didn't remember either of their names.

"Good to know," Ellie said.

Kade's mouth edged up. "Anything else I need to confess?"

She smiled. "Actually I came in to tell you I got a lead on Frank Keller." Reaching into her pocket, she pulled out a slip of paper and handed it over. "Keller has a cousin in Phippsburg. His name is Earl Dunstan. No address. That's his post office box number."

Kade looked at the note and felt a rush of excitement, followed by a sweep of anger. "You call the sheriff?"

"Not yet. I wanted to let you know first."

Kade unsnapped the pocket on his denim shirt and shoved the note inside. "We'll phone the sheriff from the road. Carver may need to call the Routt County sheriff, since Phippsburg's in his jurisdiction. We're closer than either one of them."

"You think we can find Dunstan?"

"It's a very small town." His jaw flexed. "We'll find Dunstan, and when we do, I got a hunch we'll find Keller."

"If he's there, he's likely armed. Are you sure you wouldn't rather let the cops handle this?"

Kade walked back to his desk, pulled open the bottom drawer, and punched the code into his gun safe. Reaching inside, he picked up the holstered Colt Classic .45 that had belonged to his dad.

He looked at Ellie. "Keller shot two of my steers, one of my men, and my dog." He strapped the big semiauto around his waist and tied the leather thong around his thigh. "I'm damned sure." Kade grabbed his hat and tugged it low, caught Ellie's arm and propelled her out of the study.

"Wait a minute." She pulled free. "I need my purse, my jacket, and my weapon. I'll meet you outside."

Kade just nodded. He wanted Frank Keller. If Keller was in Phippsburg, Kade was going to find him. He was going to end this. One way or another.

CHAPTER TWENTY-ONE

*P*HIPPSBURG, IN ROUTT COUNTY, COLORADO, WAS LITTLE MORE THAN a wide spot in the road about thirty miles north of Coffee Springs. A post office, a ranch supply store, a couple of boarded-up businesses, and a small settlement of houses marked the rural community. A few hundred people lived close to town; a few more made their homes in the surrounding hills.

Because it was Saturday, the red-brick post office was closed. Instead, Kade turned the pickup into the parking lot of Flatt's Ranch Supply and pulled into one of the diagonal spaces out front. He'd known the owner, Charlie Flatt, for more than a decade.

Ellie walked beside him across the asphalt, and Kade pulled open the door to the long wooden building. The place was stacked high with bags of horse feed, cans of dog food, tack and tools, fuel for pellet stoves, automotive parts, tires, and farming equipment. You name it, you could find it at Flatt's.

Charlie stood behind the counter, a man in his sixties with iron-gray hair and a paunch over the waistband of work jeans held up by colorful striped suspenders.

He spotted them as they walked up and smiled. "Well, Kade Logan! Long time no see."

Kade smiled back. "Been a while, Charlie. Though I don't think you ever really change."

"Well, if you didn't notice, I've put on a few extra pounds." His hands smoothed affectionately over his belly, as if Kade might have missed it. "Who's the pretty lady?"

"Charlie, meet Ellie Bowman. She's helping me out while my cook is on vacation."

"Nice to meet you, Ellie."

Ellie smiled. "You too, Charlie."

"So what can I do for you two?"

"Actually, I need some information," Kade said. "I'm hoping you can tell me where to find a guy named Earl Dunstan. He lives in Phippsburg, but I'm not sure where."

"No problem. I know Earl. He's a good guy. Lives out at the end of Pine Street. Just keep going after you get to where the dirt road narrows. Earl's place is over the hill, down on your right."

"Thanks, Charlie. You drop by for supper next time you're in Coffee Springs. I promise you Ellie's a damn fine cook."

"I'll just bet she is." Charlie winked at Ellie, and Kade didn't miss the twinkle in his eyes. He figured Ellie and Kade were an item, and at least for the moment, they were.

Kade shook his head. Small towns thrived on gossip, and Charlie had gotten a juicy morsel in return for his help. Kade waved at him over his shoulder as they left the store and headed back to the truck.

The day was still sunny, the temperature on the warm side for this time of year. The road heading west out of town was narrow, with just a few scattered houses along the way. When the pickup reached the top of the hill and the lane narrowed still further, Kade pulled off and parked.

"Let's take a look." He leaned over and opened the glove box, took out a pair of binoculars, and focused them on the scene below. A small white, wood-frame house with a covered front porch sat on a parcel of land away from the road. A red barn with a chicken coop on one side sat behind the house, while a sway-backed white mare and a big bay gelding meandered around the pasture.

Kade panned the binoculars, fixed them on a recent-model

Dodge Ram truck in the yard next to a faded brown horse trailer. He handed the glasses to Ellie.

"Pickup and trailer could be Keller's rig," he said. "Doesn't look like anyone's around outside. Can't tell if there's someone in the house."

Ellie scanned the area, must have seen the same lack of activity he did. "Why don't we find out?"

Kade cranked the engine and pulled the pickup back onto the road. They dropped off the hill and turned into the long drive-way leading to the house. Pulling around back, he parked in front of the barn.

"I still don't see anyone," Kade said. "Stay here while I take a look."

"Not a chance." Ellie cracked open her door and got out. Kade bit back a curse and followed.

His sheepskin jacket covered the pistol on his belt. In this kind of country, walking up to a man's house with a gun in your hand could get you killed. In this case, going in without a weapon could get you just as dead.

As Kade neared the front porch, he pulled the Colt, and Ellie pulled her pistol, a Glock semiauto, she'd told him. She signaled that she was going around to the back and slipped off in that di-rection. With no way to call her back, Kade clenched his jaw, his tension ratcheting up another notch.

He eased up onto the wooden porch, knocked on the front door, and stepped to one side, his pistol in a two-handed grip pointed upward. He wasn't a cop, but he knew how to use a firearm, and he was a damned good shot. His tension revved higher as he knocked again. Surprise hit him when the door moved a little, creaked, and slowly swung open.

Kade counted off the seconds. No one appeared. Careful not to make himself a target, he shoved the door with the toe of his boot. Through the windows next to the couch, sunlight poured into the living room. Catching no sign of movement, he stepped inside.

Kade froze. Frank Keller slumped in a plush, brown, overstuffed chair next to the sofa, legs thrust out in front of him, arms limp at his sides. Keller's head lolled on his chest, and a black semiauto lay on the floor where it must have dropped from his hand.

Still armed, Kade eased toward the chair. Keller was dead, blood leaking down the side of his face from a bullet hole in his right temple, brain matter oozing from the exit wound on the other side. Kade looked up to see Ellie moving silently into the living room, weapon gripped in both hands. She shook her head. *No one in the kitchen.*

So far, no sign of Earl Dunstan.

Ellie spotted Keller. Her eyes flashed to Kade's, and her face turned pale. Kade signaled toward the bedrooms, and Ellie nodded. They needed to be sure no one else was in the house.

It was quiet as he moved along the hall, just the muffled thud of his boots on the carpet and the tick of a clock on a nightstand he could see through the open bedroom door. He checked the closets and under the bed, moved along the hall to the other bedroom, then checked the bathroom.

"All clear," he said, holstering the Colt as he returned to the living room. His gaze went to the body sprawled in the chair. Kade had no trouble recognizing the man who had briefly worked for him during the roundup. "Looks like Keller shot himself."

Her gun re-holstered, the color back in her face, Ellie examined the crime scene, studying the body from different angles and surveying the area around it. "That's what it looks like."

Kade frowned at the trace of doubt in her voice. "You don't think so?"

"Keller didn't strike me as the suicidal type."

Kade mulled that over. "Maybe he figured the cops were closing in on him. He shot one of my men and rigged an IED that blew up a guy in a mine. He was going to prison. Maybe he couldn't handle it."

"Maybe. Either way, it puts an end to the trouble on the ranch." She looked back at the body, down at the weapon on the floor. "Or maybe this isn't what it seems."

Kade's frown returned. "You think it was staged to look like he killed himself?"

Ellie glanced around. "I don't see a suicide note."

Kade's gaze followed hers, taking in the simply furnished living room with its brown shag carpet. The place wasn't fancy, but it was neat and clean. "Not everybody leaves a note."

"No, not everybody."

"There's no smell, so he hasn't been dead that long," Kade said.

"Maybe his cousin shot him, staged the scene, and ran."

Kade looked back at the body. "Why would his cousin shoot him? Dunstan and Keller were family. That's why Frank came to Phippsburg, the reason he came to Dunstan for help. Family counts for something out here."

Ellie glanced toward the window. "The sheriff's bound to show up soon. Why don't we take a look around before he gets here?"

"Good idea." Kade headed back down the hall, into the spare bedroom, where he figured Keller would have been staying. There was a canvas duffle on the bed and clothes strewn on the floor.

"We need to be careful not to contaminate the crime scene," Ellie said, walking up beside him.

But Kade was already in motion, heading for the rifle propped against the wall in the corner. "It's .308 Winchester bolt-action. Looks like a Leupold scope. Good hunting rifle, probably the gun he used to shoot Alejandro."

"Don't touch it," Ellie warned.

"I don't need to. I can see the bolt from here. This gun belongs to a left-handed man."

Ellie's gaze locked with his. "Frank Keller died from a bullet to his right temple. The pistol on the floor makes it look as if the gun was fired with his right hand."

Kade's expression went grim. "Keller didn't kill himself."

Ellie looked up at him with those big green eyes that had a way of unsettling him. "Not if that's Keller's rifle."

Ellie crossed the bedroom to the dresser and studied the items on top—a wallet, set of car keys, pen and pencil, and some loose change. She picked up the pencil and used it to open the wallet. Frank Keller's picture on his driver's license stared back at her.

"The room is his," she said. She went over to the closet. The slider stood open, revealing the clothes Frank had brought with him to Phippsburg.

She slid the metal hanging door open a little farther, then took down a hanger that held an XL size red-flannel shirt. "Look at this."

Kade walked up, and Ellie pointed to a small chunk of fabric missing from the sleeve of the shirt. "What do you bet the hole matches the piece we found caught on that fence post out in the north pasture?"

"If it does, that proves Keller was behind the shootings."

"There's no chain of evidence, but it doesn't really matter since Frank's dead." Ellie hung the shirt back in the closet.

"The question now is who killed him?" Kade said.

Ellie looked up at him. "And why?"

The whine of an engine sounded in the distance, followed by the noise of a second vehicle. "Looks like the law just arrived." They went back to the living room, and Kade saw two Routt County sheriff's SUVs pulling up to the house.

"We need to do this right," Kade said. He rested his weapon on the floor of the living room, and Ellie did the same. Kade opened the door, they raised their hands, and both of them walked out onto the porch.

Neither of them wanted to get shot by the good guys.

The Routt County sheriff, Webb Fischer, took their statements. He was average height with a stocky build, unremarkable except for his blue eyes and leonine mane of thick gray hair. Kade made the point that if the rifle in the bedroom belonged to Frank Keller, the guy was left-handed. If so, there was a strong likelihood Keller hadn't shot himself.

"The medical examiner's in Steamboat," Sheriff Fischer said.

"He's on his way here now. It's only about a thirty- minute drive. We'll know more after he examines the body."

In the meantime, it didn't take long for the sheriff to find out Frank Keller was the owner of a .308 Winchester registered in Denver County. The left-hand bolt said it all.

Kade answered more of the sheriff's questions, and so did Ellie. Then Kade asked a few questions of his own.

"What about Earl Dunstan? He could have killed Keller, or even if he didn't, he might know something about his death."

"I've put a BOLO out on Dunstan as a person of interest, but he's probably just off working somewhere. Earl does handyman repairs in the area. That's how he makes his living."

"You don't think he could be Frank's killer?"

"At this point, Keller's death is still a suicide. Even if the ME lists the cause of death as homicide, I know Earl. He's harmless. No way he killed his cousin."

"Then who did?" Kade asked.

Fischer drilled him with a glare. "According to Glen Carver, you think Keller is behind the trouble you've been having at the ranch. That gives you plenty of motive yourself."

Kade stiffened. "I didn't kill the bastard."

"You better hope not. Just because you own one of the biggest spreads this side of Denver doesn't make you exempt from the law."

Kade's shoulders tightened even more. He felt Ellie's hand on his arm. "Are we done here, Sheriff?" she asked.

"We're done. *For now.* Your weapons are evidence in an ongoing investigation. You'll get them back once it's over."

"Neither of them has been fired," Kade pointed out.

Fischer ignored him. "Sheriff Carver will also want to talk to you. I'm advising you not to leave the state." He turned to Ellie. "That goes for you, too, Ms. Bowman." The sheriff strode off to join his men.

Kade's jaw hardened. He stared at the house where he'd found the body of a dead man, and dread poured through him. Instead of his problems being solved, things had just gotten worse. Now he was a suspect in a murder investigation.

"Sonofabitch," he growled.

"You didn't do anything wrong," Ellie said. "If the sheriff can't figure that out, we'll do whatever it takes to make sure he does."

Kade looked down at her, took in the stubborn angle of her chin. Her copper hair blazed like hellfire in the sunlight, and her pretty lips were set in a determined line.

She was sticking by him. She was strong, and she was smart. She wouldn't leave him to deal with the problem alone.

Something expanded in his chest. Until that moment, Kade hadn't realized just how much that meant to him.

CHAPTER TWENTY-TWO

*D*USK SETTLED OVER THE MOUNTAINS, THE MOTTLED SKY TURNING soft shades of orange and turquoise as the pickup headed back toward the ranch.

Ellie rode in silence, her thoughts on the shooting, on Frank Keller's death, and what it might mean to Kade and the people on the ranch.

"The medical examiner won't report the cause of death until he does the autopsy," Ellie said, speaking over the hum of the diesel engine. "Unless something changes, we have to assume Frank was murdered."

Kade's attention swung away from the road and lit for a moment on her face. "We need to find out who killed him—and why."

"A better question might be what happens next? With Keller dead, are your troubles over? What if Frank's beef with you wasn't personal? What if it never had anything to do with payback?"

His jaw tightened. "You're thinking he might have been working for someone else. Someone who paid him to cause me trouble."

"That's right. Maybe the person who hired him wasn't satisfied with the job Frank was doing. Or he was afraid Frank was about to get caught."

Kade nodded. "We found Keller. Which means the sheriff would probably have found him fairly soon. The killer could have shot Frank to keep him from talking."

"Could be, and if Keller was murdered to silence him, whoever hired him might not be finished. You and your people could still be danger."

Kade's hands tightened around the steering wheel. "We can't afford to let down our guard. Not yet. I'll keep the security guys on the payroll and warn the hands to stay alert till we figure out what's going on."

"With any luck, Sheriff Fischer will come up with something."

Kade grunted. "Or Carver will. He's been looking for the shooter from the beginning."

As they got closer to the ranch, Ellie phoned Zoe to tell her to forget about Frank Keller, that they had found him dead. Zoe promised to call on Monday with updates on the rest of the info Ellie wanted.

By the time Kade parked the truck behind the ranch house and Ellie walked through the back door into the kitchen, supper was in progress. The men had already loaded their plates with steaks off the big stainless grill, baked potatoes, salad, and French bread. It was Saturday night. Sunday was a well-deserved day off for most of the men.

Ellie recognized a couple of guys from the security detail. There were always one or two men who showed up to eat at the end of their shifts.

Maria was still working, getting ready to serve dessert. "Sorry I'm late," Ellie said to her.

Maria flashed a proud smile. "Everything went smoothly. Turtle helped, and the steaks turned out very good."

"Better than good," one of the men called out. "Maria did great."

Ellie looked over to see Alejandro among the hands seated around the table. His arm was in a sling, his shirt unsnapped partway to make room for the bandage around his shoulder. Maria blushed at his compliment and looked away.

Kade hung his hat on a peg and strode toward the injured man. "You sure you ought to be out of bed?"

"The doctor says I should move around if I want to get well."

"You look a little better. How are you feeling?"

Alejandro flashed his bright white smile. "Much better. Maria's a very good nurse."

Kade flicked her a glance but returned his attention to Alejandro. "All right, but don't press too hard. Just take it easy."

Ellie touched Kade's arm. "You must be hungry. Why don't you grab a plate and have some supper?"

He just nodded. He'd been distracted all the way back from Phippsburg. His mood was dark, his jaw tight. Worry weighed heavily on his broad shoulders. Ellie felt sorry for him.

Kade filled a plate and sat down in his usual place at the head of the table. For a moment, the hands fell silent.

"Couple of things I need to tell you," Kade said, cutting into his steak. "But they can wait till we finish Maria's delicious meal." His gaze went to Ellie across the kitchen. "I know Ellie hasn't eaten. There's room at the table. It's Saturday night. Why don't both you ladies join us?"

There was always plenty of food. Ellie sometimes took a plate back to her room, or she and Maria sat together after they finished in the kitchen. The young woman made a point of not looking at Alejandro as she carried her plate over and sat down on the opposite side of the table. Ellie sat down next to Turtle, whose round face turned a little red.

It didn't take long for the men to relax and go back to talking and laughing. Since there were often women working in the kitchen, bawdy jokes and bad language weren't tolerated. These were western men. There was a certain code of honor when it came to females in their presence.

Dessert was served, a sweet Spanish egg dish called flan, one of Maria's specialties.

Kade talked as the men dug into their dessert. "This afternoon I made a trip to Phippsburg. Ellie has a friend who came up with a lead on where to find Frank Keller." Several heads came up. "By the time we got there, Keller was dead. Shot to death in the living room." Silence fell, not even the clink of silverware.

"Couldn't happen to a nicer guy," Slate drawled, digging back into the flan with a little extra gusto.

The men rumbled their agreement.

"What happened?" Wyatt asked.

"His death was meant to look like a suicide, but there's a very good chance he was murdered. The sheriff is waiting for the medical examiner's report. But unless Webb Fischer's an idiot—which I don't think he is—he'll be hunting for Frank's killer."

The men went back to eating. Ellie wondered if they were putting the pieces together, beginning to see that their troubles might not be over.

"What do you think, boss?" Roy asked. "You think we're in the clear?"

Kade set his napkin down next to his empty dessert bowl. "I think it's too soon to let down our guard. There's a chance Keller was hired by someone and that someone might have killed him to keep him from talking. If that's the case, Frank was just a tool for whoever wants to make trouble for me and the ranch."

"Any idea who it might be?" Wyatt asked.

"I'm working on it. If any of you have ideas, I'd like to hear them."

No one spoke.

"Looks like I've still got a job." Trace Elliot, Delaney's right-hand man, was a former army ranger, good-looking, with wavy brown hair and intense blue eyes.

Amusement touched Kade's lips. "I'm sorry to say you're right." The men chuckled. "We're going to need your help till this is over. Eventually it will be—one way or another."

"Tomorrow's Sunday," Riley said, his white plaster cast angled beneath the table. "Maybe we should stick around instead of taking the day off."

Kade shook his head. "We aren't letting this bastard win. You all work hard. You deserve time off. Whatever's going on, we'll figure it out." The men looked relieved. "In the meantime, I need you all to stay alert. More than that, I need you to stay safe. We're all family here. Your safety is the most important thing."

Kade slid back his chair and shoved to his feet. "Great job,

Maria. I know the men enjoyed it as much as I did." He looked at the group around the table. "Enjoy your evening."

As he strode out of the kitchen and headed down the hall, the hands began to disperse. Some of them would head back to the bunkhouse, others would drive into Coffee Springs or down to Eagle to enjoy a night out before their day off.

"Tomorrow I move back into my grandmother's house," Maria said as she and Ellie put the last of the dishes into one of two dishwashers. "I'd rather stay with Alejandro, but he doesn't need me anymore." She looked at Ellie. "I wish he wanted me to stay a little longer." Her lips trembled. "I wish he loved me, but he doesn't."

Ellie wiped her hands on a dish towel. "Did Alejandro tell you that?"

Maria shook her head. "He wouldn't want to hurt me."

"Maybe you should talk to him, tell him the way you feel, ask him what he feels for you."

Maria sadly shook her head. "I don't have that kind of courage." Untying her apron, she hung it on a peg on the wall, grabbed her coat, and walked out the back door.

Ellie thought of Kade. She had no idea what Kade felt for her. She had heard his heavy footfalls on the stairs, so she knew he had gone up to his bedroom. He hadn't asked her to join him. She didn't think he would come to her room tonight.

She thought of his weary expression, the worry lines digging into his forehead, the tiny creases beside his eyes. She thought of what might lie ahead for him, the danger his men could be facing, the danger he might be facing himself.

By now, she knew him well enough to know he would struggle tonight with all of those things. Ellie left the kitchen and headed for her bedroom to shower and change. Whether he admitted it or not, Kade needed her tonight.

Ellie intended to give him what he needed.

Kade had just walked out of the bathroom, a towel slung around his hips. His hair was still damp from the long, hot shower he had taken. He'd needed to get the smell of death scrubbed from his body.

He wished it were as easy to erase the memory of Frank Keller's brains leaking from a hole in his head.

He sighed as he crossed the room to his dresser and took out a pair of sweatpants. He was about to pull them on when a soft knock sounded at the door. He knew that knock, knew Ellie stood in the hallway, and his body stirred to life.

Kade silently cursed. In the mood he was in, Ellie was the last person he wanted to see. Apparently his body disagreed.

He pulled open the door, managed to ignore how beautiful she looked with her face clean of makeup and her burnished hair loose around her shoulders. "It's been a long day, darlin'. I figure we could both use some sleep."

Those big green eyes ran over his bare chest, must have noticed the bulge at the front of the towel. "Aren't you going to invite me in?"

His pulse quickened. She was barefoot, wearing her fleecy robe. He remembered the first time she had worn the robe to his room and the heated lovemaking that had followed.

His arousal strengthened, but his big head wasn't in the game. Not after the scene at Earl Dunstan's. "I'm not in the best mood tonight." He didn't move, just stood there blocking the door. "You'd be smart to go back downstairs."

Ellie reached for his hand, walked past him, and led him over to the bed. "I'm going to help your mood improve. Lie down on your stomach."

"Ellie, I don't think I can do this tonight."

She looked up at him with a trace of pity, then down at the towel, and laughed. He couldn't believe it.

"You don't have to do anything. Not tonight. The bed, Kade. Now."

His interest—among other things—was piqued. He climbed up onto the big four-poster and sprawled on his stomach. Ellie pulled off the towel, leaving him naked and more than a little aroused. Tossing her robe on the foot of the bed, she climbed up beside him in a short, silky lavender nightgown that barely covered her fine little ass.

He hadn't noticed the bottle of lotion she'd brought with her. He'd mostly been trying to control his building lust. He felt the cooling moisture as she leaned over him, ran her palms across the muscles in his shoulders, began to knead away the tension in his neck.

"Close your eyes," she said, spreading the lotion over the tired muscles in his back.

"If I do, I'll see Frank Keller's dead body."

"Not for long. I promise." Her hands never stopped moving, digging into tendons and sinews, smoothing over his skin, moving lower, gently easing away some of the fatigue. He closed his eyes and, little by little, began to relax.

Ellie massaged his thighs, his calves, spent extra time on his feet. He wasn't sure when he drifted off or how long he slept, but it was a deep, untroubled slumber.

It was midnight when a sound in the house awoke him, and his eyes slowly opened. Rain on the roof, he realized, nothing to worry about. For a moment, he couldn't remember why he was lying facedown on the quilt on his bed.

Then he remembered. *Ellie.* He glanced around in search of her, but she was gone. He felt better, just as she'd promised, his mind refreshed and back in control, his focus returned. He wished she had stayed.

The thought unsettled him. She'd come to help him. She had given him what he needed in a manner he hadn't expected. Not sex, though he thought that she would have responded to him if he'd wanted.

Instead she had sensed a different sort of need. Relief from the burdens he carried, the chance to ease his troubled mind, if only for a while. Ellie had given him a valuable gift.

In his mind's eye, he saw her in her silky lavender nightgown, all soft, welcoming woman. Kade tossed off the covers, grabbed his jeans off the chair, and slid them on. Barefoot, he headed for the stairs.

CHAPTER TWENTY-THREE

SOFT GRAY, EARLY DAWN LIGHT FILTERED THROUGH THE CURTAINS AT the bedroom window as Ellie slowly opened her eyes. She came fully awake to find herself in a tangle of arms and long, muscular, hair-roughened legs. Curled around her, Kade slept soundly. He had never come to her room before.

Everything about last night was different. The same fierce passion had burned between them, but Kade's attention had been focused wholly on her. For the first time, he had made love to her, pleasured her in a deeper, almost reverent manner. He had worshipped her body with his and, in doing so, destroyed every barrier she had so carefully constructed between them.

She didn't want to fall in love with Kade. Neither of them was interested in a long-term relationship. Kade had made that clear from the start.

That was the way she wanted it too. Or thought she did.

But last night confused and frightened her. Heartbreak lay ahead if she didn't find a way to protect herself.

Slipping out of bed, she went in to shower and dress for the day. Kade was still asleep when she returned to the bedroom. Certain he wouldn't want the hands to know where he'd spent the night, Ellie gently shook his shoulder.

"Wake up, Kade. I have to go to work, and you need to go back to your bedroom."

He rolled onto his back and looked up at her, a lazy smile on his lips. "You tossing me out, darlin'?"

She would have smiled back, but it was time to start distancing herself. "I've got work to do, and you need to get dressed."

Gloriously naked, he rolled out of bed. "Thanks for last night," he said as he pulled on his jeans and zipped the fly.

Ellie felt the heat creeping into her face.

"The massage, darlin', not the sex." He grinned. "But I enjoyed that, too."

Ellie glanced away, the endearment warming her as it always did. She was already half in love with him. After last night, it was time to rein in her emotions.

"I'll see you at breakfast." She pulled open the door and walked out into the hall.

Maria had the day off, but so did most of the men, which made the cooking light and on Sunday, the meal was served a little later. It wasn't until breakfast was over and the kitchen cleaned up that she saw Kade again. He walked up behind her, slid his arms around her waist, and nuzzled the nape of her neck.

"I think it's time we told the men the truth about who you are," he said. Surprised, she turned in his arms to look up at him.

"You came here to find Heather's killer," Kade continued. "You need time to do that. That means you can't spend your day in here cooking."

Ellie didn't disagree.

"I'm pretty sure you've already checked out all the hands," Kade said. "Unless you found something that points to one of them as a suspect—"

"I've looked at them hard, Kade. I don't think any of your men would go behind your back to have sex with your wife. Or hurt her or you in any way. As near as I can tell, these are men you can trust."

Kade's shoulders relaxed. "I was hoping you'd say that. Wyatt and the others . . . they're more than just employees. They're guys I rely on every day with the most valuable things I own. My land and my cattle."

She considered the advantages of having more time to do her job. "Maria can probably handle the cooking—she's more capable every day." She glanced around the big stainless kitchen. "But it's not a small job. She'll still need someone to help her."

"Mabel's due back in a couple of days. Turtle can help out until she gets here. That frees you up to do whatever you need to."

"All right, that sounds good. Why don't we tell them tonight at supper?"

He nodded. "We can do that. Most of them will be back by dinnertime, ready to go to work first thing in the morning. Might not go smoothly, though, not at first. These guys aren't stupid. They're going to figure out you've been investigating them, too."

"I won't lie to them. I'll tell them the truth. I just need to find a way to make them understand."

Kade flashed one of his devastating smiles, and Ellie's stomach lifted. "If anyone can, you can, darlin'."

Kade pressed a quick kiss on her lips. She watched his long-legged strides as he crossed the room, grabbed his hat off the peg, and tugged it on.

"It's Sunday," he said. "Put on something pretty, and I'll take you to church."

"Church? What about supper?"

"I'll have you back in time to cook. Tonight'll be the last time you have to worry about it." He touched the brim of his hat in farewell and walked out the back door.

Ellie heard the fading crunch of Kade's boots and leaned back against the kitchen counter. Her stomach was fluttering; her knees felt weak. She had never met a man who could make her feel this way. She wasn't good at relationships. She was in way over her head with Kade. She didn't know how to deal with a man like him, didn't want to think of the consequences of getting in so deep.

Ellie wished she knew what to do.

Kade left the house in search of Conner Delaney. He needed to bring the security team up to speed on the situation with Frank Keller. Turned out Trace Elliot, who'd been at supper last night, had already filled his boss in.

Kade spotted Delaney walking toward him at the same time Delaney spotted him.

"I was on my way to find you," Kade said.

Delaney nodded. "I heard what happened with Keller. I figured you'd want to talk. There's coffee on the stove in the cabin." He was over six feet and built like a brick house—all of them were.

"Sounds good." Kade followed Delaney into the former guesthouse-turned-barracks.

A fire burned low in the potbellied stove in the corner, and the forest-green pillows on the hand-hewn log sofa needed to be straightened. Sleeping bags were strewn over the oval braided rugs on the wide pine floors, along with canvas duffels. Boxes of ammunition sat open on the coffee table.

"Looks like you're ready to fight a war," Kade said.

Delaney just shrugged. "You never know what situation you're going to find yourself in. Better to be prepared."

Since Kade couldn't argue with that, he accepted the steaming mug of coffee Delaney poured and handed over. "I wanted to make sure you understood that, just because Frank Keller's dead, it doesn't mean we can lower our guard. Good chance he was killed by someone who was paying him to cause trouble. We're pursuing that avenue. So are Sheriff Fischer and Sheriff Carver. Sooner or later, one of us is bound to come up with a lead."

"We're here as long as you need us." Delaney sipped his coffee.

Kade blew across the top and took a drink, gathering himself to approach the next subject. "There's always a chance a situation may come up, something unexpected, someplace other than the ranch. If I need backup—"

"You need any or all of us—you just call. You've got my contact number. Trace Elliot is second-in-command. You can't reach me, you call him." Delaney gave him Elliot's number, and Kade relaxed as he punched the man's contact info into his phone.

"Thanks." Setting the mug down on the counter, Kade stuck out his hand. "I'm glad to have you and your men here."

Delaney shook, his grip firm.

Kade left the cabin feeling a little better about pursuing the shooter, as he and Ellie planned to do. But they needed a lead, and so far that hadn't happened.

Which meant the priority returned to finding Heather's killer. They could discuss their next steps on the way to church. Kade didn't go often, but he was a prominent figure in the community, and it was important to stay connected to neighbors and friends.

Kade figured, with everything that had happened, having God on his side wasn't a bad idea.

Nobody was in the kitchen when he walked into the house, so he headed upstairs. Pulling on his lizard boots, he grabbed his western sport coat and custom-made, dark brown, 30X beaver Stetson.

Ellie was waiting when he walked back into the kitchen, her dark copper curls loose around her shoulders the way he liked. She looked pretty as a picture in her pale blue cashmere sweater, ankle-length tweed wool skirt, and knee-high, mid-heeled boots. He managed not to suggest they skip church altogether, that he strip off her clothes, and have his way with her right there in the kitchen.

"You look real pretty, darlin'." He walked over and drew her close, captured those soft lips in a kiss. "You smell pretty, too. Like wildflowers in the spring."

Her eyes widened in surprise. He wasn't the type for hearts and flowers. A little embarrassed, his next words came out husky. "You ready?"

Ellie just nodded. "I'm not sure this is a good idea, the two of us being seen together."

"We're working to find a killer. So what if they think you're my woman? They won't really be surprised. They've been speculating since the day you arrived."

"True. Small towns are notorious for gossip."

"Besides, lots of local folks will be there. Might learn something useful about the murder."

Ellie cocked a brow. "Which murder? Heather's or Frank's?"

Kade scoffed. "Both." He led Ellie outside but didn't stop at the big Ford dually parked behind the house.

"Where are we going?"

"We're taking my car instead of the truck. I don't drive it often enough. Church is a good excuse." While Ellie waited, Kade went to the west end of the barn and pushed a code into the keypad, unlocking a garage door that rolled up to reveal a year-old, diamond-white Mercedes S550 with saddle-brown leather interior.

He didn't drive the car much, mostly when he went to Denver or spent the night in one of the fancy hotels in Vail. He'd never spent much money on himself, but the car was a temptation he couldn't resist. Once in a while, it did a man good to indulge himself.

He drove the Mercedes up beside Ellie and left the powerful engine running as he got out, went around, and opened the passenger door. The astonished look on her face was worth the extra trouble it had taken to fetch the car.

"I can't believe you own a Mercedes-Benz." She ran a hand over the burlwood dash as she slid into the deep leather seat.

"I bought it in a moment of insanity," he said as he slid back in behind the wheel. "Grace said I worked too hard. She kept saying I should do something special for myself, said I deserved it. A couple days later, I saw this in the window of a showroom in Denver. I took it for a test drive and bought it on the spot." He put the Mercedes in gear. "I hardly ever use it. I probably ought to sell it, but—"

"I think for once I agree with Grace. If you like it, keep it. You deserve it."

He smiled as he stepped on the gas, and the car leapt forward, rolling off the hill toward the big timber front gate. "I promise you one thing. This little beauty doesn't bounce you around like the pickup. Might as well relax and enjoy the ride."

Ellie sighed with pleasure and settled back in the seat.

Kade was just beginning to get the feel of the car when, a few minutes into the trip, his cell phone started ringing. He checked the caller number on the screen built into the dash; it began with 702, a Boulder County area code. Something about the number pricked the back of his mind, and a ball of unease settled like a rock in his stomach.

Kade had a bad feeling the phone call meant trouble.

Ellie noticed the knot bunched in Kade's jaw as he hit the hands-free button on the wheel. "Logan."

"Logan, this is Matt McBride, Boulder County Chief of Police."

Kade eased the big Mercedes over to the side of the road. "Chief McBride. Been a while. Six years, as I recall."

"Close enough."

"What can I do for you, Chief?"

"You going to be around this afternoon? We need to talk."

Kade's shoulders tightened. Ellie wasn't sure what information the police chief might have, but she knew Boulder was where Heather's body had been found.

"I'll be around," Kade said. "What time?"

"We're flying in. The chopper only takes about an hour."

"Must be important," Kade said.

"I'll see you in an hour." The voice faded from the speaker, and Kade leaned back in the driver's seat.

"What do you think's going on?" Ellie asked.

His gaze swung to hers, and she could read the turbulence there. "McBride was head of the department when they found Heather's body. Maybe they caught the guy who killed her."

"I hope that's what it is." But there was something in McBride's voice . . . Ellie didn't think he was bringing good news.

Kade turned the car around in the middle of the road and drove the short distance back to the ranch house. He let Ellie out, pulled the Mercedes back into the garage, and closed the overhead door.

Maria was in the kitchen when Ellie walked inside with Kade.

"You're supposed to have the day off," Kade said.

Maria just shrugged. "I was going to take my grandmother to

church, but she wasn't feeling well, and there were some things I wanted to take care of."

Kade nodded. "Well, I'm glad you're here. I'm making some changes, starting in the kitchen. From now on, you're in charge. I'll talk to Mabel when she gets back, tell her it's time to let you take over."

Maria's gaze shot to Ellie.

"Don't worry about Ellie," Kade said. "She isn't leaving. She has other work to do."

"What about Mabel?" Maria asked. "I don't want to steal her job."

"Mabel's family. She's been working here since I was a kid. Now she'll be able to work fewer hours for the same money. I think she'll be relieved to have less responsibility." He took off his hat and ran a hand through his hair. "Can you handle the job? The position includes a nice, fat pay raise."

Maria's gaze flashed to Ellie, who gave her an encouraging nod, then returned to Kade. Her chin went up. "*Sí*, Señor Kade. I'll be the best cook the Diamond Bar ever had."

Kade seemed pleased. "I know you will. Turtle's going to help you till Mabel gets back. I saw him out by the corral when we drove in. I'll let him know." He rested a possessive hand on Ellie's waist. "One more thing. The police are on the way. The chopper is due in an hour. Since you're here, coffee and sandwiches might be a good idea."

"I'll take care of it."

"Thanks." Kade urged Ellie out of the kitchen, down the hall to his study, where he firmly closed the door. "You sit here." He settled her in the big leather chair behind his desk, facing his computer.

"Let's see if we can figure out what's happened in Boulder that might bring Chief McBride all the way out here."

Kade left for a moment, and Ellie went to work. She was reading an article in the Boulder *Daily Camera*, the city's online digital newspaper, when Kade returned. By then, she had discovered that the police weren't coming to tell him they had found his dead wife's killer. According to the paper, a woman's body had been found in a shallow grave in the hills at the edge of the city.

Ellie caught Kade's grim expression as he leaned over her shoulder to read the article, and her heart went out to him.

The last thing Kade needed was more trouble. But it definitely looked as if more trouble had arrived.

CHAPTER TWENTY-FOUR

*P*OLICE CHIEF MATT MCBRIDE WAS A MAN IN HIS LATE FIFTIES, WITH a lean, wiry build and curly brown hair. He and the other man who got out of the helicopter were both dressed all in black: cold-weather jackets, uniforms, black-billed caps with emblems on the front.

Ellie stood next to Kade, who waited in the brisk, late-morning air to greet them.

"Sorry for the short notice," McBride said to Kade, but his dark expression said he wasn't sorry at all. "Kade Logan, this is Detective Clay Meadows, Denver PD."

Kade made a cursory nod. "Detective." He drew Ellie forward. "This is Eleanor Bowman. She's a private investigator."

"Nice to meet you." Meadows was about five-ten, attractive, with his sandy hair and dark brown eyes.

"So you're working for Logan?" the police chief asked Ellie.

Kade answered for her. "After my late wife's car was found, I hired Ms. Bowman to take another look into Heather's murder."

"I see." The chief looked at Ellie. "Come up with anything?"

"I'm still working the case," she answered.

"Why don't we go inside out of the cold?" Kade suggested.

"Good idea," the chief agreed.

The men followed Kade into the house through the tall wooden front door. He led them through the entry beneath a huge elk antler chandelier into the living room, which was done with the same wildlife motif and Native American designs as the rest of the house.

"We've got coffee and sandwiches," Kade said. "Soft drinks, if you'd prefer."

The men exchanged glances. "It's been a long morning," said McBride. "I could use something to eat. But I'd prefer to take care of business first."

"I'll let Maria know." Ellie headed for the kitchen, delivered the message, then returned. She sat down next to Kade on the burgundy leather sofa as the men sat down in matching wing-backed chairs around the thick slab of varnished pine that served as a coffee table.

"So what's going on, Chief?" Kade asked.

"Two days ago, a female jogger out at Rainbow Lakes Campground veered a little off the path, following a squirrel. She walked past a mound of earth and noticed a couple of human fingers protruding through the dirt where the rain had washed the soil away. She immediately called 911. Officers arrived at the scene. The CSIs were called in, and they found the woman's remains."

Ellie felt a chill. Tension vibrated in the sinews in Kade's neck and shoulders.

"Have they identified the body?" he asked.

McBride nodded. "A Denver woman named Barbara Meeks. Disappeared about three weeks ago. Name mean anything to you?"

"No."

"You sure?" McBride pressed.

Kade shook his head. "I don't know the woman."

McBride studied him a moment more, then leaned back in his chair. "Barbara and her husband were Denver residents, so Denver PD is working jointly with us on the case."

"I was leading the missing person's investigation," Detective Meadows said. "But there wasn't much to go on. She was just home one day and gone the next. Now I'm heading up a murder case."

"Husband a suspect?" Kade asked.

McBride cast him a glance. "The husband is always a suspect."

A muscle ticked in Kade's jaw.

"What can you tell us about her?" Ellie asked.

The detective answered. "Barbara was in her late twenties, married, no children. Her husband, Bryan, is CEO of a software company based in Denver."

"Attractive?" Kade asked.

"Based on her photos, she was beautiful."

"What was the cause of death?" Ellie asked.

"Denver medical examiner will be doing an autopsy, but initial findings at the scene were that she was beaten, then strangled to death. We think she was murdered somewhere else and moved to that location to hide the body."

Silence fell as the implications mounted. "That's why you're here," Kade said. "Because the circumstances are similar to Heather's murder."

"That's right," McBride said.

"Have you come up with DNA, fingerprints, anything that points to the killer?" Kade asked.

"Truth is, we haven't found much of anything," Detective Meadows said. "ME on the scene believed she was murdered within days after she disappeared, maybe that day. There were signs of a sexual encounter, but it didn't look forced. The killer was meticulous and most likely used a condom."

"So you've got nothing," Kade said. "Same as last time."

McBride's lips thinned.

"Eight years between murders is a long time," Ellie said. "If it's the same man, why did he wait so long?"

Detective Meadows's gaze shifted in her direction. "If the murders are connected, we may find other bodies."

Ellie's stomach knotted. "You're thinking he might be a serial?"

"At this point, there don't appear to be any of the usual ritualistic elements," the detective said. "No torture, no rape, nothing weirdly out of the ordinary. The beating and strangulation suggest it was more a crime of passion."

That followed Ellie's line of reasoning. Like Barbara Meeks,

Heather had also been beaten and strangled. And Heather was famous for leading men on, then dumping them. Which brought
Ellie back to Sheriff Glen Carver or another of her lovers. Was it
really possible the same man had murdered Barbara Meeks?

"Anything else?" Kade asked.

"Just keep in mind that we're working on it," Meadows said.
"This creates a fresh opportunity to look into your wife's murder,
as well."

Kade nodded. He signaled to Turtle, who had appeared in the
doorway holding a silver tray heaped with neatly halved sandwiches and a carafe of coffee. Turtle set the tray on the coffee
table, Maria followed with cups, plates, and napkins, and then
both of them quietly disappeared.

Everyone helped themselves to the food, including Ellie and
Kade, all of them eating in silence for a while. Kade finished the
first half of his sandwich, thin-sliced ham and Swiss cheese, and
settled back against the sofa.

McBride wolfed down his sandwich and wiped his hands on a
paper napkin. He looked over at Meadows, who downed the last
of his coffee and set the cup down on the table.

Both men rose. "We may have more questions," Chief McBride
said. "I hope you aren't planning any lengthy trips in the near future."

"Not at the moment," Kade said. "I'd appreciate your keeping
me informed."

"As much as we can," the detective promised. The men left the
house, and a few minutes later, Ellie heard the sound of a helicopter lifting away.

"You think the murders are connected?" Kade asked, as they returned to the house.

Ellie's mind was churning, running through the information
they had just learned. "The police think so. There are certainly
enough similarities to make it plausible. Both beautiful women
who disappeared without a trace, then turned up murdered, pre-
sumably killed just days after they went missing."

"The cause of death is the same," Kade said.

She nodded. "Both beaten and strangled. And the timing is interesting."

"How so?"

"Barbara Meeks disappeared three weeks ago. Your wife's vehicle was found a month ago—a week before Barbara disappeared. If it's the same guy, the discovery of the car could have been a trigger of some kind."

Kade's golden eyes darkened. "The story was in all the newspapers, at least in this area and Denver. They rehashed the murder, finding the body two years later, and then the car turning up in the lake."

"So maybe the killer reads the article and remembers the way it happened. Remembers what it felt like to murder Heather—or why he did it. If he's a local, it's possible he was even there when they pulled the car out of the water."

Kade's jaw flexed.

"I'm not saying that's what happened, or even that the murders are connected. But it's a possibility we need to consider."

Kade paused at the door to his study. "I'm glad you'll be working the case full-time now." He looked hard at Ellie. "I don't want to see another woman turn up dead."

Though it was Sunday and most of the hands had the day off, Kade needed to be working. While Ellie dug around on the computer, Kade changed out of his church clothes, walked out to the barn, and saddled Hannibal. He needed to do some physical labor, something that would keep his mind off Barbara Meeks and the man who had killed her. Possibly the same man who had murdered his wife.

The hands had been pulling wire and mending fence posts in the north pasture, so Kade rode in that direction and arrived twenty minutes later. Swinging down from the big buckskin's saddle, he tethered the horse where there was graze and went to work.

It was a bright day, and the sun was warm on his back through his flannel shirt. It felt good to stretch his muscles, ease some of the tension in his neck and shoulders.

He was pleasantly tired, the sun riding low on the horizon, when he headed back to the ranch house. He was surprised at the way it cheered him to walk in and find Ellie in the kitchen.

"You're home," she said, smiling. Damp heat curled fine ruby strands of hair at her temples, and a soft red sweater curved over her breasts. She was female temptation personified. "You rode off by yourself," she said. "I was starting to worry."

Warmth spread through him. "It's nice to have someone worrying about me, darlin'. But I'm fine. Better after a little hard work."

Elle grabbed a potholder and pulled a tray out of the oven. This was her last night working with Maria in the kitchen, and both of their aprons were dusted with flour. Some of the hands were already seated at the table, back from wherever they had gone on their day off.

Alejandro stood near the window, his arm in a sling, but the bandage was gone from his shoulder or at least was smaller, hidden beneath his denim shirt. Kade didn't miss the intense dark gaze that tracked Maria's every move across the floor, or the soft look on the girl's face whenever she noticed.

Damn.

Maria was destined for heartbreak, and aside from firing one of his top hands, there was nothing he could do.

Kade walked over to Alejandro. "How are you feeling?"

Those dark eyes swung toward him. "Much better. I moved back into the bunkhouse. I think I'll be able to return to work in a day or two."

"Maybe. If you put in shorter hours and leave the heavy lifting to the rest of the men."

Alejandro just nodded. Maria was laughing at something Ellie said, and Alejandro was clearly distracted by the softly feminine sound.

"You got something on your mind?" Kade asked.

Alejandro shook his head. "It's nothing."

Kade's glance went to Maria. "I don't think it's nothing. I think it's a woman, and we both know which one. The question is what are you going to do about it?"

Alejandro's jaw firmed with resolution, but there was something bleak in his eyes. "I'm not the man for her. She's too innocent, too sweet. She deserves someone better than me."

"I'm not going to argue with you," Kade said. "Maria is everything good in a female. On the other hand, you shouldn't sell yourself short. You're a good man, Alejandro. I guess it just depends on how much the woman means to you, and if she were yours, how you would treat her." Kade set a hand on the man's uninjured shoulder. "Give it some thought."

Kade headed for his seat at the head of the table, and Alejandro sat down next to Seth on one of the benches. The meal was served, pot roast, always a Sunday favorite. They ate and talked. Kade mentioned he had worked on the fence in the north pasture.

"I got that last stretch done just before it started getting dark."

"You didn't have to do that, boss," Wyatt said.

Kade swallowed a mouthful of the succulent roast beef. "I've had a lot on my mind. I needed a little exercise."

Wyatt nodded. The men all understood how tough it was to run a ranch the size of the Diamond Bar, the stress Kade was often under.

"Seth spotted some strays up on Bear Tooth Ridge." Roy grinned. "We can always use an extra hand."

Kade chuckled. "I've got another project I'm working on. Which brings me to a topic I've been wanting to discuss." He stood and motioned for Ellie to join him at the head of the table.

"I want to introduce you men to someone. You already know her name, but not the real reason she's here. Ellie's a damn fine cook—as you all know by now. But that's not why I hired her. After Heather's car turned up in the lake, I decided to start digging again, see if I could find the man who killed her. Ellie's a private investigator. She's looking for the man who murdered my wife. That's the reason she's here."

Nobody spoke.

Seth turned a hard look on Ellie. "You're a private investigator?" He made it sound like a crime, and Kade felt the tension building in the air.

"That's right," Ellie said. "I work for a company called Nighthawk Security in Denver."

"So you came here to dig up dirt on all of us?" Slate accused.

"I don't appreciate being spied on," Roy added.

"Neither do I," said Riley.

Ellie raised her hand. "Before all of you go completely ballistic, I want you to know that I've been looking at anyone and everyone who knew Heather Logan. I focused on you men first because you live on the ranch. I checked you out very thoroughly—and I'm pretty good at finding pertinent information."

"And?" Wyatt pressed, clearly not happy he hadn't been trusted with the truth.

"I found out that Kade has some very fine men working for him. You aren't perfect—nobody is. But near as I could discover, you guys are loyal, honest, and trustworthy. Kade's lucky to have you."

Silence fell.

"Ellie's still looking for the killer," Kade said. "She'll be doing that full-time from now on. But none of you are on her suspect list. I want this guy. I want him to get what he deserves. I hope you'll give Ellie whatever help she needs."

"That's it, then?" Roy asked. "No more spying?"

Ellie smiled. "Where you guys are concerned, the spying is over. Anybody have any questions?"

"I do," Wyatt said. "You been here a while. You got any idea who this guy is?"

"We got a little sidetracked with Frank Keller," Kade explained. "Now that Keller's dead, Ellie's back to work on Heather's murder."

Ellie surveyed the men, who seemed satisfied with her answers. She turned. "If that's all, I think it's time for dessert. Maria?"

The young woman smiled. "We have hot apple pie with vanilla

ice cream." She lifted the heavy tray and started walking. Turtle rose and took the tray. Anticipation wiped away the last of the men's hostility. It was hard to stay mad when you were stuffing your face with hot apple pie.

Kade sat back down and returned to eating. Once the evening was over, he planned to persuade Ellie to join him upstairs in his bed.

A different sort of anticipation poured through him, making his body stir to life. He glanced at Ellie. He wasn't sure what there was about her that fired his blood. He just knew he wanted her.

Tomorrow they would start working again to find a killer. Tonight he had plans for Ellie that had nothing to do with murder.

CHAPTER TWENTY-FIVE

*T*HREE DAYS PASSED. THREE NIGHTS THAT ELLIE SPENT IN KADE'S bed. It was wonderful—and it was terrifying. She wasn't an emotional risk-taker, and she was definitely taking a risk with Kade.

In the end, she was bound to get hurt, but the time she spent with Kade was worth it. In the meantime, she was a private investigator. She intended to do her job.

Now that a second victim had been found, she needed to know if the two women's murders were connected, and if so, what that connection was.

She figured McBride and the Denver police would be working that angle, but she wasn't sure how much information they would be willing to share.

Yesterday, Detective Meadows had phoned Kade with the coroner's report on Barbara Meeks. Strangulation was confirmed as the cause of death, which made it a homicide. The victim had been badly beaten, and there were signs of recent sex, but no indication of rape and no DNA.

Nothing new there.

Kade had also heard from the lab in Eagle, which had called with the results of the water sample from the hole that had sickened his cows. According to the lab, the waterhole had definitely been poisoned. But the cows had recovered, and with Keller dead, it seemed a moot point now.

Late Wednesday afternoon, a deputy from Routt County showed

up at the ranch to return the weapons taken at the scene of Frank Keller's murder. Ballistics proved no shots had been fired from either pistol. Keller, left-handed, had been shot in the right temple. No powder residue on either hand. His death was officially a homicide.

Sitting in front of her laptop on Thursday morning, Ellie studied the screen, her focus once more on Barbara Meeks. There were dozens of articles written about her. Barbara was a well-known member of Denver society, the wife of the CEO of an important company. With her long brown hair, high cheekbones, and full lips, she was beautiful. According to the articles, she was charming, born into a wealthy family, accepted in the highest ranks of the Denver elite. The couple had no children.

Articles published after her disappearance focused on pleas from friends and family, including her husband, for any information that might help bring her home. After her body was discovered, the articles recapped her disappearance and speculated that she had been murdered. After the autopsy, the assumption was officially confirmed.

Ellie had just printed several photos of the woman when her cell phone rang. She grabbed the phone off the writing desk, recognized the number, and smiled.

"Hey, Zoe, I'm glad you phoned." It was a FaceTime call. Zoe's short blond hair and pixie features moved animatedly on the screen. She really did look like Tinkerbelle.

"Hey, girlfriend. How's ranch life?"

"Kind of feels good to be back in the country after so many years in the city. I'm out of the kitchen now, working the murder case full-time."

"That should speed things up."

"I hope so."

"So here's what I've got. First, the bartender at the Elkhorn, Rance Sullivan? His father's Irish, and his mother's Italian. Not Native American at all."

Ellie laughed. "So now we know Rance is a liar."

Zoe chuckled. "I'm guessing he's the kind of guy who's willing to say anything to get a woman in bed. But aside from a few speeding tickets and a drunk-driving arrest ten years ago, I don't see anything that looks suspicious."

"I'm not surprised. He didn't really strike me as dangerous, or the sort to get emotionally involved enough to commit a crime of passion."

"You think that's what it was?"

"That's the theory I'm currently working."

"Speaking of passion, you'll be happy to know I didn't find any indication of abuse in Heather Logan's medical records. Your guy doesn't appear to be a threat."

Your guy. Ellie felt a pinch in her chest. Kade was hers for a little while longer; then she would return to the life she'd had before. She felt a pang at the thought.

"Kade's kind of old-fashioned when it comes to women," Ellie said. "Sort of a white-hat kind of guy, if you know what I mean. I didn't expect you to find anything, but it's always better to know for sure."

"Have you come up with any new leads?" Zoe asked.

"Boulder police came out Sunday. The body of a woman named Barbara Meeks turned up. She disappeared not quite a month ago, was strangled and buried in a shallow grave. Lots of similarities between her death and Heather Logan's. I'm trying to find a connection between the two women. So far without much success."

"Eight years is a long time. You want me to take a look?"

"I do, but not yet. I need a little more information first. How's it going with you and Chad?"

Zoe sighed. "We decided to take a break from each other. We'll stay friends—with benefits, of course. I'll still see him once in a while."

Ellie smiled. "When you get the itch, right?"

Zoe didn't laugh. "I guess so."

"But cooling things down was your idea?"

"Sort of. Let me know if you need me."

"Will do." Ellie ended the call, a little worried about her usually carefree friend.

She went back to perusing information on the net. Barbara Meeks came from old money. She'd been married to Bryan Meeks, CEO of Red Tag Advanced Software, which specialized in designing programs for big international companies. In the early interviews, Bryan appeared to be devastated by his wife's disappearance. After her body was found, he seemed more angry than grief-stricken.

It reminded her of Kade and the rage that still simmered inside him. Was there a chance that Barbara, like Heather, could have been having an affair? She wondered again if it were possible both women were involved with the same man. If that man could have killed them both.

It was a big leap without more information. But the police were certainly considering the possibility, and it fit the theory she was working.

She dug around a little more, searching for a link in the women's lives, people they both might have known, business acquaintances, hobbies they both might have enjoyed. Neither had children, so there were no connections along those lines. She searched for something that would link Barbara to Coffee Springs but also turned up nothing.

And the eight-year gap made it even harder to establish a connection.

An article mentioned a women's charity golf event at the exclusive Cherry Creek Country Club, in the neighborhood where Barbara and her husband lived. Barbara also played tennis, but Ellie didn't think Heather had been involved in either of those sports, and there was nothing in the articles about riding or anything to do with horses.

Ellie sighed, the task seemingly hopeless. She needed to make a trip to Denver to talk to Bryan Meeks. Maybe Barbara's husband could help.

Ellie left the bedroom in search of Kade and found him behind the dark oak desk in his study. She knocked on the open door, and Kade rose.

"Come on in." He shoved back his chair and rounded the desk, crossed the room in several long strides. Her eyes widened as he hauled her into his arms, bent his head, and very thoroughly kissed her.

"That isn't . . . isn't why I came," she said breathlessly.

His golden eyes were hot. "No? Close the door, darlin', and tell me what you want. I'm more than happy to oblige."

Ellie laughed. "You're insatiable."

He chuckled. "Only when it comes to you." He ran a finger down her cheek. "So what's going on?"

"I need to go to Denver. I want to talk to Bryan Meeks, see if I can find something Barbara and Heather had in common, a way they could have met the same man, the man who eventually killed them."

Kade tugged her over to the leather chairs in front of his desk, and both of them sat down.

"What have you got so far?"

"Well, we know both women were in their late twenties, beautiful, and childless. Both were married to wealthy, successful men, which gave them access to plenty of money."

"Heather loved to go shopping in Denver. Maybe she and Barbara bought clothes from the same store."

"An exclusive boutique is definitely something to consider. The Cherry Creek Mall is one of the most exclusive shopping areas in the city, and the Meeks's family home is in the area. It's certainly worth checking out."

"What else?"

"I haven't found any mutual friends or hobbies, but after I talk to Barbara's husband, that might change. It's going to take some time. I'm planning to stay overnight."

Kade nodded. "All right. I'll go with you."

"You don't have to do that. I have an apartment there, so I have a place to stay. I know how busy you are."

"I've got things pretty much under control around here, at least for the moment. When do you want to leave?"

"I was thinking I'd drive down this afternoon, but I need to call Meeks first, find out if he'll see me sometime tomorrow."

He nodded. "We can leave whenever you're ready. We'll spend

the night at the Brown Palace. It's one of my favorites. Lot of good restaurants in the area." His smile returned. "I'll buy you the best steak in Denver."

Ellie started to suggest they simply stay at her place, but the Palace was a luxury she had never enjoyed. She imagined the evening ahead and what would happen when they got back to the hotel, thought of Kade's lovemaking and the way he could make her feel, and desire curled through her.

"How can I turn down an offer like that?"

Kade flashed one of his sexy smiles. "A king-size bed at the Brown Palace definitely beats the desk in my study."

A noise slipped from Ellie's throat as she eyed the desk. "I . . . umm . . . I'll go pack." Determined to keep her mind on work, she turned and walked out of the office.

CHAPTER TWENTY-SIX

THINKING OF ELLIE AND THE NIGHT AHEAD, KADE HEADED UPSTAIRS to pack an overnight bag. He was going to Denver. He figured he would enjoy the trip, but he didn't like the reason he had decided to go.

The idea of Ellie spending the night without him in Denver made him uneasy. He'd finally accepted that Heather had been cheating on her trips out of town. The notion of Ellie sleeping with another man sent a wash of fury into his blood.

He didn't understand it. He wasn't a jealous man.

Not until now.

But Ellie belonged to him—at least for a little while longer. As long as she was his, he wouldn't tolerate another man's hands on her. He wouldn't play the fool a second time.

Kade strode into his bedroom and pulled down his leather overnight bag. He packed enough for a couple of days in case they needed to stay, grabbed his shaving kit, changed into his dark blue city jeans and a white western shirt, and grabbed his Stetson. He was zipping the bag when his cell phone rang.

He checked the screen but didn't recognize the number. "Logan."

"Mr. Logan, this is Earl Dunstan. Frank Keller's cousin."

"I know who you are. How did you get this number?"

"I got it from Charlie Flatt. I need to talk to you, Mr. Logan. I know who killed Frank. I know who hired him to come after you. Now the guy is trying to kill me, too."

Kade frowned. "Why don't you go to the sheriff?"

"I'm afraid he won't be able to protect me. I need to get out of the country. I didn't have anything to do with any of this. I didn't even know Frank was causing trouble for you out at the ranch. He was just my cousin, so I gave him a place to stay. Now the guy who killed him wants to shut me up, too."

"Who? Who are you talking about?"

"Meet me behind Flatt's at midnight. Bring enough cash for me to buy a plane ticket and rent a place to stay till I can find a job. That's all I want. I wouldn't ask, but I got no choice."

"Dammit, give me a name."

"Flatt's. Midnight." Earl hung up the phone.

Kade left his suitcase on the bed and headed downstairs. Looked like his trip to Denver would have to be postponed.

He made his way to Ellie's bedroom. He figured, her being a woman, packing for a night on the town would take at least an hour. He rapped twice and opened the door, found her seated at the antique Victorian writing desk, her laptop open in front of her. Her suitcase was packed and waiting on the bed.

She was ready to leave. Another wrong assumption about her.

"We got a problem," Kade said.

Ellie rose. "What is it?"

"Earl Dunstan just phoned. He says the guy who killed Frank Keller is trying to murder him, too. Apparently Dunstan knows too much. He wants enough money to get out of the country in exchange for information. He's meeting me at midnight."

She walked toward him. "Why doesn't he call the sheriff?"

"I got the impression whoever is hunting him has enough power to go around the sheriff to get to him. Or at least that's what Earl believes."

Ellie went over to the bedside table, pulled open the top drawer, and took out her Glock 19, the gun the sheriff had just returned.

"You're going to need backup," she said, dropping the mag to check the load, then shoving it back in and holstering the weapon. "I'm going with you."

Kade didn't argue. He'd learned that Eleanor Bowman was a strong, capable woman who knew how to handle herself. He knew he could rely on her. "I thought about handing this over to Sheriff Fischer, but if things went sideways, Dunstan might disappear."

"Or Earl could be right about Frank's killer and end up dead."

Kade nodded. "We need to find the guy and shut him down."

"Dunstan didn't give you any idea who it was?"

"No. Earl's desperate. He's not talking until he finds a way to get himself somewhere safe."

"I guess we'll find out at midnight," Ellie said.

"I sure as hell hope so." Maybe they could solve at least one murder and end any threat to the ranch.

Maybe. But Kade wasn't so sure.

It was black as pitch, no stars, a layer of low-hanging clouds blocking the moon. Ellie sat tensely as Kade drove the pickup through Coffee Springs, heading north toward Phippsburg. Ellie gripped the seat as Kade swerved to dodge a deer that stepped into the road. A few minutes later, an owl swooped down in front of the windshield but made a safe escape.

"I'd forgotten how many animals live out in this kind of country," Ellie said, breaking into the silence. "It was one of the things I liked best about living on our ranch."

"All kinds of varmints out here," Kade said. "With any luck, Earl Dunstan will give us one of the human variety."

"Maybe Earl knows why the man who hired Frank wanted to cause you trouble."

Kade's features tightened. "I plan to ask him."

They drove through the darkness a while longer, until the big, barn-like structure of Flatt's Ranch Supply appeared in the headlights off to the left. No cars in the lot, and the interior was completely dark behind the windows. Kade pulled around to the back and killed the engine, turned off his headlights, but left the parking lights on. No sign of anyone moving around.

Ellie checked the time on her cell phone. Three minutes to midnight. Kade turned off the dome light before he opened the door and stepped out of the truck. Ellie got out on her side of the pickup.

She could see a hay shed, bales stacked six high under the metal roof. As she and Kade approached, a small, rotund man in boots and a beat-up cowboy hat stepped out of the darkness and started toward them. In the glow of the parking lights, his face had a sickly yellow tint.

He was ten feet away when a rifle shot rang out, and Earl Dunstan went down.

Ellie pulled her Glock, Kade pulled his Colt, and both of them hit the ground. More shots rained down from a spot in a cluster of trees on the side of the hill, some of them pinging on the metal struts holding up the building. She and Kade split up and crawled to cover, Kade back behind the pickup, Ellie behind a stack of gray cement blocks.

Another shot rang out, drilling into the truck near where Kade crouched behind a front tire. Ellie fired two return shots, then started moving, darting behind the base of a big pine tree closer to Dunstan, who lay unmoving on the ground. While Kade laid down a barrage of gunfire, Ellie eased into the deep grass and crawled toward Earl.

A shot thumped into the dirt a few feet away from him, and Kade fired again in the direction the shots had come from. Ellie caught a glimpse of Kade running low, circling around to the shooter's position in a copse of trees on the side of the hill.

Her heart was pounding with fear for him and worry for the man on the ground. When no more shots rang out, she crawled over to where Earl sprawled in the grass. She could hear his shallow breaths as he gasped for air.

"Everything's going to be okay, Earl. I'm Ellie. I'm with Kade.

I'm calling for help." Quickly she punched in 911. "A man's been shot in Phippsburg behind Flatt's Ranch Supply. Whoever shot him is still out there shooting at us."

"What's your name?" the female dispatcher asked.

Ellie tucked the phone between her neck and shoulder, opened Earl's bloody jacket, then tore open his shirt. In the dim glow of the parking lights, she could see he'd been shot in the chest, and it was bad.

"I'm Eleanor Bowman. I'm here with Kade Logan. Both of us are legally armed. We need an ambulance. Please hurry."

"They're on their way. Stay on the line until they get there."

Ellie dropped the phone into the grass beside her, peeled off her puffy jacket, and pressed it against Earl's chest to slow the bleeding.

"Just take it easy, okay?"

"He . . . he did it. He . . . he shot me."

"Who, Earl? Who shot you?" But Earl was already fading, his body jerking and his eyes losing focus.

"Frank said . . . said he knew him from . . . from the mine."

The mine? "Who, Earl? What was his name?" She reached out and took hold of his hand. Earl's fingers curled around hers, but they felt icy cold. "Tell me who shot you."

Earl's eyes slowly lifted to hers. In the faded yellow beam of the distant truck lights, his mouth opened and closed, but no sound came out.

Ellie's heart went out to this man who had gotten caught up in something far bigger than he could have imagined. "Just rest and take it easy, Earl, okay? The ambulance is on its way." She smoothed a hand over the little man's forehead and tightened her grip on his limp hand. "You're going to be okay."

The words seemed to comfort him. His features relaxed, and the tightness around his lips softened. Then a trickle of blood slid from the corner of his mouth, and his eyes slowly closed. Air whispered out of his lungs, but his chest never rose again.

Ellie's heart squeezed. Earl Dunstan was just another victim, like Kade's dead steers, like Alejandro, and Smoke. Like the sick cows, and the man who'd lost his leg at the Red Hawk Mine. Frank Keller had pulled his cousin into something sinister, and now he was dead. Both of them were.

Ellie wiped tears from her cheeks and looked up as Kade approached. "Earl's dead." She swallowed past the painful lump in her throat. "We didn't get here in time."

Kade's jaw hardened, and he glanced off toward the trees. "Whoever it was made it back to his vehicle and took off into the hills. There are a couple of feeder roads that'll take him to the main highway. No way to catch up with him."

Ellie picked up her phone and rose from the grass next to Earl's body. Without her jacket, she was shaking, but she didn't think it was from the cold.

Kade pulled off his sheepskin coat and settled it around her shoulders. It smelled like him, like pine forests and horses.

Clutching his jacket around her, Ellie looked up at him. "Earl died before he could give me the shooter's name, but he said something that could be important. Earl said Frank knew the man who murdered him from the mine."

"The mine. Earl was talking about the guy who shot Frank?"

"That was the way it sounded. The guy who hired Frank, then murdered him and Earl."

Kade's brows drew together beneath his hat. "According to your friend, Zoe, Frank Keller worked in mines all over the world."

"I know, but—"

Red and blue lights flashed in the distance as a pair of sheriff's vehicles crested the rise and rolled toward them down the road.

"Let's keep that information to ourselves for a while," Kade said. "See where it leads before we muddle things up by bringing in the law."

"Good idea."

Ellie watched the SUVs closing in. "I wish we could just go home."

Kade's arm went around her, and he pulled her close. "So do I, darlin'. So do I."

But they would have to wait for Sheriff Fischer to take their statements. They would have to convince the authorities that the bullet that killed Earl Dunstan hadn't come from one of their guns.

CHAPTER TWENTY-SEVEN

*I*T WAS ALMOST FOUR IN THE MORNING WHEN KADE LED ELLIE INTO the ranch house, nearly time for Maria to arrive and start breakfast.

"It's been a long day," Ellie said. "We both need to get some rest." Wearily, she raked back her thick, dark auburn hair. "Maybe I should stay in my own room."

Kade frowned, not liking the notion. "I'll sleep a lot better if you're beside me, but it's up to you."

Ellie's gaze flicked to his, and her pretty lips curved. "I'll probably sleep better, too."

Kade felt a sweep of relief that surprised him. He was getting used to having Ellie in his bed. It was probably a bad idea. Sooner or later, she would be leaving.

If you're dumb enough to let her go.

The thought came out of nowhere. Kade shoved it aside, and they headed upstairs to his room. Ellie's clothes were covered in blood, so she went in to rinse off her jacket and take a quick shower. Kade didn't join her, though he wanted to. As she had said, they both needed to get some sleep.

It was light outside when he awoke hours later with Ellie snuggled against him, her glorious, fire-touched hair spread over his chest. His erection stirred to life, but he didn't wake her.

Last night had been difficult for both of them. Watching a man die was never easy, and it had been only days since they'd found Frank Keller's bloody, lifeless body.

Kade left Ellie sleeping, showered, dressed, and went downstairs. Breakfast was long over, the kitchen cleaned up, Maria gone, the hands off at work. The big stainless coffeepot was on, as always, and a couple of left-over sack lunches sat on the counter for whoever might need them, but Kade wasn't in the mood.

Instead he turned on the stove, grabbed a skillet, and started frying strips of bacon, enough for him and Ellie. He made some toast and was stirring a pan of scrambled eggs when the kitchen door swung open.

"Good morning," she said, smiling as she walked into the kitchen. Without makeup, she looked clean and wholesome, young and vibrant. His possessive instincts arose, and arousal slid through him. There was just something about her.

"I've got breakfast ready. You're just in time."

Her smile widened. "That smells delicious, and I'm starving." She reached over and snagged a piece of bacon. "I didn't realize you could cook."

He chuckled as he turned off the stove and dished up their plates. "Just one of my many talents." At the moment, there was another talent he'd like to show her, but that would have to wait.

They sat down at the long oak table and dug in. "You never talk about your brothers," she said out of the blue. "Gage and Edge, right? Gage is the middle brother. Edge is the youngest."

"You being a detective, I guess you looked us up."

"That's right. Both your parents are gone. So why don't you ever talk about them?"

Kade lifted his coffee mug but didn't take a drink. "I don't see them much anymore. Gage is always off on some adventure. Half the time he's out of the country. Same with Edge. He's Army Special Forces. Only thing he ever wanted to do."

"Doesn't sound like the three of you are very close."

Regret filled him, and he set the coffee mug back down on the table. "We were when we were kids. After Mom died, we kind of drifted apart."

"That's too bad." Ellie started eating again. Kade was glad she had dropped the subject.

He missed his brothers, wished they had parted on better terms. Kade had wanted them to stick around, help him run the ranch. Neither Gage nor Edge was interested. They had fought about it. It wasn't until after they were gone that he realized they had made the right decision. They had their own lives to live, and ranching had never appealed to them.

Kade was right where he belonged, and so were Gage and Edge. Still, he wished he could see them, make sure they understood he respected them for being strong enough to stand up to him and follow their dreams.

Ellie sipped her coffee. "I've been thinking about Earl Dunstan and what he said last night."

He took a drink of coffee. "And?"

"According to Earl, the man who hired Frank and then killed him had something to do with the mine."

"You think he was talking about the Red Hawk?"

"It's the only mine Frank worked that has any connection to you."

Kade shook his head. "I don't know. We've talked to Will Turley. Will and I have known each other for years. No way he hired Frank to get back at me. Will and I never had a problem."

"I didn't pick up any bad vibes, either. What about the miners? Ever had any trouble with one of the men?"

"Aside from Will, I don't know any of the guys who work there. And I have to think whoever hired Frank paid him plenty. Those miners don't make that kind of money."

"Why don't you call Will, get him to give you the names of anyone and everyone who has any connection to the mine? Maybe one of the names will ring a bell."

Kade nodded. "I'll call him before we leave."

Ellie's gaze shot to his. "We're still going to Denver?"

"You worried about the guy who shot Keller and Dunstan showing up while we're gone?"

"I don't know. But two men are dead, and if it's you he's after—"

"The ranch has first-class security twenty-four seven, and the hands are all on alert. If it's me he's after, he'll have to go to Denver to find me."

"Okay, then. Because I've still got a job to do. You hired me to find Heather's killer. At the moment, finding out what happened to Barbara Meeks is the best chance we've got."

Built in 1892, the Brown Palace Hotel in downtown Denver was a Colorado landmark. Nearly every president since 1905 had stayed in the luxurious hotel, with its eight-story, open atrium lit by a beautiful, multicolored, domed glass skylight.

Walking through the brass front door, Ellie felt as if she were stepping into the age of Old World glamour. Kade's big hand rode at her waist as they traveled the open corridor, following the bellman toward the suite Kade had reserved.

He opened the door, and they walked into a living room warmed by pale yellow walls, molded ceilings, and Persian carpets. A traditional sofa in soft shades of amber sat in front of a mantled fireplace. In minutes, they were settled, their clothes unpacked in the bedroom.

Kade flashed a look at the huge four-poster bed, hand-carved in a West Indies design. Graceful, gold-silk draperies hung at the windows. Ellie's gaze met Kade's across the room. She could almost feel the heat simmering beneath his surface calm, and her stomach lifted.

"I know what you're thinking," she said. "But we have work to do before we can . . . umm . . . relax."

Kade chuckled. "Always practical. Fine, we'll wait. For now."

Ellie just smiled. "We've got an appointment with Bryan Meeks in forty-five minutes, and it's a twenty-minute drive. We need to get going."

She was already dressed for today's meeting in a forest-green, knee-length skirt suit, cream silk blouse, paisley scarf, and heels. Kade wore crisp blue jeans, a pale yellow western shirt with pearl snaps, and his dark brown, western-cut tweed jacket.

The valet had kept the Mercedes waiting out front, and they settled themselves inside, out of the frosty cold. Kade followed North Broadway to I-25, then merged south toward the Denver Tech Center in Greenwood Village.

Red Tag Advance Software Developers was a multistoried building on a grassy knoll in the 4600 block of Ulster Street. In the two-story lobby, a security guard behind the counter checked to see if they had an appointment.

"Yes, here you are." The guard, a chubby little man with a beard, scanned the computer screen in front of him. "Eleanor Bowman and Kade Logan to see Bryan Meeks. You can go right on up."

The elevator ride was brief, the doors opening onto the eighth floor, where a receptionist with a cap of short blond hair sat behind a desk with a black granite top.

The blonde stood up behind the desk. "Mr. Meeks is expecting you. If you'll please follow me." She led them through one of the double doors leading into Meeks's massive office. The view through the big glass windows reached all the way to distant, snow-topped peaks.

Meeks rose from his chair and strode toward them, a handsome dark-haired man with sad brown eyes. "Mr. Logan. Ms. Bowman." He extended his hand to each of them, and they shook. "I understand you wanted to see me about what happened to my wife."

"Ms. Bowman is a private investigator," Kade said. "I hired her to look into the murder of my wife, Heather, which, according to police, has a number of similarities to the recent murder of your wife, Barbara."

Meeks's shoulders sagged. "Why don't we sit down?" He led the way to an ultra-modern, black leather sofa and matching chrome-and-black chairs in front of a glass-topped table. All of them sat down, Kade next to Ellie on the sofa. He rested his Stetson on his knee.

Bryan leaned back in his chair. "So, Mr. Logan, apparently we share a similar pain."

"It's just Kade, and it looks that way."

"We're here to see if we can find a common thread between the two women," Ellie said. "Something that could link them to the man who killed them."

Meeks frowned. "I don't understand. From what I was told, your wife was murdered eight years ago. You don't really think there's a chance it could be the same man, do you?"

"The police think it's possible," Kade said. "Maybe you can help us find out if it's true."

Bryan's features tightened. "I want to find out who killed her. What would you like to know?"

For the next twenty minutes, Ellie asked questions, everything from the names of Barbara's closest friends to her activities, both as an individual and with her husband. She made a few notes on her phone.

"What about sports?" Ellie asked.

"Barb played golf and tennis. She was a really good tennis player. And skiing. She loved the winter as long as she could spend some time on the slopes. She was a pretty good athlete all around."

"Barbara liked to snow ski?" Ellie asked, picking up on the only possible link between the two women so far.

"Yes. We skied every winter. I didn't go the last couple of years. The company was expanding. I had too much to do."

On the sofa beside her, Kade's tall frame shifted forward. "So Barbara went skiing alone?"

"With her friends, yes. Why?"

"My wife often went skiing with her girlfriends. Like you, I was too busy working."

The unspoken question hung in the air. Bryan held Kade's stare, then glanced away. He took a deep breath. "You think my wife was cheating." It was more a statement than a question.

"Mine was, and it's not an easy thing for a man to admit."

"No, it isn't," Bryan agreed. "Truth is, it's possible. We were fighting a lot toward the end. I wasn't giving her as much time as she wanted. I began to suspect something was going on, but I didn't know for sure. Now it doesn't matter."

"Maybe it does," Ellie said. "Heather Logan's been dead eight years, but your wife's murder is recent. We're going to focus on her death, see if we can find out who killed her. If we find him, there's a chance we'll also find the man who killed Kade's wife."

"Maybe we'll get lucky," Kade added. "Get justice for your wife and for mine."

Bryan swallowed. The glint of tears appeared in his eyes. He blinked, and it was gone.

Kade rose. Ellie stood, and so did Bryan. "One last question," she said. "You mentioned Barbara loved to ski. There are lots of places to ski near Denver. Was there any place she preferred?"

"Barbara liked Aspen. Breckenridge is a little closer, but Vail was her favorite, and she had friends there. Tom and Judy Springer. Their names are on your list."

Ellie's gaze locked with Kade's. "Thank you again for your time, Bryan, and for being so honest."

"If there's anything else I can tell you, please call. I want this man found as much as you do." He stuck out his hand. Kade gripped it, and a look passed between the two men.

Ellie led the way out of the office. Kade put on his Stetson and followed. They didn't speak until they reached the car and were settled inside, out of the blustery cold.

"Vail," he said, cranking the engine, the heater roaring to life.

Ellie nodded. "It keeps popping up."

Kade's features darkened. "From the start, people said Heather ran off with some guy she met in Vail. The gossip was all over Coffee Springs. Even I believed it."

"You reported her as a missing person. Didn't the police check it out?"

"I'm sure they followed up on the rumor, but they never came up with anything."

"After her body was found, you hired a private detective. Did he check it out?"

"Boulder County's a long way from Vail. It changed the direction of the investigation. The detective never came up with anything, and neither did the police."

"Doesn't mean Heather couldn't have left with a guy she met when she went skiing. There's no way to know how she ended up where she did."

Kade's hands tightened around the steering wheel. "Looks like we're going to Vail," he said, and drove the Mercedes out of the parking lot.

CHAPTER TWENTY-EIGHT

"*I*'D LIKE TO STOP BY MY APARTMENT WHILE WE'RE IN TOWN," ELLIE said as Kade drove back to the hotel. "I need to check, make sure everything's okay."

"No problem. What's the address?" It was getting late. Kade had promised Ellie a night on the town, and he was looking forward to it. After everything that had happened, they both needed a break. They would head for Vail tomorrow to continue their search.

"My apartment's on Speer Boulevard. It's only a ten-minute walk from my office." She gave him an address in the 200 block, and he punched the number into the Mercedes's GPS system. A soft female voice guided him directly to the location.

Kade pulled into a guest parking space, and they took the elevator up to Ellie's third-floor unit. She used her key to let them in, then began a quick check to make sure everything was in order.

"There's a couple of things I need to grab while I'm here," she said. "I'll be right back."

Ellie disappeared into the bedroom, leaving Kade to survey the apartment, a basic one-bedroom, one-bath with dark hardwood floors and windows opening onto a courtyard with a pool. A compact living room with a dining area contained a built-in desk and bookshelves, which, by the look of the stack of files and the reference books on the shelves, Ellie made good use of.

The place wasn't fancy, and decorations were sparse. Clearly she didn't spend a lot of time there. He wandered toward the open kitchen, which was roomy and modern, with granite countertops and stainless appliances, the best feature of the apartment. Ellie was a good cook, so it made sense.

She walked out of the bedroom smiling, a garment bag in hand. "I thought I'd pick up something a little more interesting to wear tonight."

Kade thought about the evening he had planned and what she might be wearing, and his blood headed south. "I can't wait to see you in it," he drawled. Meaning *I can't wait to strip you out of it.*

Ellie glanced around. "Everything in the apartment seems to be okay."

"Doesn't look like you spend much time here."

She laughed. "That's why I have artificial plants."

He took the hanger from her hand and started across the living room. Before he reached the door, a solid knock sounded.

Ellie walked up to check the peephole, then pulled it open. "Justin."

"Hi, Ellie, I thought I heard you in here. Haven't seen you in a while." He was younger than Kade, maybe thirty, with thick blond hair a little too long and a pale, close-cropped beard. The T-shirt he wore showed off a sculpted body and solid biceps. GYM RAT was printed on the front.

Kade disliked him instantly.

"Justin, this is my friend Kade Logan."

Friend, my ass, Kade thought.

"Kade, this is my next-door neighbor, Justin Cooper."

Justin's lips barely curved. "Logan."

Kade tipped his head. "Cooper." Neither offered a handshake. A look passed between them that said Justin wasn't pleased to see Ellie with another man. Kade wanted to take the damn garment bag and wrap it around surfer boy's blond head.

Ellie must have felt the tension. "I'm sorry, Justin, we were just leaving." She walked over to the still-open door and waited for her neighbor to walk past her into the hall. "Thanks for stopping by," she said.

"Way it goes, I guess. I'll see you next time." Justin sauntered away.

Ellie waited for Kade to walk out and joined him in the hall. Justin's door closed behind him as they headed for the elevator.

It was quiet in the car on the ride back to the hotel. Ellie could tell by the knot in Kade's jaw exactly what he was thinking.

"Justin is just my neighbor, okay? Nothing more."

He flicked her a sideways glance. "So you two never dated?"

"He took me out for pizza a couple of times. If you're asking if we've had sex, the answer is no."

Kade grunted. "Not because he doesn't want you. He hardly took his eyes off you the whole time we were there."

"That's his problem. I'm not interested in Justin."

Kade pulled the car up in front of the hotel, and the valet opened her door. They walked through the gleaming brass doors into the lobby, but instead of looking up at the colorful skylight or the wrought-iron balustrades that wrapped around every floor, she headed straight for the elevator.

When they reached the suite, Kade carried the garment bag directly into the bedroom. He had only said a few short words since they'd left her apartment.

Ellie eyed him across the bedroom. "Surely you aren't jealous of Justin Cooper? You make him look like a little boy."

She thought he would smile, maybe even laugh. But the brittle look remained on his face. Ellie walked over, took off his hat and tossed it on the bed, dragged his mouth down to hers, and very hotly kissed him.

It took a second for his cool demeanor to melt. Then he was kissing her back, hauling her against him and ravishing her lips. His tongue swept in, and the heat intensified, spreading like flames through her body.

Kade shoved her jacket off her shoulders, unbuttoned her blouse, and stripped it away. In seconds, her bra was gone, one of Kade's big hands cupping her breast. Then his mouth was there, sucking hard, spiking need into her core.

"Kade . . ." She arched her back to give him better access, and he turned his attention to the other breast, suckling and tasting until she started to tremble. He shoved her skirt up around her waist and slid her pink thong down over her hips to the floor.

She barely noticed when he turned her around, bent her over the bed, and came up behind her. Big, talented hands aroused her, stroking till she was repeating his name and begging him to take her. Buzzing down his zipper, Kade freed his erection and buried himself to the hilt.

Ellie moaned. Distantly, she heard herself begging him not to stop, but the words got lost in a jumble of pleasure as Kade gripped her hips and took her deeper, pounding into her until she couldn't think of anything but him. Nothing had ever made her feel so hot, so wild, so desperate.

She rushed headlong into climax, then came again before Kade followed her to release. Still trembling, she leaned back against him. *Who is this person I've become?* she thought, a thread of worry slipping through her at the power he held.

Kade eased her back against him, and his arms tightened around her. She could feel the drumbeat of his heart, the brush of his lips on the nape of her neck.

Long minutes passed. Kade pulled her skirt down over her hips and turned her to face him. She heard his deep sigh.

"I shouldn't have pushed you so hard. I meant to slow down, take things easy, but somehow . . ." He raked a hand through his hair. "You were right. I was jealous. I don't know what's the matter with me. I've never been a jealous man."

She reached up and touched his face. "What about Heather? Surely it bothered you the way she behaved with other men?"

"I learned to ignore it. With you, it's different."

Ellie slid her arms around his neck. "I've never been with a man who cared enough about me to be jealous." Still, it bothered her.

Kade bent his head and softly kissed her. He hadn't worn a condom. They had discussed it. She was on the pill, and both of them were medically safe. Surely that was the reason the sex had been so good.

Or maybe it was just Kade. She was falling for him. Falling hard. But the closer they got, the more control he seemed to want. Ellie wasn't willing to give up the independence she had carved out for herself. Not for Kade or any other man.

"Why don't we take a nap before we have to get dressed," he said as she returned from the bathroom.

One of her eyebrows arched up. "A nap? That's what you're calling it?"

He chuckled. "The suggestion was sincere. If a nap is what you want, that's what we'll do."

She shouldn't encourage him, not when every day with him pulled her deeper under his spell. But she really wanted to curl up with him for a while.

Ellie stripped off her clothes and climbed up in bed, and Kade undressed and joined her. At first they snuggled, then things got heated. As always, making love seemed the most natural thing in the world. Afterward, they actually did get a little sleep.

Then Kade's phone signaled an incoming text. Will Turley, with a list of names, everyone who had worked at the Red Hawk Mine for the last twelve months, including support personnel, along with a list of people in management: regional, state, and international, all the way up to the CEO.

The hunt for Heather's murderer would have to be put on hold once more. Kade held up his phone, showing her the list. Will Turley was nothing if not efficient.

Nap time was over.

CHAPTER TWENTY-NINE

*T*HEY DIDN'T LEAVE FOR VAIL THE NEXT MORNING, AS KADE HAD planned. Instead, Ellie set up appointments at the headquarters of Mountain Ore Mining. Last night, after he'd received Will Turley's text message, Kade had spent an hour going over the names on the list. Nothing popped.

He'd pondered the information throughout the dinner he'd shared with Ellie at John Elway's swanky downtown steakhouse and done his damnedest to enjoy the meal. In a sexy little black number that showed off her cleavage as well as her pretty legs, Ellie had managed to distract him enough from the murders to actually taste the food.

They had lingered over after-dinner brandies, and by the time they got back to the suite, he'd been relaxed enough to make slow, leisurely love to her—the way he should have done that afternoon. He'd slept better than he had in weeks, but by morning, his thoughts were back on Frank Keller and Earl Dunstan and whoever had murdered them.

Kade had never believed Keller had been hired by one of the Red Hawk miners. According to Turley, he wasn't the sort to make close friends. If Keller was shooting steers, Kade's dog, and one of his ranch hands, he wasn't doing it as a favor to someone. Keller had been paid, and for a high-risk job that could land him in prison, the payment would have been substantial.

Whoever had hired him was someone with plenty of money. According to Earl Dunstan, that same man had killed him. Killed them both.

"I've been thinking," Kade said as he closed the snaps on the cuffs of his western shirt that morning. "If Keller wanted to kill me, he had every opportunity to do it. I wasn't hiding. I was out with my men almost every day. Even Alejandro. I think Keller could have killed him if he'd wanted to."

"So why didn't he?"

"I don't know."

"Maybe whoever hired Keller just wanted him to harass you," Ellie said. "Maybe they wanted to cause trouble but not actually murder you."

"It's possible. Even if it's true, it doesn't change what we need to find out—who's behind it and why."

"I know." Ellie straightened the turtleneck on the pale blue cashmere sweater she was wearing with navy blue wool stretch pants and a pair of black ankle boots. Kade said a silent thanks that she hadn't put on another skirt. His behavior yesterday afternoon still embarrassed him.

Sweet Jeezus. His reaction to the bozo sniffing after Ellie had been way over the top. He'd fought an urge to grab the guy by the back of the neck and the seat of his pants and toss him out into the hall.

By the time they'd returned to the suite, his anger had faded. *Mostly.* Then Ellie had kissed him, and the heat had bubbled back to the surface. The urge to claim her overrode his good sense, and his body reacted.

He'd still be apologizing if Ellie hadn't responded so wildly. Her passion matched his own—one more thing that drew him to her.

"Are you ready?" she asked.

Kade grabbed his Stetson and settled it on his head, tugged the brim low. "Let's go."

The valet, a young blond kid doing his best to grow a mustache, had the car waiting in front. He opened the passenger door, and Ellie slipped into the seat. Kade handed the boy a tip, and they headed south again on I-25, turned east, and followed GPS directions to an address on East Tufts Avenue.

The building was impressive. Brick and glass, twenty stories high. According to the list of names, the man Will Turley reported to was the Breckinridge-Leadville District manager, the guy in charge of all Mountain Ore mines in the area.

Above him in the pecking order was the Southwest Regional Senior Vice President, one of four in the state. According to info Ellie had dug up on the web, there were also VPs of Marketing, Sales, and Production for each of the four regions, who reported to the senior VPs.

At the head of the food chain was a CEO, a CFO, and a COO.

Helluva lot of names, none of which meant a damn thing to Kade.

Still, they moved forward, starting with the District Manager, a guy named Clive Murphy. They went through all the steps and were finally admitted to Murphy's fifth-floor office—desk, credenza, bookcase, two chairs, standard management level, nothing special.

They completed introductions, and both of them shook Murphy's hand. He was in his mid-forties, with medium-brown hair cut short, a dark suit, and a yellow-striped power tie. Nothing about him rang any bells, but he was high enough up the company ladder to afford to pay Frank Keller.

"I understand this has something to do with the explosion at the Red Hawk Mine," Murphy said as they sat down in front of his desk.

"That's right," Kade said. "We're looking for information on a guy name Frank Keller, a former Red Hawk Mine explosives expert."

"We suspect he's the man who set the charge in the tunnel," Ellie added. "Keller was recently murdered. We think the incidents are connected."

Murphy's features sharpened. He leaned forward and started typing on his keyboard.

"I knew the name sounded familiar. Looks like Keller worked

for the company for quite a few years. He was hired on a contract basis. Never was a full-time employee."

"Did you know him personally?" Kade asked.

"I think I met him a couple of times during the years he worked for us, but I really didn't know him. According to this, he was originally recommended by the Colorado Springs District Manager. Keller did some work for one of the coal mines we operate in that area. I had no reason not to support the recommendation."

"Any chance we can speak to the Colorado Springs manager?" Kade asked.

"Let's find out." Murphy leaned over and picked up the phone, spoke to someone, then turned back to them. "His name is Anthony Russo. Tony's got time right now. He's just down the hall."

They said their thank-yous and goodbyes and headed for Russo's office.

Tony was a black-haired, olive-skinned man of Italian heritage, attractive, with a killer smile. The result of the conversation was the same. Keller did a good job at the mine where he'd first been hired. Russo had recommended him to Murphy for the job at the Red Hawk Mine. He had met Keller somewhere but said didn't really recall much about him.

"It's hard to believe Keller's the man behind the explosion," Russo said. "The reports we received on his previous jobs showed him to be extremely competent. As far as I know, there was never a problem with any of the work he did for us."

Kade flashed Ellie a look. *Another dead end.* Both of them rose. "Well, thanks for your input."

Russo smiled. "Sorry I couldn't be more help."

Once more out in the hall, Kade walked next to Ellie. "Murphy knew him, and so did Russo. But they don't know me, and I don't know them. No reason to think they would have hired Keller to cause me trouble."

"So it's someone else."

"I'm not sure, Ellie." Kade scrubbed a hand over his jaw. "So far this is getting us nowhere."

Ellie just smiled. "That's the way it is with detective work. You ask questions, you get answers, then you try to fit the pieces of the puzzle together. We need to keep climbing the chain of command."

Kade sighed. "Fine. Who's next?"

Ellie looked down at the list. "We move up to the Senior VPs. There are four of them, one for each quarter of the state. The VP who covers the southwest area, where the Red Hawk is located, is a guy named Richard Egan. He's a member of the family that owns the company."

"Never met him or anyone else in the family," Kade said.

"We still need to check him out. I spoke to his assistant and requested an appointment. He said his boss would be in the office all day and his schedule was flexible."

They headed back to the lobby. An older woman with freckles and carrot-red hair sat behind the receptionist's desk, conversing with a tall woman standing a few feet away. Next to her, a handsome man with thick dark hair was deep in conversation with a squat, bald man in an expensive suit.

The woman was extremely attractive, with brilliant blue eyes, and glossy black hair swept into a tight knot at the back of her head. Ellie didn't miss the expensive, saffron-yellow designer suit, Hermès scarf, and Louboutin heels that marked her as one of the executives.

The woman spotted Kade and didn't look away. Few women could resist a man in a cowboy hat, especially one as handsome as Kade Logan. She removed the reading glasses perched on the end of her fine, straight nose, neatly folded them, and tucked them into the black Chanel bag dangling from her shoulder.

"You look a little lost," the woman said with the hint of a smile. "I'm Jane Egan Smithson. Perhaps I can help."

"Kade Logan. I own the Diamond Bar Ranch. Your company leases acreage from the ranch to operate the Red Hawk Mine." He tipped his head toward Ellie. "This is Eleanor Bowman, a private investigator. We'd like to speak to Richard Egan in regard to some trouble at the mine. We think it may be connected to problems we've been having at the ranch."

One of Jane's perfectly shaped black eyebrows arched up. "I see."

"Actually, we're looking for anyone in the company who might know a man named Frank Keller," Ellie said. "He was an explosives expert who worked for Mountain Ore."

Jane shook her head. "I'm sorry, I don't know him."

"What about your husband or your father?" Kade asked.

"It would be unusual for those of us in upper management to interact with an employee at that level. There's a chance my husband, as Chief Operating Officer, may have had contact with Mr. Keller through one of the Regional VPs."

She turned to the incredibly handsome man beside her and ran a manicured nail down his arm, drawing his attention. "I'm sorry to bother you, darling, but this is Kade Logan. He owns the land we lease to operate the Red Hawk Mine. Kade is looking for information on a man named Frank Keller."

Smithson's dark gaze lingered for a moment on Kade, but his features remained bland. "Sorry, I don't know anyone by that name." His glance flicked to Ellie, skimming over her in a subtle appraisal most people would have missed.

"Ellie Bowman," she said. "I'm a private investigator working for Kade." She extended her hand, and Phillip took it warmly in his.

"Nice to meet you," he said, his gaze lingering for a moment too long before his attention swung back to his wife. "I've got to go. I've got work to do in my office, then meetings the rest of the day and into the evening. Now it seems your father wants to see my weekly report a day early. He's expecting it on his desk first thing in the morning so don't wait up."

Smithson's gaze met Ellie's for an instant, then he turned, strode toward the elevator, and disappeared inside.

As the elevator doors slid closed, Jane's attention went to Kade, and the frown on her face slipped away. "As you can see, my husband is a busy man." And not happy at the moment, Ellie thought.

"My brother, Rick, is Senior VP of the Southwest Region," Jane continued, "so there's a chance he might know something about your Mr. Keller. Why don't I escort you up to his office? That way he'll be sure to make time for you."

Kade nodded. "Appreciate that."

Ellie followed the woman into the elevator, and they got off on the nineteenth floor. Jane smiled at Kade as she led them down a wide corridor to a tall mahogany door, opened it without knocking, and ushered them into an upscale waiting area done in pale blue and gray. Kade removed his hat and raked a hand through his thick, golden-brown hair.

Jane's smile went from Kade to the young man behind the desk. "Daniel, Mr. Logan and Ms. Bowman need to speak to Rick. Tell him I said it was important." Jane was CFO of the company, Ellie knew, a far more powerful position than her brother's job as only one of four Senior VPs.

"Certainly, Ms. Smithson." Daniel rose from his desk. A lean, elegant man in his twenties with sandy hair and an East Coast, cultivated accent, he disappeared into the inner office.

Jane took a business card out of her purse and smiled at Kade as she handed it over. "My office is on the top floor. Let me know if there's anything else you need."

Ellie wondered if Jane was extending a subtle invitation. The relationship between Jane and her husband certainly didn't seem all that warm.

"It was nice to meet you," Jane added with a last glance at Kade. If she was interested, Kade didn't seem to notice.

Jane left the office, and Daniel returned a few minutes later with a good-looking black-haired, blue-eyed man following in his wake, clearly Jane's brother.

"I'm Rick Egan," he said to Kade. "I understand you're the owner of the Diamond Bar Ranch."

"That's right."

"Since the mine falls under my jurisdiction, I'm familiar with the property. A pleasure to finally meet you, Mr. Logan." He offered a hand, which Kade shook. Egan turned. "Ms. Bowman." They shook. "Why don't we all go inside, and you can explain why this visit requires the presence of a private investigator."

They followed Egan into his office, which was also done in blue-and-gray tones, but had a big plate-glass window looking out over the city. Egan suggested they dispense with formalities and use their first names.

Ellie flicked a glance at Kade, urging him to take the lead since he owned the property. He started by asking if Rick knew a man named Frank Keller.

"I met Keller a couple of times," Rick said. "I understand he recently killed himself."

"You spoke to the sheriff?" Kade asked.

"Sheriff Fischer phoned Will Turley, the supervisor out at the mine."

Interesting that the sheriff hadn't told Egan that Keller's death had been ruled a homicide.

"I know Will," Kade said.

"According to Turley, the sheriff believes Keller might have been behind the explosion that caved in one of the tunnels and cost one of the miners his leg."

"What do you think, Rick?" Ellie asked. "Is there any reason Keller might have done something like that?"

Egan shook his head. "No idea. But as I said, I didn't really know him."

"We've spoken to District Managers Murphy and Russo," Kade said. "Is there anyone else in the company we should talk to? Someone who might be able to give us a little more insight?"

"Not that I can think of." Rick checked his watch and rolled his chair back from the desk. "Looks like my time has run out. I'm afraid I've got an appointment." He rose, and so did Kade and Ellie. "Sorry I couldn't be more help."

"We appreciate your time," Ellie said.

Rick smiled. "Let me know if you need anything else."

Kade settled his hat back on, and they walked out of Egan's office just as a heavyset man in a three-piece suit and slicked-back, iron-gray hair burst into the waiting area. Daniel rose behind his desk, but the man ignored him, yanked open the door to Rick's private office, and stormed inside.

"Where the hell have you been? You were supposed to be in a meeting with your marketing, sales, and production people half an hour ago! And don't tell me you forgot—again!" The door slammed closed behind him.

Daniel glanced nervously at Kade. "Sorry about that."

"Wasn't that Mose Egan?" Ellie asked. His photo on the internet, along with the three-piece, pin-striped suit and expensive silk tie, reinforced the assumption.

"That's him."

"Some kind of father-son dispute, I gather," Kade said.

Daniel cleared his throat. "Mr. Egan can be a difficult man at times." The look on the assistant's face said Mose Egan was a real bastard.

Kade opened the door, and Ellie walked past him out into the hall. She said nothing as they left the building and returned to Kade's Mercedes.

"Looks to me like we're back to square one," Kade grumbled as he started the engine.

"Maybe not. We can eliminate the CEO and CFO from our list, as well Phillip Smithson, the COO, if we take him at his word. That leaves three people employed by Mountain Ore who knew Frank Keller. One of them could have paid him to blow up the tunnel. Maybe the shootings at the ranch were only done as a distraction."

Kade flicked her a sideways glance. "A distraction. It's possible, I suppose." He sighed. "None of it makes any sense."

"Not yet. But sooner or later it will." At least for Kade's sake, she hoped so. She prayed that with Keller and his cousin both dead, the threat to Kade and the ranch was over.

Ellie wished she could make herself believe it.

Sunlight slanted through the big plate glass window where the man stood looking down on the grassy area below. As he watched the white Mercedes pull out of the parking lot, his jaw clenched and his hands balled tightly into fists. Hatred even stronger than he felt for Mose Egan rushed through him.

Kade Logan. In the flesh. Until today they had never met. But for years, just the mention of Logan's name was enough to send him into a blinding fury.

His gaze tracked the Mercedes as it drove off down the street. He didn't regret the trouble he had caused Kade Logan or the arrogant, demanding, overbearing man whose power dominated his life.

He had no regrets. The only decision he had to make now was what to do next.

A hard smile curved his lips as he thought of Logan's latest conquest. Ellie Bowman. *Private investigator.* That was a laugh. No man could mistake the sexual heat that simmered between them. The woman belonged to Logan. Which made her fair game for him.

He just needed to figure out how to proceed. Planning was everything and he was extremely good at it. There was no reason to rush things. Anticipation was part of the thrill.

And while he was at it, maybe he could find a way to make more trouble for the controlling old man in charge of the company—the billion dollar corporation *he* deserved to control.

Maybe he could even find a way to make him dead.

CHAPTER THIRTY

AFTER CHECKING OUT OF THE HOTEL, KADE DROVE THE MERCEDES back toward Coffee Springs. The Keller investigation seemed to have stalled, but there was no way to know for sure if the trouble was over. Though Wyatt hadn't reported any new problems at the ranch, Frank Keller and Earl Dunstan had both been murdered, and whoever had killed them was still on the loose.

Hoping Sheriff Fischer would come up with something new, Kade's mind returned to the reason he'd gone to Denver in the first place.

He'd hired Ellie to find Heather's killer. Kade itched to stop in Vail and talk to the Springers, friends of Barbara Meeks, see if there was any connection between Barbara and Heather. But the urge was equally strong to get back to the ranch.

"It's only an hour's drive from the Diamond Bar to Vail," he said. "I'd rather go home, makes sure everything's okay. We can go to Vail tomorrow."

Ellie nodded. "That's probably better. Gives me a chance to phone ahead, find a time when the Springers are available."

Thinking that was a good idea, Kade continued on I-70, turned onto Highway 131, and started up into the hills. They rode in comfortable silence, winding through the countryside, the grass a faded gold this time of year, the trees leafless with the approach of winter. Ellie gasped and Kade smiled as a big golden eagle swooped out of a tree next to the road, its impressive wingspan lifting it easily into the air.

"So beautiful," she said.

Like you, Kade thought, *with your fiery hair and big green eyes*, but he wasn't a man who could easily speak words like that.

He drove into Coffee Springs, turned onto the paved road, then the gravel lane leading to the ranch. Pulling through the big timber gate, he drove up the hill and parked the car, walked with Ellie into the kitchen. Kade stiffened at the sight of Maria standing at the sink, her face bathed in tears. Embarrassed, she quickly turned away.

Ellie flicked Kade a glance. "Can you give us a minute?"

He didn't want to. He wanted to know what the hell was going on. "No problem."

Walking over, Ellie wrapped her arms around Maria, and Kade clenched his jaw. Striding out of the kitchen, he let the door swing closed behind him, then stopped in the hall. No way was he leaving until he knew what Maria was crying about. Though unless he was mistaken, he had a pretty good notion already.

"It's okay," Ellie said. "Tell me what's happened."

Maria sniffed back tears. "It's nothing. I'm just being foolish."

"Tell me," Ellie softly urged.

"It's not his fault. It's mine."

"You're talking about Alejandro."

"I shouldn't have done it. I knew it, but I did it anyway." She dragged in a shaky breath. "I sent him a note. I asked him to meet me after supper in the cabin where we'd stayed when he was injured. He was worried, so he came to make sure I was all right."

"Go on," Ellie gently pressed when Maria fell silent.

"I-I seduced him. I kissed him, and when he tried to pull away, I just kept kissing him until he kissed me back and then . . . then things happened. In the morning, when I woke up in the big bed, he was gone."

Out in the hall, Kade softly cursed. Eavesdropping wasn't his style, but he wasn't leaving until he got the whole story.

"Have you seen him yet?" Ellie asked.

"No, but he left me a note. The note said he was sorry. He said he never meant to hurt me. He said I deserved someone better."

Maria started crying, and Kade ground his jaw. He headed down the hall, went out through the mudroom, off to the bunkhouse.

He yanked open the bunkhouse door, but there was no one there. *Sonofabitch!* The bastard was off working with the rest of the hands. If Ramirez thought for a minute he was getting out of this by running away, he was sorely mistaken.

Kade strode back into the house and went into his study. Alejandro would be back before dark.

Kade had plenty to say to him when he got there.

Ellie wiped a fresh tear from Maria's cheek. "Everything's going to be all right. I know how painful a broken heart can be, but in time you'll get over it."

"I have to leave. I can't stay here and see him every day. I can't face him after what I've done."

Ellie caught Maria's slim shoulders. "You didn't do anything. You fell in love with him. That isn't a crime."

The younger woman looked up at Ellie with big dark, troubled eyes. "What must he think of me now?"

"Stop it! You stop that right now. Alejandro could have chosen differently. If he hadn't wanted you, he could have refused. Whatever happened, he has always respected you. He cares for you or he wouldn't have made love to you. That isn't going to change."

Maria glanced away, her face as white as the kitchen cabinets. "Supper's ready to go into the oven. Do you think you could . . . could take care of it tonight? Just this one more time?"

"Yes, of course. We're friends. Anything you need, you just have to ask."

"I'll be back in the morning. I won't leave Señor Kade without a cook."

Ellie leaned over and hugged her. "We'll talk again tomorrow. Everything's going to be okay."

Maria just nodded. Hanging up her apron, she walked out of the house.

Ellie surveyed the kitchen, saw that everything was in order, and began to finish the last small tasks necessary to serve the meal when the hands came in that night.

As she worked, she thought of Kade and remembered the look on his face as he had stalked out of the kitchen. Kade had been running the ranch for years. He knew men. Ellie was sure he knew exactly what was going on with Maria and Alejandro.

Heading down the hall, she rapped lightly, then walked into his study. Kade sat behind his desk, his features hard, his jaw clenched tight.

"He's not getting away with it."

Ellie walked toward him. "He's a man. She's a woman. Things happen."

"She's a young girl, and he's a full-gown man. He's damn near as old as I am. He had no right to touch her."

"Maria's a young woman, Kade, not a girl. Not anymore. And so what if Alejandro is ten years older? She loves him. Maybe she shouldn't have done what she did, but it wasn't entirely his fault."

"That it?"

Ellie sighed. Clearly Kade wasn't backing down on this. "At least give it some thought."

Kade made no reply. As Ellie left the study, she felt sorry for Alejandro Ramirez.

The hands were trickling in. Kade stood out by the barn, watching as they arrived, some on horseback, others on ATVs. While the men tended their horses, Billy pitched in. Smoke trotted along beside him as Turtle and Alejandro rode in on four-wheelers.

Kade intercepted Alejandro. "We need to talk," he said. "Now."

Hard lines formed around Alejandro's mouth. He nodded. "Where?"

"Follow me." Kade led the way around the side of the barn out of sight, stopped and turned.

"You should be real proud of yourself, Ramirez. You stole a young woman's virtue and walked away like it was nothing. You bragging about it to your friends? Or are you at least man enough to keep your mouth shut?"

Alejandro's hand balled into a fist. *Good*, Kade thought, his own hand fisting.

"I don't deny it," Alejandro said, his jaw still tight. "I should have walked away."

"But you didn't."

"No."

Kade fought a wave of fury. Before he could talk himself out of it, he threw a punch that damn near knocked Ramirez off his feet. Alejandro staggered backward, but managed to regain his balance. He wiped the blood off his mouth but made no effort to defend himself.

"You want to hit me," Ramirez said. "Go ahead. I deserve it."

"You sure as hell do. You'd get a whole lot more if you hadn't just taken a bullet." Kade's hand throbbed. The man was tough. He'd give him that. "You took that young girl, then discarded her as if she were nothing—just another of your besotted women."

Alejandro's spine jackknifed straight. "That's not true! Maria isn't like any other woman. She is special. She's everything a man could want in a woman! I told her that. I tried to stay away from her. I tried to tell her I wasn't good enough for her, but she wouldn't listen. Last night, when she offered herself to me, I should have walked away, but I couldn't. I could no longer pretend I didn't love her. And I couldn't send her away."

At the anguish in Alejandro's face, Kade's anger deflated. "Jesus Christ, man. If you love her that much, you'd better marry her. You're going to be even more miserable than you are now if you don't."

Alejandro sighed. "What kind of life can I give her? We wouldn't even have a place to live."

Kade walked over and rested a hand on Alejandro's shoulder. "We'll figure it out. Let's go inside where it's warm. We can talk about it after supper."

Ramirez just nodded. By the time they got to the house, Ellie had dinner laid out. Kade cast her a grateful glance. The men were still washing up, but they'd be arriving any minute. Seemed she was always there when he needed her.

"You'd better put some ice on that eye," Kade said, but Ellie was already walking toward them, a plastic bag in her hand. One step ahead of him, as usual.

"Here, this ought to help." She handed Alejandro the bag of ice, which he pressed against the side of his face.

He glanced around the kitchen. "Where's Maria?"

"She wasn't feeling well. She went home early. She'll be back in the morning."

Alejandro handed back the ice bag. "This can't wait until morning. I need to see her now, tell her the way I feel." Turning, he strode toward the door.

"Tomorrow's Saturday," Kade called after him. "Why don't you take the day off? This may take more time than you think."

Ramirez tossed him a look of thanks and kept walking. The door closed firmly behind him. Quieter than usual, the men served themselves, ate, and headed back to the bunkhouse. As Ellie cleaned up the kitchen, Kade pitched in to help her, shortening the task considerably.

Ellie wiped her hands on a dish towel and hung it on the handle of the stove. "From the bruise on Alejandro's face, I guess you didn't take my advice."

Kade figured Ellie would get around to the subject sooner or later. "Ramirez got what he deserves, and he knows it."

"So what happens now?" she asked.

"With any luck, we're about to have a wedding—if the groom can figure out how to get his future bride to forgive him."

Ellie smiled broadly. "That shouldn't be a problem. The man just has to look at her, and Maria will forgive him anything."

Kade bent his head and softly kissed her. "How about me? That the way you feel about me?"

Ellie laughed. "You? You have to work a little harder."

Kade chuckled. His gaze went to the door. "He's worried he can't give her the things she deserves."

"I don't think Maria requires all that much," Ellie said.

Kade nodded. "Mabel has her own place. Now that Maria's head cook, seems only fair for her to have a place of her own too. There's an old cabin just off the road. Ramirez can fix it up, make it a decent place to live. Be doing both of us a favor."

Ellie tipped her head back and kissed his jaw. "That's very sweet of you."

Kade glanced away. "Just a good business decision. Important to keep the head cook happy."

Ellie simply smiled and walked away.

Kade watched her go. Ellie knew the truth, knew he cared about his people, wanted them to be happy. She had a way of reading him no other woman ever had. Kade studied the sway of her sexy behind and felt the familiar pulse of desire for her.

He sighed. Ramirez wasn't the only one who needed to figure things out.

CHAPTER THIRTY-ONE

AFTER A NIGHT IN KADE'S BIG BED, ELLIE ROSE EARLY AND HEADED downstairs. She figured Maria would be with Alejandro, planning their future together. Instead, as she opened the kitchen door, she caught the smell of frying bacon and the pungent aroma of fresh brewed coffee.

"What are you doing here?" she asked. "Did you talk to Alejandro?"

Maria's chin went up. "*Sí*, I talked to him. He came to my grandmother's house last night."

"And . . . ?"

"And I sent him away. I saw his battered face. I know what Señor Kade did to him. I won't have a man who's only marrying me because he has been told he must." This was a different Maria from the heartbroken girl Ellie had found in the kitchen last night. It seemed there was a strong will beneath the soft exterior of the sweet young woman.

"He loves you, Maria. He told Kade that."

Maria turned away. "I need to finish breakfast. The men will be here soon."

Ellie went along with the change of subject. Things would work out for the couple—or at least she hoped they would.

Kade arrived a few minutes ahead of the hands. He spotted Maria and started to say something, but Ellie shook her head. "*Later*," she mouthed, and Kade nodded.

The next arrivals were Conn Delaney and Trace Elliot. Kade intercepted the men as they walked through the door. Conn and Trace were both good-looking and extremely well-built. Kade's tall, masculine figure fit right in.

"I'm glad you're here," Kade said. "I figured I'd run you down after breakfast. Let's eat, and we'll talk." Motioning for Ellie to join them, they filled their plates and sat down at the end of the table.

"I had a hunch you'd be looking for me fairly soon," Delaney said, shoveling in a mouthful of eggs. "My team hasn't run into any new problems, and your biggest problem is dead."

"There's a chance whoever hired Keller will make more trouble, but there's no way to know unless something happens. And I can't keep guards on the payroll twenty-four hours a day unless there's a credible threat."

Ellie silently agreed. With Keller dead, they had to hope the danger was over.

"You're right," Conn said. "No way to anticipate what might happen." He took a drink of coffee. "I'll tell my guys to stand down. We can pack up and be gone by the end of the day."

On the bench next to him, Trace crunched a strip of bacon. "I'll ride out, make sure everyone gets the word."

Kade took a drink of coffee, set the mug back down on the table. "Your boys have done a damn fine job. I know my men felt safer having your team around. If a problem comes up—"

"If a problem comes up," Conn said, "you know where to find us." He looked over at Ellie. "If there's anything you need, just call."

Ellie smiled and nodded.

As the hands filed in, she felt Kade's thigh against hers beneath the table, and a sweep of heat settled low in her stomach. Kade had given up pretending their relationship was merely professional. Ellie wasn't sure how she felt about that, but they were sleeping together every night. Not easy to keep something like that a secret.

As breakfast came to a close, Kade glanced over at Maria, anxious for information.

"Let's go for a walk," he said to Ellie. "Haven't had a chance to look at the new foal yet." Grabbing their jackets, they walked out in the morning chill.

They'd only taken a few steps toward the barn when Kade's questions started. "What's going on with Maria? The girl looked ready to do battle with anyone who glanced at her sideways. Especially me."

"Apparently, Alejandro's proposal didn't go well. Maria refused him. She thinks you forced him into it."

Kade swore foully. "Well, hell."

Ellie smiled. "I don't think Alejandro will give up that easily."

"He'd better not if he knows what's good for him," Kade grumbled.

Ellie bit back a laugh.

"That reminds me," Kade said. "Mabel called this morning. Her family wants her to move to Arizona permanently. She really wants to go. She was thrilled when I gave her the news Maria is taking over as head cook. Apparently, she felt guilty for leaving me without a replacement."

"Maria will still need help."

"I'll find somebody."

Ellie heard a bark as Smoke ran toward them. Billy was already hard at work. Dressed warmly in jeans, boots, and a winter jacket, he hurried along at the dog's side.

"Have you seen the new foal?" Billy asked, his blue eyes bright with excitement. "He's really something. The little guy's already up and walking around."

Kade chuckled. "They learn real quick."

They walked together into the barn, which was shadowy, with the sun barely up, and smelling of hay and horses, familiar and pleasant to a rancher. Or a woman with ranching in her blood.

Over the past few weeks, Ellie had come to realize how much she missed her old life. She would be sad when her time here was over.

She glanced at Kade, whose hat brim shaded his face, and a sharp pang rose in her chest. She would miss the ranch, but she would miss Kade Logan even more.

She stepped up on the bottom rung of the stall and looked down at the tiny colt nuzzling his mama for breakfast. "He's beautiful." A bright sorrel color, shiny as a newly minted penny.

"He's got great breeding," Kade said. "Be worth a good price when he's older."

"He's the same color as the horse I had when I was a girl. Rusty was amazing."

Kade's gaze found hers. "You mean before the bank took him away," he said darkly. "Along with everything else your family owned."

An unexpected jolt of pain rolled through her. She'd thought she was over the loss of her home and family. She'd told Kade about losing the ranch when she'd first arrived. She didn't think he'd remember.

Kade said nothing more, but for long seconds, his eyes remained on her face.

He glanced away. "We need to call the Springers. Sooner we talk to them the better."

Ellie nodded. She couldn't help wondering if he was thinking that the sooner they solved his wife's murder, the sooner she would be leaving.

A fresh pang returned to her chest.

Ellie sat behind her laptop on the writing desk in her sitting room. She had phoned the Springers earlier, told Judith Springer she was a private investigator looking into the murder of their friend, Barbara Meeks, and asked if they could meet. Judith had been out shopping when she took the call, but she would be home a little later.

Ellie and Kade were due in Vail at five o'clock that afternoon.

In the meantime, Ellie wanted to look into anything that might connect Frank Keller's murder with the three Mountain Ore Mining executives who knew him. With his dying breath, Earl Dunstan had said the man who'd hired Frank was connected to the mine. So far, these three were the only people who qualified.

Though Ellie hadn't been hired to solve Keller's murder or figure out why Kade had been targeted, she cared about him—way more than she should. She didn't want Kade or any of his men getting hurt.

Digging around on the internet, she pulled up info on Clive Murphy, Anthony Russo, and Rick Egan.

Murphy was a married man with a family. Nothing exciting about him. Russo was divorced with two kids. He had weekly visitation, but the kids weren't living with him. No hint of scandal, and lots of praise for his work.

Since nobody was perfect, she dug a little deeper, saw that Russo liked to play poker and he was good at it. Good enough to participate in some fairly big games. Gambling could become an expensive addiction. *Interesting.*

Rick Egan was a bachelor with a very public social life. His family was extremely wealthy and influential. They were active in the Denver social scene, especially Jane Egan Smithson and her husband Phillip, who were big philanthropists.

There were lots of pictures of Jane and Phillip at charity events, as well as photos of Rick. Jane and Phillip were the perfect couple, Jane beautiful and Phillip handsome.

A memory surfaced of their meeting, of Smithson's gaze running over her in an intimate way that hinted he might be a player. He had said he didn't know Keller, but there was no way to know if it was true.

Like Phillip, Rick was beyond good-looking, with his black hair and intense blue eyes, which Ellie couldn't help but notice when she'd walked into his office. Though neither of the two handsome men appealed to her the way Kade's fierce masculinity did, she wasn't dead, either.

In an Italian designer tuxedo, Phillip looked as if he belonged on a terrace overlooking the Mediterranean, while Rick, with a glamorous woman on his arm, was a tabloid photographer's dream.

Ellie sighed and closed down her laptop. So far she'd come up with no reason for any of the executives to hire Frank Keller, or any connection to Kade Logan or the Diamond Bar Ranch.

Feeling the heavy weight of failure, she rose from the chair and started for the door. Her feet slowed. It wasn't like her to give up, at least not so soon. Pulling out her cell phone, she hit the contact button for Zoe.

"Hey, girlfriend," Zoe said.

"I hate to bother you, but—"

"But you need info." Zoe's smile came through the phone. "I work for you these days, remember? What do you need?"

Ellie smiled. "I guess I'm still getting used to it. So you like working for Nighthawk?"

"I do. Never a dull moment around here."

Ellie laughed. "Isn't that that the truth. So what I need is something that connects Kade Logan or the Diamond Bar Ranch to Clive Murphy, Anthony Russo, or Rick Egan. They all earn the kind of money it would take to pay Keller enough to cause Kade trouble." Her mind returned to Smithson. "And if you get a little spare time, take a look at Phillip Smithson."

"Why don't I just take a look into Keller's finances and see if I can find any large deposits?" Zoe said. "Follow the money, you know? If I find something, I might be able to track the money back to where it came from."

"That sounds even better. I won't ask how you're going to do it. I don't think I want to know."

"Trust me, you don't. Anything else?"

"Just a personal question. What happened with you and Chad?"

A long pause. "I saw him the other day."

"Great. So the two of you are dating again?"

"I said I saw him. Chad was with another woman." Zoe sniffed. "I didn't know I loved him until it was too late."

"Oh, Zoe, you've got to tell him. You can't just give up."

"It's too late, Ellie. Chad warned me if I wouldn't commit, he'd find someone who would." Zoe's voice held a hint of sadness. "Listen, I've got to go. I'll let you know if I come up with anything."

The line went dead, and Ellie felt a rush of sympathy for her friend. For the first time in years, Zoe had found someone she cared about. But she'd been afraid to commit, afraid of getting hurt. By the time she'd accepted her feelings, it was too late.

Ellie thought of Kade. Beyond enjoying each other in bed, she had no idea how he felt about her. And Kade knew nothing of her feelings for him.

Maybe it was time they talked about it.

Or maybe it was better that she didn't know.

CHAPTER THIRTY-TWO

*U*NTIL SOMETHING SOLID ON KELLER CAME IN, THEY DECIDED TO focus on Heather. It was the reason Kade had brought Ellie to the ranch in the first place. A little after three-thirty that afternoon, they left for Vail in the pickup, giving Kade plenty of time to locate the Springers' address once he reached the county line. Kade hated to be late.

He barely noticed the trip through the mountains, but Ellie seemed to absorb every dip and curve in the road. The scenery was beautiful, mountains and forests, bridges across rushing streams. Vail was one of the foremost ski resorts in the nation, a favorite of the rich and famous.

Kade had been there with Heather a few times, but he wasn't much of a skier, and most of the time he'd been edgy and worried, his mind back at the ranch. In the end, Heather had persuaded him that she should go by herself and stay with her friends, who loved skiing as much as she did. At the time, he'd been relieved.

The hard truth was he'd been too busy to give his wife the attention she needed—and too naïve to realize that other men wouldn't hesitate.

If he'd been there, maybe she wouldn't have cheated. Maybe he wouldn't have decided to file for divorce.

Maybe she wouldn't be dead.

"Where are you, Kade?" Ellie snapped her fingers as the pickup rolled down the road, her voice finally penetrating his thoughts. "You look like you're miles away."

He cast her a sideways glance. "More like years away." He crested a hill and pulled out to pass the car in front of him. "Heather went to Vail every year. After the first couple of seasons, I stayed at the ranch while she drove down and stayed with Anna or Gretchen. It was winter. I told myself anything could happen on the ranch—I couldn't afford to be gone."

"You said half the town, including you, thought she'd run away with someone she met in Vail."

"At the time, I did. She'd threatened to do it before, just take off, disappear and never come back. I figured she'd finally done it."

"But eventually you called the police and reported her missing."

He nodded. "Even when they came up with nothing, I stayed in touch with Gretchen and Anna. I thought she might call them, let them know she was okay. At first, they were evasive. They figured she'd left me for someone else, and they didn't want to betray her. In the end, nothing turned up until two years later when they found her body."

"And you still feel guilty."

He kept his gaze firmly on the road. "Yeah, in some ways, I do."

"You didn't kill her, Kade. Heather made a series of bad decisions. That's what got her killed."

He was beginning to actually believe it. Some of the tension he was feeling started to ease. "I don't come here often, but this is where I met Grace. My friend Sam convinced me I needed to get out more. Vail's about the closest place you can go where anything's happening."

"Sam was right," Ellie said. "Getting away was probably good for you."

"Plus nobody knew me in Vail. Everything I did in Coffee Springs was fodder for the gossip mill."

"I know how much you hate gossip."

He flicked her a glance and smiled. "After I met Grace, we got together whenever she was in town and I could get away for a day or two. She owns a condo, so she comes up from Denver fairly often."

"I didn't realize your relationship with Grace was serious."

"It wasn't. Not for me. But after we'd been seeing each other a while, Grace got the idea we should make things permanent. That's when I broke it off."

He didn't mention the times he'd come up in the months that followed, times he'd been looking for female companionship of the one-night variety. It wasn't his style even then. Now that he'd been with Ellie, a night with a nameless female held not the slightest appeal.

It was a sobering thought.

"That's the turn." Ellie pointed to a street sign that read Spraddle Creek Road. It led into the pricey, gated community where the Springers owned a home.

Kade made the turn and stopped to speak to the gate guard, a thin, ruddy-faced man with sparse gray hair. The guard found their name on his list and opened the gate, allowing them to wind on up the road to a house on Riva Glen. The property, a beautiful home surrounded by leafless aspens this time of year, was a castle-like structure with a couple of turrets and a rock façade.

Kade walked next to Ellie up the flagstone path and climbed the stone steps onto a covered front porch. The heavy wooden door opened as they arrived, and a pretty brunette in her thirties stood in the entry.

She smiled. She had very curly hair that didn't quite reach her shoulders but seemed to fit her friendly face. "You must be Ellie and Kade."

"That's right," Kade said.

"I'm Judith Springer. Please come in." She stepped back to invite them inside, and they crossed a slate-floored entry beneath a frosted glass chandelier into a high-ceilinged living room. Tall, French-paned windows looked out toward the ski slopes on the mountain across the valley.

"Beautiful view," Ellie said.

"We enjoy it." Her eyes darkened with sadness. "Barbara loved to come here. We're really going to miss her."

Kade's gaze traveled around the house. It was beautifully furnished in warm shades of beige, with traditional sofas and heavy damask silk draperies, a real showplace.

"Will your husband be joining us?" Ellie asked.

"Thomas wasn't able to make it up for the weekend. My husband is president of Integrity Insurance National Health Care. Once the mountain is open, he tries to come up more often." She smiled. "I'm fortunate to be able to spend most of the fall and winter up here, as well as several months in the summer."

Kade wondered if that much time apart could actually work in a marriage. He'd been with Heather almost every day, and it still wasn't enough.

Or maybe Ellie was right, and his wife's unhappiness wasn't entirely his fault.

One thing was certain—he didn't want a marriage where he and his wife lived apart. And why the hell had the word *marriage* even popped into his head?

"Why don't we get comfortable in the library?" Judith suggested. "There's coffee in there, or something stronger, if you prefer."

"Coffee sounds good," Kade said, and Ellie nodded. They made their way into a study paneled in heavy, dark wood. Built-in bookshelves held hundreds of leather-bound volumes. As Judith poured coffee into three mugs and passed them around, Kade sat down beside Ellie on a comfortable, chocolate-brown leather sofa and rested his hat on his knee. Judith joined them in a matching armchair.

"First, we'd like to express our sympathy for the loss of your friend," Ellie said. "We didn't know Barbara, but she certainly didn't deserve what happened to her."

"No, she didn't." Judith was attractive in a girl-next-door sort of way, with thick-lashed green eyes and a trim figure. She wore loose-fitting blue jeans and a cable knit sweater. "That's why I agreed to see you. I want the man who murdered my friend brought to justice."

Ellie leaned over and set her mug on a coaster on the coffee table. "If you really want to help us, you'll have to be completely honest. I can promise that anything you say will not be repeated unless it's absolutely necessary."

Kade watched Judith's expression, caught a look of understanding pass between the two women.

"I'll tell you as much as I can," Judith said. "Is there something specific you wanted to know?"

Ellie's gaze didn't waver. "Eight years ago, Kade's wife, Heather, was also murdered. The circumstances of her death were very similar to what happened to Barbara. Enough so that the police suspect the crime may have been committed by the same man. Kade and I believe that man may have met Barbara, as well as Heather, somewhere in Vail."

Judith's eyes widened. "Are you sure?"

"We can't be certain," Ellie said. "At least not yet. But it's a possibility we're looking into."

Judith took a sip of her coffee, cradled the mug in her hands. She took a shaky breath. "I tried to warn her. I worried every time she went out by herself. Barbara wouldn't listen."

"What happened?" Ellie asked.

"Bryan was always busy, and Barbara was lonely. She called, asked if she could come up. It wasn't unusual. She was bored, she said. She just wanted to have some fun. Of course I told her yes. We'd known each other for years."

"When was this?" Kade asked.

"The last time she came up was the weekend before she disappeared. Barbara arrived late Friday afternoon. I wasn't feeling very well, so she went out for a drink by herself." Judith looked at Kade and fell silent.

Ellie leaned over and touched her hand. "Barbara went looking for company, right? She went out to meet a man."

Judith's eyes filled with tears she dashed away. "It wasn't the first time. She and Bryan came up a few times during the ski season when Thomas was here. The four of us always had a good time. But on the weekends when my husband had to work, sometimes Barb would come up by herself. She'd go out alone, and she wouldn't come home till morning. I didn't approve. It wasn't something I would ever do. But I knew she was lonely, and she was my friend."

Kade's adrenaline was pumping, the story all too familiar. "So she met a man that Friday night and went home with him," Kade said.

"She went to the bar hoping to meet someone, and apparently she did," Judith said. "She called me a couple of times over the weekend to tell me she was okay and having a great time. It wasn't until late Sunday afternoon that I saw her again. She asked if she could come back the following weekend. I knew Bryan wasn't coming up, so I said yes. It's a big house, plenty of room."

"Do you think she planned to meet the same man?" Ellie asked.

"I don't know. It was usually a one-night thing with her."

"But that weekend she spent both nights with the same guy," Kade pressed, just to be clear.

She nodded. "She said he was really into her, easy to talk to, and good in bed. She said that was how it used to be with Bryan. Barb thanked me, hugged me, and drove back to Denver. That was the last time I ever saw her."

"Did you tell the police?" Ellie asked.

Judith shook her head, moving the springy curls around her face. "The police have never talked to me. Barb was with Bryan in Denver when she disappeared. I didn't see any reason to mention a hookup that had happened in Vail. The two didn't seem connected, and I didn't want to hurt her husband."

Kade got up and paced over to the window, turned his hat in his hands as he stared out across the mountains to the empty ski slopes trailing down the side of the hill. Whatever trace of snow they'd had was gone. It would be weeks before the season officially opened. He turned back to the women, who were speaking quietly, their heads close together.

Ellie rose from the sofa. She took a business card out of her purse and handed it to Judith. "If you think of anything else, I hope you'll call."

"I will. I promise."

"One more thing," Kade said. "Was there any place Barbara particularly liked to go when she went out? Someplace she might have met this man?"

"There were a couple of places. She said she always had a good time at The ShakeUp. It's a late-night spot. Live music, lots going on. We went there together a couple of times, but I'm not into that kind of scene anymore. She also liked Bullwinkle's. It's great for after-ski. People can sit outside on the deck if they want. That's where the two of us usually went for a drink if we were by ourselves. If Thomas and Bryan were with us, we went to The Remedy. It's one of the nicest places in town."

Kade walked back to where Judith stood next to the leather ottoman in front of her chair. "We really appreciate your help, Judith. I know how tough it is to lose someone you care about."

She must have read the darkness in his eyes. Heather's death had haunted him for years. Judith took his hand and gave it a gentle squeeze, turned, and led them out of the library, back to the front door.

She stopped and looked up at him. "Whoever he is, I hope you catch him."

If he did, the bastard was a dead man. Kade's jaw hardened. "So do I."

CHAPTER THIRTY-THREE

"**S**O I GUESS YOU'RE BUYING ME A DRINK," ELLIE SAID AS THE pickup reached the interchange and drove under I-70 to the frontage road that ran along the base of the ski hill. It was already dark, the cold setting in, especially in the mountains.

"We're trying to find a guy who could have killed both women," Kade said. "So far, Vail is the only common denominator. Maybe they met him in the same place. The ShakeUp wasn't around when Heather was alive, but Bullwinkle's has been here as long as I can remember."

"We might as well follow the trail as far as it leads."

Kade nodded. "Bullwinkle's is basically a local's joint. Gets lots of tourists in winter, but people who own condos, anybody who spends time in the area winds up there sooner or later."

There was something in his voice. "Is that where you met Grace?"

He scoffed. "Not her style. I met Grace at The Remedy. It's in the Four Seasons Resort. That's where I stay when I'm in town."

She flicked him a glance. "You're just full of surprises, Kade Logan. First a fancy white Mercedes. Now I find out you have five-star tastes in hotels."

His hard mouth faintly curved. "You should have figured that out at the Brown Palace."

A memory arose of the hours they had spent in the luxurious four-poster bed. She squirmed in her seat, thinking of sex, wanting more of him and trying not to let him know. "Good point."

His golden eyes met hers and heated as he read her thoughts. "We'll come back, spend a few days here once things settle down."

Her heart gave an unexpected lurch. She wanted that, she realized, wanted something that lasted beyond the end-of-the-job farewell she had planned.

The pickup pulled into the lot. Bullwinkle's was a big wooden structure with plenty of parking. No snow on the mountain yet, but the place was definitely ready to handle the crowds.

"There's a deck in back that looks out at the slope. During the season, dozens of skiers collect out there after the lifts close. But it's busy pretty much all year." He got out of the pickup, walked around to help her out, and they headed inside.

Bullwinkle's was the kind of place that made people feel welcome. The walls were covered in bric-a-brac: old wooden skis, bent license plates, antique snowshoes, neon beer signs, Coca Cola posters from the forties—junk to some, treasures to others. Lumped together, it gave the bar a friendly, exciting vibe that drew locals, tourists, and skiers alike.

Kade set a hand on her waist as Ellie made her way through the crush of customers seated at wooden tables. The place was noisy, people in jeans, sweaters, and winter boots laughing and talking, but the late-October crowd was probably minimal compared to the throng that showed up after the mountain opened for the season.

"Do you know any of the bartenders?" Ellie asked.

Kade glanced toward the two guys working behind the big rectangular bar in the middle of the room. Then his gaze traveled to the sexy young women serving food and drinks. In a town like Vail with so much to offer, the competition for jobs was fierce. Businesses had their choice of the best-looking, most competent employees.

"I might know some of the servers."

She frowned, catching a faint note of that same something she had heard earlier in his voice. "How long since you've been here?"

Kade looked at her, then away. "I was here in August, a month or so before they found Heather's car."

"Why do I have a feeling there's something you're not telling me?"

"Hey, Kade!" One of the female servers with a tray flat on her palm sashayed toward him. She slid an arm around Kade's neck and pressed a quick kiss on his mouth. "I wondered when you'd get around to coming back."

A flush rose in his lean cheeks. He glanced down and read the name badge pinned to the twenty-something's impressive chest. "Savannah, this is Ellie. Ellie, meet Savannah."

Savannah's assessing glance swung from Kade to Ellie and back. She flashed him an unrepentant grin. "I thought you said it was like bringing sand to the beach."

The flush deepened. "Yeah, well, I guess in this case that doesn't apply."

Savannah shrugged, lifting the high, round globes beneath her tight white sweater. A pair of black stretch pants were tucked into her tall black boots, and a silver-studded belt rode low on her waist.

Savannah flashed him a sexy smile. "Well, that's too bad."

Kade ignored the comment. "Ellie's a private detective, Savannah. If you get a minute, maybe you could help us."

Savannah seemed intrigued. "Sure. I have a break in about fifteen minutes."

"We'll wait," Ellie said.

As the female server hip-swayed toward the bar to refill her drink tray, Kade led Ellie over to a wooden table, and they sat down.

"Pretty girl," Ellie said. "I get the impression you two are more than just friends."

Kade's gaze found hers across the table. "Depends how you look at it. I barely remember her. I know I had sex with her. If I'd seen her somewhere else, I might not have recognized her."

Ellie glanced at the long blond ponytail swishing back and forth above Savannah's sexy behind. "Seriously?"

"Yeah." His gaze settled on Ellie's mouth, leaving no doubt as to what he was thinking. "I'd remember you if I saw you twenty years from now."

Some of the awkwardness she was feeling slipped away.

They ordered local beers from a different server and sipped them as they watched the crowd.

Fifteen minutes slipped past, and Savannah returned. Kade rose and pulled out a chair for her, gallant as always. Ellie ignored a thread of irritation.

Savannah smiled. "So what can I do for you?"

One look at those plump, pink lips, and Ellie could guess what Kade would like her to do. Forcing herself to concentrate, she pulled out the photo of Barbara Meeks she had printed off the internet.

"We think this woman may have come in here a few weeks back, a little less than a month ago. Does she look familiar?"

"A lot of people come in here," Savannah said. "Not sure I would remember her if I saw her. Any reason I should?"

"Because she was murdered," Kade said darkly.

Savannah's heavily mascaraed blue eyes widened.

"She would have come in on a weekend," Ellie continued. "Sometimes she was with a friend, a woman who owns a place here in Vail. That weekend, she came in by herself."

Savannah took the photo from Ellie's hand and studied it more closely. "I might have seen her . . . she looks kind of familiar."

"If she was here by herself, she would have been trolling," Ellie said. "Looking for a hookup."

Savannah ran a finger over the photo. "Was she as pretty as she looks in the picture?"

"According to people who knew her, she was beautiful," Kade said.

Savannah looked up. "I think I remember her. Sometimes, I . . . umm . . . like to do something a little different. You know, with a guy and another woman." She didn't glance at Kade, thank God. Ellie was feeling insecure enough without imagining Kade having sex with two women at the same time.

"It was a while back," Savannah added. "Close to a month, I'd say. She sat down at the bar, and I remember thinking how sexy she was."

"Did she leave with a man?" Kade asked.

Savannah nodded. "I remember watching them walk out the door. I remember wishing I had said something to her myself."

"Do you remember the man?" Ellie asked.

"I remember he was a nice-looking guy. Dark hair, athletic build, designer jeans. You know the type."

"So, not fat," Kade said. "Tall or short?"

"I don't remember him being either, so I'd say he was probably average or a little above."

"Any tats?" Ellie asked. "Any scars, anything like that?"

"Not that I recall."

She looked back down at the photo. "I know he had to be attractive. A woman that beautiful can have her pick." This time she did look at Kade. "I don't recall seeing him in here after that, but that doesn't mean he hasn't been in."

"Would you be willing to talk to a police artist?" Kade asked. "Let him do a sketch of the guy?"

It was a good idea. Ellie should have thought of it, would have if she hadn't been sidetracked by the green-eyed monster. Kade was the only man who'd ever affected her that way, and she definitely didn't like it.

Savannah bit her full bottom lip. "I don't remember the guy well enough to describe him."

"A sketch artist knows the right questions to ask," Ellie said. "You'll be surprised what you'll be able to recall."

"I don't know. I'm not crazy about police."

Ellie finished the last of her beer and set the glass back down on the table. "Maybe not, but until they catch this guy, you and any other woman in the area could wind up dead."

Savannah's blue eyes flashed with understanding. "Oh, my God, you're right. I'll do it," she said.

Kade climbed in behind the wheel of the pickup and fastened his seat belt. Ellie hadn't looked at him since they'd left the building. Sitting stiffly in her seat, she stared out the window into the dark beyond the parking lot.

"I met her at the bar, okay? I took her back to my hotel room. She spent the night and was gone when I woke up in the morning. That was the end of it."

When he didn't start the truck, she turned to look at him.

"I won't apologize, Ellie. I'm a man. I've been alone for eight years. Aside from the time I spent with Grace, and a few one-night stands here and there, I haven't dated all that much. And I'm not into threesomes, if that's what you're thinking."

The stiffness went out of her shoulders. "I'm sorry. You're right. I shouldn't have let it bother me."

Kade leaned over, caught her shoulders, dragged her toward him and kissed her, kept kissing her until she grabbed the front of his shirt and kissed him back.

"Neither of us can change what we've done in the past. But dammit, I don't want Savannah or some other one-night hookup. You mean something to me, Ellie. You're the woman I want in my bed." Kade kissed her again, more softly this time, coaxing a response from her, then deepening the kiss until she was clinging to his shoulders, making erotic little sounds in her throat.

He was hard, aching to have her. The hour drive back to the ranch sounded like forever. He ran a finger down her cheek. "I want you, darlin'. You and nobody else. Let's go home, and I'll show you."

Her features softened. She released a slow breath and nodded.

It didn't take long to reach the city limits and start winding through the hills. Deer were a constant hazard, so he focused on the road, let the miles unfold ahead of him.

"We need to call the police," Ellie said, returning the conversation to where it belonged as the truck rolled through the darkness. "We need to fill them in on everything we've learned."

"You got Savannah's contact info, right?" The blonde had been more than happy to cooperate once she realized the threat the killer still posed.

"I've got it. Savannah Nightingale. Can you believe it?"

Kade fought not to grin. Now was definitely not a good time.

"The police will want to interview other employees," Ellie said. "Anyone who might have information."

"Maybe they'll come up with something," Kade said.

"Setting up a session with a sketch artist was a good idea. I should have thought of it myself."

He cast her a glance. "You were sidetracked. My fault. I should have warned you."

"True," she said, not cutting him any slack.

Kade smiled. "I was playing the odds. It was kind of a long shot that she would be there."

"Even more of a long shot that she would remember Barbara." Ellie pulled the photo out of her purse. "Or maybe not, considering how spectacularly beautiful she was."

"Like Heather," Kade said darkly, his mind dredging up a memory of the day he had married her. *Like a blond, blue-eyed angel,* he'd thought when she'd started toward him down the aisle, her beautiful face framed in exquisite Belgian lace. When her body was found, he refused to look at the crime-scene photos. He never would.

He felt Ellie's hand on his thigh, the warmth penetrating his jeans and his morbid thoughts. "She's always there, isn't she? In the back of your mind."

For an instant, Kade's eyes left the road and swung to Ellie. "Not when I'm with you."

Ellie said nothing.

Kade wondered if she believed him. He hoped she did, because it was true. Heather's death still haunted him and would until the bastard who'd killed her paid for what he had done. But the woman who was his wife had been erased from his heart long ago.

He was free of her, he realized, and found his gaze straying back to Ellie. Maybe it was time to reconsider the future he had once wanted and figured he could never have.

Maybe with the right woman, it wasn't too late.

CHAPTER THIRTY-FOUR

*I*T WAS MONDAY AFTERNOON, THE SKY OVERCAST AND CLOUDY. IN A grove of leafless aspens on a hillside overlooking the Diamond Bar Ranch, he studied the activity in the valley below.

His dark green Hummer had made the trip up the muddy, rocky back road without a hitch. A loose stone had put a ding in the lower panel on the driver's side door, which pissed him off, but the vehicle had done its job, and the thrill of looking down on his prey was worth the cost of the repair.

Focusing the lenses of his two-thousand dollars a pair, crystal-clear Swarovski binoculars—worth every dime—he studied the flow of men moving between the barn, the outbuildings, and the sprawling, log-and-stone ranch house.

He followed the progress of a man exercising a palomino horse in an arena next to the barn, lanky, with sandy brown hair escaping beneath the brim of a battered felt cowboy hat. Not a man, he realized, grateful again for the high-quality lenses. More like a teenage boy.

He panned the glasses, saw the back door open and a woman walk out, wearing tight jeans, battered cowboy boots, and a blue flannel shirt. The thick auburn hair pulled into a single braid was a dead giveaway. Logan's woman. He had noticed the possessive gleam in the man's dark eyes the minute he had seen the two together.

His groin pulsed as anticipation poured through him. In the

back of his mind, he saw the scene unfold like a rerun of his favorite movie.

Through the lenses, he watched Ellie cross the yard to the arena and step up on the bottom rail. The kid led the horse over, and the two of them started talking. They laughed together at something he said.

The kid could be useful, he thought, his mind racing ahead as a plan began to formulate in his head.

His thoughts went to the memories that had plagued him, nightmares that shifted between ecstasy and horror. He'd told himself he just needed to take back control, needed some kind of payback, a way to put things on an even keel again.

Frank Keller's name had popped into his head, a man who worked for Mountain Ore; he had used him before to resolve unforeseen problems. Keller was a conscienceless SOB willing to do just about anything if enough money was involved.

Harassing Logan after all these years returned some of his sense of control. When Keller suggested blowing up a tunnel in the Red Hawk Mine, which sat on Diamond Bar property, he had jumped at the chance to cause trouble for Logan and at the same time shove a little dirt in the old man's face.

Then Keller had gotten sloppy and begun to worry about getting caught. He'd demanded more money and a job at a company-owned mine in South America, threatened to tell Logan the truth. In the end, he'd had no choice but to deal with Keller himself—Keller and his hillbilly cousin.

His back teeth clenched together so hard it hurt. He'd hoped the anger inside him would disappear, but the trouble Keller had caused was a pittance, not nearly enough to settle his debt with Logan.

He watched Ellie Bowman with the kid and the horse. He had time, he reminded himself. He'd taken a week off from work for a backpacking trip. He'd be out of phone range for a while, not unusual, since he hiked into the high country at least once a year. Everyone understood that in a stressful job like his, he needed a break.

He looked back down the hill to the woman with the fiery, dark red hair. There was no need to hurry.

The longer it took, the more he could savor the rush.

Ellie leaned over the top of the arena fence. The wind was picking up, the sky turning dark. Rain was predicted tonight, but tomorrow was supposed to be sunny.

She smiled as she watched Billy exercising the six-month-old palomino filly Kade planned to start training. The horse was a beauty, and Billy was obviously in love. He was such a good kid, always so ready to lend a hand.

Lately Billy had been spending more and more time at the ranch, often staying overnight in the bunkhouse. Today he'd confided that his dream was to own his own place one day.

"I'm gonna finish high school, then go to City College," he'd said. "Kade says I'll make a better rancher if I understand business. I also gotta know how to grow hay for the livestock, so that's what I want to study, business and agriculture."

"You talked to Kade about it?"

He nodded. "Kade said he'd help me get through school, long as I keep up my grades."

It didn't surprise her. Kade had a soft spot for Billy, whose family life was pretty grim: a deadbeat dad who had disappeared years ago and a working mom who never seemed to have time for him. Ellie was glad he had Kade.

"I think you'll make a great rancher, Billy."

The boy grinned. "Thanks." He was a good-looking kid, almost six feet tall, with a lean, rangy build. The work he did built solid muscle. Once he had a little more self-confidence, the girls were going to love him.

Ellie watched him work the horse a few minutes more, then climbed down from the fence. Smoke gave a yip, rose from his place at her feet, and nuzzled her hand. Ellie gave him a rub, and they set off for the house.

It was Monday afternoon. Yesterday Kade had phoned Denver Police Detective Clay Meadows and brought him up to speed on

Barbara Meeks, her trip to Vail just before she was killed, and the man Savannah Nightingale had seen Barbara with at Bullwinkle's. The police were moving forward. They planned to question employees and set up an appointment for Savannah with a sketch artist.

The sound of an engine caught her attention, and Ellie's gaze swung toward the gate to see an Eagle County Sheriff's black-and-white SUV driving up the hill toward the house.

The vehicle stopped in front of the back door, the engine went silent, and Sheriff Glen Carver stepped out. A tall, broad-shouldered man, even with his thinning dark hair, Carver was good-looking. Ellie thought of Heather and the handsome man Carver must have been eight years ago.

He started walking toward her, and Ellie met him halfway.

"Ms. Bowman," he said.

"Sheriff Carver. If you're looking for Kade, he's out with the men. If there's cell service, I might be able to reach him."

"I'm here about the Barbara Meeks case. I gather you have pertinent information you shared with the Denver PD."

"That's right. There's a chance whoever killed Barbara may have also murdered Heather Logan."

He nodded. "I got a call from a detective named Meadows. He filled me in, but I thought it might be worth a follow-up call."

"Why don't we go inside and I'll buy you a cup of coffee," Ellie suggested.

Carver followed her in. She poured two mugs from the big stainless pot that was a permanent fixture on the kitchen counter, and they carried them over to the long rectangular table in the corner. Ellie sat on the bench on one side; Carver sat down on the other.

He took a drink of coffee. "How did this lead come about?"

"I imagine by now you know I'm a private investigator. Kade hired me to look into his wife's murder."

Carver nodded, looking uneasy. "I ran your name a while back when I heard you'd been talking to some of Heather's friends. Any reason you didn't tell me you worked private when we met?"

She cupped the mug in her hands. "A couple of reasons. Mostly, I wanted to keep my involvement as quiet as possible. I was questioning people in the area, hoping I might come up with something useful."

"Have you?"

"Maybe. Heather's murder had a number of similarities with Barbara's, which the police pointed out. Kade and I've been working the theory that the two of them may have been killed by the same man."

He paused a moment. "Go on."

"Turns out Vail is the link between the two women. That and the fact both were known to cheat on their husbands. Are you a skier, Sheriff Carver?"

Carver nodded. "Loved it since I was a kid. Don't get a chance to go that often anymore." He frowned. "You don't suspect me, do you?"

"Actually, for a while, your name topped my suspect list. You and I both know you and Heather had an affair. Word was she dumped you, and you weren't happy about it. Revenge can be a prime motive for murder."

The color leached out of Carver's face. "Does Kade know about the affair?"

"I saw no reason to mention it unless the evidence pointed in your direction. At the moment, I'm not convinced it does. "

"I didn't kill Heather. I was in love with her. I thought it was mutual."

"I gather that was the way she liked to play the game. Looks like you were just one of many."

"Yeah, eventually I figured that out. It's not a time in my life I'm proud of."

"As I said, I have no intention of telling Kade if I don't have to. His wife hurt him enough. He doesn't need a reminder."

He studied her closely, and one of his eyebrows edged up. "You'll keep quiet—unless I go back to the top of your suspect list. Is that it?"

"Be better for everyone if you don't."

He managed the faintest of smiles. "Any idea who this guy you're looking at might be?"

"No idea. But I have a feeling we're close to finding out."

Carver drained his mug and set it down on the table, his expression unreadable. "Any more trouble on the ranch?"

"Not since Keller died. With any luck, the guy who financed his dirty work got the payback he wanted."

Carver rose from his chair. "For Kade's sake, I hope so."

Ellie walked him back outside.

"About Heather . . ." he said. "If you come up with anything, I hope you'll let me know. Doesn't matter what happened between us. She didn't deserve to be murdered."

"No, she didn't." Ellie watched Carver stride back to his vehicle. If the regret she had seen in his face was any indication, Glen Carver hadn't killed Heather Logan. But, at this point, she couldn't be sure.

Ellie was determined to find out.

CHAPTER THIRTY-FIVE

SUPPERTIME ARRIVED. ELLIE HELPED WITH THE EVENING MEAL, BUT starting tomorrow, one of Maria's cousins from Eagle would be assisting her in the kitchen. Apparently, Dolores wanted to be a chef, and this was a good place for her to get some experience.

Maria refused to talk about Alejandro. She said it would only make her cry. Alejandro was clearly miserable, but Maria continued to ignore him. She was determined to put the episode behind her and Alejandro out of her life. Ellie felt sorry for both of them.

The succulent aroma of meatloaf, mashed potatoes, and gravy filled the kitchen as the men filed in for supper, pausing at the door long enough to hang up their hats and jackets. Maria greeted them warmly, all except Alejandro, who received the same icy welcome he had been getting since his failed marriage proposal.

It cooled the atmosphere in the kitchen and made everyone uneasy. The hands looked forward to the evening meal as a time to relax at the end of a long, hard day. Kade wanted his men happy. Ellie wasn't sure how much longer he was going to put up with the impasse.

She caught the look he flashed her way as he walked in with his men. Apparently, time was up.

Kade started to move toward the front of the group, but he had only taken a few steps before Alejandro stepped forward. Apparently the handsome Latino was as tired of the situation as Kade. He climbed up on the one of the benches at the dining table, his gaze sweeping the room for Maria, then his attention returned to the men.

"You all know me," he said. "You know the kind of man I am. Does anyone here believe I'm a liar?"

The men shifted uneasily. "Hell, no," Riley shouted, and the rest of the men chimed in.

"So if I say I'm in love with Maria Sanchez, do you believe me?"

There was laughter and someone cheered. "Yes!" The men were grinning, beginning to see where this was going, and their answer rang across the kitchen.

"I love her," Alejandro continued. "I've loved her for years. She told me she loves me too, so I'm asking you, my friends, to help me convince this woman I love to marry me and end the misery I've been suffering since I lost her."

"He loves you, Maria!" Turtle shouted. "You have to marry him so the rest of us don't have to put up with him moping around anymore."

"Take pity on him, Maria!" Riley chimed in.

Ellie's gaze went to the young woman, who stood at the kitchen counter, tears trailing down her cheeks. Alejandro strode toward her, went down on one knee in front of her.

"I love you, *querida*. Please say you will do me the great honor of becoming my wife."

"Oh, Alejandro." Maria threw her arms around his neck. "I love you so much."

He whispered something in Spanish meant just for her. "Will you marry me?"

A watery smile broke over her beautiful face. "*Sí, mi amor*, I'll marry you."

A cheer went up from the men, and Ellie's throat closed up.

"About damn time," Kade grumbled. Striding out of the kitchen, he went to the wine cellar in the dining room and returned with bottles of champagne. Glasses were retrieved. Turtle helped him pour, and toasts were made to the happy couple.

It was a good night in the ranch house. Even the rain battering the windows couldn't dampen the mood.

The sun was up, breakfast over, the men off to work the next morning. Kade had spent a satisfying night in bed with the prettiest lady around. He'd slept better the last few weeks than he had in years.

Ellie was still on his mind as he dumped a can of grain into the trough for the little palomino Billy had been tending. The kid had a real talent with horses, animals in general. During school hours, when Billy couldn't be there, one of the hands took turns mucking out stalls and feeding the livestock in the barn. Roy Cobb was handling the chores this week.

Leaving Cobb to his work, Kade pulled out his cell and phoned Webb Fischer. Though there hadn't been any more incidents on the ranch—no more dead steers, poisoned waterholes, or backshot cowhands—it bothered him that the man who had murdered Frank Keller and poor ol' Earl Dunstan was still on the loose.

The line picked up on the second ring. "Sheriff Fischer."

"Kade Logan, Sheriff. Figured I'd call, see if you've got any news on the murders in Phippsburg?"

"I was planning to give you a call. We were able to get a set of tire tracks from a vehicle parked behind Flatt's the night Earl Dunstan was killed."

"It was raining. I didn't figure you'd get much of anything in the way of tracks."

"Vehicle was parked beneath a tin roof covering a stack of hay bales. Once the guy drove out from under the shed, the tracks turned to mud and disappeared. We didn't find the ones under the shed right away, didn't connect the dots till later."

"So what kind of car was the shooter driving?"

"That's the interesting part. Looks like a big-ass Hummer. Not something you usually see country folk cruising around in. It's impractical on the narrow roads, and any kind of rancher would rather spend his money on something more versatile. A pickup's something you can haul stuff around in. Hummer's more a city-boy pretending to be a tough guy kind of rig."

That was pretty much true, though a flashy Mercedes wasn't much of a rancher's car, either. Kade kept the thought to himself. "You got a way to run it down?"

"No plate number, nothing like that. The tires were an upgrade on a 2019 H2 model."

"That narrows it down."

"We'll be searching DMV records, but there's bound to be a lot of those cars in Colorado. Deputies have been asking questions, trying to find a witness who saw a rig like that in the area. Car like that is memorable. Might get something that'll help us refine the search."

"It's a good lead, Sheriff. You try asking around in Coffee Springs?"

"Not my jurisdiction. I can ask Carver to send a couple deputies out to canvas the shops in town."

"Could be worth it." And Kade was thinking he might do a little asking around himself. "Thanks, Webb."

"Keep your hat pulled low, Kade. We still haven't caught this guy."

"I will." The line went dead. Kade returned to the house to find Ellie seated behind the laptop in her bedroom. Since the door was open, he walked right in.

She looked up and smiled, and he felt the familiar warm stirring. "What's up?" she asked.

"Just talked to Webb Fischer. Guy who killed Dunstan was driving a Hummer. Not many of those around these parts. Fischer's got his deputies asking questions. Coffee Springs is out of his jurisdiction, so I thought we might go into town, pitch in, and give him a hand."

"Since I'm getting nowhere on the internet, and I haven't heard from Zoe, that sounds good to me. Yesterday, I called Heather's friend, Anna, and left a message, but she hasn't called me back. We need to know if Bullwinkle's was a place Heather used to go by herself. If she did, it'll give us an even more solid link between the two women."

Kade remembered the only time he and Heather had gone to the pub together. It was the noisy, crowded kind of place she loved. He didn't want to think of the men she might have met there.

Ellie must have read his dark thoughts. She walked toward him, slid her hands up his chest, and pressed a soft kiss on his lips.

Kade felt the rush, along with a different sort of need he hadn't expected. Pulling her against him, he kissed her the way he'd wanted to since he'd walked into her room, deeply and thoroughly, a fist full of her thick dark copper hair anchoring her in place.

"Wow," she whispered breathlessly when the hot kiss ended. "I was just saying hello. I didn't expect quite so much . . . enthusiasm."

His jeans felt too tight. "Keep looking at me like that, and my enthusiasm is going to end up with both of us back in bed."

Ellie laughed, a richly feminine sound that cut right through him, stirring him up all over again. Wisely, she changed the subject.

"So we're going into Coffee Springs. When do you want to leave?"

"How about right now? I'll buy you lunch in town."

She nodded, grabbed her purse and puffy down jacket, and they headed for the door. It had rained last night, leaving the ground wet and muddy, but the storm had drifted on. A few low clouds hung over the mountains, and a damp chill frosted the air, but the sun broke through here and there.

Kade's big Ford dually navigated the sloppy road without a problem. He parked in a space in front of the post office, and they got out of the truck.

"We can cover more territory if we split up," Ellie suggested.

Kade nodded. "I'll take the far side of the street and meet you at the café when you're done."

She glanced at her watch. "That should work out just about right."

Ellie headed off in one direction, while Kade crossed the street and went into Fred's Gun Shop and Dentistry. Fred sat behind the counter, cleaning a long gun. He was short and stout, with a fringe of gray hair around a bald head, a friendly guy, usually good-natured. Probably a good thing when you were in the gun trade.

Fred stood up and smiled. "Good to see you, Kade. Been a while." He lifted the long gun, and Kade recognized the antique weapon. "Just got my hands on this little beauty. Sharps Model 1874, .44 caliber, 30-inch octagon barrel with double-set triggers. Come outta Texas. Got it here on consignment." He lovingly rubbed the oiled rag over the barrel. "Just like the one Matthew Quigley carried in *Quigley Down Under*. Give ya a good price on it."

It was a beautiful rifle. They were rare, and they didn't come cheap. This one was in great condition, a real prize. "What are you asking?"

"The price I'm asking is seventeen grand, but I can let you have it for a thousand less."

"It's tempting, I have to admit. Actually, I just came in to ask if you'd seen anyone driving around in one of those big Hummers. Would have been in the area sometime last week, maybe ten days ago." When Keller was killed or, later, Earl.

Fred shook his head. "Can't say as I have. Vehicle like that . . . I'd probably recall if I had."

Kade nodded. "Well, thanks anyway."

"Think about the gun. Look real good over that big rock fireplace of yours."

Kade smiled. "I'll keep it in mind. Thanks, Fred." But with trouble stalking the ranch and murder still in the air, indulging himself didn't feel right, even if the antique weapon was a good investment.

He made a quick stop at the dentist's office next door, talked to Dr. Purcell's assistant and the doctor himself. Had no luck and moved on.

Kade hoped Ellie was having more success than he was.

CHAPTER THIRTY-SIX

*E*LLIE CAME OUT OF THE POST OFFICE AND WALKED NEXT DOOR TO the ornate, slate-blue Victorian house down the street, the Coffee Springs Bed and Breakfast. Ellie had never met the owner, but her name was Nola Myers, an energetic woman in her fifties who was cheerful and didn't mind answering questions.

"We're trying to locate the owner of a vehicle," Ellie said. "A big Hummer SUV. Any chance you happened to see a car like that passing through?"

"Nope, sure haven't. And none of my guests have registered that kind of car."

"If you see one, would you call my cell or the Diamond Bar Ranch?"

"Sure, be happy to."

Ellie gave Nola her cell number. "Thanks, Nola." She started for the door.

"You're Kade Logan's new girlfriend, right? Word gets around, and I saw you get out of his truck. That is some man you got there."

Kade's girlfriend. Ellie wasn't sure how she felt about that. But Kade was definitely all man. "We're umm . . . dating." Not exactly, but the best she could come up with. "The two of us are just getting to know each other."

Nola sighed. "If I were twenty years younger, I'd try to lasso that man myself. Be a hard man to tame, though."

Ellie nodded. "You have no idea."

She made her way along the street. Jonas Murray had stepped out of the store on an errand, but the sign on the door said he'd be back in fifteen minutes.

Ellie walked on down the sidewalk to Rocky Mountain Supply and spoke to Frances Tilman. Fran hadn't seen a Hummer anywhere in the area, nor had any of the other people who worked in the building.

The day had warmed into the sixties. Ellie took off her jacket as she walked back to Murray's. She found the door unlocked and Jonas behind the counter. She hadn't seen him since their failed lunch date, but the look in his vivid blue eyes said his interest hadn't waned.

"Hey, Ellie. I wasn't sure you were still around. Maria comes in now. I guess she's taken over kitchen duties."

"That's right. Mabel decided to stay with her family in Arizona."

He took off his dark green grocer's apron and came out from behind the checkout counter. His gaze slid over her, took in her stretch jeans and the sweater that curved over her full breasts.

"You're looking great," Jonas said. "Better than great. I really hoped you'd let me cook you supper, the way we talked about. The offer's still open, if you're interested. Give us a chance to catch up."

"I've been busy. I still am. I just came in to ask if you or anyone in the store had seen one of those big Hummers in town or passing through on the road. It's part of a sheriff's investigation."

One dark eyebrow went up. "That so?" It wasn't a secret, and she figured she might get more cooperation if she mentioned law enforcement.

"I wish I could help," Jonas said. "But I'm afraid I haven't seen anything. I'll ask my son, Sean, see if he's noticed a car like that. Give me your number, and I'll call and let you know." He was a very good-looking man, confident and self-assured. Given no choice, Ellie told him her cell number, and he punched it into his phone.

She should have been paying attention, should have noticed he had moved closer.

"Maria is cooking these days," he said, "so you're doing . . . what? Aside from being Kade Logan's bedmate."

She bristled. "What I'm doing is none of your business, Jonas."

"Maybe not, but the day we met, I thought we made some kind of connection. I thought you felt it too."

A noise in the backroom distracted her, and the next thing she knew, his hand was beneath her hair at the nape of her neck, and his mouth came down over hers.

Stunned, Ellie jerked away just as the door swung open. The hard set of Kade's jaw said he had seen them through the window.

"It's not what you think," she said as he strode toward her.

Kade ignored her. One hand shot out and grabbed the front of Jonas's pristine white shirt while the other drew back and Kade threw a punch that sent the store owner flying backward onto the checkout counter, sliding across the top, and landing on the floor.

"You fucked one of my women," Kade said. "You touch this one, and you won't live through it."

Ellie gasped as Kade propelled her out the door and slammed it solidly behind him. He didn't slow down and didn't let go until they had reached the truck. He opened the passenger door and shoved her in, rounded the front, and climbed in behind the wheel.

"Dammit, Kade, he just surprised me. I had no idea he was going to kiss me, and I didn't kiss him back. I'm not interested in Jonas Murray. I told you that before."

Kade started the engine. Ellie reached over and turned it off. "Your jealousy is getting old, Kade. And it's completely misplaced. I'm not like Heather. Not in any way. If you can't understand that, this isn't going to work."

Kade leaned back, took off his hat and tossed it on the dash, raked a hand through his hair. "Goddammit!"

"Jonas Murray isn't even my type. He's smug and arrogant, and he thinks he's God's gift to women."

Those golden eyes found hers across the distance between them. "I can't apologize for hitting some sonofabitch who's poaching on my territory."

"That's what he was doing? *Poaching*?"

"He was doing his best. I don't think he'll try it again."

"He can try all he wants. He isn't going to succeed."

Kade said nothing.

"Jonas could have you arrested for assault, Kade."

He drilled her with a look. "Not if he wants to live."

Ellie rolled her eyes.

"You still want lunch?" Kade asked, clearly not backing down.

She would have said no if she hadn't been so hungry. "Have you talked to the people who work at the café yet?"

Kade shook his head, settled his hat back on and tugged the brim low. "Not yet. I figured we could do that together."

She released a slow breath. "All right, fine. But no more jealous tantrums and no more fistfights."

His eyes found hers. "I wasn't having a tantrum. I was administering a lesson."

"A lesson. *Men*."

Kade grunted, cracked open his door, and went around to her side of the truck while Ellie climbed out to join him.

"Jonas," Kade said. "He slept with her, didn't he?"

She should have seen this coming. "I'm not a hundred percent sure."

"How sure are you?"

She sighed. "Ninety-nine percent."

"I knew it. I've always known. God, I was an idiot."

She stopped and turned, reached up, and set her palm on his cheek. "You loved her. She just wasn't worthy of your love."

Kade caught her hand, laced her fingers with his, and held it as they headed down the street to the café.

The good news was Wendy Cummings, the café owners' daughter, had seen a dark green Hummer passing through town just after closing last week. She wasn't sure which night, but she had definitely seen the car on her way home, after she had left the café.

"They're kind of cool, you know?" She smiled at Kade as if she knew he would agree. "That's why I remember it."

Wendy couldn't think of anything specific about the vehicle, no dents, no antennas, nothing like that, just that it was "cool," and it was a dark forest green.

But the make and now the color of the killer's car were more than they'd had before. And something about the car got Ellie to thinking. Kade phoned Sheriff Fischer to let him know, but Ellie was quiet on the ride back to the ranch.

"You still mad at me?"

At the rumble of his deep, masculine voice, she turned. "I should be."

"I found you kissing another man. What if it had been me with another woman?"

"I wouldn't like it, that's for sure. I doubt I would have punched her in the face."

"So you are still mad."

She sighed. "Unfortunately, you're tough to stay mad at."

Kade smiled. "Good to know."

Ellie didn't smile back. She wasn't sure how to deal with Kade's jealousy. If they were truly involved, his possessiveness would be a threat to her independence. She had men friends. She worked with men in her office. She wasn't willing to give them up for Kade or anyone else.

It was something to think about on the long, quiet ride back to the ranch.

The afternoon sun slanted across the barns and paddock below. Rising from behind a granite boulder, his favorite spot deep in the aspen grove on the hill above the ranch, he looked down on the scene below. He'd parked some distance down the dirt road, then hiked to the spot.

When he'd arrived, Logan's big dual-wheeled Ford was nowhere in sight. Now, as he looked through the binoculars, he spotted the truck rolling through the tall timber gate, grinding on up the road, then coming to a stop behind the house.

Ellie got out and rounded the vehicle, heading for the kitchen door. She was wearing dark blue stretch jeans that drew a man's attention to her sexy ass, carrying her jacket, which gave him a solid look at the full breasts moving beneath her sweater.

His dick stirred as he imagined the way he planned to use her. She wouldn't willingly give him what he wanted, but the thought of taking her while she fought him turned his arousal rock hard.

Since the day six weeks ago when the dark green Subaru had been found in the lake where he had hidden it, he'd been haunted by nightmares. Driven by memories of the beautiful woman he had loved to the depths of his soul, the deceitful bitch who had betrayed him.

Even now, memories of how it had felt to wrap his hands around her slender throat and end her pathetic life filled him with satisfaction.

Heather had loved him, she'd said. But when the time came for her to leave her bastard husband so they could make a life together, she'd faltered. She'd been pathetically weak where Logan was concerned, too spineless to stand up for herself. To stand up for *him*. She'd decided instead to beg her husband's forgiveness, try to make her marriage work.

Even now it sickened him to think of it.

Heather had deserved to die, and he didn't regret it.

Every time he thought of Kade Logan, the fire inside erupted again, scorching through his veins like a blaze flashing out of control. He wanted Logan's woman. He wanted to feel that power surging through him as it had before.

He took a last look at the ranch house. As he blended into the trees and started back the way he had come, the plan in his head expanded.

And the flames burned hotter.

CHAPTER THIRTY-SEVEN

NIGHT SURROUNDED THE RANCH HOUSE. STRETCHED OUT IN HIS big, king-size bed, Kade stirred at the sound of men's voices coming from outside, growing louder as the hands streamed out of the bunkhouse. The glowing hands of the digital clock read three a.m.

Ellie stirred as he lifted her head off his chest and eased her aside, tossed back the covers, and strode to the window.

"What is it?"

"Can't be anything good." He pulled on his jeans and zipped them, heard his cell phone ring and grabbed it off the nightstand. Wyatt's number appeared on the screen.

"What the hell's going on?" Kade asked.

"Turtle spotted flames on the mountain near Bear Tooth Ridge. We've called it in, but the wind's blowing toward the east pasture, so we've got to move the cattle."

"I'm on my way." He turned to Ellie, who sat up in bed, anxiously clutching the blanket over her breasts. "Looks like there's a fire on the mountain near the east pasture. I need to get up there."

"You might need an extra hand. I'll go with you."

He started to argue, caught the mulish expression he recognized as trouble, and nodded. "All right, but we need to get there as fast as we can."

She was dressed in minutes in jeans and boots, her fiery hair pulled back in a ponytail. They grabbed their jackets off the hooks in the kitchen. Kade grabbed his hat, and Ellie grabbed a bill cap with the Diamond Bar emblem on the front.

The men were ready to leave. The back of a pickup had been loaded with a water tank, picks, shovels, axes, and rakes. The truck towed a horse trailer, the animals inside saddled and ready to go. A Bobcat had been loaded into the bed of a second pickup. Men not riding in the trucks rode ATVs.

Kade brought out his four-wheeler, Ellie climbed on behind him, and they moved to the front of the caravan heading up the hill toward the mountain.

It took twenty minutes to get there with everybody hauling ass. The fire was burning in a stand of timber at the edge of the far side of the pasture. Once it hit the dry, brown grass in the flat open meadow, it would spread like flaming oil across water.

"Let's set up a fire break between the edge of the forest and the fence line," Kade told Wyatt. He pointed. "Right about there looks like a good place to start."

Wyatt's gaze followed. "Thirty feet of clear-cut might do it."

"Fifty would be better, but we'll do what we can."

Slate backed the Bobcat down the ramp out of the truck, fired the engine, and started scraping a path through the shrubs on the other side of the grass. Men grabbed shovels and picks, then spread out in a line and went to work. The water tank in the truck bed held only enough for spot fires that managed to jump the line, but it was the best they could do for now.

Ramirez backed the horses out of the trailer. Riders tightened cinches, mounted up, and headed off to move the cattle to a safer spot away from the blaze.

Kade traded his hat for a Diamond Bar bill cap, grabbed a shovel, and looked up to see Ellie grabbing a rake and heading for the fire line.

"You're with me," he said in the voice he used to command his men, and for once she didn't argue. He didn't like the idea of her working a fire, but she was there, and she refused to stand by and watch. Kade admired her for it, but he was worried about her.

All kinds of accidents happened in a firefight. Drifting chunks of burning ash could set your clothes on fire, a blazing tree could fall and kill you, just breathing the thick damned smoke could make you sick, even kill you if the air was too hot.

Around them, he could hear the crack and roar of the fire as the wind whipped the blaze down the mountain. Red and orange flames leaped from the tall pines into the night-black sky. Sparks exploded, catching another tree afire. The greasy smell of smoke hung heavy in the air.

A couple of deer bounded out of the woods to escape the flames, but so far the area burning didn't appear to be more than a hundred acres. That could double if the wind kicked up. At least the air was cold, and the fire department was on its way.

Kade wet a bandana from a plastic water bottle, tied it around his nose and mouth, and saw Ellie doing the same. He'd hired her for her skills as a detective, but she was a real hand when it came to ranching. His admiration grew, and his chest tightened with emotions he didn't have time to feel. At the moment, he just needed to keep her safe.

As they worked beside the men to clear a swath wide enough to deprive the fire of fuel, he glanced at the flames licking their way down the hillside, and an unwelcome thought occurred.

Had the man who'd hired Keller set the fire to cause more trouble? Was it arson? Had the blaze been set to kill cattle and men?

Kade clenched his jaw, tugged down the brim of his bill cap, and kept working, digging up dry bushes, small trees, and dead grass while Ellie raked the debris out of the way.

They worked hard for over an hour. Sam Bridger and some of the cow hands off neighboring ranches showed up to join the fire line. A few minutes later, Kade looked up to see the flashing red lights of fire trucks, two engines plus a water tanker.

In the eerie red glow of the blaze, he could read the emblems on the doors. Coffee Springs Volunteer Fire Department on one truck. The other truck and the water tanker were from Eagle.

The vehicles drove through the hole in the fence the hands had made and pulled to a halt on the opposite side. Men in helmets and firefighting turnout gear streamed out. Two firemen went for the hose attached to the water tanker, while others grabbed shovels and axes.

A big man in a helmet, a tan coat with neon-yellow stripes, and high rubber boots headed toward the hands working the line, and Kade walked over to meet him.

"Chief Wayne Gifford, Eagle Fire Department." Gifford was darkly tanned, had lots of working-man wrinkles on his face.

"Kade Logan. I own the ranch. Glad to have you here."

Gifford dipped his chin in greeting, then turned to look around. "Nice work on the break. If the weather holds, we should be able to keep it manageable till the sun comes up. As soon as it's light, they're sending in a helo to do some water drops."

That was good news. "Any idea what caused it?"

"Fire investigators will be here in the morning. They'll be looking for accelerants, specific burn patterns, something that might suggest arson or whatever natural events could have caused it."

"What else do you need us to do?"

"Just keep working on the break. The farther along the tree line you can make it, the better chance we have of stopping this thing before it really sinks its fangs into us."

"Will do."

"Give me your cell number, and I'll keep you posted." Gifford and Kade exchanged numbers, and the fire chief left to join his men.

Kade turned as Ellie walked up.

"They've got a helo coming in at first light," he said. "I'm going to keep the men working until it gets here. In the meantime, I'm sending you back down the hill with Turtle."

"You're staying?"

He nodded. "I want to make sure Gifford's got everything he needs."

"I'll stay with you."

He just shook his head. "No use both of us staying up all night." He didn't tell her he wanted to talk to the arson investigators when they arrived.

"I'm staying, Kade. Turtle has work to do here, and I can move branches and dirt as well as any of the men."

"I'll feel better if you're home and safe."

"I'll feel better if I'm here doing my part," Ellie said stubbornly.

He shouldn't feel amused, but he admired the way she stood up to him. Reluctantly, he agreed. "All right, fine. If you're sure that's what you want, let's get back to work."

They continued the backbreaking labor till the sky lightened, turned to a washed-out gray-blue, then orange and gold as the sun came up. The sound of a chopper signaled the beginning of the water drops that would help bring the fire under control.

"Time to go home," Kade said to her. "And no more arguments. We'll let Chief Gifford and his men take over from here."

Ellie stretched her neck and tiredly rubbed her lower back. "All right."

"I've got a couple more things to do," he said. "I'll see you back at the ranch."

Soot-smudged and exhausted, she just nodded. Kade sent her home on the back of Turtle's ATV, watched until she was safely on her way down the road toward the house. The rest of the hands were heading back right behind them, all except Wyatt, who, like Kade, wanted to know what—or who—was responsible for the blaze.

Kade looked at the smoldering remains of the fire, thought of the two dead men in Phippsburg, and a chill ran down his spine that should have been impossible in the hot air generated by the flames.

Worried about Kade and wishing he had returned with her, Ellie headed for her bedroom. She intended to shower off the soot and smoke and get some sleep, but in the end, she decided to check her email first.

It took longer than she'd expected, but finally she headed into the bathroom to shower off the grit and grime, hoping to get a little sleep before Kade got home.

Pulling the elastic scrunchy off her ponytail, she shook her hair out, then climbed into the shower beneath the warm spray.

A deep, exhausted sigh escaped. As she washed her hair and scrubbed away the soot, worry for Kade hovered at the back of her mind, along with a notion that had been circling round in her head.

Two women dead, killed by their seducer, perhaps the same man. Two men murdered to keep them silent. Four dead people. Three in the past six weeks.

She heard a noise in the bathroom, felt an instant of fear as the shadowy figure of a man appeared through the frosted glass. Recognizing the height and solid, broad-shouldered build, she relaxed as Kade stripped away his clothes and opened the shower door.

"Mind if I join you?" He stepped in without waiting for permission, which he could surely read on her face. Just looking at him turned her on, the long, powerful legs, the ladder of muscle across his flat stomach. She rested her palms on his chest and felt the warmth of his skin, hotter than the spray rushing over them. Ellie's insides softened in anticipation.

"Did you get the fire out?" she asked, forcing herself to concentrate.

Big hands settled at her waist. "We got it out, and it wasn't arson. Lightning strike from the other night. Hit a tree and been smoldering in the trunk. Wind finally whipped it into a blaze. Out now, and everyone's safe."

Relief trickled through her. "That's really good news. I was worried about it."

"So was I." He bent his head and softly kissed her. "Want to help me celebrate?" His skillful hands slid over her wet skin to cup her breasts, shaping and molding, turning her nipples hard and her knees weak.

Ellie moaned as his mouth moved down to replace his hands, his tongue licking over her skin, circling her nipple, then pulling the fullness between his teeth. Desire washed through her, and an ache settled between her legs.

Her fingers slid into his wet, dark hair. She loved his hard, workingman's body, loved the masculine taste of him, the lips that were softer than they appeared, the way they molded so perfectly with hers.

Kade crouched in front of her. Cupping the cheeks of her bottom, he trailed kisses over her stomach and ringed her navel with his tongue. Ellie tipped her head back against the tile as his wicked mouth moved lower and pleasure burned through her. Her limbs trembled, her bones melted, and the world spun away.

Ellie thought that she had never known a man who understood her the way he did, as if he knew every secret her body possessed and exactly how to please her.

Kade lifted her up and wrapped her legs around his waist, his heavy arousal pressing against her, setting off little flares of heat that curled low in her belly. Kade took her, sliding deep inside, moving in a steady rhythm that drove her up again. No matter what happened, there would never be another man who could touch her the way he did, who could know the deepest needs of her body and satisfy them the way he could.

She was in love with him. More every day. But Kade was Kade, and she was a woman who valued her independence above all things. Every day she spent with him would only make their parting more painful.

Ellie clung to him as he moved inside her, carrying her once more toward the peak. In the end, she would have to give him up, but for now Kade was hers. Ellie intended to enjoy every moment.

CHAPTER THIRTY-EIGHT

*A*FTER THEIR EXHAUSTING NIGHT OF FIREFIGHTING, THEY SLEPT LATE into the day. It was early afternoon. Ellie was buttoning her plaid flannel shirt, Kade pulling on his jeans, when her cell phone rang. Recognizing Anna's number, she pressed the phone against her ear.

"I got your message," Anna said. "I meant to call sooner, but one of the neighbors stopped by, and it just slipped my mind."

"It's easy to do. With kids and a husband, you have a lot going on. I wanted to ask about a pub in Vail called Bullwinkle's. You know it, right? I think most of the locals do."

"I know it. My husband and I go there sometimes, mostly during ski season."

"It's been there a while," Ellie said. "Do you remember if Heather went there when she came to visit? You said she went out by herself sometimes."

"We went there nearly every time she came to Vail. We were younger. Sometimes Heather went alone. It was the place everybody went back then. I guess if you're single, it still is."

"There's been another murder, Anna. A woman from Denver named Barbara Meeks."

"Oh no."

"Barbara was killed under circumstances similar to what happened to Heather. They found her body in the same mountain park on the outskirts of Boulder."

"That's terrible news. I feel so sorry for her family. But surely the police can't believe it's the same man."

"I know eight years is a long time, but there's a chance it's him. A woman who works at Bullwinkle's saw Barbara with a man the weekend before she was killed. She's doing a sketch with the Denver police. I'd like you to look at it once it's finished. You might have seen him somewhere back then."

"Yes, absolutely. I'll talk to Gretchen, make sure she sees it, too."

"That would be great. I'll let you know as soon as I have something to show you." Ellie hung up and looked over to find Kade watching her.

"So Heather went to Bullwinkle's to pick up men," he said darkly.

"We don't know for sure that's what she did there, but it's certainly possible." She walked over to him, gently laid a hand on his cheek. "I warned you when we started that dredging up the past would be painful."

He caught her hand, turned his face into it, and kissed her palm. "I'm not sorry. If we're right and the same man killed both women, he could kill again. We need to find him and stop him."

"We're going to find him," Ellie said. "Which means I need to get to work. I've got some things to check on the internet." Ellie's cell phone rang. She grabbed it off the dresser.

"It's Zoe," she said to Kade. Zoe was working the Keller case, looking for proof that the man had been paid and, if so, figuring out who'd paid him.

"I've got good news and bad," Zoe said. "The good news is Frank Keller made two ten-thousand-dollar deposits into his Wells Fargo account in Denver."

Adrenaline jolted through Ellie. "Which confirms what we figured, that someone hired him to cause Kade trouble."

"Yes, that's the good news. The bad news is the deposit was made in cash, so there's no way to track who paid him."

Ellie looked over her shoulder to find Kade anxiously watching. "Even so, that's good work, Zoe."

"I wish there was more I could do. Maybe one of us will think of something." There was a different tone to her voice, a lightness that hadn't been there the last time they had spoken.

"You sound good." Ellie turned away from Kade's impatient glare. "You sound happy. What's going on?"

"Chad and I got back together. I really love him, Ellie. When I saw him again, I knew he was the one for me. Chad said he'd never stopped loving me, and I realized when it's right, it's really not that hard to commit."

Ellie ignored a pang. "I'm really glad things worked out. I'll call you back and get all the warm and fuzzies when Kade isn't standing here glowering at me for news."

Zoe laughed. "Talk to you later."

The call ended, and Ellie turned to Kade. "Keller made two ten-thousand-dollar deposits into his bank account in Denver. Unfortunately, they were made in cash."

"So no way to track who they came from." Kade tucked his denim work shirt into his jeans. "At least we know for sure Frank was working for someone else."

"Yes, and according to Earl, that was the person who killed him."

"Someone Frank knew from the mine." Kade sighed. "It's something. Just not enough."

Ellie silently agreed.

It was late afternoon of the following day, the sky graying toward dark, when Kade swung down from Hannibal and glanced around for Billy. It took a moment to spot him, riding next to Ellie toward the barn, leading the little palomino filly.

Lately, Kade had been giving the boy more and more responsibility. He was planning to hire another stable hand so Billy could spend more time working with the horses.

Kade led his buckskin into the barn at the same time Ellie and Billy rode in. Ellie dismounted from Painted Lady and flashed Kade a smile so warm it made him wish they were back in the shower.

"I was desperate for a little fresh air," Ellie said. "Billy was work-

ing Sunshine on a lead line. I talked him into combining his ef-
forts and going for a ride with me. I didn't think you'd mind."

"Not a bit. I was glad to be out of the house myself." He turned
to Billy, who swung down from a very reliable bay gelding named
Ringo that he was using to pony Sunshine. "The filly needs the
work," Kade said to him. "Looks like you're doing a good job."

"Sunshine likes to learn, and she's really smart. She's going to
be one of your best horses, Kade."

Kade ran a hand over the palomino's golden neck. "You just
keep doing what you're doing, and I'm sure she will be."

While the hands washed up for supper, Kade walked Ellie back
to the house. The aroma of baked ham and biscuits filled the
kitchen. Maria and her new assistant, her cousin Dolores, were
bustling around, their movements not quite in sync. Learning
each other's routines took time. As Dolores hurried over to set
the table, she bumped into Kade, and her cheeks reddened.

"Please excuse me, Señor Kade." She was a year younger than
Maria, round-faced and a little plump, with a sweet disposition.
Kade liked her.

"It's just Kade, Dolores, and we'll get out of your way till supper's ready."

"All right . . . Kade."

Kade felt the pull of a smile as he urged Ellie out the door toward the living room. "It's been a long day," he said. "I could use
a drink."

"I wouldn't mind a glass of white wine," Ellie said as they
walked into the high-ceilinged room that didn't get used nearly
enough.

Kade went over to the cedar-slab bar, pulled a chilled bottle out
of the under-counter fridge, and poured a glass, then took down
a heavy, crystal rocks glass, added ice, and poured himself a
whiskey, Stranahan's Rocky Mountain single malt.

The first sip spread the burn out through his limbs, relieving
some of the tension. They carried their drinks over to the sofa
and sat down on the burgundy leather. As Ellie took a sip of wine,
Kade noticed the faint worry lines across her forehead.

"Something's going on in that head of yours." He caught her chin, forcing her to look at him. "What is it?"

Ellie sighed. "I'm afraid to say it out loud. I'm afraid you'll think I'm crazy."

"Try me."

She set her wineglass down on the coffee table. "Okay, but don't say I didn't warn you."

Kade just waited.

"Coffee Springs is a rural community, right? Aside from what happened to Heather, murder doesn't commonly occur around here."

"Couple of rustlers were hanged back in the Wild West days, but that was over a hundred years ago."

"And yet we have two dead men in Routt County—Frank Keller and Earl Dunstan, murdered about thirty miles from here, just across the county line. Eight years ago, Heather was murdered, and now Barbara Meeks, who may have been killed by the same guy who killed Heather. Four people dead, Kade. I keep asking myself why they all have some connection—no matter how re-mote—to you."

Kade frowned. "Wait a minute. You think Keller, Dunstan, and the dead women are connected? Tell me how it fits together."

Ellie picked up her wineglass, walked over to the window, and stared out at the snow-capped range in the distance. "I'm not sure." She turned to face him. "I told you it was going to sound crazy."

"Maybe it's all just coincidence."

"As I recall, neither of us believe much in coincidence."

Kade carried his whiskey over and joined her at the window. "All right, just for drill, let's run with it, see how it plays out."

"We'll have to theorize some of it."

"We have to start somewhere."

She nodded. "Okay, let's begin with Frank Keller. Someone hired Keller to cause Kade Logan trouble."

He nodded. "We've always figured the man who hired him wanted payback for something I did."

"And he shot two men in cold blood, so we know he's a killer."

"True enough," Kade said.

"So let's go further, say he wants more than just payback. Say he hates you, he's obsessed with you for some reason."

"Well, he sure as hell doesn't like me."

Ellie grinned. "Right. So what if he's the guy who killed Heather all those years ago? Maybe he murdered her for the same reason he hired Frank Keller. Because he hates you and wants to punish you for whatever it is you've done—or he thinks you've done."

Kade took a drink of whiskey. "If he killed Heather because he hated me, why did he wait eight years to come after me again?"

"I'm not sure, but . . ."

"But what?"

"All of this started after the police found Heather's car. More coincidence?"

The ice rattled in his glass as he took a drink. "I see what you mean."

Ellie sighed. "I don't know all the answers, but it's my job to find out." She looked back at the snow-capped mountains. "And I still think all of this—even Barbara Meeks—has something to do with you."

CHAPTER THIRTY-NINE

*E*LLIE'S THEORY DROVE KADE CRAZY THAT NIGHT. HE WOKE UP groggy and foul-tempered, tried not to take it out on his pretty bedmate and instead made love to her before he got up to shower and pull on his jeans and boots.

Desperate to clear his head and keep his mind off the possibility he was somehow responsible for the deaths of four people, he rode out with his men and didn't return until dark. He couldn't make sense of it, but he had come to trust Ellie. If she thought it was possible, he'd keep an open mind.

He found her in her bedroom when he walked into the house at the end of the day. Ellie rose from her seat at the Victorian writing desk, came over, and looped her arms around his neck.

"So how was your day?" She smiled and pressed a soft kiss on his lips, and something warm expanded inside him.

It had been years since anyone had welcomed him home at the end of the day. As he thought back, Heather had usually been busy doing something else when he came in at night.

He lifted a russet curl off her cheek. "Long and exhausting, but better now that I'm home." *With you.* But he didn't say that. He was still trying to get a handle on the feelings that continued to grow inside him.

"You want a drink before supper?" she asked. "That seemed to help last night."

"Sounds good. Let me go wash up first. I'll meet you in the living room."

He returned ten minutes later in fresh jeans and a dark gold thermal to find a cozy fire burning in the big rock fireplace. Ellie greeted him with a glass of the same whiskey he'd poured himself last night.

"A guy could get used to this." He accepted the drink, took a swallow, and enjoyed the burn. They carried their glasses over and sat down on the sofa as they had before.

"I talked to the fire guys mopping up the blaze near the east pasture," he said. "They should be done by tomorrow, latest."

"They did a good job."

"They're good men." He sipped his drink, leaned back on the sofa, and stretched his arm across the back. "Between moving cattle and working on that road we're building up to the summer camp, I thought about your theory off and on all day. I couldn't get it out of my head."

"Come up with anything?"

"My mind keeps going back to Earl Dunstan. Before he died, Earl said Frank knew the guy who killed him was from the mine. Frank worked at the Red Hawk. The only three people we could find at Mountain Ore who knew Frank and could afford to pay him the twenty grand we know he got were Clive Murphy, Tony Russo, and Rick Egan."

Ellie nodded. "The top execs make enough too, but Phillip Smithson said he didn't know Keller, and Jane says she and the CEO don't deal with employees at Frank's level."

"I can't figure why Murphy, Russo, or Egan would have a beef with me, and none of them looked like a killer."

"You can't tell by a person's looks, Kade."

Amusement touched his lips. "I know, but it always seems to dead-end there."

Ellie nodded. "I guess we were thinking alike, because I went online and made another run at the same three men."

"And?"

"I didn't find anything that raised an alarm. I've got Zoey looking at DMV records. If one of them owns a Hummer—"

"Sheriff Fischer is looking into that."

"The sheriff doesn't have any evidence that connects those three men to Keller."

Kade took a drink of whiskey, and Ellie sipped her wine.

"I don't know what Murphy and Russo drive," she said, "but I found pictures of Rick Egan on Facebook in front of a white Porsche 911 GT3."

Kade nodded. "Guy definitely looks like the foreign sports car type. Can't see that pretty boy driving a Hummer."

Ellie cocked her head in his direction. "Maybe not, but then most people wouldn't peg you for the Mercedes-Benz type."

He smiled. "Good point."

"Zoe's going to text and let me know."

"So how does Frank's killer connect to Heather and Barbara?"

"Savannah said the guy Barbara left the bar with was dark-haired, athletic, and attractive," Ellie said. "To some extent, Murphy, Russo, and Egan all fit that description."

"I guess. All three of them are decent-looking men."

"So maybe you *can* tell a killer by his looks. From the beginning, I've been searching for someone Heather would have been attracted to. Unless Clive Murphy was a lot better-looking eight years ago, I think we should move him down our list. He just doesn't look like a guy Heather would have been interested in."

Kade thought of how beautiful Heather had been. She could have had any man she wanted. Clive Murphy wouldn't have stood a chance. "You're right. At least for now, let's concentrate on the other men."

"Phillip Smithson has the kind of good looks that would attract a beautiful woman."

"He said he didn't know Keller."

"That's what he said, but there's no way to know if it's true. Maybe Smithson, Russo, or Egan is the guy Barbara slept with. Maybe he's the same guy Heather slept with years earlier—and he's the same guy who killed them. It would link you to all four murders."

Kade fell silent, his mind spinning at the thought. "We need to see that sketch Savannah is working on."

Ellie's phone started ringing. She pulled it out of her jeans and pressed it against her ear. "Hello, Jonas."

Kade could only hear half the conversation, but when her gaze cut to him, his jaw tightened even more. Just the fact the bastard was calling her set his teeth on edge.

"Okay, great," she said. "We'll follow up with Mrs. Morgenstern. Thanks for calling." She flicked Kade another glance. "I'm afraid I'm busy," she said into her phone. "No, that won't work, either. I have to go, Jonas. Thanks again for the help." Ellie hung up her cell.

Kade had to force out the words. "How the hell does Jonas Murray have your number?"

Ellie's chin went up. "I gave it to him when we were in town asking about the Hummer. Jonas said he would check with his son and his customers, see if anyone had seen a vehicle like that around. Apparently the lady who lives in a house just south of the post office, Mrs. Morgenstern, got up in the night to let her dog out and saw a Hummer on the road through town. It was a little over a week ago on Wednesday night. No idea why she remembers the date, but that was the night Earl Dunstan was killed."

Kade ignored the information they already knew. "Jonas asked you to go out with him. He has no business asking you for a date." His voice was stone-cold.

Ellie's hand trembled as she set her wineglass down on the coffee table and rose from the sofa. "We've talked about this, Kade. I just can't handle it anymore. I'm not like Heather. Either you trust me or you don't. I have a life, a job I enjoy, and friends. I'm not giving any of that up because you're too jealous to deal with it."

Kade said nothing.

"I'm going back to Denver in the morning. I shouldn't have stayed this long in the first place."

Kade's chest clamped down. "You can't leave. You work for me, and you haven't found Heather's killer yet."

"I'll keep working the case. I can do everything I need to do back in the city. I'm sorry things didn't work out, but it's probably for the best. Good night, Kade." Ellie walked out of the living room, and Kade felt as if the breath had been sucked out of his lungs.

He didn't want her to go. Ellie was everything he'd ever wanted. She represented the kind of future he yearned for but had given up on long ago. He wanted Ellie to stay. But deep down, he was afraid of making the same mistake he had made before.

Kade's worst fear was falling in love with a woman, then finding out she had betrayed him. He couldn't handle it again.

He heard Ellie's footsteps receding down the hall toward her bedroom. She wouldn't be joining him in his big bed tonight. Or any night in the future.

Pressure built in his chest. Kade lifted his whiskey glass, downed the contents in a single long swallow, and headed upstairs.

CHAPTER FORTY

*E*LLIE WIPED TEARS FROM HER CHEEKS AS SHE WALKED INTO HER BED-room. She had known this was coming. It was just a matter of time. No matter her feelings for Kade, she couldn't live with a man who didn't trust her.

Stripping out of her clothes, she showered and changed into a Denver Broncos sleep tee. Tomorrow, she'd pack her things and drive back to the city. She didn't think Kade would stop her.

He'd told her from the start he wasn't interested in a relation-ship. At the time, she'd thought that was what she wanted too. Ex-cept the man was Kade, and she had fallen in love with him.

She dragged in a shaky breath. She'd keep working the case, follow the theory she had come up with that the same man was re-sponsible for all four murders.

Which would eliminate the sheriff, who had no connection to Frank Keller or the Red Hawk Mine. Any of the Mountain Ore execs could be the killer, but Murphy was off the list, and Tony Russo didn't have the handsome, sophisticated demeanor that Phillip Smithson had or the sexual allure and movie-star looks Rick Egan possessed. She didn't know Barbara's tastes in men, but Phillip and Rick were both handsome as sin, and a woman on the prowl would be easy prey. On the way back to Denver, she'd stop and talk to Savannah, show her internet photos of the two men.

Weariness settled over her. And sadness and a deep sense of loss. She climbed into bed and tried to read, but it was impossible to concentrate. Worry about a killer warred with thoughts of the man upstairs.

She'd been a fool to let things go so far, to let herself fall so hard for Kade. She was desperately, hopelessly in love. Tears formed a lump in her throat, and her eyes burned. She wanted to cry, but she refused to give in to the urge. At least Zoe had a chance for a happy ending. And Maria.

Ellie closed her eyes, but tears leaked from beneath her lashes. She was in love with Kade. But whatever Kade felt for her, it wasn't enough. Real love required trust, and after the way Heather had betrayed him, Kade would never trust a woman again.

It was two a.m. when she finally gave up, took an Ambien, and managed to fall asleep. Exhausted, she overslept the next morning and woke up groggy, her chest aching with the tears she'd held back last night.

Breakfast was over, the men all gone to work.

As she had guessed, she didn't see Kade. Instead, she carried her bags out to her rented Jeep Cherokee and loaded them into the back. A leaden sky and thick gray clouds promised rain, and the temperature had dropped below freezing. The prediction for tonight was even lower as an early-winter storm swept in.

Dreading the drive back to Denver, she returned to the kitchen to say goodbye to Maria and Dolores. Maria must have read the sadness in her face because she followed her out to the car.

"You should stay," Maria said. "You should fight for him. Señor Kade loves you. Sometimes a man needs time to figure things out."

She almost smiled. "You mean like Alejandro?"

"Sí. Alejandro is happy, and so am I. But Señor Kade . . . he is not happy. He told me you were leaving, and I could see in his heart that he wants you to stay. He needs you, Ellie."

She just shook her head. "Kade doesn't love me. Or at least not enough to trust me. I'm sorry, but it has to be this way." She leaned over and hugged the girl who had become a woman since they had met and also a very good friend. "Say goodbye to Alejandro for me."

Maria wiped a tear from her cheek. "I will. *Vaya con Dios, mi amiga.*" May God go with you, my friend.

"You too, Maria."

As Maria walked back into the house, Ellie swallowed the tears clogging her throat. She was going to miss this place, more than she ever could have guessed. But it was past time to leave. She headed for the barn. She had one more goodbye to say before she left the ranch.

It was Saturday. The barn doors were closed against the storm, but she could hear Billy moving around inside. Entering through the side door, she heard the shuffle of horse's hooves and the sound of Billy's voice as he spoke quietly to Sunshine.

He looked up, spotted her, and smiled. "Hey, Ellie. You come out to go riding?" Smoke stretched out on his belly just outside the stall, patiently waiting for his best friend.

Ellie barely managed a return smile. "No, Billy, I came to say goodbye. It's time I went home."

"Home? I thought this was your home."

"Denver's where I live. I've done what I needed to do in Coffee Springs. I can finish my work just as well from my office in the city."

Billy walked out of the stall, closed and latched the gate. Smoke rose and joined him. "What about you and Kade? I thought the two of you might . . . you know, get together."

Her heart squeezed. "I thought that might happen too, but things didn't work out. Kade's a good man. I wish things could be different. I just came to say goodbye before I left."

"Are you sure you can't stay a little longer? I think you should give Kade another chance."

She leaned over and hugged him. "He knows where to find me." Though she didn't think Kade would come after her. He just wasn't ready. She didn't think he ever would be.

"Take care of Smoke," she said, stroking the dog's shiny coat.

Smoke gave a soft woof, as if he knew how sad she was, and butted his head against her hand. Ellie gave him a last rub and started back toward the Jeep.

"Stop right where you are." The voice came from behind her. Turning, she saw a man in a ski mask standing next to Billy, pointing a semiautomatic pistol at his head.

Shock and fear tightened a knot in her stomach.

"Ellie . . . ?" The boy stood frozen, his blue eyes big and anxious.

"Just stay calm, Billy. Everything's going to be all right." Her heart beat frantically. She looked at the man with the gun. "What do you want?"

"My car's up the trail. We're all going to take a little drive."

Adrenaline poured through her. She thought about the gun in her luggage. No way to get to it. Her phone was in her purse. She looked at Billy, whose face was the color of sun-bleached straw. The gun pressed to his head didn't waver.

Running wasn't an option. If she screamed for help, Maria and Dolores would rush to her aid, and both of them could be killed.

"Who are you?" Her pulse hammered. Her mind raced as she tried to figure out what was going on.

"You're the detective. You figure it out."

"Let him go, and I'll do whatever you want," Ellie said.

"You're both going to do exactly what I tell you. You don't, and the kid dies."

A low sound came from Billy's throat. Ellie realized he was thinking of making a move, doing something to take the gunman down.

Her pulse leaped. "Billy, listen to me. Do what the man tells you, and everything is going to be okay. All right?"

Seconds passed.

"You hear me, Billy? We need to do what he says." If he didn't, one or both of them was going to get shot, maybe killed.

"Billy?" she pressed, her eyes locked with his, silently relaying a message—at the first opportunity, they would resist.

"Okay, fine."

The thoughts whirling around in her head began to slow and point in one direction. He knew she was a detective? Was this the man who'd shot Frank and Earl? Was he one of the men at Mountain Ore she and Kade had talked to? With the mask on, she couldn't tell anything about him. Still, there was something familiar about his voice.

"Put your hands behind your back," he said to Billy.

Ellie cast the boy a warning glance, and he complied. Pressing the pistol into Billy's side, the gunman dropped a zip-tie loop around Billy's wrists and pulled it tight.

"Now you," he said. "Turn around."

She wanted to fight him. But she didn't have an opening, and there was every chance he would kill them both. She needed Billy safe before she could resist. She felt the barrel of the gun press into her ribs, put her hands behind her back, but kept her wrists slightly spread, a trick she had learned in self-defense class.

The gunman used the same technique as before, dropping a thin loop of nylon over her wrists and pulling it snug. Ellie glanced around, praying one of the men would ride in, then praying he wouldn't. She didn't want anyone getting killed.

Smoke was whining, jumping up and down on Billy's legs, sensing the boy's fear.

"Tell the dog to stay. Do it, or I shoot him."

"Sit, Smoke! Stay there, boy. Stay!" The dog sat down at Billy's feet.

"Be stupid to yell for help. You'll only get someone killed."

Billy's mouth thinned, but he nodded.

"Now get going." He shoved Ellie forward. "Walk out the door at the back of the barn and head up the trail. Take the path to the right and follow it to the top of the hill."

Ellie started walking. The gunman shoved Billy, and he stumbled into line behind her. "I've got the gun pointed at the back of the kid's head," the man said. "Either of you try anything, the boy is dead."

Ellie kept walking, out through the back door of the barn, her legs trembling as she took the fork in the path to the right. She heard the barn door slam shut, locking Smoke inside so he couldn't follow. She wondered what Kade would think when he returned and found her car still there with all of her stuff inside.

She bit back a bubble of hysteria. Kade would probably think she'd run off with Jonas Murray.

CHAPTER FORTY-ONE

*K*ADE SPENT THE MORNING REPAIRING THE DIRT ROAD UP TO THE summer camp. Clearing weeds, removing fallen trees, using a chain saw to cut the dead logs into firewood hadn't done a damn thing to keep his mind off Ellie.

An image of her pretty face rose in his head, her big green eyes and fiery auburn curls, her sexy curves, the passionate woman he couldn't get enough of. He remembered the way she'd slid her arms around his neck and smiled up at him. *How was your day?* Simple words that banished his troubles and filled his heart with warmth.

Ellie. She was the best thing that had ever happened to him, and he was letting her walk out of his life. Letting her walk away because he was too much of a coward to tell her the truth. Tell her he was in love with her. That the reason he had behaved like such an ass was because he was afraid of losing her to another man.

But Ellie was nothing like Heather. She was honest, and she was loyal. She was there when he needed her, always stood by him, and never let him down.

She was everything he wanted and more.

His gut tightened. He wanted her. Hell, he needed her. Instead, he had driven her away. Now he wasn't sure he could convince her to come back to him. Even if he asked her to marry him, it might not be enough.

Marriage. He wanted that, he realized. Wanted to build a life with her. Maybe even have kids. The thought filled him with quiet determination. Ellie was his. Deep down, she must know they belonged together. They were a perfect fit.

He'd been a fool to let her go. And Kade was no fool.

Now that the fog had cleared from his brain and he'd admitted the truth, he took the four-wheeler and headed down the mountain, arriving back at the ranch a little after noon. Dark clouds had settled over the valley, and drops of rain had begun to fall.

When he spotted Ellie's white Jeep Cherokee, he breathed a sigh of relief. She hadn't left yet. He still had a chance.

His long canvas duster flapped around his legs as he walked into the kitchen. No one was there. Maria and Dolores wouldn't be back to start supper for at least a few more hours.

He walked through the house calling Ellie's name, but got no answer. There was an emptiness in the rooms that said she wasn't there.

Beginning to worry, he went back outside to look for Billy, figuring the two of them must be together, but as he glanced through the window of the Jeep, he saw Ellie's suitcases in the back, her purse in the passenger seat.

His unease built. Kade opened the car door and looked inside her purse, saw Ellie's cell phone. A knot began to build in his stomach. She always carried her phone. No way would she go off somewhere and leave it behind. He took the phone out and checked her recent calls. Her friend Zoe's name appeared as the last call she'd made, and that was yesterday.

A sense of urgency had him moving faster, striding rapidly toward the barn.

"Billy!" Sunshine was there, nickering softly at his approach. A can of grain had been spilled on the ground in front of her stall and hadn't been cleaned up. Lady was in another stall. She hadn't been grained, and there was no sign of Billy.

The knot tightened as Smoke raced toward him, whining, and barking, yapping frantically. The dog raced off toward the back door of the barn, turned around and raced back, started barking again, then rushed back to the door.

Cold fear replaced worry. "Where are they, Smoke? You know where they are? Show me where they are, boy."

The dog ran back to the door and starting scratching to get out. When Kade pulled the door open, Smoke shot off up the trail. The dog paused a moment where the path forked and sniffed the ground, then headed up the path to the right, Kade just behind him.

The dog moved faster, and so did Kade. The rain was picking up, steady drops that began to pool on the ground. He pulled up the collar of his duster and kept moving. Neither of them stopped till they reached the top of the hill.

No sign of Ellie or Billy. He took a look around and noticed a place where the grass had been flattened and boulders formed a barrier that made the perfect place for a watcher to survey the ranch from above.

Fresh fear shot through him, and his pulse accelerated. Turning, he followed Smoke on up the trail, which was rapidly turning to mud. As he hurried behind the dog, he pulled out his cell and phoned Wyatt.

"Ellie and Billy are missing. We need to start a search."

"Maybe they just went for a hike or something."

"Someone's been watching us from the hill above the barn. I'm calling Sheriff Carver. I'm not waiting this time."

"Where are you?" Wyatt asked, his tone shifting to dark and serious.

"I'm at the top of the hill. I'm going after them. I'll stay in touch as long as I can." Until there was no cell service. Kade ended the call. Smoke was bouncing anxiously up and down, winding around his legs.

"Go on, boy. Go find Billy and Ellie."

Smoke barked and took off running. As Kade followed the dog along the trail, the narrow path winding through a grove of aspens, then climbing into the pines, he phoned the sheriff. He figured Carver would give him some guff about it being too soon to worry, but surprisingly he didn't. Too much had been happening. Too many people were dead. The thought chilled him.

"I'll put the word out and get some men together for a search party," Carver said.

"This may be the same guy who shot Keller and Dunstan. If it is, he could be driving a dark green Hummer."

"I saw the BOLO, and Webb Fischer called me about it. My deputies are on the lookout for a car like that in the area."

"I'm following the trail up the mountain behind the barn. The path goes over the ridge, then in a half mile or so, it starts down the back side of the hill."

"Listen, Kade. Don't try to handle this on your own. You could get people killed, including yourself."

"Sorry, can't hear you. Signal's fading. I'll let you know if I find them." He heard Carver curse as he ended the call. No way was he waiting. Not when Ellie and Billy's lives could be in danger.

Smoke raced back to him, then turned and ran back along the trail. Kade followed. He wished he were armed. Everything inside him warned that Ellie and Billy were in serious trouble.

And if Ellie's theory about the killer was correct, it was all his fault.

The gunman had forced them off the trail some distance back, taking a longer, more circuitous route through a stand of downed pines, a field of dry grass, then over some boulders, so they couldn't be followed. The rain was falling steadily now, washing away their tracks. With every step farther away from the ranch, Ellie's fear swelled.

Ahead through the trees, she spotted what appeared to be a vehicle, which had pulled off a dirt road into a knot of trees where it was mostly concealed. The car was a dark green color, and as they drew near, she saw it was a Hummer.

Her blood ran cold. This was the guy who had murdered Frank and Earl. She had no doubt that if she and Billy got in the car with him, they would be dead.

"Where are you taking us?" She needed to get him talking, draw things out, look for an opening.

"I've got a nice spot prepared for you. A place we can enjoy ourselves. And we won't have to worry about anyone interrupting us."

She started to ask about Billy, beg him to leave the boy and just take her. But Earl Dunstan was dead because he'd known too much. The only way they were going to survive was to escape.

Ellie kept walking. She'd been steadily working her hands free of the zip tie, twisting her wrists one way and then another, tugging the stiff loop up and down, looking for a way to pull her hands through the narrow nylon ring.

"I need to catch my breath," she said, stumbling to a halt beneath a tree. Turning around, she flicked a glance at Billy. *This is the place,* she silently told him. *It's now or never.*

The boy gave an almost imperceptible nod.

"I told you to keep going," the gunman said.

"I just need a minute." She dragged in a couple of deep breaths, as if the climb had been too much, and yanked on the plastic cuffs as hard as she could. A layer of skin came off with the plastic, but her hands were free, and so was she.

Billy moved at the same time, whirling toward the gunman and kicking out, knocking the man's gun hand upward, but his grip on the pistol didn't falter. As Ellie rushed him, the gunman swung at Billy, using the weapon as a club, hitting the boy in the side of the head hard enough to knock him down. He didn't get up.

"Billy!" Ellie punched the man in the face, then slammed her fist into his stomach. She tried to knee him in the groin, went for his eyes, but he was taller and stronger, his body lean and fit.

He leveled the pistol at Billy as he wiped a trickle of blood from the corner of his mouth. "I knew you'd be a fighter." Billy was unconscious, and there was no way she could abandon him and run for help.

"Leave him here, and I'll go with you," she said. "I won't give you any more trouble."

"Oh, you're going with me."

That voice. Anger burned through her. She forced herself to stay calm. "I know who you are. You're Richard Egan." She had to keep him talking. Every minute out of the car was a chance to survive. "Earl said something about Frank knowing you from the mine. The more I searched, the more I thought it was either you or Phillip."

"Frank should have kept his mouth shut. If he had, Earl wouldn't be dead." He reached up and pulled off the ski mask, stuffed it into the pocket of his jeans. "Now get going. It's going to take us over an hour to get there."

"Where? Where are you taking me?"

"You can't guess? I bet you'll figure it out on the way."

She looked into Rick Egan's too-handsome face. *Dark-haired and good-looking,* Savannah had said. *Solid athletic build.* Ellie had theorized that the man who'd killed Frank and Earl was the same man who'd killed Heather, the same man who'd killed Barbara Meeks. She thought of the ski mask. Vail and skiing, the common denominator. Icy fear clawed at her insides.

She glanced down at Billy, couldn't tell if he was breathing and prayed that he was.

Egan followed her gaze. "The kid was just a means to an end. He doesn't know jack shit. If he lives through the ball-freezing night, maybe he'll make it. Now head for the car. I won't ask you again."

It took a few minutes to reach the Hummer, which she could now see clearly through the trees. Ellie waited until Egan pushed her toward the passenger side of the car and opened the door. Knowing it was her last chance, she went for the gun, but Egan jerked his hand free and backhanded her hard across the face. Ellie stumbled but didn't fall. When she regained her balance, she saw the pistol pointed at the center of her chest.

"You little wildcat. I'm really going to enjoy you." Egan's fist hit her squarely in the jaw, and she went down. Ellie groaned as he kicked her in the stomach with a heavy leather boot, once, twice. Then he kicked her in the head, and everything went black.

As Rick drove the Hummer toward his destination, his thoughts strayed from the unconscious woman and the pleasures that lay ahead to another woman he had known. Barbara Meeks wasn't as beautiful as Heather, but she was undeniably lovely. He figured fate had played a role in bringing the two of them together.

After the police had found Heather's car, emotions returned that he had managed to bury for years. Memories of Heather and how deeply he had loved her. How happy he had been when they were together.

Thoughts of her swelled inside his head, pounding, pounding, like a hammer battering the inside of his skull until the pain was nearly unbearable. Warm memories clashed with ugly dark images, the memory of her last-minute refusal to leave her husband, the rejection that had sent him spiraling out of control.

Fighting to crawl out of the quagmire of pain that had started when the cops found her car, he'd returned to Vail, the place he and Heather had met, the first time he had made love to her.

That Friday night, he'd gone to the same pub, one of their favorites, and just as before, a beautiful woman had sat down beside him at the bar. Rick recognized Barbara Meeks from the Denver society pages, had even met her and her husband once at a charity benefit in the city.

Bryan Meeks was a corporate executive, CEO of some big software company. A powerful man—like Rick's father, who held the fate of his employees in one of his godlike hands. Like Mose Egan, who disrespected Rick again and again, even chose Rick's sister and her husband for the highest positions in the company, instead of his eldest son.

Seducing Barbara was easy. Just a few sweet words to a woman starved for affection, followed by a few lusty hours in bed.

Nothing gave him a rush like cuckolding a wealthy, influential man, to secretly know he had taken what the man held most dear—his wife's fidelity.

For a while, sleeping with Barbara had been enough. Then everything had fallen apart, and once again he'd been forced to deal with a deceitful, lying bitch.

Now he had Logan's woman. Rick smiled, already anticipating the outcome.

This time Rick would make sure Logan knew she was dead.

CHAPTER FORTY-TWO

*K*ADE FOLLOWED SMOKE UNTIL THE DOG STOPPED ON THE TRAIL and began to run in circles. Smoke ran up the path and then back. Ran off into some downed pine trees, out into the wet grass, then ran back. The rain had washed the scent away.

Kade swore foully, rage and fear mixing until it was nearly impossible to think. He decided to go back and continue up the main trail, follow the path until he came to the old logging road that wound up the back side of the mountain. He prayed he would find a vehicle, but when he arrived, no one was there, and the dirt road was too muddy to find any tire tracks.

Kade's chest felt leaden, pressing in on him until he could barely breathe. Billy was just a kid, a boy just starting out in life. Ellie was the woman he loved. He had to find them. Had to clear his head enough to make rational decisions. He wanted to keep searching, but sounder thinking told him he needed help.

He started back down the mountain, pausing to phone Wyatt and the sheriff as soon as he got in cell range. By the time he reached the barn, the hands were assembled there, some of them ready to ride off on ATVs, the rest planning a mounted search. Wyatt bent over a table set up in the middle of the barn, drawing up a search grid.

He looked up as Smoke rushed in. The pain on Kade's face must have said it all.

"We'll find them," Wyatt said. "Sheriff Carver called. He's got men and equipment on the way. In the meantime, we'll start looking where you left off."

"Tell the men to arm themselves. If this is the guy who murdered Keller and Dunstan, he won't think twice about killing someone else."

"That's what you think happened? You think he came back for Ellie and Billy?"

"It's worse than that. Ellie thinks he might be the same guy who killed Heather. If he is, Billy was just a way to get to her. I think he's been watching us from up on the hill. He must have seen her with the boy. She wouldn't do anything to put Billy in danger. I think he had this all worked out."

"Jesus, Kade."

A muscle flexed in his jaw. "If he planned as well as I figure, he had a vehicle parked somewhere along the old logging road on the back side of the mountain. He's taken them somewhere. We need to figure out where that is."

Kade heard a noise outside and walked out of the barn as a caravan of sheriff's SUVs and pickups rolled through the big timber gate toward the ranch house. Carver pulled up in front of the barn and turned off the engine.

He walked right up to Kade. "We're going to find them."

Kade didn't argue. He wasn't giving up until he brought Ellie and Billy home. He filled Carver in on his search and the theory that the kidnapper had a vehicle parked on the old logging road and was already out of the area.

"We'll check the road, see if we can find any evidence, but with the rain—"

"The question isn't if he was there. The question is where would he take them?" Kade took a deep breath and walked away, leaving the search strategy to Wyatt and Carver. He needed to think. Needed to put the pieces of the puzzle together.

He started with the basics, the connection between Keller and Dunstan and the shootings on the ranch. Dunstan had mentioned the mine.

He and Ellie had gone to Mountain Ore Mining in Denver.

Murphy, Russo, and Egan all had connections to Keller. Zoe was running DMV records to see if one of them owned a dark green Hummer.

As the search parties dispersed, Kade retrieved Ellie's cell phone from her purse and hit Zoe's number. He'd rather be on the hunt, but he trusted Wyatt and his men. If Ellie and Billy were out there, the men would find them.

But Kade believed they were already gone. Finding where the killer had taken them was the only chance they had.

The phone kept ringing, but Zoe didn't pick up. Kade swore softly and left a message, telling Zoe that Ellie was missing, possibly abducted by the man who'd killed Frank Keller, and urging her to call him as soon as she could.

"Let's go inside where it's warm," Carver suggested. "No use working out here in the cold."

Kade just nodded. It was getting dark, the clouds a thick low barrier over the mountains. The rain was turning to freezing sleet, and the wind had come up, blowing the frozen rain sideways. By the time he and the sheriff walked into the house, Maria and Dolores were back in the kitchen. Maria rushed toward him.

"Wyatt told us what happened. Señor Kade, I'm so sorry."

Kade pulled in a steadying breath. "We're going to find them. We won't quit until we do."

Maria touched his shoulder in sympathy, turned, and went back to work. The women had made coffee and sandwiches for the search crew. Webb Fischer pounded on the back door and walked into the kitchen. He spoke to Kade, grabbed a cup of coffee, and joined Carver at the kitchen table.

Kade turned away from them, grabbed his oiled-canvas duster, and walked back out to the barn, hoping the icy chill would clear his head. The temperature had dropped into the twenties, and the light was almost gone.

Soon they would have to call off the search until morning. If he believed for a moment that Ellie and Billy were anywhere near, he would be out there with the search teams. Instead he was here, trying to piece things together, make the information fit and tell him what he needed to know.

Kade walked through the barn to the door at the back. Smoke was lying there, his head on his paws. Worried brown eyes stared forlornly at the door. The dog struggled dejectedly to his feet.

"We'll find them," Kade said, running a hand over the dog's thick, damp fur. "We'll bring them home."

The dog's ears twitched, then went up. He lunged toward the back door and started barking. Kade's heart jerked. Striding over to Smoke, he opened the door to see Billy stumbling down the path toward the ranch. Blood covered the side of his head and the front of his shirt.

Kade ran toward him. "Billy!"

The boy looked up and took a couple more staggering steps. "Kade . . ." Billy collapsed in his arms.

"You're okay, son." Kade's throat tightened. "You're home. I've got you. Everything's going to be okay."

The blood on Billy's face was beginning to congeal, and his icy body trembled with cold. Kade lifted the boy over his shoulders in a fireman's carry and strode back through the barn, across the yard, and into the kitchen.

"Billy!" Maria rushed toward him. Carver shoved up from the dining table, took out his phone, and dialed 911.

"Let's put him in Ellie's room," Kade said; it was downstairs and the closest. "Get a heating pad and some blankets. He's hypothermic. We need to warm him up." Maria and Dolores both went into action.

The boy remained unconscious. As Kade got him undressed and under the covers, put the heating pad on his feet, and heaped more covers on top of him, Billy stirred but didn't wake up.

"Get the medical kit," he said, and Maria raced off once more. Kade headed for the bathroom, grabbed a couple of towels, and returned to Billy's bedside as Maria ran back into the room with the medical supplies.

Working together, they cleansed the wound and wrapped a white cotton bandage around Billy's head, but the boy didn't stir. The cut wasn't as bad as it looked, but it would still need stitches. It wasn't the blood Kade was worried about. It was the concussion.

"I'll take care of him," Maria said. "You go find Ellie."

Kade nodded, his jaw tight. "Let me know the minute he wakes up."

"*Sí*, I will."

Kade strode out of the bedroom and returned to the kitchen. "Boy's still unconscious," he said. "No idea when he'll wake up."

"Ambulance is on its way," Sheriff Carver said. "I called for a chopper, but the weather's got them all grounded."

"Son of a bitch." Kade had been hoping they could add an airborne search, but it wasn't going to happen now. He paced the kitchen floor, trying not to think of Ellie and what might be happening to her, trying to keep his mind functioning, desperate to solve the riddle that meant life or death.

He went back to the basics, the connection between Keller and Dunstan and the shootings on the ranch. Dunstan had mentioned the mine. He and Ellie had gone to Mountain Ore Mining in Denver. They had spoken to Murphy, Russo, and Egan. All of them knew Frank Keller. All three were suspects. According to Ellie, so was Phillip Smithson.

Kade headed down the hall to his study, found Jane Egan Smithson's card on his desk. Her cell phone number was listed. He punched in the number, and Jane picked up.

"Jane, this is Kade Logan. Sorry to bother you on a weekend, but this is an emergency. Is your husband at home?"

"Yes, he's in the living room." So it couldn't be Smithson. "What's this about?" Jane asked.

"As I said, it's an emergency. I need to speak to Clive Murphy, Anthony Russo, and your brother, Rick. Any chance you have their cell phone numbers?"

"I don't have Clive or Tony's number. My brother's on a hiking trip into the mountains. He's been out of cell phone range all week. He isn't due back until Tuesday morning."

Kade tipped his head back and sucked in a deep breath of air. *Egan.* Had to be. "Any idea where he went?"

"No idea. He backpacks into the high country every year."

"Any place special?"

"Not that I know of."

"Thanks for the help." He started to hang up. "By the way, does your brother own a dark green Hummer?"

"Mostly he drives his Porsche, but the Hummer's what he drives in the mountains."

Kade felt sick to his stomach. "Thanks." He hung up the phone and headed back to the kitchen to speak to the sheriff.

"Glen, the man who took them is a guy named Richard Egan. Calls himself Rick. He's one of the VPs at Mountain Ore Mining. Drives a dark green Hummer, and he's supposedly off backpacking in the high country, somewhere out of cell range."

"We've got a BOLO out on the car. I'll add his name and get out a photo." Carver went to work, and so did Sheriff Fischer.

Kade's cell phone rang. "Logan."

"Kade, it's Zoe. You said Ellie was missing. What's going on?" Kade filled her in. "Oh, my God. Richard Egan is the guy at Mountain Ore who owns a Hummer. I should have gotten back to her sooner, but I was working on a child-abduction case."

"Not your fault."

"The plate number is QXA 555."

"Thanks, Zoe."

"If you need anything—anything at all—let me know."

"I will, thanks again." He turned to the two sheriffs and rattled off Egan's plate number.

Carver frowned. "How'd you come up with that? Only law enforcement can access DMV owners' information." At the hard set of Kade's jaw, he shook his head. "Never mind. I'll tell them the suspect should be considered armed and dangerous."

Kade just nodded. "One more thing. Ellie's been working the theory that the guy who killed Keller and Dunstan is the same guy who murdered Heather and Barbara Meeks."

Fischer's head came up. "That's a helluva stretch."

"You think she could be right?" Carver asked.

"She's good at what she does, Glen."

"I'll have the department pull up everything they've got on the sonofabitch." Carver got back on the phone, and Fischer continued his call.

Kade thought of Ellie and forced himself to stay calm. Egan was out there. Kade just had to figure out where.

Maria appeared in the doorway. "Señor Kade, come quick!"

Kade raced after her, following her down the hall to Ellie's bedroom. Billy lay on the bed, his face as pale as the bandage around his head. Worried blue eyes fixed on Kade's face as he strode through the door.

"Y-You have to find her, K-kade. H-he . . . hit her. H-he hurt her. You h-have to f-find her."

Kade gripped the boy's shoulder. "I'm going to find her, Billy, I promise you. Do you know where he was taking her? Did he say anything? Try to remember."

Billy moistened his lips. He was still shaking from the cold, barely able to force out the words. "I h-heard some of what h-he said. H-he told her h-he had a place all fixed up for h-her."

"Where, Billy? Did he say where he was going?"

"H-he said the place was over an h-hour away."

"Anything else?"

"H-he said she should be able to f-figure out where it was." Exhausted from the effort, Billy lay back against the pillow.

Kade took the boy's cold hand and gave it a final squeeze. "Help's on the way, son. You just take it easy. In the meantime, I'm going after Ellie."

Billy looked up at him with eyes full of hope; then he drifted off again. Kade turned to find Maria hovering in the doorway.

"He's got a concussion. Don't let him go to sleep for more than fifteen minutes at a time."

"*Sí*, Señor Kade. I'll take care of him."

Kade just nodded, thinking how lucky Alejandro was to have this woman. Thinking of Ellie and vowing that once he found her, he wasn't letting her go again.

Kade strode back into the kitchen, his mind clear for the first time since he'd walked into the barn and found Ellie gone.

"Egan's taking her to the mine," he said. "The Red Hawk. It's on the old Diamond Bar spread. Everything comes back to the mine. Billy heard some of what Egan said. He told her it would take more than an hour to get there. He said Ellie should be able to figure it out. The mine's the only thing that makes sense."

"All right, I'll get things rolling," Carver said.

"Be faster if we had a chopper," Fischer grumbled. "Doesn't look like that's going to happen."

Kade strode toward the back door. "I'm heading there now. You and your men can meet me there."

Carver shot up from the bench. "Dammit, Kade. You can't do this on your own. If you're sure that's where she is, we can call in deputies from Summit County, have them head over and intercept him."

Kade shook his head. "No way. Something goes wrong, Ellie could wind up dead. I'm leaving right now. You want to come along, let's go."

Webb Fischer pushed his sturdy body up from the table. "We could have you arrested, you know. For interfering in a sheriff's investigation."

A muscle flexed in Kade's jaw. "You need me, Sheriff. My brothers and I spent half the summer up at the Red Hawk when we were kids. I know my way around up there." The three of them had loved to explore the old abandoned tunnels. It was dangerous, but things had been more lax back then. They were lucky they hadn't been injured or killed.

"You go in blind," Kade continued, "you won't know where to look. All you'll do is let Egan know you're there. Ellie will end up dead and maybe some of your men, as well."

Carver looked at Fischer. "He may be right."

Fischer nodded. "All right. This has been our case from the start. It's our folks who've been killed. We'll bring that fucker down together. Let's go."

CHAPTER FORTY-THREE

*E*LLIE STIRRED ON THE MATTRESS AND FORCED HER EYES TO OPEN. Though she blinked and stared, she couldn't see through the penetrating darkness. Her head was pounding. Her jaw ached from ear to chin. When she moved, pain shot through her ribs, and she hissed in a breath.

For a moment, she just lay there panting, trying to get her bearings, to remember where she was and what had happened. As the pain receded, a jolt of clarity struck her, and it all came rushing back.

Leaving Kade. Leaving the ranch house. Going into the barn to look for Billy. An image appeared of the man in the ski mask holding a gun against the boy's head. Her whole body tightened as Rick Egan's face swam into focus, and suddenly Ellie knew exactly where she was.

Her breath stalled. The darkness pressed in on her, and fear gripped her, a terror far worse than the pain throbbing through her body.

Where are you taking me?

You can't guess? You're the detective. You figure it out.

Oh, God, he had brought her to the mine!

Panic surged through her, and the fear deepened, threatening to swallow her whole. Her breath came in sharp, ragged gasps, and her heart thundered. The panic attack grew more fierce, shutting her body down until her lungs seized and she couldn't drag in enough air.

Dear God, help me. Ellie closed her eyes and fought to stay calm, to remember the lessons Mrs. Scarsdale, her school nurse, had taught her all those years ago.

Quiet your mind. Breathe in and hold it. Count to five as you release it. Breathe out and hold it. Count to five as you release it. She did the breathing exercise over and over until her body began to relax and the tightness in her chest began to ease.

She could do this, she told herself. If she wanted to live, she had no choice.

It took longer than she'd hoped to steady her nerves, calm her mind, and regain control. It was past time to take action. Groping in the darkness, she touched the dirt wall beside her. A wooden barrier closed off a portion of the tunnel, forming some sort of room. She pictured it in her mind, realized the mattress lay on the ground in the corner.

She continued to move around in the darkness, feeling her way along the walls, searching for the tunnel entrance, the way back out of the mine.

She came to a turn and, now that her eyes had adjusted to the pitch-black interior, saw a thin ray of light in the distance. As she approached, she realized the light seeped in through another wooden barricade. The tunnel was abandoned, boarded up to keep people from wandering into the dangerous interior.

She hurried toward the light, feeling the first ray of hope since she had awakened in the pit of Egan's hell. She could hear the steady patter of rain and remembered it had been raining when they had walked along the trail leading away from the ranch. Her clothes were damp but a little drier than they had been. She figured she had been here a couple of hours.

A second wave of fear struck her. *Billy!* Had Billy survived the fierce blow to his head? Dear God, she hoped he had. And what about the freezing cold? He could die before morning.

She took a shaky breath. One thing she knew. The only way to help Billy was to help herself. That meant she had to escape.

She reached the barrier at the entrance, made from scraps of wood, and peered through the narrow cracks. It was dark outside, faint rays coming from distant overhead lighting that illuminated an open area surrounded by chain-link fencing. She grabbed one of the wooden boards and frantically started tugging, trying to rip it off.

She just needed a hole big enough to squeeze through, but the boards were nailed together from the outside, and the task was daunting. She could do it, she was sure, but it was going to take time, and she had a bad feeling she didn't have much of that left.

The sound of a vehicle engine grinding up the mountain came from somewhere outside. Tires rolled over the muddy ground and came to a stop out in front. The engine paused, then went silent. Her heart beat faster as the car door opened and a man got out. She prayed it was one of the workmen, someone who would help her if she cried out. But it was Saturday, and she hadn't heard any heavy equipment moving around.

She took a last look through the tiny crack. *Egan.*

Her heart jerked. She glanced wildly around, searching for something to use as a weapon. Perhaps there was something in the makeshift room with the mattress, but this part of the tunnel was empty.

Adrenalin pumped through her as footsteps began to move toward the entrance to the mine. Ellie retreated into the darkness, her pulse hammering in her ears. The sound of rusty hinges was unmistakable. Egan had fashioned a door out of the scrap wood, disguising it as part of the barricade. As the door swung open, a spot of faint, yellow light flooded into the tunnel.

Ellie retreated farther into the darkness. She could see Egan's silhouette, see he was holding the handle of an old-fashioned kerosene lantern, lighting the way ahead of him.

Ellie braced herself against the wall and began moving sideways through the darkness, praying she would find something she could use against him. Instead, she found a pile of rocks that partially blocked the way. Beyond it was an opening that led deeper into the mine.

The memory of being half-buried in the old dirt fort sent a crushing wave of terror into her chest. No way could she could go deeper into the blackness that left her paralyzed and barely able to function.

Ellie picked up a rock and gripped it in her hand, but as the light from the kerosene lantern grew closer, her feet refused to move backward.

She bit back the sound of fear that tried to escape her throat. She only had one chance if she wanted to live. With a deep breath for courage, Ellie made her way past the rubble and slipped deeper into the mine.

Driving through the rain at a speed that edged as close to perilous as he dared, Kade shaved minutes off the trip to the Red Hawk Mine. Sliding off the road into the mountainside wouldn't help Ellie.

Carver and Fischer were a few minutes behind him. He had promised to wait if he got there first. Wait for them before he went in after Ellie.

Kade wasn't waiting. The problem was he had to find her.

He slowed as he neared the top of the hill. The mine was shut down on the weekends, the front gate locked. But the main tunnel wasn't where Egan would take a woman.

Turning off the steep road, Kade turned down a narrow lane around the side of the mountain toward the back of the mine, where he and his brothers had played. The shafts were old there, abandoned, and long boarded up.

As a kid, they'd played cowboys and Indians there. He'd been a cowboy, of course. Gage and Edge were Arapaho warriors. He wished his brothers were with him now, wished he hadn't let the rift between them go unmended for so long.

The big diesel slopped through the muddy, little-used road, around to the back of the mountain. Kade parked in a spot the pickup wouldn't be heard or easily seen, got out with his flashlight, and started walking. The Colt .45 in the holster on his belt felt comforting. He was dealing with a killer. He wouldn't hesitate to use the weapon.

As he searched for the place he and his brothers had used to sneak through the fence, the flashlight formed a yellow circle in front of him. He figured Egan must have a key to the gate leading into this area, what had been, years ago, the main ore-producing tunnels of the mine.

Continuing along the fence, he looked for the gnarled old pine that marked the spot he recalled. He'd told Carver and Fischer about the back entrance, told them to bring a bolt cutter for the lock on the gate. They were rounding up deputies and on their way to join him.

He thought of Ellie and what Egan might have done to her, and a rush of fury nearly blinded him. Kade clenched his teeth and forced the image away. He had to keep his head on straight if he was going to help her. He prayed she would stay alive long enough for him to get there.

Kade lengthened his stride and kept walking.

CHAPTER FORTY-FOUR

*U*SING THE WALL TO GUIDE HER THROUGH THE THICK VEIL OF BLACK-
ness, Ellie inched slowly backward, away from the approaching
light. The kerosene lantern gave off a dull yellow glow that al-
lowed her to see her surroundings: fallen rock and sagging timbers, rubble that included piles of rotten boards, old nails, and
rusty miners' picks and shovels.

There was a stack of old wooden boxes with the words HIGH EX-
PLOSIVES and DANGEROUS printed on the sides. She carefully edged
around them, figuring they were probably extremely unstable.

She studied the ground, and her heartbeat quickened as she
spotted a shovel, put down the rock, and grabbed the handle,
only to have it disintegrate in her hand. She caught the blade before it landed noisily on the ground, set it aside with relief, and
grabbed one of the picks, a smaller weapon but perhaps more
useful. She would have to get closer to use it, but the pick was in
better condition.

With luck, it would stay in one piece long enough to use it
against her attacker.

Her gaze came to rest on a small metal trowel lying half-buried
in the dirt. Pulling it free, she stuffed it into her back pocket.

The will to live strengthened inside her, giving her a fresh rush
of courage. As long as she was thinking and planning, she was
able to keep the panic under control. She wasn't going down
without a fight. If she lost her struggle with the devil, she would
do her best to send Rick Egan straight to the hell he deserved.

The lantern light shifted, casting eerie shadows on the walls as Egan searched the partial room he had created and realized she was hiding in the darkness beyond.

"There's no way out, Ellie. You can go deeper, but you'll only get lost down there. Unlike you, I know my way around these tunnels. My father made me work here when I was a boy. He thought it would be good for me to learn the business from the ground up." Eerie laughter echoed through the cavernous interior, and goose bumps rose on her skin.

"Ironic, isn't it? I finally made use of what I learned."

Ellie's hands shook as her fingers tightened around the handle of the pick and she raised it above her head.

"If you don't come out, I'll be forced to come after you. You won't like what will happen when I find you."

Ellie said nothing.

"This is your last chance, sweetheart." Quiet fell. The silence stretched into what seemed an eternity.

Then the lantern went out.

Ellie gasped as suffocating darkness once more enveloped her. She could hear the faint sound of Egan's footfalls coming in her direction, but she couldn't force her feet to move. He was closing the distance, moving confidently, almost silently through the blackness, as if he could actually see.

Devil that he was, maybe he could.

Straining to hear his movements in the dark, her body tensed, preparing to attack. When he bumped into her, she screamed and swung the pick. Egan grunted, dodged the iron head, and caught her wrist. Ellie tried to fight him, to hang on to the pick, but in the darkness, it was like struggling with a ghost. His grip tightened on her wrist and twisted until she bit back a cry of pain.

"Drop it," he demanded and twisted harder. "Do it!"

The pick fell from her nerveless fingers.

Egan turned her around and shoved her back the way he had come, and Ellie stumbled forward. A flashlight went on behind her as Egan followed.

Back in the room, he shoved her into the wall behind the mattress, and she went down. Egan set the flashlight on a narrow wooden table, the only other furniture in the room, re-lit the kerosene lantern, and turned off the flashlight.

"Is this where you murdered Heather and Barbara?" Ellie asked, glancing around at what was really just half a room constructed by blocking off part of the tunnel.

Egan sighed. "I didn't bring them here. I made this place especially for you, sweetheart. Kade Logan's woman." His smile turned savage. "You can't imagine how good it feels to have you here. And I didn't intend to kill Heather and Barbara. It was an accident."

"An accident? That's what you call it?"

He shrugged. "We argued. Things got heated, and I lost my temper."

Ellie forced herself not to think of the women he had brutally murdered. "What did you argue about?" As long as he kept talking, she stayed alive.

"Heather wanted to end our affair because she wore Kade Logan's ring." He scoffed. "Kade didn't even love her. Not the way I did. Heather told me she loved me, but it was a lie." He moved a little, and his shadow shifted on the wall, making him look like the monster he was. "I hadn't planned to kill her, but the minute I put my hands around her neck, I knew what I had to do."

Ellie's insides trembled. She realized Rick had forgotten all about Barbara. This was about Heather. Had been all along. Barbara was just a substitute.

She rubbed her injured wrist, which was sprained and starting to swell. Sooner or later, she would have to fight him. The trowel in her pocket was her only hope.

"I'd really like to understand," Ellie said, playing for time. "What about Barbara?"

Rick's gaze slid over her like cold grease. "I didn't mean to kill Barbara. Or maybe I did. I'm not really sure anymore. After spending the weekend together, we planned to meet in Denver the following week."

"And you did," Ellie said when he fell silent.

"That's right. I picked her up at a park three blocks from her house, and we drove to a motel not far away. The sex was even better than before, but as soon as we were finished, she started in on me. 'It was fun,' she said. 'But we won't be able to do this anymore. I've got a husband, you know. I can't risk Bryan finding out.'

"I watched those painted lips moving and thought of how Heather had said the same thing. Then the rage set in, just like before." He looked at Ellie. "I loved Heather so much. But she was still in love with Kade."

Ellie swallowed the dryness in her throat and tried to breathe past the mine dust in her lungs. "If you wanted to get back at Kade, why did you wait eight years?"

His lips thinned. "When they found Heather's car in the lake, everything came flooding back. How much I loved her. How Heather had chosen Logan over me. I went to Vail, the place we'd met. I thought it might help."

"And that's where you met Barbara."

"That's right. Everything about her reminded me of Heather. When she tried to end things, I felt the same uncontrollable anger, the same thrill when I slammed her head against the bedside table. I wrapped my hands around her throat and felt the same rush as before." His mouth curled in a sick, wolfish smile. "I look forward to feeling that rush again tonight."

Rick reached down and stroked a hand over the front of his jeans. Ellie realized he was aroused, and her stomach rolled with nausea.

"You made a mistake when you showed up at my office," he said. "The moment you and Logan walked in, I knew what I was going to do."

Kade spotted the old pine tree that marked the loose spot in the chain-link fence and hurried toward it. Pulling up the unattached section, he ducked through the opening, then hurried toward the abandoned tunnels, trying to stay out of sight. He prayed he could figure out which tunnel Egan had chosen to take Ellie.

As he rounded the side of the mountain, he stopped. A vehicle sat in front of the boarded-up entrance to one of the old tunnels—Egan's dark green Hummer.

Kade's hand fisted. Cold fury washed over him, while white-hot rage burned inside. Pulling the Colt, he eased closer to the mountain and made his way toward the boarded-up entrance. Shining the beam of the flashlight over the old, discarded boards, he spotted what looked like a wooden door camouflaged to go unnoticed.

Kade turned off the flashlight and stuck it in his pocket, pulled the door open, and eased silently inside. Muffled voices came from deeper in the mine, a man and a woman. *Ellie.* His heart raced as gratitude filled him. She was still alive.

On my way, darlin'. Just hang on a little longer.

A faint yellow glow lit the path ahead as he slipped farther into the tunnel. Kade edged quietly through the dimly lit interior, following the source of the light.

"We've talked enough," Egan said. "I'm going to have you, Ellie. Every way I can think of. You can make it easy on yourself and give me what I want—but I really hope you fight me."

Anger tore through Kade, and his hand tightened around the Colt. He forced himself under control. One mistake and he could get Ellie killed.

"You want me to fight you?" she said. "Don't worry. I intend to do just that."

Kade swore foully and started running. Gun in a two-handed grip, he rounded the corner just as Ellie leaped from a thin mattress in the corner of a room inside the tunnel. She tackled Egan, and both of them went down.

"Ellie!" Unable to get a clear shot, Kade holstered the weapon and went after Egan, who rolled Ellie beneath him and slapped her hard across the face.

Kade grabbed the man by the back of the neck and dragged him off her, spun him around, and slammed a fist into his face. Blood flew, spraying drops of crimson over the front of Kade's jacket, and Egan went for his throat, wrapping his hands around Kade's neck, trying to cut off his air supply.

Kade pried Egan's fingers loose and punched him hard in the

jaw. The men struggled back and forth but managed to stay on their feet.

Egan swung a hard punch that slid off Kade's jaw. "I'm going to kill you, Logan!"

Kade buried a fist in Egan's gut, then punched him in the mouth. Egan staggered but didn't fall, bounced back with a series of blows that Kade managed to counter. Egan was tougher than he looked, his body lean and wiry. A hard blow sent Kade crashing backward into the narrow table along the wall. The kerosene lantern went flying, spilling fuel all over the ground, and Kade went down.

"Kade!" Ellie's warning came an instant too late as Egan grabbed a heavy flashlight and hit Kade in the head. His vision blurred, and everything went black.

By the time Kade opened his eyes a few moments later, a sagging timber was ablaze, Ellie was struggling with Egan, doing her best to fight him with the sharp metal trowel in her hand, and there was ice-cold fury in Egan's blue eyes.

Kade swayed a little as he came to his feet, just in time to see Ellie dodge Egan's powerful fist and shove the blade into his stomach.

"You bitch!" he shouted, grabbing the trowel and pulling it free. He gazed down at the blood pouring out of the wound as if he couldn't believe his eyes. The mattress was blazing, more timbers catching fire. As Kade started toward him, Egan cupped his hands over the bloody wound in his stomach, turned, and ran, heading deeper into the tunnel.

Kade started after him. No way was he letting the bastard escape.

Ellie grabbed him from behind and spun him around. "There isn't time! We have to leave! The timbers are on fire! The tunnel is going to collapse!"

The fire was moving fast, licking over the debris on the floor of the tunnel, lighting the timbers along the walls and overhead.

Kade took a last look into the darkness and caught a glimpse of Egan's retreating figure through the growing wall of flames.

"Let's go!" Grabbing Ellie's hand, he tugged her forward, and the two of them ran toward the mouth of the tunnel.

Kade shoved open the makeshift wooden door, helped Ellie through to the other side, and ducked through behind her. There was blood on the side of her head, and more oozed from the corner of her mouth. She was clutching her side, he saw, more injured than he had realized. When she took a shaky step forward, Kade swore an oath, scooped her up in his arms, and started running toward the half dozen sheriff's vehicles pulling through the gate in the chain-link fence.

A safe distance away from the blaze that now licked through the boards across the entrance to the mine, Kade set Ellie back on her feet, then eased her to a sitting position on the ground.

"How bad are you hurt?" he asked, crouching beside her.

But Ellie's gaze was fixed on the mine. "What . . . what about Egan?"

Kade looked back at the mouth of the tunnel. Flames enveloped the entire entrance. Unless there was another way out, Egan was doomed.

Kade's jaw felt like granite. "Fire doesn't kill him, I will. Either way, Richard Egan is a dead man today."

Kade held onto Ellie's hand as they watched the vehicles braking to a halt, red and blue lights flashing. Car doors flew open, and deputies began pouring out. Then fire belched out of the mouth of the tunnel, and the entire side of the mountain exploded. A deadly shower of dirt and rocks flew into the air, and everyone hit the ground.

CHAPTER FORTY-FIVE

*E*LLIE SPENT THE NIGHT IN THE HOSPITAL. SHE HAD A MILD CONcussion and two fractured ribs, so they had given her a sedative to help her sleep. She stirred, and her eyes slowly opened. Weak light poured in through the windows, marking the dawn. Groggy and disoriented, she managed to remember where she was and what had happened the night before.

Egan! Kade! The mine exploding! The memories had her heart racing. Her body ached all over, and her head pounded. Her jaw throbbed, but she was alive.

She shifted on the mattress and turned to see Kade sleeping in the chair beside the bed, his lean, broad-shouldered frame bent at an uncomfortable angle, his handsome face lined with fatigue, a day's growth of beard along his jaw. Blood stained his shirtfront, and his hat was gone.

As she studied his hard, masculine profile, Ellie felt a sweep of longing. Love for him washed through her, this man who had risked his life to save her. This man who had come for her, as she had known he would.

The knowledge loosened something inside her. In her heart, she had never doubted him. She had known in every cell of her body that once he discovered she was missing, nothing could keep him away. A feeling she didn't quite recognize swelled inside her. She realized it was hope.

Kade's tall frame shifted in the uncomfortable chair. Clearly, he had been there all night, unwilling to leave her alone. His whiskey-brown eyes opened and came to rest on her face.

"Ellie . . ." Sitting up in the chair, he reached over and took hold of her hand. "How are you feelin', darlin'?"

She raked back her messy auburn curls. "Better than I should, considering." After the explosion, the ambulance had taken her to the nearest hospital. Kade had followed in his pickup. While she was being treated for the blow Egan had dealt to her head, which included a CT scan, Kade had given the deputies his statement. Sometime later, Ellie had given hers.

Though the concussion didn't appear to be life-threatening, the doctors had insisted she spend the night for observation. Kade agreed.

Ellie shifted on the bed, trying to sit up a little straighter. Kade leaned over to help, plumping the pillows behind her back.

"The doctor said if I was feeling all right, I could go home today," she said. "That's what I want, Kade."

His gaze ran over her face. It felt like a caress. "That's what I want too, darlin'. I want you to come back with me to the ranch."

Her heart squeezed. She wanted that more than anything in the world. Ellie shook her head. "I don't think that's a good idea."

"It's the best idea I've ever had. I shouldn't have let you go in the first place." His hold tightened on her hand. "I love you, honey. I should have told you long before now."

The hope inside wanted to blossom, but she ruthlessly crushed it down. "I love you too, Kade. You must know that by now."

His features softened. "I was hoping, but I wasn't sure."

"I love you, but sometimes loving someone isn't enough. You don't trust me, Kade, and without trust, what we have could never work."

He ran his thumb over the back of her hand and little tingles raced up her arm. "I know that. Believe me, I've spent plenty of time thinking about it."

Ellie remembered the man she had married. Kade wasn't the only one who knew about cheating and the harm it caused. "I would never hurt you, Kade. I wouldn't lie to you, and I would never betray you. We both know what it's like to live with some-one who does those things."

Kade lifted her hand to his mouth and pressed his lips against the back. "I trust you, Ellie. I know I acted like an idiot, but I've never met a woman I trusted more. I've trusted you with my life, and I'd do it again."

Her heart was throbbing. It was impossible to tamp down the hope.

Kade sighed. "It was never you. It was me. The truth is, I was afraid I wouldn't be able to keep you. You're beautiful and smart, you're courageous, and the sexiest woman I've ever met. I was afraid some other guy would come along and sweep you off your feet. I couldn't handle the thought of losing you."

Ellie's eyes filled. "Oh, Kade." She was beginning to under-stand. He had loved Heather and lost her. He was afraid of losing her too. But Ellie was a very different woman.

He sat up a little straighter. "I love you, honey. So damned much. I was never really jealous of Heather because I never loved her the way I do you. It took me a while to figure that out."

He leaned over and pressed a soft kiss on her lips. "Say you'll come home with me. I want to marry you, darlin'. But I don't want to ask while you're lying in a hospital bed, hurting all over. I need you, Ellie. If you love me, we'll figure a way to make the rest of it work. What do you say?"

She was smiling and crying at the same time. Kade loved her. He wasn't a man who spoke those words lightly.

Her smile widened. "I told you once, Kade Logan, you're a hard man to resist. The answer to just about anything you ask me is yes."

Kade flashed one of his devastating smiles, leaned down, and very thoroughly kissed her, and though it made her bruised body ache all over, it was worth it.

EPILOGUE

THERE WAS A WEDDING GOING ON IN THE BIG LOG RANCH HOUSE. IT seemed as if half of Eagle County had shown up for the event. The overflow streamed in and out of a big white canvas tent set up outside, with heaters to keep the place warm against the dusting of snow that covered the ground. The mountains and pastures surrounding the ranch house sparkled with last night's snowfall, making it look like something out of a fairy tale.

Beneath twinkling lights, guests sat at round, linen-draped tables decorated with bouquets of white and pale peach roses sprinkled with white lilies. The fragrance of gardenias drifted in the air.

Along one wall of the tent, a beautiful buffet served Diamond Bar Hereford beef, with every side dish Maria and Dolores could think of. A three-piece western band played a Brad Paisley slow song.

It was time for the bridal dance. Ellie's heart did a soft flutter as Kade looked down at her, and she couldn't miss the love reflected in his whiskey-brown eyes.

For the wedding, she had chosen a pale peach silk gown, street-length, with a square-cut bodice. Cream lace flirted with the swell of her breasts, while butter-soft, peach-leather cowboy boots with roses on the front carried out the western theme.

When she'd mentioned wearing her hair swept up with pearl combs, Kade had grumbled something that made her laugh. She hadn't told him she'd left it down especially for him, but the heat in his eyes when he looked at her said she'd made the right decision.

Kade reached for her hand, drew her onto the dance floor and into his arms for their first dance as husband and wife. He was dressed like the rest of the men in the wedding party, in a black, western-cut tuxedo, black felt hat, and black alligator boots. The guys all looked delicious, especially Kade.

She thought of the wedding gift he had given her, the little sorrel colt that reminded her of Rusty, the horse she had loved and lost. In a sweet moment, he had given Billy an early Christmas present, Sunshine, the palomino filly he had been training. "For helping save Ellie's life," Kade had told him.

As she'd watched the two of them together, she'd thought what a wonderful father Kade would make, and smiled at the decision they had made to start a family sometime soon.

A few weeks after the incident at the mine, Kade had taken her to the old Diamond Bar homestead to finish her recovery. She had loved the old cabin on sight. While they were there, she and Kade had talked about the future, what she wanted to do after they were married.

"There's plenty for me to do on the ranch," she said. "And it feels exactly right to be here with you. If I decide later that I want something more, I can always take cases on the side. There's bound to be plenty of work for a private investigator in Eagle County."

Kade had grinned and kissed her.

Her mind returned to the present as they made a sweeping turn around the dance floor, Kade's cheek pressed to hers. "You look so damn beautiful," he said. "You have any idea how happy you've made me?"

Ellie smiled. "You make me happy too, Kade."

"I'm going to make you even happier tonight." He grinned and kissed her, hot and sweet, giving her a sample of what to expect.

Ellie laughed.

The music swelled, and other couples joined them. Alejandro, handsome as sin in black jeans and a black western-cut jacket, swept Maria onto the floor. The beautiful, black-haired young woman he was going to marry beamed up at him. There was going be another ranch wedding in the spring.

Kade's friend, Sam Bridger, was there, dancing with Libby Hale, the little blonde he'd told Kade he planned to marry. Maisie Yates was there, flirting with the ranch hands. Currently Slate Crawford seemed to be the center of her attention. Wyatt was there, Roy, Riley, Seth and his fiancée, and Turtle Farley.

Half the town of Coffee Springs was enjoying the party. Even Jonas Murray had been invited. Kade no longer seemed worried about Jonas or any other man. He was the man she was marrying, and she had shown him in every way a woman possibly could that she wasn't interested in anyone but him.

As the song came to a close, he took her hand and led her off the dance floor.

"I think your friend Zoe is looking for you," Kade said.

Ellie's attention swung to her tiny blond friend. "Looks like Chad has gone for fresh drinks," she said. "Zoe's probably hoping for a little girl talk."

Kade nodded, smiled. "I'll be over there with my brothers."

Ellie went up on her toes and kissed his cheek, then walked over to visit her friend. Kade headed for the bar, where his brothers, Gage and Edge, stood sipping Kade's favorite whiskey, Stranahan's Rocky Mountain single malt.

Gage was as tall as Kade, but brawnier, with the same dark brown hair. Unlike Kade, his eyes were a piercing shade of blue, made even more dramatic by his darkly suntanned skin. Gage had been all over the world on one adventure or another. His company in Denver specialized in finding lost treasure, lost bits of history, sunken ships or just about anything else.

Edge was an inch taller, with a lean, hard-muscled build. He had even darker hair than Gage, and the same blue eyes, but there was a watchfulness in them that set him apart from other men. Edge was Army Special Forces, a subject he rarely discussed.

The brothers' presence had been Kade's wedding gift from Ellie—best gift ever. They had shown up three days ago.

"Ellie called me," Gage had said when they walked into the

house. "I was in Mexico. Your lady tracked me down—God knows how—told me she wasn't going to marry you unless I showed up. And I was to bring Edge with me. She said it was time we started acting like brothers again."

He'd had a helluva time talking with a lump in his throat the size of an egg, which seem to be affecting all three of them. Kade couldn't think of anything that pleased him more than seeing the family he had let slip away. He'd vowed then and there he wouldn't let it happen again.

The sounds of the band playing returned his attention to the moment.

"You two make a good-looking couple," Gage drawled, taking a drink of whiskey.

"Ellie's beautiful," Kade said, his gaze finding her at a table with Zoe a few feet away. "Inside and out."

"You must really love her," Edge said. "I've never seen you look at a woman the way you look at her."

Gage sipped his drink. "Not even the beautiful-but-deceitful Heather."

Only Gage would be bold enough to mention her, but Kade just shook his head. "Not even the same species."

"I didn't think so," Gage agreed, and Gage knew plenty of women.

"I'm really glad you both came," Kade said. "I should have called you years ago, done my best to mend fences."

"Ellie did it for you," Edge said. "And you're right. It was way past time for all of us."

"I knew I was going to like her when she called and demanded we show up," Gage said. "I admire a woman with the courage of her convictions."

Kade laughed softly. "Oh, yeah, my bride is no wilting lily, that's for sure." He reached for the glass of whiskey the bartender poured for him. "She probably saved my life that night in the mine." Gage and Edge both exchanged glances. They knew about Richard Egan, knew how close Kade and Ellie had come to dying that night.

Egan was dead, crushed as he'd tried to escape through an old back tunnel, his body only partially recovered. God's justice was harsh but well-deserved.

"You heading back to Mexico after the wedding?" Kade asked Gage.

"I'm finished down there. I've got a possible client. A woman. Says she inherited a map from her grandfather. Wants me to help her find the treasure."

"You think it's real?"

"No idea. Usually it's just a pipe dream, but you never know."

Edge's blue eyes swung to Kade, and he released a slow breath. "There's something I need to tell you. I already talked to Gage about it, but I wanted to tell you myself. I left the army, Kade."

Surprised jolted through him. "The army's all you ever wanted. I thought you were a lifer."

"Something happened between me and one of my superiors. The army gave me two choices. Face a court martial or leave the service. Twenty years in Leavenworth held no appeal, so I resigned my commission and came back to the States."

Kade wasn't sure what to say. "Maybe that's good. At least you won't be off somewhere, risking your life every day."

"It could be a good thing," Gage agreed. "You've got skills. You just need to figure out what you want to do with them."

Edge took a big drink of whiskey and set the glass back down on the bar. "Yeah, I guess. In the meantime, I think I'll dance." Striding away from them, he headed for the sexy blonde Kade recognized as Wendy Cummings, the waitress at the Coffee Springs Café.

"He'll be okay," Gage said.

"You know what happened?"

"Not yet. In time he'll tell us."

In the meantime, from the seductive smile Wendy gave Edge as he led her onto the dance floor, there was a good chance he'd be able to forget his troubles at least for tonight.

As for Kade, he'd be spending the night with his beautiful bride. They were talking about having kids, a notion he had abandoned long ago. He wanted a family, and so did Ellie. Inwardly, he smiled. They could start practicing tonight.

Kade looked up to see Billy hurrying toward him across the dance floor, a worried look on his face. He was still dressed in the black tux Kade had rented for him, but his windblown hair said he'd been outside.

"Looks like something's come up," Gage said.

Kade nodded. "Always does." He started toward Billy, only to be joined by his pretty wife.

"I think we may have trouble," Ellie said, her gaze on Billy.

One thing he could count on, there would always be problems on a ranch the size of the Diamond Bar. "Maybe we'll get lucky, and it won't be anything too bad."

Ellie reached for his hand, laced her fingers with his. "We're already lucky, Kade."

Kade looked down at their linked hands. There would always be problems. But now that he had Ellie, he wouldn't be facing them alone.

Kade lifted her hand and kissed the back. "You're right, darlin'. I'm the luckiest man in Colorado."